Cloud City

Jack Taylor Cases:
Cloud City

by C. N. Wynn

CNW PUBLICATIONS

Written by Christian N. Wynn
Cover illustration by Nick Street
Edited by Michelle Ellen
Interior chapter illustrations by Zachary Woomer
Full Character illustration (Sonny) by Kip Ayers

ISBN 978-09855709-7-2

 Library of Congress Control Number: 2014908245

Visit www.jacktaylorcases.com

CNWynn Publications
P.O. Box 328, Cheswold, DE 19936

Special thanks to my family for always being understanding and encouraging, the Guidetti family for the time and patience to find my way, and my readers who give me reason to continue. Because of you all, my dreams become more and more possible.

For Cassandra, who kept me moving forward and allowed me to continue. You don't need a billion dollars, a million fans or ten thousand followers to do what you love. All you need is enough. Just enough to keep you going.

Evidence

Cloud City

Chapter 1
Travel Arrangements

Finally tomorrow happened. It was December 22 in the small town. Jack's mother awaited his return at the Blue Mountain Hotel. Only a few blocks away, the source of the last ten repetitious days stood looking over the area: a building where moments could have lasted indefinitely and the trickle of time had almost slowed to a sudden surrendering stop. Forceful winter winds continued to press on with persistence against the surrounding buildings as if nothing unusual had occurred at all. People shopping by the rest area were forced to scurry inside for shelter, grabbing tightly at their warm coats and wool scarves to wrap around them as securely as the gifts many carried for the holidays.

Clouds began blocking the late afternoon sun, developing a large amount of shade over the town. One shaded building in particular overlooked the area as if in a grimace. The windows were solidly boarded up, blocking any view inside the darkened interior. French doors with colorful stained windowpanes guarded the only entrance. The stones around the building had faded and peeled after years of neglect, and gargoyle statues at the foot of the stairs peered out at the street full of onlookers with mischievous grins. Only a single gold plaque secured to the building shined brightly as if freshly bolted on the east side of the aging stones. The only movements were the sudden firm slams of the French doors from the one-story building's interior, containing the many more stories it held inside as they closed shut and where a new year had already begun.

Inside, the building was immense and tall with multiple stories unseen from the outside. People in red, gold, and black uniforms hurried in every direction, cleaning rubble left from the destruction the night before or attending to departing guests down the long east and west halls. A stern looking dark-skinned man dressed in a neatly pressed black suit ordered his employees with precision as if he'd been directing traffic from behind his desk.

Of 365 doors in the extended hall, the store Teas, Tees, and Ts of room 222 had recently been entered. This particular room had been created with the outer aspects of a country club's golf course. Here Jack, a thirteen-year-old aspiring detective with curly jet-black hair and pearl-brown eyes, looked away from the sun as the early morning rays made him yawn. He couldn't help but notice how it caused the glass table he sat at to mimic the ink-stained jeans of the girl sitting across from him. Colors danced through the prism effected table onto the white T-shaped patio they'd been seated at. His eyes drew to the girl's slender hands with their many paper cuts as she brought a teacup to her lips, and then brushed her blonde hair back. She sipped unconsciously looking onto the vast green landscape of hills in the distance. It wasn't nearly the same shade, but it made him think of his detective's flashlight and the trouble it caused by those searching for it.

A few people were teeing off on the first hole of the golf course when the young woman went to speak. "Strange." Sonny curiously peered up at the sky. Her green eyes reflected the light, causing the appearance of sunflowers in her pupils. "I was quite sure it was later in the afternoon when we walked in, but the sun still appears to be rising…"

Jack looked up at the hills as a server walked up the patio steps with a fresh steaming pot of tea. "Time is different here. Think it has something to do with the two existing planes and the New Year Spirit's artifact. Probably the least strange thing about this place really. Kind of like how a fourteen-year-old girl sounds like a fifty-year-old woman drinking tea," he said slyly.

Sonny narrowed her eyes at Jack as she held her cup steady for the server. "I suppose that makes sense with the days not repeating here."

"Why are we here drinking tea anyway?" Jack asked, folding his arms in frustration. "I should be out there looking for my dad before that fake attendant does something to him."

Smiling slightly at Jack, Sonny watched the server as he began switching out their pot of tea for the other. "That is precisely why we are here. My Granddad used to serve tea whenever I needed help thinking. We need a plan of rescue, and besides the name of a city we have never been to, we have no reports of who took your father or where to begin searching." She brought the cup to her lips. "So we drink tea."

"Plan a way to Cloud City?" Jack understood. "Well, if we're here just to think, we should have just asked for that Fiz drink." A loud horn blew twice from a distance.

"What was that sound?" Sonny asked. The horn blew twice more as both Jack and Sonny looked past the golf course.

"Ah, that would be the ship," the server interrupted. "I didn't mean to listen in. The horn's just signaling the arrival of the cruise ship leaving for the city capital shortly."

"A cruise ship?" Sonny asked. "That's rather convenient."

"Well the Spirit of New Year does it every year at the end of his vacation," he continued. "The celebration continues on the ship and concludes at his mansion by midnight. That is if you can get an invitation. I believe he left on the first ship. It's one of the biggest events in Cloud City next to the challenges. Last day the spirit is seen until the end of the year. I doubt two heroes won't be denied invites." The server finished then carried on down the steps and onto the field.

Jack and Sonny had been thanked and congratulated since they'd walked into the hotel. The events from the night before spread quickly that morning, and many called them heroes. Sonny hadn't mentioned much, but Jack didn't feel heroic at all. The only reason he'd began the case was to escape the hotel. It wasn't until the young detective learned of his father's existence inside that he really cared. As far as he was concerned, it was a matter of selfishness that motivated him. He wasn't proud but would continue to look for his father.

He removed his flashlight from his jacket pocket. Passing it between his fingers, he gazed at the door leading out of the tea shop, and back into the west hall. The gold writing gleamed in the sun where the words *Light up the Darkness* were inscribed and that the magnifying glass handle reflected back. He could see himself in the green finish. Details from the night before flooded back all at once.

"You know, Phoenix invited us to stay at his party last night. One of the other holiday spirits there must know something about the attendant if he's going to the city. Who he is, or who may want this?" Jack held up his flashlight. "That cruise ship could be my ticket there. Just have to find a lead to him afterward."

Shooting up from her chair, Sonny reached into her pocket. She retrieved her red and silver pen and notepad. Clicking the pen, the aspiring investigator flipped through a few pages of the notepad. Paragraphs and notes appeared, and she scanned the first few lines of a specific page.

"Come with me." She said on her way to the door. "I may have an idea where that lead begins."

Rushing out of the doorway and into the hall, Sonny led Jack past multiple doors down the hall. It wasn't until they made their way past room 189 toward the lobby before Jack asked. "Where are we going?"

Sonny checked over her notepad. Jack noticed she had flipped to the pages of illustrated maps from the hotel. "I know she was in the east hall, but I'm not quite sure which room," Sonny replied lightly as Jack followed behind.

The attendants were still working to check out guests and fix the mess left behind by Trick's rampage the night before. The sounds of crumbling rock made Jack hesitate momentarily, thinking back to the security system of the Saint Valentine's Day spirit's villa and the statues that guarded it. All of the attendants seemed too busy to notice as they passed by the entrance doors. Only Number Fifty-Two was able to get out a "good morning" before Sonny walked by hastily with no more than a nod and smile.

Before Jack could ask her who she referred to and where they were rushing to, Sonny had stopped. They were to a door across from a blank wall. The hall had become drastically colder since the lobby. Jack's lungs filled with the cold air like icicles piercing his chest when he realized why the blank wall he stared at was so familiar. Turning on his flashlight, he pointed the light at the wall where a doorway to the Spirit of Christmas' villa was located.

"Feels like it's been longer since we were last here." He pointed the light, preparing to knock on the wreath decorated door.

Sonny grasped Jack's fist just before he was able to tap on the door. "Not that one." She pointed to another across the hall a few doors down.

Walking with her over to a different door, he blinked a few times recognizing this one as well. It was the only door without a handle. "Luminista?"

"We need a lead to find your father, correct?" Sonny asked rhetorically. She held up her notepad after locating several paragraphs of notes in orange ink. "Well, who better to ask than someone who we know last spoke to him? I wrote down everything you told me of the conversation you had with Luminista our first night at the hotel. I remembered notes I'd written when you mentioned the Fiz at the tea shop. Your father sent her to this hotel to do a reading for you, remember?"

"That's right." Jack nodded in agreement. He thought back to the night before he watched part of his father's past. "She told me he was sent to have a reading done himself, and after his, dad paid her to do one for me. That fake attendant kept demanding a totem back from my dad. I'm guessing that's why he sent the flashlight to me in the first place."

"He must've known this would happen from his reading," Sonny added.

Something about it all didn't connect correctly for Jack. "Except, the plane crash hadn't happened until after he sent it to me. When would he have met her?"

Sonny shrugged. "Another detail we have to inquire about."

Jack made his way over to the door. He remembered the last time he had been there, Luminista advised him the room would only open for those she allowed in. This time, however, the door was already slightly agape, and with a light touch, it swung open.

"It's just how I left it." Jack scanned the semi-dark room for a moment, stopping at the same place he had met the fortune teller before. "She's gone."

Besides a few autumn colored throw pillows and a card left behind on the same table Jack had his reading, the tent that had once been the fortune teller's room was abandoned. Following Jack inside, Sonny brought out her notepad and began investigating the other interior rooms. Jack couldn't help but feel how much more empty. It was now compared to how she'd vanished in the darkness. The small amount of light inside seemed to come from nowhere and was dimming. Jack was sure she had left voluntarily as there were no new damages. He flipped over the card on the table as Sonny rejoined him in the main room.

"What is it?" she asked, hopeful, watching Jack's peculiar gaze. "Do you recognize it?"

"One of the cards she read me last time I was here," he replied casually, tossing the magician's card onto the table and turning toward the doorway. "Let's go. Maybe the manager knows something."

The hall became progressively warmer as they walked back to the lobby. Number Fifty-Two, among a few other attendants, gave a respectful nod as they passed the front doors. Number One was walking back from the broken fountain when Sonny spotted him. "Good morning Manny."

Number One's expression went from a pleasant, yet determined, smile to a grimace very similar to the rundown exterior of the building in an instant. He stopped short in front of them with his guest list in hand and a slight scowl. "If you refuse to call me by my proper name, you are welcome to call me by my position."

Sonny smirked quietly. After a curious glance, the manager placed the list down onto the front desk. "To what or whom exactly do I owe the pleasure of seeing our latest young heroes return so presently? Not running rampant in my hotel again, are you?"

"Luminista," Jack said hopefully. "Do you know where she is?"

The manager's eyes narrowed. "Possibly, why is it that you need to know another guest's whereabouts?"

"We believe she may know where we can begin locating Jack's father since he was the one who sent her here," Sonny answered promptly.

"The owner?" the manager confirmed, sighing. "He's always held high regards for me over the years and promoted me accordingly. Although I do believe I am more than capable of controlling the matter, recent events worry me of what may come. I do hope he is found soon. In time we may be lost without him." He spoke more to himself than to Jack or Sonny.

"I would be happy to assist you, but I'm afraid guest information is still private and cannot be freely provided, even to you Mr. Taylor. However, as she has recently checked out, you may want to check your options for travel arrangements. If I were you, I'd start by asking attendants on the ship below to Cloud City."

"Wait, the ship's here?" Jack asked.

"Indeed." Emanuel continued. "I have siblings who work in the city. As I recall, a district for people with Luminista's genre of abilities can be found. It would make sense she would be going there."

The manager walked over to an attendant Jack had only seen twice before. However, it was difficult to forget her as each occasion had been a different person. She still looked shaken up as Emanuel instructed her.

"Number Two, would you escort our young guests to the fifty-third floor? They may need information on the boarding list of the ships. See that they are fully taken care of and if necessary, have the director provide board. I'll approve of it."

Jack and Sonny exchanged curious looks as Number Two agreed nervously and lead them to the televator. Sonny nearly burned a hole into her notepad as she wrote hastily. "Did I hear him correctly? A fifty-third floor?" she asked

"It's technically not a hotel floor," Number Two replied with a shaky voice. "More of a port for the ships docked below the lobby. It's accessible through the televators like any other hotel floor if you have access."

Entering the televator, Jack gazed at the wall of buttons he'd become used to. Searching, he realized he'd never noticed a button for a fifty-third floor. Only the fifty-two keys were visible just as always.

From around her neck, Number Two removed a long thin chain necklace. Attached to it was a standard silver key, unlike the key cards they used for rooms. She continued by pressing each bottom button around the silver cylinder walls producing the usual bright blue glow. However, after completing the circle with the final key, every button surrounding them turned to a bright shade of red like stoplights. A small square opening in the center of the floor appeared where a keyhole lay hidden. While Jack and Sonny watched, Number Two placed her key into the floor's opening and turned. With a shutter, the lights turned purple. A moment later, a bell rang, and the door opened.

Number Two lead them outside. "This is the fifty-third floor." She walked Jack and Sonny through a massive aircraft hangar much too large for planes. Plasma cutters, forklifts, giant cables, and mobile access units lined glass walls where people worked on giant propellers, glass panels, and ship sidings. The opening could be seen a few hundred yards down where sunlight poured in.

"This is where our maintenance people work on our ships when not in use."

Sonny scribbled notes occasionally stopping from paper cuts. "Aren't hangars like these made for airplanes?" she asked.

Number Two either hadn't heard her or was confused about the comment as she carried on down the long hangar without a response. Jack's mind was on a different matter. He noticed the nervous mannerism of the attendant; it was unlike any of the others they'd come in contact with. She was pale and exhausted looking. He assumed she was still shaken up about being taken by Trick and his associate. The first and last time he'd met her—the real Number Two—she brought him five minutes of infinite sand from Phoenix to view the past. Several other attendants had guarded her, and although Jack believed it was for the sand's protection, now he wondered if it could've been for hers as well.

"Are you all right?" He asked her finally. "What exactly happened when you were taken?"

Number Two continued walking but took a shaky breath. "They threw me into the closet shortly after the manager. It was Trick who put me in, disguised of course... I thought he was Number One when he walked up to me. Twelve years hiding as the April Fool, he had plenty of time to research us all. He was persuasive. I remember he asked me to search the closet for the maintenance schedule. He must've put me to sleep because I woke up and there was nothing but darkness and plastic. No light until I was released days later. Wasn't sure how much time passed, but you two saved me. You saved all of us."

Sonny grinned widely, but Jack felt a mixture of anger and guilt. Someone had attempted to stop time permanently and ending existence. He was sure Trick must've been insane to willingly put himself into that fate too. He struggled to make eye contact with her. His concern had never really been about anyone else except his father. Being praised for what he considered a selfish endeavor, he doubted his father would be as approving. "Do you remember anything else that may be helpful? Like what the other attendant may have been doing, or saying?"

"Yes, actually." She said after a few moments. "Inside, I thought it was my dream, yet I remember the voice too well. I couldn't see who, but someone mentioned a promised totem, but no one answered him. It was like he was talking to himself, but with pauses for responses. I guess that doesn't make sense. It was the only change when I was trapped inside the bag."

Jack remembered a similar situation himself during his time in the Leap Room as they approached the port opening. A bald man with a crooked nose and an impressive beach tan firmly grasped his clipboard and stood waiting. His open-collared shirt and matching pants were similar to the hotel attendants except more casual in white and blue. A small gold hoop earring hung from his right ear, making it difficult for Jack to get the image of a pirate missing a parrot out of his mind.

"Two more boarding the iPlane?" the man asked, sliding a finger down the clipboard. "Names?"

"This is the owner's son Jack and his friend Sonny," Number Two introduced. "I believe they will be attending the New Year celebration today after visiting the craft district."

"Oh yes, Number One sent a message about it," the bald man replied. "My name is Kurt, the cruise director for the Solar iPlane."

Sonny checked her notepad. "I was positive we were to board a ship, not a plane."

"I'll leave you to your work, Kurt." Number Two smiled and turned to Jack and Sonny. "The first ship's already departed, but you won't be too far behind if the fortune teller was aboard. Enjoy your cruise folks."

The cruise director ushered them both to follow him to the dock where an immaculate, white, majestic ship stood beaming in glory outside the hanger. Although they were taken outside, the weather was fair, unlike the dreary winter scene from the hotel's masked exterior. On this existence, it was closer to an eternal spring. A body of water stretched out beneath the ship along a grand shoreline.

"The Solar iPlane is actually the cruise ship we will be boarding." The director laughed. "Common misconception for first time passengers that the iPlanes are only intended for aquatic travels or that it's a plane. What they are actually capable of is more impressive."

Kurt's voice traveled in and out of Jack's ears as he continued looking ahead, wondering where the fortune teller could be. His mind drifted as he hoped she would have the answers he needed about his father. Growing impatient of Kurt's lecture of the ship, Jack interrupted. "Do you know where we could find Luminista? It's important I talk to her."

Kurt looked back with an eyebrow raised. "The fortune teller? She and a few holiday spirits were persistent on leaving with the first ship, understandably. They boarded our other ship, the Lunar iPlane, shortly after the disruption. It left a few hours after midnight. Everything that happened the last few days is already news. The whole city's been talking about it since the paper released."

"The paper?" Sonny beamed. "As in a newspaper? With actual reporters?!"

"Of course. I would suggest you subscribe to the Cloud City Journal when we arrive. Nina is the editor. They always seem to be in the know before anyone."

Jack had lost any interest in their conversation. Lately, time was always against him, and he had no way of knowing how long Luminista would be in this craft district. Getting to her as quickly as possible was his new priority, and with minimal clues, he had to hurry.

She could be there already, he thought to himself in disappointment. "How long will it be to get there?"

"The answer to that is plentiful, to say the least," Kurt replied, leading them up. "It will be a day's worth of time that we travel, yet the power of the iPlane is so impressive... Well, I should let the captain explain the mechanics to you. He did engineer it. This way, please."

Walking up the steep ramp, Jack only now realized just how incredible the ship was. Colossal in size, it maintained a gleaming white body that matched the clouds above and was a quarter mile in length. Multiple windows in numerous rows and columns connected into one massive digital welcome sign scrolling across that advertised Presto the Illusionist's big performance. Blue neon lights reflected from the water below as the ship hummed quietly. People on the top deck were enjoying activities such as rock climbing, low gravity water gun fights, and surfing on one side, then volleyball, a waterworks carnival, and a 16-player first-person shooter video game on the other. An inflatable screen towered over them all as they battled in a tournament.

Over the center, waterslides intertwined together like twisty straws into a pool. The outer ring was lined with an incased aquarium of fish growing brighter with the sun's rise into the sky. Jack's gaze drifted up as he followed the vertical line of window monitors to where they boarded, realizing just how much taller it was than any ship he'd ever seen or heard of.

"Twenty-six deck levels on each of our two ships," Kurt continued as they reached the top of the ramp. "When it was engineered, they called it moveable perfection. Once inside, I'll take you to the top deck for your room processing, and we'll be on our way."

Eight attendants from the hotel walked up the ramp behind Sonny in their red and gold uniforms. They surrounded a ninth attendant who carefully carried a covered item with a unique clamping tool. It reminded Jack of Number Two and the infinite hourglass.

"We have the last item to be shipped," reported the lead attendant.

Kurt's eyes became huge, and he stammered for a moment. Stepping further beyond the ramp and into a hall of the ship, he reached for a wall phone. "The following attendants, Letters R through Z, report to boarding for security transport immediately."

"Why are there so many attendants?" Sonny directed at Kurt.

He didn't respond right away. With so many attendants around, it was easy to tell whatever was beneath the tarp was important to someone. "I apologize. This item is the property of a former passenger and is under high security."

Nine of the cruise ship's attendants had arrived. They wore neatly pressed blue uniforms with white pearl buttons and matching stitching. They clashed with the uniforms of the hotel attendants, like two factions of janitors going to war. Jack felt an odd tingle as the wind picked up and blew a corner of the tarp off the secured item. Before they hurriedly recovered it, he caught a partial glimpse. It was only a letter, resembling an initial, much like the name of his father's company.

The attendants cautiously shifted places with the hotel attendants and simultaneously handed off the item. It was a strange yet precise exchange. There were never less than eight attendants surrounding it at once before it was handed off. After completing the switch, the hotel attendants returned to the building.

"Take the package to deck X," Kurt directed. "Room six should be fully secured for it already and try not to forget the password again. The reminder isn't difficult to use." The attendants hurried down the hall and soon after disappeared.

A bell rang followed by the same loud horn. "We should hurry to the top level, we're about to set sail," he advised Jack and Sonny.

Following the cruise director into the hall, they passed between security gates and a few more attendants until they reached a televator. This one was different than the hotel's as there were only half as many keys. As they illuminated the walls, however, a corresponding letter was inscribed to each instead of numbers as Kurt pressed key A.

"Each deck on the ship is cared for by an attendant. They are positioned by letters beginning with myself, Letter A." He gestured to himself. "The lowest deck is deck Z. I believe you were familiar with a similar system at the hotel under Number One's supervision, although in personality we do differ."

He continued his instruction as they arrived on Deck A. The doors opened to a vast new level of guests sunbathing and drinking at a juice bar. "On the ship, it's not about the comforts of home, but your new enjoyments. A dream experience, so to speak. You'll each be staying in one of the twelve rooms on Deck B in our King of Hearts rooms."

"Peculiar. Why exactly twelve rooms and twenty-six decks?" Sonny asked, still taking notes.

"J.E.T. Enterprises," Kurt answered in apparent tones. "All of the owner's designs have themes. The two ships have twenty-six decks each combing to equal fifty-two, the same number of stories in the hotel. The ship that left last night is powered by the moonlight and this one by solar energy. The twelve rooms represent twelve hours for daytime on this ship and twelve on the other for night. Your father is a very clever man. Of course, that should be obvious — he did hire me."

Kurt chuckled and led them up a few steps to the top deck where they were able to see the attractions up close. The surface had been designed to look like a beach covered in sand with a lake-sized pool centered as an oasis. People surfed and slid down slides as some dove deep down into the incredible depth of the water. The water sparkled in the morning sun like crystals as the mist picked up slightly from splashes. It was breathtaking and beautiful, like a vacation dream cruise should be. With his father always working, Jack's family rarely enjoyed vacations together.

Strolling past the pool, they advanced upon a thin man with narrow eyes behind glasses and thin white hair in jeans and a dark turtleneck shirt with the sleeves rolled. He held a small touch screen device and was typing in codes when the cruise director interrupted.   "Looks like all passengers are aboard Captain," Kurt stated. "Mr. Taylor had a question about the duration of the trip. I thought better explained by you."

The captain placed his device an arms-length away, pointing it toward the sky. "Perfect timing Letter A, just about to set sail and I didn't feel up to finding a new director so soon." He responded smugly. Switching his attention to Jack and Sonny, he glared at them both for quite some time as if searching for the best way to explain complicated matters to inferior beings. "As I hope you can understand with today's proceedings, I must make this explanation as brief as possible. My name is Stephen. I am the captain and engineer who designed the Solar iPlane to travel at its current phenomenal speeds, absorbing the sun's enormous energy with specially created panels to recycle, transform, then infuse it with the first ever perpetual source. With the energy driving the propellers beneath the ship, it allows us to use that solar energy and mimic it. This creates the speed of the earth's revolutions as we rotate around the sun. I've recently upgraded the software to all J.E.T. Enterprises owned facilities except for the hotel, which is long overdue."

Jack and Sonny exchanged glances of confusion but nodded anyway. The captain rolled his eyes and lowered the touch screen device. "So to sum up the time duration it will take to get to Cloud City, we will travel for twenty-four hours, but in such haste following the earth's revolution, we will arrive at the same time we depart, as if time hasn't passed."

Jack stood, dazed over the time that would elapse. *Twenty-four hours will actually pass. Luminista could be anywhere by then*, he thought to himself.

Sonny, however, seemed thrilled about the trip. "That is remarkable," she said, looking over the ship's railing excitedly. "It's almost like time travel! The ship can really move that swiftly on water?"

"The iPlane?... On water? I haven't heard anything so outdated since windows." Pressing a combination of buttons on his touch screen device, the captain glared at Sonny with a confident smile. "Water?..." he mocked, showing her the handheld device. "With my iPilot controls, where we're going we don't need water."

With that, the Solar iPlane began to shutter as the spinning of enormous propellers could be heard coming from the bottom of the ship's twenty-six decks. It hummed like a million fans circulating all at once. Gusts of air picked up beneath the boat forcing water to separate. The body of water it rested on parted in half away from the ship into giant pillars along the sides. Jack was barely able to run to a railing as Sonny gripped her arms around the rails tightly. Trees on the shoreline bent away from the ship like a tropical storm. Within a few moments, the boat had risen from the water; steadily moving with the captain's every motioned gesture on his device.

Jack had trouble leveling himself, as the force from the propellers pushed off the ground like a fleet of helicopters until the ship was fully ascending. From this view, he was able to get his first real glance at the hotel's exterior. Over fifty floors jetted up to the sky with un-aged red blocks separated by gold accents, large gaping windows with delicately engraved frames, expanded balconies, pointed white pillars, and spotlights aimed at a large sign that sparkled like diamonds. The building's body gleamed as they pulled farther away from the dock. Within minutes they were up in the air and gaining speed heading north by northeast, leveling out when an attendant ran up to them. "I have the welcome package for the new passengers sir."

"Wonderful Letter B, show them to their rooms and make sure they take proper care before we get to too high an altitude," advised Kurt. "I'll be checking over the new security precautions with the other staff."

Letter B nodded. "I'll show you to your rooms."

Sonny and Jack released their grips from the railing and were guided by the attendant Letter B to the televator then down one deck below. The televator doors opened, revealing a tall portrait of an eighteenth-century king of hearts holding a broad sword against a white backdrop. It was displayed in a gold frame hung from floor to ceiling. The deck itself was similar to the lobby of the Holiday Hotel. They walked on the same-style white marble flooring with black etching, which had matching white walls. However, across from each of the twelve doors leading to rooms was a cursive gold *B*. They sparkled as if made from actual gold dust.

"This ship is so incredible." Sonny smiled. "I wish there were blueprints I could copy."

"I wouldn't be surprised if the captain had it all locked up somewhere or destroyed," the attendant responded. "He's very particular about the work on his ship. Even the glass plates for the monitors outside the ship aren't made conventionally. They're all made of fulgurite. Sand struck by lightning creates the glass then it's reshaped and molded for the ship. And the Lunar iPlane has a much bigger ice cream mountain."

"Difficult not to admire a person's passion for creativity and genius," admitted Sonny.

"Not sure if it's genius or insanity," Jack muttered in frustration. "Planes already exist, why would ships need to fly?"

Letter B stopped partly down the hall and grinned. "Well, no one told your father that when he thought of it."

The attendant led them over to two rooms and handed a welcome packet to them each. "You will be in rooms four and five. If you feel at all light-headed, it is perfectly normal as we continue to climb higher into the sky. Your packets include a tonic that reduces the effects of high altitude pressure. Deck N is the main lobby for merchants and dining halls, and if you require my services, the phone inside your rooms will contact me. Once we arrive in the city, the tour guide will escort you to the celebration. I'll leave you now."

"Odd that our room numbers are the same as before," Sonny stated as she opened her packet. Removing the key card, she opened her door and stepped inside. "Exploring the ship in a few if you'd like to join me?"

"Yea," Jack responded half-heartedly. There was a lot on his mind, but very little he could do until they reached the city. "That sounds perfect."

Opening his door, he experienced a familiar tingle staring at a room identical to the one he had recently checked out of. The walls were in his favorite shade of blue with the mural of his favorite football player. A large stack of movies and a plush bed (he knew better than to lie on it just yet) waited for him. The only difference was where the television had once been now displayed a clear view of the clouds and a balcony. He could easily see the expanding sky as they climbed higher when a message appeared across the glass.

Be sure to enter the limbo contest and come see what fabulous creations your imagination holds with unlimited vacant space. Turn to channel seven for viewing and thank you for choosing the Solar iPlane as your choice of travel!

Jack finished reading as the window became completely transparent again. It was easily the largest monitor he'd ever witnessed in a single room, other than a theater like in the hotel. He could still vaguely taste the chalky dryness in his mouth from his time inside the screen as if he had recently chewed on coal.

Removing the items from the clear cellophane wrapped welcome bag, he laid out a map of the ship, a welcome note he didn't bother reading, and a tonic with a few instructions.

To reduce the effects of high altitude. Warning: May cause strong sleeplessness. (Insomnia) <u>Drink Me</u>!*

Still curious about the heavily secured item being transferred on the ship, he looked over the map for deck X and noticed the room itself was missing. The room number and pictures were gone completely. Before he had time to register the information, Sonny walked into his doorway.

"Are you ready to explore the ship?" she asked.

Jack gathered the tonic and map together, placed them into the pockets of his black bomber-style leather coat, and met her at the door. "Yeah, let's get started."

Throughout the day, Sonny practically dragged Jack throughout the ship's levels, activities, and functions. Deck N had several game rooms, a large dining hall overlooking the sky, and stores selling cruise ship merchandise. They didn't accept the type of money Jack was used to, instead trading clear orbs with a unique element in the center as currency. Luckily, as the owner's son, Jack had no need for either.

Quite a few of the game rooms and stores were fashioned after the most popular ones located in the Holiday Hotel. Other activities like go-carting up tracks that traveled up the ceilings and snowboarding down a mountain made of ice cream quickly became two of Jack's new favorites. Diving deep into an oasis led them through a large tube that traveled throughout the ship. It allowed them to swim with sea creatures neither Jack nor Sonny had seen before. Jack ignored her suggestions that they were from an ancient race brought from meteors.

Hours had gone by, but the sun hadn't seemed to change its arc as they sailed through the morning sky. It was difficult to tell what time it was and when to sleep, but Jack and Sonny managed to get a nap in for a few hours before a horn alerted them. After leaving the dining hall eating brunch, they tried their first pieces of stratus candy from a center shop—an arid tasting sweet mixture of cotton candy wrapped in a crunchy fruit shell. Sonny seemed to notice the sweets had no effect in changing Jack's mood. He threw the wrapper onto the floor. Sonny quickly picked it up, clearly irritated.

"What is the matter with you?" she scolded him. "You should not litter."

Jack shrugged with a confused expression. "What's the big deal, we're not even outside?"

"For now, you live here just like the rest of the planet." She shoved the wrapper into his hand. "Clean up your own messes."

He looked at the wrapper, found a recycling bin, and tossed it in with a mocking smile. Sonny shook her head. "Something new has you preoccupied today." She observed. Jack leaned against a tube filled with water. A few fish and some scuba divers stared at him from inside the chamber then swam off. His hands were in his pocket, fumbling with something absentmindedly.

"I can't stop wondering about that thing they brought in behind us," Jack said as the fish behind him scurried. "Pretty sure I saw letters written on it. I think it may have something to do with my dad. But if they won't tell us anything, it has to be really secured."

Still fiddling in his pocket, he removed an object from his pocket, believing it was his flashlight. He paused, realizing the shape and size were off. With the bottle in his hand, he instantly remembered where it came from.

"You haven't taken the tonic yet?" Sonny asked. "No wonder you've been so moody today. It wasn't long after we elevated before my headache began. I can only imagine how much pain you must be in." The thought hadn't actually occurred to Jack in the least. He did feel slightly dizzy, but it was mostly the thoughts running through his mind. However, he was relieved when he found his flashlight in his other pocket.

Sonny rummaged through her notepad, locating a replica map of the ship and clicked her pen. "I thought it would be to our advantage if I copied the map from the introductory packet. I noticed something strange scanning it. A room was missing, but I didn't understand — ouch!" She dropped her pen on the floor and grasped her hand quickly, shaking it vigorously.

"Are you OK?" Jack asked.

"Just…still stings when I grip too tight." She stopped, eyeing something to Jack's right.

Jack followed her gaze. "What is it?" he asked as he picked up her pen.

"Luck," she said as she confidently looked toward a doorway down the hall. "Opportunity meets preparation."

The only headache Jack currently experienced was sourced from the confusing statements Sonny regularly came up with. However, scratching his head and checking over his shoulder, he did understand one thing. "You must have a plan."

"More like an idea," she corrected. "The room Letter A mentioned before was room six, which I noticed was the same room missing from the map. I seriously doubt, however, that it means the room doesn't exist. In the hotel, there were hidden villas. You were able to find them with your flashlight."

Jack rolled his eyes. "Yeah that could work, but what about security or guards? With all the attendants surrounding it when we boarded, you know it'll be protected by both."

Smiling triumphantly, Sonny pointed over to an attendant assisting a guest at the end of the deck and retorted. "Come on, where's your sense of adventure? I thought of that part too. Did you notice there is no lobby here? Without a lobby like the hotel contained, there's only one attendant on each deck at all times. Meaning we would only need to distract the attendant of deck X. I'm sure we can easily handle that task while finding a way in."

"Why do I feel like there's a *but* coming?"

"But…" Sonny added. "There's one obstacle that leaves me perplexed. I'm certain there will be some sort of door mechanism or alarm to keep us out."

It took a few moments, but Jack's eyes widened, and he lifted his head and walked over to the televator. "Think I have a way around that one."

After a short discussion inside the televator, Jack walked Sonny to her room. "Make sure you count to ten before you make the call." Jack reminded her. Rushing back to the televator, he silently counted to ten as well, waiting for the precise moment to take it down to deck X. In no time at all, the doors opened, revealing a new hallway. Much like his deck, the floor of this deck was etched in black and white marble, and the walls were decorated in gold, but with a large letter X on the front of each door. The only other noticeable difference was the portrait hanging up in a matching gold frame depicting an eighteenth-century knight in mail armor, a heart centered on his chest plate, and the number seven on each of his shoulders.

Luckily, two things were vacant in the hall as he dashed to the area between rooms five and seven, and promptly removed his flashlight. Room six and any attendant watching over the deck were both missing just as he'd planned. Reassured that Sonny's distraction was working, he pointed his detective's flashlight at the space between the two visible rooms. Sliding his thumb up the switch, the light turned on, beaming through the wall and exposing a vacant space, hidden door, and a small grin on Jack's face. Walking forward through the wall, he dreaded the challenge that lay before him, and how far he'd have to go to see his father again.

The door was familiar to him. One he had seen recently, in fact, protecting the safe room his father used in the leap year. It was heavily armored with thick metal plates, yet there was no keypad to stop Jack's entrance inside. Only a slot for keycard access separated him now. His hand shook slightly as he removed a small plastic card from the inside pocket of his leather Jacket. The skull imprint almost appeared to be staring back at him as he hoped, with both the cruise ships and hotel owned by his father, he would have access inside. Taking in a deep breath, he slid the card and waited.

A small light next to the door handle lit green, and the lock clicked. Yet, the young detective's relief was short lived as a second confirmation appeared beneath a sliding plate. This one was on a touch screen monitor similar to the engineer's device but larger. A three digit code was requested with four attempts remaining. Jack first tried his birthday as it worked in the hotel but here failed. Then the current month and year 113 but it too failed. When two attempts remained, Jack found letters among the keys to choose from. Believing he discovered the proper code, he pressed in each letter, *JET*. However, this too proved to be incorrect.

With his last attempt remaining a slide option for a hint became available. Following the prompted gesture, the tip appeared on the screen with just two words: *Daily, Weekly*.

His fingers hovered over the letters, then the number pad. He hesitated and closed his eye, trying to remember what he learned about the cruise ship. *Two ships. One for day, one for night. Twenty-six decks. iPlane? No that's too many keys.* He thought to himself. *A ship for day and night. Seven rooms per deck. That doesn't make sense… not unless.* Punching each key in firmly with precision, he typed in three numbers: 247. A new light lit green and the second bolt unlocked.

"Twenty-four, seven," Jack whispered, shaking his head. "Why is it always on the last try?"

Unsure of how much time he had, Jack shoved the door open abruptly. The room was small but empty of anyone, like a standard wood ship cabin built for storage. It looked as if it hadn't been used in a while. There were no beds or chairs to be used for comfort, and no windows to be seen in or out of. A single bulb on the ceiling provided the only light. A few items on a shelf such as a silver heart-shaped locket, film canister, and a framed picture of a man and woman were inside. The girl in the photo, Jack thought seemed familiar, but it wasn't pertinent when his eyes finally met the sheet covered crate.

It was placed near the furthest wall, but Jack could feel something pulse inside it. He reached his hand toward the sheet cautiously, remembering the guard using a unique tool to handle it. With one quick pull, the cover fell from the crate and landed in a clump on the floor, allowing him to read three words marked on the front.

"Fragile. Extremely dangerous," Jack read aloud. On the top, it was addressed to the Spirit of New Year, and the only other distinction was where he saw the content information. However, only the initials had been printed for the content. Initials, he was not familiar with, but as Jack read them aloud, he wondered why he felt he already should be. "B. S. H.?"

Seconds later, Jack heard a loud familiar ding and knew immediately he had run out of time. It was the arrival of the televator to the deck, and he was positive Sonny's distraction had run its course. As fast as he could, he threw the sheet back over the crate and exited the hidden room, slamming the door shut, and racing through the wall just as the televator doors opened.

An attendant stepped out muttering to himself. "Honestly, how does someone get ink on the walls in so many different colors and not know how?" He stopped, spotting Jack. "Oh…is there something I can help you with sir?" he asked suspiciously.

Attempting his best to have a casual demeanor, Jack tried to think of a good reason for him to be on the deck. "I um, just pressed the wrong key."

The attendant continued toward him. "I see. Well, it's easy to remember where to go using what I do, sir. Deck A for All, Deck B begins the balconies to Deck C., And Deck D is for departure. Makes it easy for me, anyway. I can help you to Deck D now."

The attendant walked Jack back towards the televator, but Jack stood outside of them, confused. "I'm actually on Deck B. Not D."

The attendant held the door open politely responding. "You didn't hear? We're preparing to dock now sir. We've arrived in Cloud City."

Chapter 2
Cloudy Trails

The altitude of the ship caused a chilling stir of air. Outside, around the edges of the ship's screens, a thin layer of ice crystals had developed. Below the boat, many of the iPlane's propellers were no longer running as it began to slow and decline. Jack had gone up to Deck A, where Sonny agreed to meet him if their investigation succeeded.

 The top deck had changed over the last few hours. Where the sandy beach and oasis had been was now covered in a thick layer of white glittering snow surrounding a frozen pond. People used sleds to travel down long curved slides carved from ice, fully dressed in winter apparel of snow hats, gloves, and thick coats.

 Sonny stood at the bow of the ship, looking out at the large mass of clouds they approached. Even in this newly chilled environment, she was dressed lightly in a t-shirt and jeans. Her pink and white knit hat covered most of her short blonde hair as the chilled wind passed through the rest. She had just taken a deep breath and sighed when Jack approached.

"About time you decided to show up," she whispered. "Almost believed they caught you."

Jack glanced beyond the rails and out into the clouds as they sped on. "Not before I find who I came for. How did you get them to come to your room so fast? I went to deck X, and it was already abandoned."

She pointed at her notepad and showed Jack the colors through the pages. "A few clicks of my pen and I had all of the writing go onto the walls. They couldn't figure out how to remove it. They decided to switch my room to another when the arrival announcement came."

Looking out into the mass of clouds they traveled through, Jack felt cold dampness over his entire body. "Well, I don't get how we arrived anywhere. Nothing's here but empty sky and…well, more sky."

Passing through the last cloud clumps, Jack noticed a tall four-sided clock tower made of stone in the distance protruding from the center of a circle road. A road spiraled up around it to the cloud above. Houses, streets, and shops had been built into a surrounding ring. Behind these houses were several larger circled roads and more buildings that surrounded each other in nine total rings. They were protected by a final cloud barrier on the outside, enclosing them all. An intersecting vertical and horizontal road connected all roads together.

Jack couldn't help but appreciate the architectural layout. The white cloud barriers beneath rose up the building's sides like pizza crust. They surrounded the outer buildings like a barrier, making it difficult to see the others. They sailed toward the outermost ring where there was a large gap that held the only space that was both unprotected by clouds and level with the base of the buildings. It was, however, blocked by gold spiraled gates with two large letter C's entwined. As the ship inched forward, it hovered into the dock and came to a complete stop.

Four guards stood at the gates dressed in white trench coats that blended into the clouds. Silver helmets with tinted protective visors covered most of their face. One stood on either side of the gate with transparent shields that held a blue light that pulsed like electricity from the center and out to the edges. The other two guards processed new arrivals and allowed passage through the gates. Strangely, the gates never moved but became intangible when a guard escorted them through, then became stable once again. Little leather pouches were attached to their belts in a dull shade of gray. Jack assumed it was better not to find out the contents.

As the ship released passengers, Jack and Sonny continued to gaze out at the glistening city. Letter A had arrived on the top deck exiting the televator when he spotted Jack and Sonny at the ship's nose. "Good morning once again, you two. I hope you both enjoyed the trip," Kurt said brightly. "Tour Guide Morris will be waiting for you just beyond the city gates when you are ready. He will escort you through the city and to the celebration."

"You won't be joining us?" Sonny asked earnestly.

Kurt shook his head, gesturing them both to the televator. "We will be docked here until just before sunset and continue back to the hotel. No worries though, we return once a week and every cloud nine holiday, traveling by the rabbit hole and other lands."

"Every what holiday?" Jack interrupted.

"What was that about rabbit holes?" Sonny asked.

Kurt smiled as they stepped into the televator down to Deck D. "You'll find out soon enough."

Taking the ramp down from deck D, they stepped gently onto a cloudy mass, as if walking on drying sponges. The pearly white swirls were soft and airy with a mist that smelled like fresh laundry. The cruise director left them and a few other passengers at the golden gates where Jack and Sonny would be processed. She found silver letters spelled out across the back of the guards' trench coats, hiding their padded armor as they were asked to step up.

"J.A.C.K." Sonny spelled aloud. "Why, *Jack*?"

The guard processing her removed his badge from the inside of his coat, waving it over her. "Not *Jack*, ma'am. J.A.C.K.s," the guard corrected. He checked his insignia and scanned her again. "Jurisdiction Approved Cloud Keepers. We ensure the safety of those within the gates of Cloud City under the approved jurisdiction appointed by the four judges." The guard continued scanning her with a puzzled expression until the badge finally approved. She was escorted through the golden gates, shortly followed by Jack, into a whole new world.

The guards departed, leaving Jack and Sonny in front of thousands of people touring, selling, performing, and shopping. Dozens of stores, carts, and stands placed together outlined the streets like a modern marketplace. Looking to his left, Jack could see the inn for visitors to stay. It wasn't as impressive as his father's, but with seven floors and a cottage-like outer shell, it held a warm, casual, and inviting feeling. The buildings continued around where he discovered Marilyn's Candy Labyrinth, Tinker's Toys, The Cloud City Bank, an impressive city library, and toward the first turn, Birthday Blowout. People came bustling in and out of buildings to the likes of New York City and Paris.

Some were wearing clothes from different periods. More than most were wearing sports jerseys with varying designs of animal. They were in assorted colors displaying different team names. Pictures of animals in fierce poses stretched across the chest. Some people even branded animal tails like a scorpion's or a bunny's, and others had winged backs like dragonflies.

The clock tower chimed loudly eight times from the inner ring alerting the hours of the morning. Jack could hear it clearly projected out as if it were placed beside him. It shook the posters on the walls that displayed the great illusionist's next performance at the New Year celebration. As if right on time, a tall, athletic, dark-skinned man with a goatee, sporting grizzly bear ears atop his head approached them promptly.

"Well, you two look pretty lost," he said in a loud, barking voice. "No need to fret. Every cloud has a silver lining. City slogan an' all. Must be my VIP group? Dreamers, right? I'm Tour Guide Morris."

He offered his hand to Jack and Sonny and shook them wildly and a bit harder than he probably meant. Jack tried not to wince too much. Instead, he grinned politely as Sonny introduced them. "Hello, Morris. I'm Sonny, and this is Jack."

"Tour Guide Morris," he corrected. "Makes it easier to tell us Morris's apart. Now me, I can provide practically any information you'd like about the city."

"Number One mentioned an information expert," Jack recalled. "At the Holiday Hotel. Did he mean you?"

"Ha, first time I've been told my brother called me an expert in anything except smashin' stuff and running," Tour Guide Morris laughed. "Yup he'd be the oldest of us. I know he's a stick-in-the-mud, and kind of the oddball of the family, but still family."

Jack recognized the irony examining the man wearing bear ears but didn't say anything.

"Well come on, there's a lot to see." The tour guide waved them on.

He began escorting Jack and Sonny down the firmer gray brick road walking by Gifted the gift shop, the Cloudy Day Inn where they would later be staying, and a few restaurants. "The Cloudy Day Inn was originally established in 1885. A seven-story building, it was the first hotel built before Lucky's. The burnt orange roof and white siding represent the sun touching clouds. By the way, sunny days are usual around here, but the dryer air takes getting used to. Hasn't rained in nearly a hundred years. Hope you took your tonics. Over there is Tinker's Toys, one of the first few shops built in Cloud City, but two different owners. The store used to be very popular, but since Santa's workshop was built, no one goes in much. O'er down the center of the road, those carts are where most of the food and small holidays display," he continued.

Tour Guide Morris waved to a food vendor as Jack and Sonny trailed behind. With his taller stature, the long strides made it challenging to catch up. More and more people seemed to know of him as if he were a local celebrity. People who passed by sported grizzly bear ears atop their heads and some with matching sports jerseys walked by cheering.

Sonny had been writing what she could as they observed people walking by. "Earlier you mentioned something I didn't understand. What did you mean about telling Morris's apart?"

"Two of my brothers are also named Morris," he chuckled gruffly. "It's a common name in my family, so we use our working titles. Kinda like the Jeff's except I'm the popular one of my brothers." He added, winking at a group of giggling women.

"The Jeff's?" Jack watched a blond-haired man become encircled by a group of people dancing as he played music. "Is that like a gang?"

"Nah," Tour Guide Morris barked. "Just another team like us that happen to have similar names."

He pointed out a few people performing in the streets. "That Jeff o'er there and with the surrounding group is Jeffery, he's a DJ. He'll prolly be playing at the New Year celebration later today."

He made a gesture to another man in a cart with a long line stretching down the street. "That Jeff there is Jeff G., not to be confused with Geoffrey spelled with a G. Jeff G. sells the meanest gourmet grilled cheese sandwiches you'll ever have."

Jack looked back at the cart. The sign Grilled Cheesus hung overhead, and there was an impressive extended line. He shook his head in disbelief. "All that for grilled cheese?"

Tour Guide Morris chuckled hard at this, almost tripping on the stone road. "Well, you never had one of Grilled Cheese Jeff's sandwiches. Best in the city! Even got a national holiday for grilled cheese sandwiches you know. That's how good it is, I tell yea. Hey Jeff!"

He shouted over to a man who had a beach sand complexion, short brown hair, and beard. Jeff G. sported an apron displaying the Epic Eagles while cooking. Nodding, he pointed at his apron and smiled.

Jack and Sonny were shown and told about many more buildings of the outer ring and the holidays supporting them. The tour guide exhausted information of each with precision. Along the way, they passed between a training center with gym equipment and a brick building with splashes of colorful bubbles and the Fiz Factory logo. The layout was enthralling, but it only made him more anxious as he thought of how much his dad would enjoy it too.

More and more people walked by proudly wearing jerseys of different teams, such as the Scorching Scorpions in black and orange flames, the Hectic Hedgehogs in brown and tan, Arctic Wolves in white fur, and the Dragon Flies in green and blue wings. Two large men were having a spat over their favorite players as the group rounded the first corner of the cobblestone road when Sonny raised her head from her notepad and pointed at them with her pen. "Why are so many people wearing animal prints and wings?"

"You've never heard of the Eclipse Tournament?" Tour Guide Morris asked with shock, pointing at his bear ears. "No better fun than the tournament. I train hard every year for it. The games are a full-on battle between two teams of four players. Each team has two blockers at their goals and two runners after the balls. Runners try to score by throwing either the sun or moon ball into the goals. Each goal scored gets ten points. The first team with twelve scores wins."

He stretched his hands in the air as if embracing the air around him. "Ramming into each other, stealing balls, leaping over obstacles, and the power gloves... Tonight after the New Year's celebration finishes the first game begins, and the Grizzlies are gonna beat the Wolves!" He made a deep growl as a few surrounding fans cheered. Sonny smiled uncontrollably.

"What are the gloves used for?" she asked as she jotted down the details of the game.

Jack had mostly been focusing on the architectural layout in the area, studying the columns of the candy labyrinth and an archway of the library, but snapped out of it after Sonny's new sports inquiries. It sounded a lot like football to him, using an additional ball, fewer players, and some new elements.

"See, the Grizzlies, Moles, Hedgehogs, and Chipmunks use autumn gloves that are made to vibrate trees and make leaves fall just like the season, but each team uses it differently. We Grizzly Bears use them to slam into the ground and shake it up. Throws the other teams off. Mighty Moles used to be good years ago, but no one bothers with them now. Don't even have a full team this year. We made it to the final four twice in a row, but last year the Arctic Wolves took us out. They use winter gloves to make frost, but this year's our year."

He stopped their tour near a worn wooden bench near small metal tracks. A red trolley traveled down from uphill where the cobblestone road turned upward. It came in fast, almost colliding with them but halted instantly before impact. There were no controls, but Tour Guide Morris climbed aboard as if this were normal. "This'll be our transportation as we continue to the rest of district one. Next, I'll show you where Lucky's Casino is, and the Cloud City Journal for the latest news. Better get on before it leaves us behind."

Just as he and Sonny stepped toward the trolley, Jack noticed the figure of a man in a tattered suit, with curly hair like his and glasses rushing up to them. Jack's eyes grew wider and wider, the closer he approached, in disbelief. "Dad?" he muttered to himself.

"Father?" Sonny peered around him to get a better look. "What are you doing here?"

Jack blinked a few times as the man grew closer, and a clearer image of the Spirit of Father's Day came into view. His multiple striped and dotted ties rocked back and forth, and if possible he had an even more exhausted expression then when they'd last seen him. He walked up to the group at a quick pace and answered promptly. "Well, I live in the city…but I could ask you the same thing, except there's a more pressing issue first."

Tour Guide Morris stepped off the trolley with a puzzled look. "Whatcha doin' downtown, coach?"

After an exchange of curious looks between Jack and Sonny, Father explained. "There's a situation with one of your teammates and a malfunctioning glove. She was practicing the new pillar formation and, well, she was propelled into the air instead of the ground. She's pretty banged up as if someone's been tampering with it. The team needs to decide what to do if we don't have her tonight and my advice would be to hurry son. The team needs their captain for a group decision before someone shoots their eye out next."

The tour guide gestured to Jack and Sonny. "All right, I'm gonna have to cut the tour short and handle my team. You two should go check into the Cloud City Inn while I'm gone. I'll meet you back at the hotel just before noon to take you to the celebration."

Jack and Sonny watched as the tour guide, and Father climbed aboard the trolley. In an instant, it had powered up, producing a large gust of white steam beneath it. With a burst of speed, it rushed off and disappeared out of view, leaving a streak of red blur like a raging fire truck.

Jack pointed to the clock tower. "We should probably get to the inn right away. We only have a couple hours before noon, and I have to see if anyone here knows where I can find Luminista. The cloud's only so big right? Someone must have a lead to her."

Sonny glared up at the tall emerald green building further up the hill with a glowing gold sign reading *Lucky's Casino*, then to her left, past the city's gates where the Cloud

City Inn resided. "There may be a bit of a problem with that. What are we to do about money? I'm sure it's possible, but I doubt your father owns the hotels here in the city as well."

He hated to admit it, but she had thought of something he hadn't. It didn't occur to Jack they would need money for anything. When he and Sonny first arrived at the Holiday Hotel, the manager Emanuel had taken care of everything as they were locked inside and later discovered to be the son of its owner. He considered the bank, hoping he'd be able to pose as his father when he overheard a familiar voice heading into the candy labyrinth.

Jack hadn't seen the lanky man in the apron since his first night in the hotel when he wandered into the candy garden, but he recognized him instantly.

"Yes ma'am, the island cream extract was ordered from the Fiz Factory, and we should have plenty for the new chewy taffy by tonight." Chip waited in the doorway of the store, speaking to someone as Jack, followed by Sonny, crossed the street.

"We had an odd order for some moon rock candy too," a woman replied sweetly to Chip. Her words washed over Jack like a lullaby. He couldn't see her in the doorway as Chip blocked it, but her voice continued pulling Jack in as if it were the sweetest sound he'd ever heard.

The woman handed Chip a clipboard. "Some oddly mysterious woman with an even stranger name just popped in and out of here not too long ago. Lulu-something asked me to have it ordered for her but disappeared before I got an address. Can't imagine what she would want it for. Terrible taste after all but be sure to get enough of it while you're up there just in case she comes back. I don't want you getting used to the gravity and then get all squishy when you return, sugar."

~ 39 ~

She closed the door behind her. Chip took the clipboard and ran off before Jack had realized, leaving him and Sonny in front of Marilyn's Candy Labyrinth. Jack studied the door. It was identical to the one he had visited in the hotel. Red and white striped like a candy cane, with a peppermint scent. This one was scaled a bit larger, and a sign on the door handle read *Eating may cause splinters!*

Sonny knocked a few times, but Jack became impatient and quickly squeezed the handle. The door creaked open, and a waft of fresh mint and coffee hit his senses pleasantly. The store was set up like a small coffee shop with an espresso machine, bistro tables, baked goods, and a few people on their laptops discussing plays and other literature. It had walnut-brown walls, with white swirls that actually moved like steam up to the ceiling.

A sprite man in his early twenties stood behind the counter in a plum-colored apron, bottle green pants, and gray gloves, feeding a squirrel. His chin had the stubble of a developing black goatee, and his eyes sparkled and twinkled with delight as if his job were the greatest. The squirrel seemed to be communicating with him. It stood on its hind legs and accepted a nut.

"Hello, welcome, come in, come in!" he exclaimed. His face was full of life, and sharp laughter and his head moved much like the squirrel's trying to behave. He seemed to notice their glances at the squirrel. "Rather intelligent creatures, squirrels. I considered geese laying golden chocolate eggs at first."

Jack scoffed. "That's ridiculous."

"I know." The man grinned. "Have you seen the price of geese food these days? Better to start training smaller. Squirrels are excellent at getting nuts out."

Jack looked sideways and muttered to Sonny. "Wonder how long before Marilyn gets this nut out."

"Are you here for coffee or a sweet treat to please and eat?" The spritely young man smiled.

"I was wondering if that was Marilyn who just entered and if I could speak with her?" Jack asked, approaching the counter. "Think she might have some information I could really use."

"Delightful!" he replied. The squirrel ran off into a small hole at the bottom of the wall behind him. "This way. Hurry, hurry. Come in. Come in!"

He turned around to the wall where a combination lock was placed. After a few turns and a rhyme he seemed to be saying to himself, a door opened in the wall revealing large waxy hedges. The hedges were taller than any of them could see pass and made of licorice vines with green buttercream leaves. The open-air blew in the scent of raspberry roses and peppermint tulips. The cashier took a deep breath, inhaling the aroma.

"Wonderful, stupendous smells," he said, delighted. "I can't wait to create a fully functional factory for my own inventions. Can you imagine a pillow made of marshmallow? Soft to sleep and then to eat!"

"That wouldn't make sense," Jack said. "Wouldn't it just get sticky or stale after long?" he asked.

The cashier responded with a bounce of joy. "Doesn't have to make sense. That's the fun of inventing candy, finding ways to make all flavors work!"

Sonny giggled and gazed out at the garden in amazement. Jack remembered she hadn't experienced the candy garden of the hotel, but this one was much different than the garden he'd visited.

"Where's Marilyn?" He asked impatiently.

"She should be in there working somewhere, but you'll have to search for her yourself." The sprite man sighed as if he were missing out. "You try to give the candy mixture a little punch one time by adding boxing gloves, and suddenly you're stuck at the counter."

Jack raised an eyebrow, but Sonny just shrugged and smirked.

"Well, if you two should find yourselves lost, just yell, and I'll try to direct you back here. Name's William, but you can call me Billy."

Billy shut the door behind him, resealing the wall. In front of them lay the vast candy labyrinth. An entire maze made of the tall edible hedges blocking any sight into where Marilyn was working and stretched wider than Jack could see to the left and right. An opening in front of them allowed the only entrance, and Jack immediately began walking without hesitation.

"Marilyn!" Jack yelled out continuously. "Marilyn!"

"Who do you think Billy is keeping the area guarded against?" Sonny asked between Jack's callings.

Jack refused to be sidetracked, determined to continue his search. "I don't know. I'm sure when we find her, we can ask. Marilyn!"

"Too bad we don't have any candy with us," Sonny mentioned as they walked.

"Candy?" Jack repeated. "It's all around us."

"No, I mean different candy that's easy to see, like the fairytale of the seven paths?" Sonny nodded. "Or the one of the brother and sister, and house made of candy. Some fairytales have life-changing lessons." Jack sighed and continued walking.

Turn after turn, they walked around candied red apples, blue and purple flowers, giant cotton candy spider webs, candy cane branches, giant mushrooms with cream fillings, and vines that either formed pointing arrows in misleading directions or grabbed at their ankles. It wasn't until an hour later that they turned a corner and were startled. A nearly finished chocolate Minotaur towered over them, blocking their path. Steam spewed from its nostrils while a distinct whistling came from behind it. A woman could be partially seen standing behind it with a piping bag of chocolate and a spatula, pausing as they stepped into the square.

"Who let you two in?" she asked as she made the giant bull's tail. "You're not J.A.C.K.'s, are you?"

"No, but my name is Jack," he answered. Her sweet voice washed over him, and he momentarily lost focus on why he was there. "Uh, Marilyn, right? Like the Candy Garden's Marilyn?"

She walked around to the front of the bull where she could be seen fully. Her long auburn hair with orange highlights brushed over her eyes. It flowed down to her apron, covering a purple tank top and black jeans. Specks of chocolate were on her face and hands, but she didn't appear to notice. She reminded Jack of a punk-rock singer he'd seen minus the chocolate on her nose.

"I'd think it's pretty obvious, sugar. Are ya here for a tour or just to interview me?" She pointed at Sonny's notepad. "Because the labyrinth's not nearly half done yet, and you should really leave candy as a trail here. It'll be tough to find your way out."

Sonny looked up from her notes and smiled at Jack. "Well, to be honest, I do have a question about your shop. I was wondering why this area is hidden behind a wall? Why were you concerned if we were those guards outside the gates?"

She wiped the bit of chocolate from her nose and waved the spatula, ushering Jack and Sonny to follow. Hesitantly, they followed. They walked in silence for a bit, passing more hedges and a few obstacles Marilyn quickly shut down. A giant spider made of hard candy spewing webs and a swamp of bubbling sticky caramel were both settled. They freely leaped over stones to avoid snake-sized gummy worms snipping at their feet. Jack realized she'd worked backward from the labyrinth's opposite side most likely to avoid being trapped in herself.

They continued to follow Marilyn until they reached a small secluded area where a circular path had been cleared. It surrounded a small plot where a few plants grew among grass blades. They sprouted nuts that held a silver finish. Appearing naturally metallic, the nuts reflected in the sun. Marilyn gestured to the plants as if this were all the explanation she needed.

"These nuts have an addictively sweet center, so much in fact that they are banned from being used in food," she confessed. "Well that and the silver shell are very poisonous, so you have to be extremely careful. I have to get the seeds from an island once a year. Impossible to find unless you know where to look. I combine them with a potent extract from the Fiz Factory to make it a safe mixture that will coat anything and make it delicious. Sour candies, salty treats, moon rock candy, wood. Whatever you do or don't like." She pulled candy from her apron, placing a piece into her mouth and offering them some. "Chocolate?"

"No, thank you. I don't care for chocolate actually." Sonny made a note of the silver shelled nut. The mention of moon rock candy jolted Jack's memory.

"A woman was here earlier I think," he said eagerly. "She may have some vital information for me. Her name is Luminista. Any clue where she may have gone to at all?"

"You know now that I think of it, she did mention a place she had to be before she disappeared on me," Marilyn muttered. "Something about a card from the Birthday Blowout a few stores down. I remember she mentioned Oracle Island and since I have family there I said—"

"Thanks a lot," Jack interrupted. He grabbed Sonny, who was still writing, by the hand and rushed back to the entrance. It took a bit of traveling, but thankfully, his memory was sharp, and Sonny had written directions on how they came in. After knocking on the wall to get out, Billy gawked at them, stunned as they dashed out of the entrance, startling the squirrel.

They ran by the bank, bookstore, and Tinker's Toys, where a mousy-haired potbellied man in brown overalls displayed eerie wooden puppets by their strings. Just next door to it, they arrived at the Birthday Blowout Store, an entire warehouse devoted to the celebration of birthdays. Inside were hundreds of shelves full of candles, wrapping paper, party games, and cards that produced fireworks and projected messages. Balloons hovered high above, covering the ceiling in sizes as small as a bowling ball and some larger than a truck. Calendars highlighted the date in yellow, streamers rose and fell by themselves in vibrant colors, and lanterns flickered with an ambient light floating from one to another.

Sonny was occupied by a thick pen made of wax she'd found, while Jack scanned for the fortune teller. A robust man with a huge belly, small head, and tiny neck waddled over past some novelty gifts and several birthday cakes. Jack couldn't help but wonder how the portly guy was able to maneuver around his stock so easily. His belly was within inches of multiple party hats, but he scooted by with ease as if he was able to do so wearing a blindfold.

"Howdy, folks!" he greeted loudly, shaking both their hands. "Name's Bob, you're just in time for the New Year's special. Birth of a new year, the birth of a new deal. We have decorations for regular birthdays, sweet sixteens, bar mitzvahs, quinceañeras, even un-birthdays. I see you've noticed our candles, little lady."

Sonny's attention was fixed on a mid-century pen-shaped candle. It was black and had the illusion of silver ink flowing through it. Her hand barely touched it when it began to smoke. A few black wisps emerged lightly and then just as suddenly stopped. She stared at it puzzled, and then marked in her notepad.

"So they light themselves when you come in contact?" she asked.

"Actually my candles are enchanted," Bob corrected. "Emits black smoke if your birthday hasn't passed this year, white smoke the week of, and fully lights up on your birthday. Perfect for that one special wish. When's your birthday?"

"February 23," she replied.

"Less than two months away." He beamed. "Well if you blow out a proper flame on your birthday and make a wish, it'll come true. Any wish at all. Well almost, can't exactly turn back time, wish someone gone, or anything life changing like that but practically anything probable. Maybe something you once had or small things you want to happen. The general rule is if the candle blows out, your wish will come true."

Jack sighed. "Wishes?... Wish someone would tell me where Luminista was."

The birthday store owner turned to him. "Well, there you go. Wishes do come true. You just missed her a little bit ago, on her way to see the doctor."

"Doctor?" Jack muttered his eyes widening. "You mean Dr. DeLuca? The Valentine's Day Spirit?"

Bob waved the black wisps of smoke from the candle away. "No, not that kind of doctor, he's more of a therapist with a green thumb. This guy's a real medicine man. Witch doctor down on Enlightened Circle, seven blocks into the center. If she's still in the city, that's where you'd find her."

In minutes, they had cleared most of the rings traveling the seven blocks into the center. Together, Jack and Sonny had walked swiftly following the long road dividing the district. Even though she was taller, Sonny had difficulty keeping up with Jack's determined march. He could feel her eyes on him, but he didn't want anything new to distract him. If his father was still in trouble, he needed every moment to count.

It wasn't hard to see the differences of Enlightened Circle when they arrived. The sun didn't shine on the area very well, as it was closer to the city's center and therefore beneath the thickest parts of the cloud above. Tiny specs like miniature stars hovered and glowed ominously. Chants echoed with the humming of a green light that shimmered from nowhere.

Some buildings were made of wood that creaked with decades of dust. Others were straw huts connected together or elaborate colorful tents. Only a few people were actually outside in the street. Four women, in particular, surrounded a sizeable black cauldron the size of a bathtub. Steam overflowed into the streets as it gurgled and bubbled. A green shimmer basked from it eerily as they stirred.

Sonny approached one of the women directing the others on how to stir. She looked young with long, luxurious red hair, but her eyes held the wisdom of a much older spirit. Her white dress draped over her arms as she searched through a thick brown book. Jack couldn't help but notice how much they all resembled witches or fairies.

The woman to her right had a black dress and held an umbrella shielding her from the popping bubbles. She was much older and paunch, with her hair twisted into three pigtails beneath a gold cap. Her eye patch twitched as she and the younger looking woman had a spat. Jack wasn't sure if she was sick or envious, but her face held an unattractive green all the same.

The other two around the boiling pot continued stirring with large wooden spoons gripped in their hands. On the north side, a kindly looking elderly woman blew kisses to no one in particular. To the eastern side a dry withered woman with no shoes gave a fierce scowl. Sonny politely interrupted them.

"Excuse me, ladies," she said with heightened enthusiasm and curiosity. "Are you women real witches, and actually brewing?"

The younger woman's blue eyes flickered, and she closed her book firmly. "Sorceresses preferably and yes, I am attempting to train them on brewing."

"I know how to brew just fine Glinda," the woman in black responded shrilly, holding her umbrella up tightly. "But if I get wet..."

"You would surely melt like the wicked witch you are." The barefoot woman snickered and turned to the woman blowing kisses. "If it would only work on this one. Locasta may finally realize her kisses aren't protecting anyone!"

"Oh hush, shoeless," snapped the woman blowing kisses. "No one even remembers your name. Next time I'll just LET the house fall on you!"

An argument began to break out between the four of them. Glinda fixed her dress, while the green one hid behind her umbrella. The kindly woman argued her kisses could shield, while the nameless woman complained about her shoes being stolen. Jack marched up to them as they all continued to bicker.

"Does anyone know where I can find the fortune teller Luminista?!" he shouted over them all.

The sickly looking woman was taken aback but quickly recovered. "Fortune teller? More of a hack if you ask me. People only care about her because of her mother's fame."

"Her mother?" Sonny chimed in. "Who is her mother?"

Glinda folded her book multiple times into a tiny square, flattening it and placed it into the waist of her white dress. "Luminista's mother is a powerful oracle. She could take simple choices and tell you what would happen the next day, month, even years beyond, your grandkids. A truly gifted seer, I believe in the islands. Her daughter, however…"

"…is an amateur," the green woman interrupted. "Never as gifted as people thought she would be and can't see much further than what's right in front of her. That's what she gets for traveling between planes so often. Just as insufferable as the city's hierarchy. If you're looking for her help, check out the doctor's huts over there." She pointed a gnarled green finger over to the straw huts linked together.

"Thanks," Sonny replied brightly.

"Yeah, yeah, good luck and good riddance," the woman cackled, ducking a final splash from the cauldron.

Although from outside they appeared separated, the straw huts were actually linked together, forming a small medical lab. It was complete with the essential hospital beds, monitors, support systems, and more. Nurses in teal scrubs rushed paperwork or attended to the few patients in need of care. Jack thought it lucky they weren't absurdly busy. A few beds were empty, and a nurse at the desk in front of them waved politely.

Before they could even ask, a man in a white medical coat stood up from his chair. He'd just finished helping a patient with a shrunken head in the corner when he turned to Jack. He was tall with dark skin and close-cut black hair. As he turned to face them, the man showed a frightening feature. The top portion of his face was covered by a mask of skeletal elements from his forehead to his nose. Below that, his mouth formed a contradicting yet welcoming smile.

"Jack Taylor, correct?" the man asked in a deep impacting voice. "I have something for you."

Jack stared at him, searching his pockets. "For me?"

"Yes." He replied. "Luminista left instructions for you. It's somewhere around here. She told me you would be here soon, but had to project herself back to your world quickly."

"My world?" Jack asked skeptically. "Are you the witch doctor? How did she leave? Does she know where my dad is?"

Jack rambled off questions like a salesman. He tried to gather as much information about the man as he could, from the man's quick glances to his ability to misplace things so quickly. The skeletal faced man continued to search the pockets of his lab coat for the card thoroughly. He removed pens, a stethoscope, and lollipops before locating it.

"Doctor, shaman, healer, whichever you like." The doctor located the card and handed it to Jack. "Luminista has unique abilities. Like many seers, usually through meditation, she can cross over between the spiritual plane and yours. Didn't you know she was alive like you?"

Jack and Sonny shook their heads in unison. It never occurred to Jack that he and Sonny were not the only dreamers. More questions were piling up, but he mostly wondered what Luminista said to his father, to send the flashlight in the first place.

When the doctor handed him the card, he wasted no time in ripping open the envelope. It was clear the fortune teller had chosen the card from Birthday Blowout, as several sparks flew into the air upon opening it. Other than that, he realized it was dull. It was an ordinary card with an empty space for a message. Jack read the note, taking it in as thoroughly as possible, recalling her voice as he read.

Young Mr. Taylor,

This is the path you have chosen, and now there is no going back. Although your path has many possible endings, only one will rescue us all. I urge you to use all of the lessons you have and will learn. Do not ignore what is right in front of you. Keep an open mind to all possibilities small and large. Accept help when it's given as well as needed and above all, be sure to remember enemies and friends can come from anywhere. You were born from a long line of essential and brave Jacks. Nimble Jack, Jack, the giant killer, and even famous pirates. The heroic bloodline can continue with you. Events will come full circle in the end. This will be the last you will hear directly from me until your journey is nearly complete. Beware of the father. Enjoy the party.

HAPPY BIRTHDAY!

The card ended, but he wasn't sure if the *Happy Birthday* was a message for him or just part of the card. Either way, it hadn't helped answer any of the questions he had except one. He wouldn't get a chance to ask the fortune teller anything about his father. He did get something small out of it as he tucked the card into his coat pocket. She wanted him to attend the New Year's party that afternoon.

Beware of the father? He thought to himself. *Whose father? My father? The Spirit of Father's Day? What kind of message is that?* Brushing his hand through his hair, he sighed. "Gypped by a gypsy. Perfect."

"Actually the term is Romani fortune teller, don't be rude." The doctor corrected sternly." Luminista has been a dear friend and brings news of medical breakthroughs to me from your plane when she visits. It's amazing what simple items we have here that can be used to cure people of harmful effects. Did you know moon rock candy will aid in anti-gravity effects like losing consciousness? And some Fiz drinks can shield you from burns? The new Green Apple Mint can even help breathe in space or underwater if it's submerged with a towel and covering the mouth. Anyways, I hope in the end she left you something useful. Sometimes it's hard to understand what matters until you get there."

Jack almost forgot he was still standing in the hospital. He muttered a soft thank you before realizing Sonny had already left. Peeking outside, he saw her silhouette disappear around the corner. *Where is she going?* He wondered as he chased her footsteps back up through the dividing street. He had to run to keep up with the sound as it ricocheted off the walls until he finally found her.

On the west side of the outer ring of the city, Sonny stood at a metal guardrail protecting onlookers from the cliff. Danger and caution signs were posted on the rails, strongly urging people to avoid the area. It overlooked a large surface of mossy valley covered in the thickest layer of fog Jack had ever seen. A few tombstones were barely visible but separated from one another by quite a bit of distance. It was eerily dark, almost completely hidden beneath the city. An oddly mixed odor of rotten eggs and burnt marshmallow lingered in the air, followed by inaudible whispers growing louder.

Sonny stood on her toes, surveying the area over the rails with a bemused brow. "I've never seen a cemetery like this before."

"Why'd you ditch me in the hospital to come here?" Jack asked, frustrated, gagging on the smell.

"I'm not sure really," she muttered dreamily. "I heard voices calling out from this place like echoes got a headache, and I couldn't help myself."

The red trolley raced around the corner and screeched loudly to a stop just a few feet away from the rails. Tour Guide Morris stepped off the vehicle with a disapproving gaze. It was almost humorous for such a tall man wearing bear ears to appear so severe, but his gloomy expression set the tone abruptly.

"You two were supposed to be at the inn," he said, glancing over the edge. "Really ought not to be here of all places. Might have a stronger effect on you."

"What do you mean?" Jack asked, taking notice of Sonny's vacant expression. "What is this place?"

"No one in the city likes to talk 'bout it." The tour guide shook his head and pointed over the railing. "It's the Valley of Lost Souls, and I'm warnin' ya, it's not a place you should travel to. But I guess better you learn from me than wander in yourself."

"Learn what?" Sonny asked.

"You see, energy is never created or destroyed, it just transfers. You have energy, and so do us spirits. When you cross planes, it comes with you. Ours exists like a glowing ball of light. Ye prolly can't see it, but in the center, there is a well swirling with such darkness, no light can penetrate it. Whether it's an accident or a punishment, that there's the final death for any spirit. You lose your energy. That big well is where the energy is funneled into to be extinguished. Prolly the most dangerous energy source in the city."

Jack turned his head slowly from the graveyard like scene. "Why is that?"

"You hear those echoes?" the tour guide asked. "The echoes come from those that are gone as the energy is taken, but the well is so deep beneath the city it takes weeks to hear it climb up to the top. If you ever heard the term ghosts, folks 'round here don't use it, and that's the reason why. Spirits hold on to a piece of who they were when they cross over, but some violent ones or those in the well…they become something else altogether. Something dark and unnatural, and might be the reason people here weren't too fond of Halloween becoming a holiday," he finished.

"Wait, did Mr. Shadow have something to do with them?" Jack guessed.

The tour guide barked, "Shadow? No. Past spirits maybe, but not him. Despite how old he looks, he's actually the newest holiday spirit we've had."

Jack and Sonny stared out into the valley, unsure of what could and could not be seen in the distant fog. The valley declined the closer it came to the rail, and continued beneath them making it impossible to tell just how large it really was. The whispers seemed eerily close the longer they stayed, and Jack noticed Sonny's developing trance. Her eyes slowly began closing much like the day she'd fallen asleep from the dream dust in the Holiday Hotel. For a moment, she seemed to think climbing over the rail was a good idea. It wasn't until Tour

Guide Morris, clasped his hands together that her foot stepped down.

"Well we should get you two to the elevator so we can get you up to the party," the Tour Guide stated.

"Up?" Sonny asked, shaking her head as if just waking up. "Where are we going?"

The tour guide boarded the trolley. It sank a little due to his size as the gears began powering up again. "Time to celebrate on the highest cloud o'course. Didn't think this was the whole city did ya? This is just the first cloud. The celebration's on Cloud Nine."

Chapter 3
Cloud Nine

The ride up was different than Jack was used to. Two televators of Lucky's Casino allowed access throughout the building. They were identical to the Holiday Hotel's except for a gold exterior and green light that illuminated from the keys. One was marked out of order by a hanging sign similar to a foreclosed sign he'd seen recently. An average elevator positioned between the two gold ones was completely clear. It traveled up through the stacked clouds just outside the building. Unlike the two televators beside it, this transparent elevator wasn't instantaneous yet still extremely speedy. It raced straight up for miles following the casino's steep ascension into the sky. Nine keys lit in gold for each cloudy level of the city. The rise up the vertical distance allowed just enough time to view the layout of each cloud they passed. The tour guide explained how each cloud in the city operated.

The first, second, and third clouds were trade districts. Each one, the home for minor or daily holidays like birthdays, anniversaries, grilled cheese day, an arena for the eclipse tournament, national soup day, and hat day. The fourth and fifth clouds were full of farming areas and country roads. The roads divided the clouds into sections like pie slices. These clouds were the homes of better known holidays like grandparents' day, secretaries' day, and nurses' day. Clouds six and seven were upscale cities containing expanded condos and a massive car dealership. The holidays there celebrated famous historical people and events like Martin Luther King's Birthday, and President's Day, and the armed services like Memorial Day, Veteran's Day, Patriot's Day, and Labor Day.

As they rocketed even higher into the sky, they passed the eighth cloud, which formed a large town with several neighborhoods. Many houses on the east side of the cloud were grouped together, forming Mother's Avenue and on the west side Father's Lane. Spread between them were plotted areas for Groundhog Day's underground tunnels, and large tents together like a circus. A winding road followed between each stacked cloud like a corkscrew, beginning on the first cloud around the clock tower, and flattening up to the last. The tour guide explained it as the original way up through the city before the casino's elevator, but an exhausting one before they had vehicles.

Finally, the elevator began to slow as it climbed just above the most enormous cloud at the very top. It shuttered to a stop, and the transparent doors slid open to the entrance of a vast hall twenty feet tall. Giant dark iron statues stood much taller on either side of the hall's entrance as if ready to clash in a horrific battle. The figure on the left was of a beautiful woman with curled locks of hair flowing down her back. Her dress cascaded out of an armored chest plate. Vines traced her arms, legs, and neck, while an impressively stretched single wing sprouted from her back ready to take flight or shield her as she held an intricate knolled staff.

Opposing her, separated by the archway, was an iron statue of a man with robust facial features, and muscular arms. He held a large sword with an etched blade. His hair was short and spiked at the top, allowing his armored shoulders and chest to be easily seen. His smile was menacing as if he knew just where to strike next. The single wing jetting from his back appeared edgier with sharper feathers and battle-worn, and his eyes were dangerous and vengeful.

Sonny gazed up at both statues for some time before reading the inscription on the ground between them aloud. "Without darkness, light is not understood."

"The two beings." Tour Guide Morris stepped out of the elevator, his arms open between them. "Leads us to Justice Hall. The two beings created all of this."

"Who are they?" Sonny asked, staring at the woman uncertainly. "They look like…angels, missing a wing?"

The tour guide walked them between the statues and into the hall, where iron fixtures hung on walls, and high ceilings had candlelit chandeliers. "It's an old legend of the capital actually. Centuries ago, the two beings used to be one angelic being with incredible abilities, greater than any symbol, holiday spirits, even the four judges. Did some incredible things like putting giants the size of a country to sleep, creating this city, and taming the elemental rock. But there was an inner conflict, and the being was forced to split itself into the two you saw outside. That was the first."

"Well, what happened to them?" Jack chimed in as they approached a four-way intersection in the hall. "Where are they now?"

"At first, although they were complete opposites, they worked together very well," Tour Guide Morris continued. "A being of natural light that was kind and lovely. She took care of your plane of existence and all the living beings, going by the name Kayla for centuries. The other was a being of darkness. He was strong, forceful, and much more disciplined. He tended to the existence on this plane and anyone that passed on, created the well in the valley of lost souls, and from what I've read, the beings worked together peacefully. Neither was good or evil or nothin', just did what needed to be done like night and day, and there was a balance, up until the second divide."

They entered the crossway of the four paths in the hall where Jack noticed the posted directions. A sign to the right labeled J.A.C.K.'s Headquarters pointed them down another hallway lined with portraits on the wall. Behind them, another arrow pointed back to Lucky's Penthouse where they could go back through Cloud City. To his left, an ominous red portal was bared off in a shorter hall. A sign pointed in its direction to the Judges' Quarters. The sign straight ahead of them pointed to Cloud Nine, where the tour guide continued leading them.

"The being of darkness grew bitter and resentful of the praise Kayla received... He was also the reason for several plagues and wars. During an argument, he challenged her for her abilities. Their battle literally shook the skies themselves, and several cities including parts of the capital but in the end, Kayla delivered the final blow. When it was over, she divided him into two parts, banishing his mind to this plane and his body to yours. Then she separated herself the same way, locked their minds away so there'd be no way the balances could cause more destruction. Been nearly a thousand years since it all happened. Only thing is, a lot of folks believe one of the beings will find their other half and come back."

Sonny recorded the story into her notepad as if it was a story her grandfather told her. "Why do some believe that?"

The tour guide's expression became hardened. Jack noticed there was a bit less cheer in his face as he finished the story. "Years back, a dreamer with a vendetta against the judges found the beings' minds and released them. Meaning one day, whenever their bodies die on your plane, if they're reunited with their memories, it could be very good, very bad, or worse."

Tour Guide Morris' expression returned to a pleasant one. "Least that's what I reckon. Well, here we are," he carried on casually.

They exited the long hall into an open area outside where the bright blue sky could be seen clearly. A circular road led out into eleven additional pathways. Inscribed wooden arrows pointed to each path leading down snaking roads, cobblestone streets, snowy paths, or grassy trails. The Overpass began off to the left beside them. Sonny continued reading the names of each route as they went around.

"Rebirth Caverns, Bicentennial Village, Ali Pillars, Shadow Manor, Plymouth Meeting, Light Festival, Holly Woods, Imani Park, Phoenix's Estate, DeLuca Gardens…" Sonny read each sign completing the circle, finally turning behind them where she read the sign directed behind them. "…Lucky's Penthouse."

"Yup, last stop of the tour," Tour Guide Morris concluded, opening his arms wide to a long line. "Cloud Nine is not only the most secured and closest to the sun but the home of the year's twelve most popular holidays. Not everyone below believes they should have it to themselves, but it's the way things have been. Each path takes you to another holiday's home, and that one with the long line there is where you two head for the celebration. I'll be off training for the big game tonight. Be sure'n root for the Grizzlies guys! Grrrrrr!"

The tour guide waved as he headed back through the hall and disappeared into the distance back to the elevator. Sonny approached the line, but Jack held back. Near the entrance of the DeLuca Gardens trail, a small person half his size draped in a green cloak from head to ankle kneeled down on the road barefooted. Through the sleeves, he could see tiny hands peeking out, making circular motions. A flower began to grow and wave as if dancing in its roots. Vines chased each other, petals waved, and together they formed into a colorful picture on the road of a dancing garden.

As if hypnotized by the swaying petals, Jack walked over to the small person, mesmerized by the movement. "I've never seen anyone affect plants like that. Are you a holiday spirit?"

The person beneath the cloak immediately became still. Stopping the hand movements, the plant shook bitterly then withered away. After a short glance up, Jack was able to see the person beneath the hood was a young Asian girl who looked no older than seven. She wore a dress beneath the cloak as if it were a costume she'd grown bored of. Her short dark hair had red accents dangling over her rainbow-colored eyes. Dirt from the ground smudged her cheeks, stained the frilly dress, and covered her hands and feet. She had an innocent stare but quickly shielded her face, then abruptly began to run before Jack stopped her.

"Wait, don't run, I'm not gonna hurt you," Jack said with open hands. "What's your name?"

The small girl stopped and replied without turning in a tiny voice. "You won't tell the old man?"

Old man? He thought to himself. The only person who crossed Jack's mind was Phoenix, but under the circumstances that didn't make things any clearer. Phoenix had been reborn as a baby the night before and was anything but old. He shook his head all the same.

"My name is Spring," she answered timidly as she removed her hood. "I'm really not supposed to leave the temple, but I enjoy being outside very much." Her rainbow-colored eyes moved to Jack's pocket. "Does he prefer it inside?"

Jack reached into his jacket pocket and removed his flashlight cautiously. The lens reflected the girl's questioning stare reversely as she looked into it. Something in her eyes was more mysterious than the others. Every color of the rainbow formed separately in her pupils like a prism hiding something beneath. If she was a holiday spirit, she was much younger than he thought possible.

He held the flashlight out with the intent to ask her how she knew. However before he was able to, she'd already taken it, placed it on the ground, and gently pet the length from light to handle. Jack had to stop himself from snatching it back in anger. It made him feel uneasy. Someone had hidden his father over it, and until he found him, Jack's sole purpose, for now, was its protection.

There was a gradual change that followed. The green metallic finish of the flashlight began ruffling into fur. The magnifying glass piece sunk into the body as the handle curved into a small fluffy tail. Four legs sprouted from beneath the middle with tiny paws. The lens formed into two closed eyes as a head, snout, little black nose, and pointy ears developed from the front casing. Finally, the gold scripture *Light up the darkness* stretched into a swirling gold stripe from its green fury head to the end of its scruffy tail.

When she stopped petting it, Jack could clearly see a miniature puppy where his flashlight had been. It curled itself up into a sleeping position and became very still. Jack bent down and scooped the puppy up as it barely filled his two cupped hands. Its eyes were closed, and soon after being picked up, it changed back. The girl bounced to her feet with wide eyes.

"His name is Rocho," she said in a wistfully delighted voice as the dog reformed itself into Jack's flashlight. "Isn't he adorable? Puppies are protective and loyal. When you hold him, he'll turn back, but I prefer him full of life. Don't you?"

Stammering, Jack tried to form the words, *Thanks*, while also asking the question, *how*, when Sonny yelled back for Jack.

"Jack! We're almost to the front," she called from the head of the line. His attention was drawn away for only a moment, but in that instant, the young girl had gone. He was left confused, holding his newly changed companion. He placed the flashlight into his pocket and caught up with Sonny.

The line of people followed a stretched tan road. It took several minutes to climb up the path as he was given disapproving looks by those waiting. A few made snide remarks of hero privileges he tried to ignore. He wasn't sure how Sonny was able to advance through the nearly half-mile line so quickly until he spotted her with someone familiar.

The tan road emptied into a massive front yard longer than the waiting line on either side. It was filled with vibrant green grass surrounded by a spiked iron gate allowing a single opening. The road split the yard into several rectangles around the estate leading to the largest house Jack had ever seen. A mansion, at least two football fields long and four stories tall, towered into view. Gray blocks with pointed dark pillars, grand windows, and pointed roofs overlooked the grounds.

Although it was during the day, spotlights waved in the sky from the doorway. Jack assumed they were from the night before. A wide arc protruded above two open doors reaching the second floor. Sonny stood at the front where two cloud keepers guarded the entrance of the mansion. The familiar person stood with her wearing unfamiliar clothes. The formal gray suit, red lapel, and name tag were different, but his strong face and bear ears were unmistakable.

"Tour Guide Morris?" Jack walked up the stairway. "I thought you went to train?"

"Butler…Morris," the suited man corrected as he adjusted his tie with his gloved hands. He stepped between the two cloud keepers with more of an average frame than Jack initially noticed. He was taller than Jack but not nearly as much as the tour guide and held a broader build. However, the face was much alike. "T. G. M. is one of my brothers. I'm in charge of the estate's staff. Phoenix has been waiting for you both as his special guests this afternoon."

Jack could see the cloud keeper's visors illuminate and scroll with his name, height, age, weight, and last known aliases as he walked by. The guards waved the next few guests in line forward after Jack and Sonny. The moment they passed through, a loud buzzer rang. Butler Morris was forced to open a side panel of the wall to input a code. When it stopped, he resealed the wall. "I'll have to get maintenance on that," he stated. "Of all the days to malfunction…"

They were led into the grand hall where clocks made of crystal chandeliers sparkled and hung from vaulted ceilings, ticking closer and closer to noon. Crimson red streamers danced from side to side above them while Butler Morris showed them nearly a thousand portraits of Phoenix's previous lives where they were affixed to the walls. One for every year he was reborn, all different in their aged appearance, yet retaining a hint of each life.

Near the end of the hall of portraits, a line of twelve men and women waited similarly dressed. Uniformed gray and red servants stood at attention. They each had their head bowed as if waiting for new orders. Only one wore all black with a chauffeur's hat and gloves. Butler Morris stopped at each servant and introduced them.

"This is the rest of the estate's staff," the butler gestured. "Our housekeepers, Tracy, Jennifer, and Seandra. The groundskeepers, John, Brooks, and Josh. The two maintenance men, Brian and Paul. Tonight's caterers, Chef Paula, Dave, and Wes, and lastly the chauffeur, Theodore. We tend to the 365 rooms of the estate."

Everyone nodded their head slightly as they were introduced except for the chauffeur, who tilted his hat. The brim hid his eyes and nose, but there was something familiar about him that Jack couldn't figure out. Disregarding it, he followed the butler to the ballroom.

Before the doors opened, they could already feel vibrations from the floor and a loud pulsing beat from behind the ballroom's doors. "What is that sound?" Sonny asked. "Why are the doors shaking?"

Butler Morris grabbed the handles of the doors. "Because behind them is the ultimate celebration."

As soon as the doors were opened, Jack thought he felt an explosion of life. Music immediately burst out flooding over them. The room was filled with thousands of people like an organized riot crammed into an enormous concert hall. More holiday spirits and symbols in a single place than Jack had ever seen were gathered. Jeffrey had his DJ equipment in the center of the room positioned onto the center of a pool, with speakers jetting out around him in a circle. Sound waves could be seen blasting out of them with silver notes. Balloons burst above people with red and silver confetti showering down onto the round glass tables. Horns blew, lights flashed in the background, and glasses filled themselves with sparkling beverages. Performers were on a hovering moving stage above the room while stars trailed around them made of fire. People laughed and danced as if they couldn't control themselves, and Jack simply mouthed the word "Epic."

As noon approached, Jack followed Sonny inside and noticed a few presidential birthday spirits, such as Abraham Lincoln and Teddy Roosevelt, discussing the evolution of civil rights with Martin Luther King, Jr. to his right. A dark-skinned woman with long braided hair wrapped in a yellow and black silk scarf and matching dress laughed together with a light-skinned woman in an elegant white dress with blue Stars of David on the hems, wrists, and necklines over a story.

He recognized several odd featured people as well. The potbellied man from Tinker's Toys stood near a door to the side. No one really paid him much attention as he performed a puppet show. He became frustrated as one of the puppets didn't move correctly. Jack watched as the toymaker took a tool from a pocket in his overalls. Oddly enough, instead of using the device to adjust the doll, it seemed as if he were threatening the puppet. The man spoke to the toy in a scratchy voice as if he'd inhaled too much sawdust and Jack wondered if he was waiting for the puppet to respond. His mousy brown hair shook as he narrowed his eyes. Shortly after, he returned to his performance as if nothing unordinary had happened.

There was a long stage stationed in the rear with a glass wall allowing a view to the open sky and neatly tended green grass of the expansive backyard. Just below the stage, a rabbit not much shorter than Jack, whom he assumed was the Easter Bunny, walked on his hind legs in a turquoise vest and bowtie. His nose wrinkled as he tried sniffing the grass blades so many yards away. Three large men in black suits, sunglasses, and green ties would whisper to each other and glance at him as if plotting something suspiciously. That's when Jack noticed it.

A unique throne chair sat on stage turned away from the group of attendees. A cloud keeper stood on either side, guarding it carefully. Jack recognized it at once as the same throne he searched on the roof of the hotel. The red plush pillows were sunken in slightly. He wondered if the extra security was because of the events with Trick.

The ticking of numerous clocks echoed in the room, and all those around ceased their conversations. Everyone began to clap and cheer as the clocks ticked down from ten, growing louder and more pronounced until there was a single loud chime. Smoke spewed from behind the throne. It rose into the air like a cloud until thunder brewed. The clouds swirled together, and a moment later, lightning struck the ground, and a thin man stood in front of the throne with a smoking jacket.

Sonny watched with excitement and a bit of confusion. "Wait, that's not Phoenix."

The man stood in a black tuxedo with his sleeves rolled, an untied bowtie around his neck, dark eyes, and a top hat. The lightning in the clouds briefly displayed his name. *Presto the Great Illusionist.* Applause followed that he relished in with open arms. A sly smile spread across his face as he rubbed his hands together. A deck of cards spread out between his hands and hovered in midair at his fingertips where a few golden rings glistened. Stepping between the cards and snatching the ace of spades, he rolled his top hat down from his head to his empty hand.

"An illusionist..." Jack said aloud, thinking of Luminista's reading of the magician card. "Wonder what the odds of that are?"

"It is my great honor to perform before such an impressive crowd," Presto announced with finesse, "and introduce such a powerful and legendary holiday spirit back from the brink of extinction and always protecting us all."

Turning around, he placed the card in his pocket and pointed at each of the cloud keepers protecting the throne. Their eyes grew large, and they dropped their hands to their sides. The illusionist brought his hands together in a spinning motion, and the guards began dancing together. Doing the tango around the stage, party guests laughed and cheered. After a snap of Presto's fingers, they clucked and pecked around the stage like two armored chickens. Once the laughter died down, the illusionist brought his hands together, eyeing the audience. "Beautiful...shake hands!"

The J.A.C.K.s bowed and shook hands, instantly snapping out of the trance, unaware what occurred except for a few peculiar feathers they coughed up. Tossing the top hat, Presto caused it to fly around the room of people and return it to the stage. Following in a chain, all of the hovering cards exploded into red flakes. The flakes spun into a cyclone and flew into the hat. In a single swoop, Presto leaped into the air, withdrew the ace of spades from his pocket, smashed it into his chest, and dove into the hat as well.

For a moment, it was quiet. The top hat rolled on its side, apparently empty. Jack immediately assumed it was finished, but Sonny stood on her toes, enthralled. It was a rare occasion where she wasn't writing what she was seeing. They watched the top hat as it flipped and rolled in front of the throne. A tall pillar of fire erupted out along with red sparks, doves, and flares.

Silver and red fireworks exploded in the background of the stage, then turned into clinking champagne glasses, and the numbers 982 appeared. As the sparks fell, they played a familiar New Year's tune hitting the ground. Acrobats in silver suits vaulted from the ceiling, doing flips in lower gravity, so they spun slowly in midair and fell gracefully to the ground. Finally, the throne chair began to turn itself, revealing a baby Phoenix in a white diaper and red sash as everyone applauded. Unable to speak verbally, he greeted them all using his unique ability.

Happy New Year to you all and welcome. Thank you all for joining me in the celebration of my 982nd new life. I have a feeling this year will be a magical one with incredible possibilities thanks mainly to our new heroes. Feels as if a whole year has gone by since last night, but hopefully, it will be a time we will all put in the past. Today we celebrate a new beginning and great fortune on this grand occasion! As this will be the last time I see most of you this year until my old age, I wish you all the best in your personal resolutions. Now mingle, celebrate with us, and enjoy this great new year!

Everyone cheered as the words washed over them all simultaneously. A few of the mansion's staff attended to baby Phoenix, and the music grew louder from the performers. Sonny pulled Jack to a table where they were able to eat and see all of the other guests. Every stand held multiple trays, displaying a variety of food from all over the world to choose from, allowing them to eat their favorites.

Shortly after eating, Sonny removed her notepad and pen. Her head moved so swiftly, it reminded Jack of the squirrel in Marilyn's labyrinth. She jotted down information on everyone who came into view. So many people were gathered in the room, it didn't take long before she exhausted the page and had to flip to another.

A woman sat down in a seat next to them with a pleasant demeanor. Jack noticed immediately how old-fashioned her attire was. She flattened out her black petticoat and white apron and then adjusted the coif atop her head. The clothes the woman wore favored a pilgrim he'd seen in history books of the seventeenth century. Her youthful, milky, white skin stretched around her mouth as she smiled at Sonny.

"Good morrow," the woman said to Sonny.

"Hello...?" Sonny replied, politely to the outdated greeting.

The woman seemed to detect it herself as she adjusted her face. "Oh excuse me I slip back into character at times without recognizing it. Happens when you're in and out of time periods and multiple personalities. That is quite a lovely pen."

Jack was positive. Sonny hadn't missed what she said about multiple personalities; however, she did her best not to let show. "Thank you. It was a gift from my grandfather."

"I can see," the woman responded. "It is so outdated."

That comment took Sonny off guard. He doubted he'd seen Sonny at such a loss for words in all the time he knew her. Looking at the woman's clothing, hearing her call anything outdated seemed backward. Jack would've been surprised if she knew electricity had been discovered. The woman stood up from her seat and held out her hand.

"Would you mind if I took a look at it, dear?" she asked gingerly. "After all, better to give than receive."

Sonny hesitated. Reluctantly, she handed her pen over. "Please be quite careful with it. It's really very important to me."

The woman took the pen in both hands. Jack wondered if she had the same sort of ability the young girl did. Bowing her head, she began to turn her entire body around. By the time she had spun completely to face them again, she had changed herself into someone completely different. The coif on her head disappeared and instead, black glossy hair unraveled from her head. Her clothes changed from the black and white pilgrim attire into a tanned animal hide dress with fringe and colorful beads. Leather footwear wrapped around her feet and ankles like boots. Finally, her face had changed, and her skin turned a beautiful golden tan.

Her hands remained clasped tightly over the pen. She opened her hands, revealing it to Sonny, yet there was no apparent change. The spiral stripes and size all appeared the same. The woman smiled approvingly, but it wasn't until she took it by the tip to present it that Sonny even reached back for it.

"May the advancements of change further your dreams and desires," she nodded politely.

"I see you two have met Nina." The Spirit of Father's Day approached their group. All of the ties around his neck matched Phoenix's colors of silver and crimson red either in multiple stripes, dots, or random splatters. The suit he wore still seemed tattered, and he again looked exhausted but progressed toward Jack and Sonny with a friendly smile. It made him think of the note Luminista had left him. Father had always been so helpful to them and provided useful advice, but sometimes there seemed to be some things he wouldn't discuss hidden beneath those tired eyes.

"She's the spirit of Thanksgiving," he said as he nodded to the Native American woman standing in front of them. "Exciting talents I've always appreciated."

Things began to click for Jack as he comprehended the Thanksgiving Spirit's transformation. The changes from her previous early American settler attire to her current Native American form, along with the multiple personality comment and old style speech made things somewhat more apparent.

"Thank you." Sonny examined the pen, obviously eager to continue her reporting on the newly discovered spirit. "May I ask what exactly changed?"

Nina squinted at Sonny then opened her hands and grinned. "As the Spirit of Thanksgiving, my abilities vary by persona. Receiving items in one form, I can give even greater gifts in another. Try pressing down and twisting your pen's top."

Sonny positioned it firmly in her left hand. Pressing down on the silver top, she twisted it. The head popped up, and a camera lens became visible near the base. A second press and a silent flash went off snapping a picture of a stooped man hiding nervously in the corner. Sonny beamed appreciatively.

"This is wonderful, thank you!" She twisted the top and pressed it back into place then checked her notepad. "Oh, and look, Jack, it's gone into my notepad with the time, date, and place."

"She also creates an incredible feast and is a contributing editor to the Cloud City News," added Father. Jack could see Sonny's attention pulled the moment Father mentioned the News. "Let me introduce you to a few others."

The Spirit of Father's Day excused himself from Nina and walked Jack and Sonny through the party of people. He provided details of different spirits, and Sonny used her pen's newly created functions.

"Over there..." He pointed to the nervous stooped fellow in the corner. "He's the Spirit of Groundhog Day. He's a bit nervous of many things, including the sun and his own shadow, but has a talent for predicting the weather. Never leaves Cloud Eight unless it's to honor the New Year... I'd say it'll be a long winter. The two women there laughing by the entrance are Imani and Anna, the Spirits of Kwanza and Hanukkah, respectively. The muscular men in sunglasses watching Easter's symbolic bunny work for the Saint Patrick's Day spirit as bodyguards. Lucky must be near here somewhere. He's confident that having that particular rabbit's foot will bring him an even greater fortune, but the Spirit of Easter will never let it happen. Oh and this spirit is..."

" — Redd Rocket!" A tall, muscular, military man introduced himself, shaking Jack and Sonny's hands firmly. "Been waiting to meet the two heroes everyone's been talking about!"

"I think you've met Usher Sam; well, Redd here is the Spirit of Independence Day," Father finished.

Redd's face was hardened as if he'd seen several wars in his lifetime. His military fatigue pants and sleeveless shirt would camouflage him or otherwise resemble current United States military branch uniforms. Depending on the angle Jack looked at him from, he appeared as an airman, soldier, sailor, marine, or a guardian. His chest was decorated with medals. On his right bicep, the American flag along with the year *1776*, was tattooed on his skin.

On his left bicep were the iconic words from the Statue of Liberty's "The New Colossus," *Give me your tired, your poor. Your huddled masses yearning to breathe free.* Dog tags draped around his thick neck, and his hair was crew cut style showing a bit of gray.

"Two hundred and thirty-seven years of service," the spirit stated confidently. "Providing the fighting spirit since the document itself was signed. Been the fighting spirit of every American war since the American Revolution, OORAH! One of the few first generations left here."

Sonny took a picture of the spirit with her pen's new function. "First generation?"

"After a few hundred years or so a lot of holiday spirits retire, or move onto other things," the spirit continued in a gruff voice. "The first generation spirits left have either been here since the tradition started or were the first spirits of their holiday. It's pretty rare after all this time now. Phoenix and Holly are the oldest of us, but don't tell her I said it, been trying to catch her under the mistletoe for years."

Sonny proceeded to follow the spirit while taking notes. Jack was tempted to as well, but seeing her take more pictures with her pen, he remembered questions he'd meant to ask someone. Luminista's letter had an unusual warning about a father, but without her available to ask about it, Jack wasn't sure who to trust. Mostly, he just wanted straight answers. In the end, he turned to Father.

"Could I ask you something?" Jack asked.

"Believe you just did," Father chuckled. "But if you have another, I don't see why not."

Jack swallowed hard, forcing a lump in his throat down. "What do you know about my flashlight? How did my dad end up with it? And why would someone want it so badly?"

Father looked nervously around him, then whispered to Jack. "Not here — in the hallway."

Shuffling past party guests, they made it back into the hall. The staff had dispersed, and the J.A.C.K.s at the doors were gone. Besides the confetti on the ground and the portraits of Phoenix's past lives, it was secluded. When they were in the clear, Father answered.

"I'm not sure who is after your flashlight now, or why your father sent it to you. After we left the hotel, rumors of the owner, your father, began to spread. As I've heard, a trip to a fortune teller in San Francisco has been the largest topic."

"You mean Luminista?" Jack asked. "When he was on his business trip?"

"It's been told he met Luminista as well, but not until after he received a message from another teller using cookies," Father continued. "His flight connected from Japan to California, and it was there he opened a fortune cookie from a different fortune teller completely. There are a lot of people who could be searching for your flashlight. It's a natural bridge between the gaps of this world to yours. A powerful totem I created, with a few unique gifts."

His head hurt, trying to keep it all together. *There was a second fortune teller in California?* He thought to himself. *That second flight is the one he died from. When did he see Luminista?* He remembered the package he received that contained his flashlight and how he brushed his fingers over the foreign postage stamps on the surface. It made Jack all that much angrier, but he tried to calm himself. "What was the flashlight for?"

"Fifty years ago, I was tasked to create a totem for a new challenge," Father explained. "The events in challenges need to be able to cross the gap for a dreamer to compete, and this specific challenge needed a totem that balanced light and darkness. One that was also able to see through hidden materials sense darkness and store light. However, the dreamer cheated during the challenge and was forced to stay."

Father rubbed his hands together, and Jack knew this was the information he'd been waiting for. "Who?" he questioned. "Someone knew enough to start all of this when my dad started in Japan. Who was it? What are these challenges? Who's the flashlight made for?"

Just then, the mansion's staff came flooding into the hallway one by one from a staircase to the left. Jack and Father had to shuffle to the side as they ran past. Butler Morris brought up the rear just as the doors burst open. With so many people, it was hard to tell what was happening, but a large container was coming.

"It's here!" the butler exclaimed. "Everyone to your marks, I don't want any mistakes."

The attendants from the iPlane had arrived at the entrance. They pushed a cart inside loaded with the covered crate and waited. The door's alarm buzzed again, and the butler had to input the code once more. It made Jack wonder if his small interaction with the covered crate had something to do with the alarm. After exchanging security with Butler Morris' staff, Jack watched as he and the chauffeur pushed the cart through the hall followed by the others. He'd almost forgotten about it entirely, but now it quickly became his new focus. *What would be inside of it for Phoenix?* He thought to himself. Jack realized sometime during the outburst that Father had gone. He assumed back to the party, so he made his way back into the ballroom as well, where he would hopefully see where the crate was going.

For an unexplained reason, he felt whatever was inside alerted him. As if his senses were warning him of something dangerous inside. He recently became open to many possibilities and believed it may even be the flashlight. Even some of Sonny's outrageous ideas hadn't seemed so ridiculous lately.

Pressing through the crowd, Jack looked for Sonny. Her ability to record into her notepad would prove useful if he could steal her away. His eyes found the Spirit of Independence Day relatively easy; the spirit was showing the handle of a large knife to Holly. Before he had a chance to approach them about Sonny, he witnessed her heading towards the side door that the chauffeur and Butler Morris had gone through.

The puppeteer stand was still set up next to it, but he was missing, making it easier for Jack to slip by. Most of the guests were now watching a small presentation from the illusionist. Presto performed close-up magic and pulled a surprised Easter Bunny from his hat. The two cloud keepers were occupied, describing their hypnotic state as imagining they were in chicken coups. Sonny had vanished from his sight. He assumed she must have seen the crate already. As stealthily as he could, he snuck past the crowd and into the side entrance, following as swiftly as possible.

The door closed quietly behind him. It led to a narrow side hallway filled with multiple doors along the right wall. He could already hear the cart returning back. With the only exit being behind him, he ducked into the first door and waited. It was very dark in this room, and he hoped he was alone as a door closed. After checking that the hall was empty, he snuck back out, scratching his head.

A strange mist clung to the air Jack wasn't familiar with. *Which one did they go through?* He wondered. With so many doors, he tried to think of a way to follow their trail and had an idea. Removing his flashlight, he used the handle's magnifying lens to see a darker track of footsteps and wheels leading into the fifth door. A door marked *Vaults* above.

The door itself was average with a standard gold knob. Beyond it, however, were heavily armored vault doors with coded access locks like the iPlane held. The doors were lined up a few yards away from each other. Individual codes had to be entered for access to each one. Signs had been engraved above each vault door that indicated its contents.

Artifacts Room, Records Keeper, Valuables, Money, and more.

Jack caught a glimpse of someone in the corner of his eye a few doors down. She vanished behind a vault with the sign *Ancient Sands.* Jack could hear Sonny's voice murmur from inside for him to follow. "When did you get in here?" he whispered, but she didn't answer. Something seemed off as the vault's door had already been unlocked and left slightly open. Sonny's voice continued to call out to him, pleading impatiently for him to hurry. He could only see her shadow, but she waved for him to follow. Against his better judgment, Jack pulled open the door and stepped inside.

The moment his foot hit the ground, he knew he'd made a mistake. It was a secure room at a level he'd never seen but was already familiar with. Hourglasses in varying sizes lined each wall on top of shelves behind transparent casings. They were the same hourglasses Jack and Sonny had discovered on the roof of the Holiday Hotel. Grains of sand fell from the top to the bottom until it was empty. Once empty, it would turn on its own starting the process again.

Sonny was nowhere to be found. Besides the hourglasses, the vault was completely empty. His footsteps echoed inside, offbeat as if they traveled further than they usually should. The mist was heavier here and his vision blurred, so he barely made out tiny dark falling crystals. As much as he rubbed his eyes, they didn't go away.

The sound of glass shattering broke the silence, forcing him to turn his head quickly. The noise came from the room's center, where a flickering red ominous glow could be seen. It was challenging to be sure, but as he approached it, he realized the red glow was from sensor lights. They flickered around a pedestal beneath the broken glass Jack had heard shatter. It was another hourglass separated from the others. One he'd seen before. The one he was sure they had just brought.

He bent down and checked the remnants of black sand that had fallen onto the floor. It was almost completely gone. The last time he saw it, the container was half full. Now only a few grains of the black mass existed.

"B.S.H.," he said to himself. "Black Sand Hourglass." Standing up, he checked his surroundings. It was suddenly clear someone must have broken it just seconds ago, yet the broken shards didn't move at all. As he'd just heard the sound, typically the glass would be rocking. It was as if something was slowing his processing. The remaining black sands whirled around the glass and shortly after blew away to nothing.

He quickly turned to leave when the corners of the room began flashing. Spotlights focused from the ceiling onto Jack, making him easily visible. Alarms rang, vibrating the entire room. Pressure descended from the ceiling as if the gravity had been increased. He strained as he attempted to walk out, but his legs felt weighted by a few hundred pounds each. He struggled even keeping his head up as the weight increased more and more. Soon his knees buckled, and he was forced down to his hands. In mere seconds, the pressure was so high he was flat on his stomach, unable to lift himself at all.

A group of people came bustling into the hall, and then into the open vault room. Many had shocked faces and muttered something about the stolen items. Jack was shocked when he found Sonny with her notepad and pen, ready to take pictures. It wasn't until she spotted him that her mouth dropped open. She made a motion as if about to run over to him when Butler Morris ran inside first.

"What happened in here?" Butler Morris keyed in a combination that turned off the alarming lights and pressure systems. Jack strained to get to his feet as he felt the gravity decrease. His head felt fuzzy and light as he lifted himself from the floor. The black sand from the hourglass had completely vanished now along with the mist that made his vision hazy. He dusted himself off while a hundred people attempted to squeeze into the hall and doorway, waiting for him to answer.

"I was looking for a bathroom," Jack lied. "I don't know what happened here. I found this broken glass when I thought I heard Sonny."

"Me?" Sonny interrupted from the doorway.

"Yeah, you kept calling me like you found…something," he hesitated.

The Spirit of Independence day interrupted, still holding his knife. "That's impossible. I've been telling her about the original thirteen colonies since you left us earlier."

Jack was confused. He saw everyone staring at him suspiciously followed by muttering from the crowd. There was movement from the back of the group as four J.A.C.K.s barged into the hall, separating the crowd. The white uniforms and trench coats stopped swaying as they blocked the only exit. The moment they spotted Jack, a cloud keeper threw his badge into the center of the vault. It scanned the area, while another made a call through his helmet.

"Rope off these areas," the first cloud keeper ordered. "Be sure no one leaves until we get a statement. Check everyone for missing items, and let the investigator know there's been an escape, but we have a suspect. This is now a crime scene."

"Suspect?" Jack questioned. "Wait, I didn't do anything. I'm not trying to escape!"

The cloud keepers ignored him and instead continued blocking off the exit using the transparent shields projected from their badges. Butler Morris answered instead, making little eye contact with Jack.

"I'm afraid that is not the case, Mr. Taylor. A hazardous item has been entrusted with the estate and is now missing."

A cloud keeper spoke into his helmet, confirming orders then approached Jack. "I have been ordered to place you under arrest by the Jurisdiction Approved Cloud Keepers under the authority of the Council of Four to be detained for further questioning."

Jack shook his head, backing away. "This is crazy. I haven't done anything!"

The cloud keeper removed a pouch from his belt and dumped the contents onto Jack's hands. He instantly felt them bind together as a gray glob formed around them. Struggling to pry his hands free, he had no use of his fingers, hands, or wrists.

"The investigator will be here shortly, and you will be escorted back to headquarters," the cloud keeper continued. "You will be charged with aiding in the release and escape of a captured political terrorist and criminal nightmare known as the Sandman."

Chapter 4
The Investigation

Murmurs and whispers bounced off the walls in the vault-like tennis balls in a gym. It felt as if time had slowed down all over again as several guests glared and the guards made motions to tackle Jack at any moment. However, as everyone focused on him, Jack's focus was on the bare floor where the swirling black sand had once been. A single question now pecked away at his mind that would hopefully produce an answer for these peculiar looks.

"Who's the Sandman?" Jack asked.

The murmurs actually increased. People began spreading doubt about his heroic gestures from the previous night. Then several started looking at Sonny with possible involvement, even with the Independence Day Spirit's backing. Two of the J.A.C.K.s continued to hold their badges, producing large transparent shields out of them. Just before the butler could answer, and the crowd began debating, a man Jack had never seen before walked into the room.

His strides immediately quieted everyone around him, reverberating in the silence with each step. The cloud keepers quickly separated as if his skin alone were dangerous to touch. He wore a similar uniform to the other J.A.C.K.s with a long trench coat, but instead of a helmet and visor, he wore dark sunglasses that appeared to display the same information the others received. A blue star illuminated from his chest a bit larger than the others, showing the title *Investigation Detective*. Instead of pouches, on his hip was a short black baton with several buttons on the hilt. It was easy to tell from the others, this man was the one in charge.

"The Sandman..." the detective began as he walked around the vault room, "...is an extremely dangerous holiday spirit from the early ninth century. A holiday we no longer celebrate."

The detective made his way through the vault, checking on the other hourglasses. His fingers fluttered over the buttons of his baton. After the hourglasses were inspected, he checked the edges and each corner of the room. No one else spoke while he searched. The investigator only allowed the occasional *hmmm* to vibrate from his lips as if discovering something amusing. It was only after glancing at the ceiling that he actually stopped and looked at Jack. He stooped down and stared at him for several seconds and then at Sonny. It was difficult to see because of the dark glasses, but it appeared as if he was making a connection between them.

Jack gave an unintentional glance to the floor where the black mass had been, then back to the investigator. He assumed the detective caught it as he brushed a hand onto the floor and rubbed his fingers together. The investigator stood up and, taking in a deep breath, directed his subordinates. "Keeper Matthews will assist me with escorting the suspect and his friend to the precinct for questioning. You three will get statements from the guests. Start with any accomplices of Mr. Taylor beginning with the estate's owner and continue with Father. Then clear the area of any hidden items, checking for clues. Use the disillusion powder to be sure nothing is missed. I want any new prints inside and out of these doors."

Cloud Keeper Matthews approached Jack with his badge. "Don't worry kid, won't be long until you're guilt comes out and…" *Crack!*

It was like a flash of lightning striking the air. The detective had removed his baton, and pressed a single button, allowing a long whip to unravel from the end. With a slight twist of his wrist and a swing of his arm, he cracked the whip within inches of the cloud keeper, which stopped him immediately.

"I will make it clearly understood that the laws and guidelines handed down by the council will be followed," the detective said, sternly retracting his whip. "Therefore, this young man is, until further notice, innocent until proven guilty as we take him into custody. Is that clear?!"

All four guards stood at attention and repeated the same two words. "Yes, sir!"

The guests and staff were forced to wait as three cloud keepers began their investigation. The room was cleared by two of them, while the third removed a sparkling white powder from one of the pouches on his belt and threw it in the air. It landed on the ground, allowing Jack to see several footsteps he'd made until he and Sonny were escorted out of the room.

They were walked back through the estate's entrance and down the long tan road outside toward Justice Hall. Some time had passed, but Jack wasn't sure just how much. His hands were still bound, but he wasn't as conscious about them. The more he walked, the more he thought of what had just happened. Thoughts of an old holiday spirit who'd been locked away spilled into his mind. He'd heard stories of the Sandman before. A man in pajamas sprinkling sand over kids' eyes so they would sleep. He couldn't imagine a figure like that could be a political enemy of the city. However, with all that had happened before, it wasn't hard for him to believe the fable was actually true, and this new tale could be as well. Being arrested in an unfamiliar place, he wondered how much more of this holiday's story he didn't know.

Sonny was being marched behind him, followed by Cloud Keeper Matthews. The detective led from the front, occasionally looking back in his dark sunglasses. Jack wished there was a way for him to say something to Sonny unnoticed, but with the J.A.C.K.s with him, he thought it best not to. He couldn't understand why she denied calling out for him inside the vault. The obvious questions finally clicked as they stepped into Justice Hall of Cloud Nine. Who else could have released the Sandman from the hourglass, and where were they now?

They followed the sign that pointed back toward Lucky's Penthouse. The hall seemed somewhat shorter than Jack remembered. They made a left turn to the J.A.C.K.s' Headquarters where the décor changed as gradually as the seasons. This hall was nearly half the length of the one in and out of Cloud Nine. Portraits similar to those in Phoenix's hall hung on the walls of this one too. However, they were different as they depicted kids around Jack's age or younger with strange backgrounds. Almost like illustrations from book covers.

"Matthews, take these two inside and have them processed," the detective ordered. "Answer whatever questions they may have and keep them occupied. I don't want any new problems to arise. I will be letting the judges know what has transpired so they can prepare *if* there is a trial."

The detective departed down the opposite hallway where the barred off portal waited. Jack and Sonny were directed to continue down the hall toward the headquarters, passing by several aging portraits from centuries prior. Jack didn't recognize most of them at first. As they grew closer to the doors of the headquarters, some of the pictures became more present and familiar.

"What are all of these people on the walls depicting?" Sonny asked finally.

The cloud keeper stopped at a portrait of a boy in green tights flying and grumbled to himself. "These are the challenges. The successful challenges, anyways."

"Challenges?" Jack asked, glaring at a tattered portrait a few yards away. "I've heard of those."

Beneath the visor, Jack could see the cloud keeper roll his eyes. "Of course you've heard of them. The challenges are the epic conclusions to a lot of the trials' decisions. A lot of stories you've heard on your plane are actually from these challenges. Like Peter, the boy who never wanted to grow up. Left in Kensington Gardens as an infant and discovered he'd been replaced, so he didn't trust adults. He was too afraid to really grow close to people and never wanted to grow up. Fighting pirates wasn't the only thing he learned to do."

They walked a bit further to the next portrait of a young blonde girl where the cloud keeper continued. "Then, of course, there was Alice following her curiosities, growing tired of the bland life she had become accustomed to. She was challenged to create a wondrous world of her own. Losing herself in it was the easy part, but finding her way back apparently became more difficult… Swear that queen reminded me of Mother."

"They were all dreamers like you," the cloud keeper continued. "Even had totems made from the Spirit of Father's Day just like you two did. Charles with that famously rare golden ticket allowed entry into a candy manufacturing dreamland. And Dorothy desperately wanting to go home, using her magic silver slippers."

"Silver?" Sonny stopped. "I thought they were red?"

"A lot of these stories get changed over the years when a dreamer makes it back to your plane," he answered bitterly. "But they were definitely silver in the original challenge. It's been quite a while since we've had one though. If I'm lucky, one of you two will be the next dreamers to go. Ha-ha!"

Jack had had enough. "What is it that you don't like about us?!"

Cloud Keeper Matthews turned on his heel with a menacing glare. Jack had a feeling if it weren't for the detective's instructions, the cloud keeper would have used something from his pouch on him. "You stumble upon a mystery in a hotel no one knew still existed. People start calling you heroes and don't believe us J.A.C.K.s are capable of our jobs. And you strut around believing it, while we continue, thankless. I solved that case, kid! Had my suspicions, Mr. Shadow was in on it all along, just to find out we brought in the wrong person. Maybe I shouldn't be irritated with you, but…all that praise, just gone."

"I believe you're doing a great job," Sonny pointed out. "But you did have twelve years to catch Trick. It took us less than twelve days."

Jack shook his head as he strolled to the next portrait. He looked at the tattered canvas of a mischievous-looking boy in a baseball cap with uncertainty. Sonny and the cloud keeper walked over to where the young detective. He continued staring at the rough exterior of this portrait as if he were drawn to it like the dilapidated building that began his journey.

The canvas was torn slightly around the edges, and it was peeling. Even the frame was tilted absurdly compared to the others. The strange thing was this portrait was obviously newer than any of the others, and it was the last one in the hall. The canvas's fabric showed little yellowing if any. Studying a single tear, he could tell someone attempted to rip this one purposely. The longer he stared into the dark eyes of the boy in the painting, the more he felt as if it were staring back.

"What about this one?" Jack asked in a severe tone without looking away. "What's his story?"

This portrait showed the boy in a cap, cuffed jeans, and a black t-shirt being attacked in a dark area by digital game characters. Although he was alone and outnumbered, he appeared confident and held a smug look to him as if he had no problem taking on the world with a few bright thoughts. What Jack noticed most was what the boy carried in his right hand. Sonny looked up at him as well, and he wondered if she saw it too. The cloud keeper walked ahead of them near the door, pointing out the details and story of this portrait.

"Another pain in the butt dreamer," Matthews pointed. "That one was of the last challenges about fifty years back. His name was Teddy. He was kind of a loner for a fourteen-year-old. Never understood what friends were good for. He preferred his emerging tech and personal thoughts over anyone's company. He was challenged to survive in a fantasy world like the ones in his comics and video games. A diverse land of future digital suburbia they called it. Built inside the largest mall conceivable filled with game zombies and alien villains not even created yet. His totem was made to signal for help from a few staged kids locked inside with him at night, but of course, he was difficult and refused. Never tried to help the other kids, only used them as bait and relied on his mind completely with manipulation. He cheated using parts from the mall's tech stores and ditched his totem. Never learned his lesson but escaped the challenge. That is why he technically beat it and escaped using a remote, but his portrait has been shamed."

"What happened to him?" Sonny asked, snapping a picture of the portrait with her pen. "I don't believe I've ever heard this story."

"This kid?" The cloud keeper opened the door to the headquarters. "I don't doubt it. When you finish your challenge, you usually collect your reward, learn the lesson to be learned, and are allowed to travel back home. Not surprised you haven't heard this story though. Only those who win get to go home, spread the stories to their children, and so on. Pretty easy since no one believes them to be true, but a failure would mean being trapped inside the fantasy world. Since he cheated, he was forced to stay here on this plane of existence. Really not sure what happened to him after that. Probably on the island prison, but I never thought much about it. Nothing's known for sure after that. I mean it's been fifty years since he's been spotted — where else would he be?"

"Why did you hang the portrait of his victory if he cheated?" Sonny asked.

The cloud keeper sighed. "The portrait appears here the moment someone wins a challenge. Somehow he figured out a way — it can't be taken down."

Jack turned. "Why would he care about a picture?"

"As long as that thing hangs on the wall, it's possible for him to find a way out of here if he hasn't already." The cloud keeper opened the door to the headquarters. "Well, if he can find his totem, that is, to bridge the gap. Come on, the detective will have a mess of questions to ask you two now. Like I said, if things don't go your way, you might get to know the rules very well yourself. You'll have your own challenge to worry about."

The J.A.C.K. Headquarters was impressively secured. They walked through four sets of doors before entering the main building. Each entry was more armored than the last, requiring a password and badge swipe combination, voice confirmations, palm scanning, and finally retina verification. Several cloud keepers stood by each door armed with a badge producing different weapons, from shields and batons to unique electrified staffs Jack had never before seen.

They were marched into a back room with no windows and a single door to allow them in and out. Besides a cold metal desk, an overhead light, and a few chairs, the room was bare. Jack and Sonny were gestured to sit in the chairs and then left alone to wait for the detective. There was an awkward silence between them that was broken when Sonny asked about the hourglass room.

"What did you think you saw me do inside the vault?" she asked in a tone as if she were unsure herself.

"I didn't really see you, just heard you call out for me," Jack stammered. "It was sort of like you were egging me on, daring me to follow. Saw a few shadows, but that's it."

She didn't say anything for a moment. Jack wondered if Mr. Shadow had something to do with it but didn't want to go down that misleading path again. Sonny held her head as if the headache bothered her again, or perhaps she was just confused.

She clicked her pen a few times as if thinking, then stopped. "That reminds me, did you notice in that final portrait..."

Sonny was cut off. Jack heard a familiar sound. The engine of a motorcycle stopped somewhere outside strangely followed by the whinnying of a horse. He'd been around police motorcycles back home enough to point them out anywhere, but the engine of this one sounded stronger. Next, he heard each door being open until the final one that led to them. The detective stepped inside appearing if possible, more determined than ever. He sat down across from Jack and Sonny and placed a book and list in front of them and folded his hands together on the table. Several seconds passed as he stared at them quietly. He didn't ask any questions until he removed his glasses and placed them onto the table.

"Well, I hope you two are comfortable," the detective said without a smile. "This could take a few hours, even days until I hear what I need. Let us begin."

If Jack discovered anything throughout the interrogation, it was that the investigator was thorough and honest, as several hours did indeed pass while they sat in the room. A hundred thoughts trickled into his mind like the minutes that passed away. He wondered why he and Sonny were being asked together instead of privately, why the detective would ask the same questions repeatedly within minutes, and what information he was really obtaining by knowing what they last ate.

"We have a list of acquaintances you frequently speak to," the detective stated as he turned a list of names on the table toward them. "Several witnesses state you were seen speaking to the spirits of Thanksgiving, Father's Day, and received a personal invitation by Phoenix. However, I believe there is information about all of the events that occurred to which you are not admitting to."

"I already told you everything," Jack said, exasperated as he noticed Sonny taking new notes. "I was talking about my flashlight to Father. There's nothing else to it. Then he disappeared when the staff came down."

"Exactly, he disappeared when your attention was taken," the detective stated. "I have been an investigator for many years and from what I've learned, you have not told me everything, and you also haven't explained why the hourglass took your attention. Witnesses prove your whereabouts are all accounted for just until the container's destruction. However, Mr. Taylor, if you had been in contact with the black sand today, it would be easy to find on your clothes, fingernails, or from the bonding material that encased your hands. Yet your distraction could mean you've been in contact before. I've also been advised you have been tracking the hourglass' destination since you exited the iPlane this morning, which is very suspicious. Therefore, I cannot rule you out unless you may have seen who did release it?"

Jack's mouth was slightly agape as he sat, stunned at the detective's revelation. "Well, except for the other hourglasses on the walls, the vault was empty when I went in. Not really much to take, right? I could just get sand from a beach if I wanted too, couldn't I?" Jack defensively.

"This is not a GAME, Mr. Taylor!" The detective slammed his fist on the table and stood up. "The Sandman is an extremely dangerous holiday spirit that will need to latch on to the first person he comes in contact with. He will use their sub-consciousness, controlling them like a puppet until he can regain his own strength by feeding on weakened shells. You are one of the few suspects without an alibi. Several eyes were on you as you entered the vaults. Now I need to know everything you remember no matter how small the detail."

"Wait, what do you mean latch on?" Jack asked. "What was so dangerous about this holiday?"

The detective took a deep breath and opened the book on the table, stopping at a page that displayed a group picture. The date showed it was taken nearly a century ago. A few holiday spirits posed in a group together. Some Jack recognized, most he didn't but could guess at. The detective pointed at one spirit who was wearing gloves and had tired eyes grinning broadly, stringy brown hair, and a small mound of sand falling to his feet. He didn't have on shoes, instead only a pair of thick socks. Among the others, he stood close to a man in crimson red robes Jack recognized as one of Phoenix's past lives.

"He was responsible for the care of the dream sand allowing children on your plane to sleep every night and giving them pleasant dreams. The substance found on your eyes when you wake up was the remainder of sand from the night before. He worked hard, and too many, he was a prodigy. Very gifted his job, he grew through the ranks to a full holiday spirit quickly and developed a day of full rest to rejuvenate. One of the very first generation holiday spirits, it wasn't long before he believed he was more deserving than others. He was refused a place on the top cloud, and that refusal began a long plan to overthrow the city."

The detective slid the book over, and Jack got a good glimpse of the names listed before the detective continued. "He became more of a politician than a holiday spirit honestly. Decades passed, and while addressing the council, he advised them he'd surpassed his time as a holiday and should be made into a fifth season following winter. It would be a period where his abilities could truly be appreciated. Sleep would be enforced for weeks until the season ended."

Jack was eager to hear more but didn't dare ask. Both he and Sonny were quiet as if interrupting would be the last thing they'd ever do. The detective stood, making slow strides around the desk. He removed a bag of glass from the broken hourglass he'd found in the vault and examined it. When he spoke again, Jack's ears perked up, listening intently as to not miss a word.

"Of course the judges denied his request," the detective continued. "A new season is no small achievement. After all, only the beings are meant to grant that power unless it's passed on from a previous judge. It can take a millennium to find a proper substitute. After his request, it was brought to their attention that a powerful sleep lasting for weeks could be endless, potentially causing comas and even death. The Sandman, unfortunately, was persistent and became vengeful. He persuaded several citizens to agree with his political stance and began brandishing his own style of justice from a small workshop. The spirit enhanced his dream sand into an even stronger substance that was reddish in color. New sands he created produced your worst nightmares into realities, quicksand that would trap, grab, and bury enemies, and the dream sand lasted years instead of hours, although you'd never know you were sleeping. Sleepwalkers would be forced over the edge of clouds or made to attack others. And his symbol was exceptionally terrible. A nightmare king, he used to punish any of his enemies and reward his followers with pleasant fantasies. Three separate sands made up his newly dangerous form, but he needed sacrifices to create them."

He nodded at one of the cloud keepers in the room who handed over an evidence bag. Jack could see the broken remains of the hourglass shards inside. He watched as the cloud keeper placed it into a lockbox with another bag containing a small bow tie and what looked like broken toothpicks. Sitting back down at the desk, the detective pointed at another man in the book next to the Sandman. "There was a fourth sand he did not have control of. It would have given him what he needed to overpower the other holiday spirits and the judges. A brave spirit used it to trap him inside the hourglass. Inside the same hourglass that has now been broken. It was his greatest friend and mentor. Some even claim their bond was like family. Almost like a father and son bond."

He didn't mean to say it aloud, but the thought left his lips before he was able to stop them. "Why are you telling us this?"

The detective paused as if controlling his anger. No one seemed sure what he was about to do. However, after clearing his throat, he continued as if the interruption never occurred.

"He grew very close to building enough power and enough support. To this day, the occurrence of the season he attempted to create still plagues us. Animals that hibernate like bears are still under these effects, and now that he has been released, there's no telling what will happen or who to trust. Some may still be loyal to him. Most of the guests and staff of the estate have alibis. Even your friend here was with Redd Rocket at the time. So, Mr. Taylor, I'm assuming if you would like to be ruled out of involvement, then you have been framed. Perhaps even multiple people are working together. I am questioning you specifically because dreamers can cross between planes easier than anyone, and they are more susceptible to be used by dream sand. We do call you dreamers for a reason after all, and you two are the only ones in the city."

"Wait, that's not true," pleaded Jack, thinking back. "There is another dreamer here. The dreamer in that portrait of the hall escaped his challenge, didn't he? Teddy?"

The detective shook his head. "Stating outlandish accusations, Mr. Taylor? No one has seen him in ages, and there's no way for him to leave the capital unseen. Why now, when no one's seen him in decades?"

"I don't know why now, but I have seen him recently. The person who took my father at the hotel, I think it was him," Jack said, remembering a chapter from his *Big Guide of Finding Clues* book that delved into information about being framed. He wondered what parts would assist him now. Having an alibi, documenting his whereabouts, and ways to establish false credibility with a partner were all covered. Usually, a family member, coworker, or someone close enough to be well trusted would be involved. If what he read was true, either Father's disappearance was part of it, working with this dreamer, or more people were working together than he realized.

The detective sat back as if gauging Jack's answer before continuing. "And if that were true, how would he have access to the hourglass? We know who brought the item inside the vault, and the transportation records to Cloud City. You were discovered closer than anyone else we've found, and it's not something you could handle alone. The more people the Sandman puts to sleep the more power he'll gain from their dreams. Their secrets will slowly become his. Their thoughts will be unknowingly encouraged by him. Are there any plausible people involved that you can think of?"

Jack sighed in frustration. "No one else I can think of."

"I see." The detective walked over to the door and knocked on it where another cloud keeper entered. "Well, until you're ready to fully accept my help, we do have to keep you two under custody. It's safer for you here, anyway. It would be wise to let me know if you do remember anything else. I can be a valuable ally if we get what we need or your worst enemy. Keep you locked away or something much worse. Whoever touched that hourglass first will be connected to him. Stopping him quickly is imperative. I hope you understand Mr. Taylor, anything you remember may be considered crucial to your own survival."

Through his expression, it was easy to see what he was saying was not only a threat but a promise. The words resonated with Jack as if the detective knew something he wasn't sharing. Placing his sunglasses on, he left the room. The cloud keeper tilted his head for them to exit the room on the other side, and marched them to a line of jail cells.

The barred door was shut firmly and locked behind them. The bonding matter dissolved from Jack's hands, allowing him to move them freely. A single small window could be viewed near the ceiling of the cell, but it too was secured. Jack wasn't sure what time it was now or how much time had passed, but it was getting darker. The sun was setting, and the stars were barely visible. A cold winter breeze whisked in, brushing against their shoulders as they sat down on a cold bench against the wall.

"So," Sonny said finally. "You don't remember anyone else at all?"

Jack removed his flashlight and placed it on the bench between them. "Not really. The only person I noticed leaving was the chauffeur and the butler, but they were the ones who wheeled it in."

"Well, I was able to copy down the suspects listed on the table, but I would think it's obvious," she responded, smiling slightly. "The butler did it. It's always the butler."

"That's Tour Guide Morris' and Number One's brother," Jack pointed out. "He doesn't fit the profile at all, and besides he wasn't alone. I really don't think he's the criminal type."

"Oh, that reminds me!" Sonny bounced to her feet, removed her notepad from her back pocket, and clicked the striped pen. "The last portrait we were shown coming in. Did you recognize it?"

Jack looked down at his flashlight and nodded his head in agreement. "You mean Teddy? I recognized the totem in the picture. I wasn't sure if you did too or not, but he was holding it. Why didn't Father just tell me? He created them all; it could've answered so many questions."

Sonny looked down at her pad where the picture she snapped of the portrait appeared, suddenly realizing what Jack meant. "It's your flashlight..."

"I know." Jack stood up, angrily. "And the worst part is he's the one who has my father. That attendant no one recognized at the hotel. It was the same guy. He must still be trying to get back home after all these years. I don't think he's aged at all in the last fifty years, but that must be why he wants this flashlight. That's why my dad's missing. So the cheating jerk can go home while his portrait is still up. Makes so much sense now."

Sonny stood up, shaking her head and holding her notepad up so Jack could see the picture clearly. "That's not all of it, Jack. I didn't realize who he was to you, but I thought I did recognize him. Remember what the cloud keeper told us about it? His name is Teddy."

Jack held his head in both hands as if there was an absurd connection she was trying to make. "I don't think I can take one of your crazy 'the butler did it' ideas right now."

~ 99 ~

"The chauffeur's name in Phoenix's estate was Theodore, smart guy." Sonny squinted at him with distaste but continued. "You didn't realize Teddy is short for Theodore? He had a hat tilted in a similar way that hid his eyes. The chauffeur is the one who took your father, and I guess he must have released the Sandman too."

His hands still covered his face, but everything she told him was connecting. It all became apparent and poured over Jack like rain. Sitting in the cell, he began to remove his hands from his face understanding these new discoveries. *The chauffeur was the last one in the vault*, he thought to himself. *Teddy was one of the people he witnessed leaving with the cart, and he's a dreamer.* He knew there was something strange about that staff member but couldn't understand why. Jack went to ask her why she didn't say anything to the detective but stopped at the look on Sonny's face. She stared with a curious expression as if something were creeping up behind him.

"What?" Jack jumped up from the bench turning around. "What is it?"

Pointing at the bench next to Jack, Sonny held a look more of curiosity than fear. Her head tilted slightly, and Jack found what she was gawking at. Jack's flashlight began growing fur much more quickly this time. In a matter of seconds, it had sprouted its legs, paws, and tail. Jack had almost forgotten about the girl providing the new transforming abilities to his flashlight. As it turned into the sleeping pup, Sonny appeared thoroughly excited.

"When did this happen?" she asked, staring at Rocho's tiny stature. "He's adorable."

"I kinda ran into a little girl who brought him to life," Jack stated. He watched the pup stand on its tiny paws fully for the first time. Rocho blinked as he stepped closer to the edge, getting nose to nose with Sonny and sniffing her. With a single stroke up, he licked her nose sweetly. She giggled and stroked his green fur.

With an impressive leap to the ground, he shook his fur abruptly and began barking. It initiated as a flicker at first, but as the barking grew louder, more and more light produced from his mouth. It illuminated the cell-like flashes of lightning parting clouds. The light would brighten the area for several seconds then slowly fade away. It wasn't long before the flashes bore the attention of one of the J.A.C.K.s.

"What's going on in there?" Shouted one of the cloud keepers as he started walking toward the cell. Jack quickly grabbed Rocho, who was now near the cell's door. In his palm, the pup transformed himself back into Jack's flashlight, and Jack hid it in his jacket pocket. The guard arrived at the cell door, his eyes searching the inside. He scanned both of the prisoners with his badge and then the cell itself.

"Keep it down in here," he spat gruffly as he lowered his badge and turned to leave. A slight tremble of the bars caused him to stop. A rumble came from outside that shook the stone walls inside. Dust fell from the ceiling as the sound of wheels could be heard coming closer to the window from outside their cell. Tremors shook the floors violently like a stampede of elephants nearing. The guard had just enough time to produce a small shield from his badge when a loud crash caused the cell's wall to crumble inward, knocking everyone within earshot back and onto the ground. Twin beams of light entered the gaping hole of the wall, obscuring any vision to the outside. The only definable source they received was a barely audible question from a strong Irish accent.

"You lads all right?" a familiar voice yelled out. Jack's vision was still blurred, and his head hurt slightly from the impact into the bars, but he could see the outline of two tall, muscular figures. Sonny sat up and rubbed her neck with a dazed look on her face. Behind them, all of the cloud keepers guarding the armored doors were knocked down. Their protective gear saved them from any real damage, but the only movement came from the subtle breathing being expelled. The short distance to the bars in the cell had apparently saved Jack and Sonny from a much harder impact.

Holding his hand up to block the light, Jack looked out through the hole where a large black vehicle dimmed its headlights. The car was built like an older limousine-tank hybrid from an old mobster movie in the 1920s. It was sturdy looking with an enforced protective grill and a transparent wedge projecting from it. It reversed abruptly, pulling more of the wall out with it and turning. Crumbling blocks fell, and the dust finally cleared enough so the vehicle's front windows could be seen through. Sitting in the front seats were two men Jack had come across before at his father's hotel. The black suits and green ties weren't items he recognized, but the red facial hair and equal stature gave the brothers away quickly.

"The bouncer brothers from the lounge?" Jack questioned as he dizzily tried to stand up. "Michael… Christopher?"

"No, I'm Michael, that's Christopher," replied the bearded brother who sat behind the steering wheel.

"Aye, no' like we're twins or nothin'. How's it no one can tell us apart?" Christopher pointed out.

Jack brushed himself off. "Maybe because you two look exactly alike."

"Well listen ta this one caught rotten," Michael replied. "Must be coddin' us. We're like chalk and cheese me and him."

Sonny lifted herself up using the bars for leverage, then scooping up her pen, and notepad approached the vehicle. "What are you gentlemen doing here?"

"Boss sent us to pay back a favor owed to youse." Christopher grinned, stretching his mustache as he leaned out of the passenger window. "Today's your lucky day!"

Chapter 5
Wanted

Night had poured out onto the streets over the last few hours as if the sky were a faucet, overflowing with moonlight, drowning the sun out of existence. The distant racket of tire screeches and engine revolutions turning corners resonated on the pavement. The smells of burning rubber and exhaust fumes stung the air sharply. A quiet calm was left, laced over the debris and gaping hole of the J.A.C.K. headquarters where Jack stood with Sonny. The cloud keepers stirred, regaining consciousness in the background, finally breaking the hypnotizing effects.

Several flashes went off from Sonny's pen as she took snapshots of the limousine rocketing down the street. "What do you believe that was all about?"

"I don't really know," admitted Jack. "A ride would've been nice though."

"Well, who would owe you a favor?" Sonny asked as she flipped through multiple pages in her notepad. "Who do those two bulking brothers work for? I don't think I took the most adequate notes on them."

"I remember the lounge in the hotel was under temporary new management," he recounted. "Irish accents, red hair, green ties. Never actually saw him but it's gotta be the spirit of Saint Patrick's Day right?"

"Or perhaps there's a city crime boss, and he wants us to assist him in a conspiracy," Sonny suggested. "They did appear to have classic gangster-like characteristics, didn't they?"

Jack turned back to the cell, where several members of the detective's team were sitting up. "How far do you think we'll need to go before we find them down that road?"

Alarms went off from inside the headquarters. Flashing blue and white lights could be seen down the alley to their left, along with a fully grown white horse connected to the building in silver horseshoes bucking violently at them. Farther, pass the horse neighing and shouting, the screeching of tires whipping around the corner could be heard. The path to his right, however, would also be hard to follow. It was a thin alley between the outside of Justice Hall and the tall fence of a holiday's home. Walking at a quick pace, they followed the upturned dirt and tire marks of the limousine.

Sonny showed a few pictures she'd taken to Jack of the limousine and the two brothers. "I doubt we would miss a vehicle like it, but the license plate did have *FORTUNE* stamped on it. Maybe your flashlight would be able to track it for us like the dream dust in the hotel?"

As she said it, Jack had already acted, reaching into his pocket. Before he could firmly grasp onto the flashlight, Rocho leaped from his palm and onto the ground. The pup shook his body as if being freed from a cage before circling Jack, then stopping at his feet. Light reflected from the swirling gold strip down his back by the street lamps as he pointed his snout to the ground and sniffed.

"Hey…" whispered Jack. "What's he doing now?"

"I think he found a trail." Sonny turned with haste as cloud keepers yelled to check in their direction, barreling down on their heels. "We should follow him quickly."

Rocho bounded down an alley only large enough to fit a single car. Occasionally he would bark releasing a light that illuminated the trail he followed. The tire marks glistened down the road, and the pup would jet off almost too fast for Jack and Sonny to keep up. It wasn't long before the trail ended to the side of the grouped televators. The two gold televators sandwiched the glass elevator they used to travel up from Cloud One. The same black limousine was parked on to the side with the license plate Sonny recorded.

"He's very talented to find Lucky's Penthouse so easily," Sonny complimented Rocho as she pet his head. "And so adorable."

"Yeah," Jack acknowledged, bending down to the pup. "Pretty impressive. Wish I had something else from my dad for him to find him but all I have IS him."

Rocho jumped into Jack's hands, instantly returning to a flashlight. He thought about it for a moment, glad to have a piece of his father with him now able to walk on its own. Almost as if a part of him was actually beside him. He noticed Sonny looking at the televators, gazing at the three of them thoroughly.

"We traveled through the clear one when we entered Cloud Nine, remember?" Sonny pointed at the elevator doors. "This right one is still not working, which leaves this one able to go to the spirit's penthouse, correct?"

He pressed a button of the working gold televator firmly. "According to the sign, yeah."

As they boarded the televator, Jack could hear the detective barking orders to his cloud keepers behind them, interrupted by the occasional siren. "Check every home on this cloud and make your way down. Start with any spirits he's been known to partner with. That means Father's Lane, Holly Woods, and Phoenix's Estate. I want that list of suspects questioned immediately after we retain the dreamers, understood?"

"Phoenix's Estate?" a cloud keeper asked. "You think he'd really return to the crime scene?"

"We are now in search of escaped suspects and the Sandman himself," the detective continued. "And criminals always return to the crime scene for one reason or another." Jack could barely hear the last words the detective yelled in the distance before the televator doors closed shut.

Jack and Sonny were transported up three stories instantly to the highest floor of the casino. Beyond the open doors lay a square outside courtyard covered in black tile like an indoor pool. Potted plants sat in the corners while a bar area and stools were stationed on the brim. On the opposite side were steps leading up to the double doors of the penthouse suite. A wide moat filled with waving water protected the courtyard on all sides preventing any access. Etched onto black tiles were large letter L's encircled with gold on each side of the moat. The moonlight emulated a gleaming shine from the water and then became darker.

"*L*?" Sonny questioned the gold encircled letters.

"Luck, I'm guessing," Jack answered with a determined expression as he watched the dark waters rise and fall. "Got any ideas on how to cross?"

Walking up to the moat, she waved for him to follow. "It's only water. How bad could it be? Not afraid to get a little wet, are you?"

As if on cue, the water began to splash violently rising above the brim of the moat. A low pitched cry like a submarine's sonar elevated from deep inside. An overflow of water splashed the dreamers' shoes and ankles. Jack's skin tingled the closer they walked to the edge. *Something's definitely in there,* he thought.

The atrium-like courtyard allowed moonlight to peer in enabling them to catch a glimpse of shiny dark green scales before they sank back down. An eel-like tail followed several feet behind whipping at the surface. The water churned and bubbled abruptly as if the creature beneath were circling its prey. All of the water at once began to change direction. Soon there was silence followed by an immediate explosion.

"Get back!" Jack yelled at Sonny. A portion of the monstrous creature's body surged out of the water. A prehistoric beast with a slimy neck longer than a giraffe's connected to a rounded head with sharp teeth. It lashed at them ferociously as if protecting its young. The quick head movements were almost too fast for either Jack or Sonny to see until it was almost too late. Sonny leaped back within inches of the monster's snout.

"So how do you think we'll get by her?" she asked, rummaging for her pen as a large splash of water landed on them. "Any magic nets or other devices hidden I don't know about?"

Jack backed up to a corner clutching his flashlight as it became warm in his pocket. "Really?! Now it's a *her*?! No, I don't exactly have a monster battling kit hidden in my underwear." He glanced around the courtyard for something to use. "Whoever comes through here must have a way of getting by. Food, a button, or maybe a giant freeze ray!"

"All right then, perhaps we'll get lucky and find something," she responded.

Jack turned to her with a scowl when the scaly monster began retreating back into its moat. The lashing stopped, and the creature's neck and head disappeared beneath the dark water. A solid floor slid in from the sides covering the moat's water. Near the penthouse staircase, Jack could see Michael and Christopher standing next to a wall switch.

"You can' be lucky all the time, but you can be smart e'ery day," Michael stated.

Christopher laughed. "Boss' waitin' fer you two inside."

The monster could still be heard beneath the floor. The water splashed loudly below the dreamers as they stepped to the solid surface. Jack glanced at Sonny and then the floor covering the moat. He tapped his sneaker on the surface as if testing the waters. Fairly sure of its sturdiness, Sonny walked across and up the steps shortly joined by Jack, where the brothers opened the doors to the penthouse.

They were escorted through the first room where a few dozen people were playing casino games. Jack wasn't sure if her notepad had gotten wet in the conflict, but her pen took pictures without issue. He could tell it was a high roller's room as the people at the tables played with high currency minimums at a time. The money they used was the same as the cruise ship. People won four small orbs in various sizes like marbles. One was the size of a dime with a flower in the center. The next was slightly larger centered with a flame. The third orb was as big as a nickel with an autumn leaf, and the largest one had a crystallized snowflake about the size of a quarter. While a few people bet with these, others loaded their winnings on greeting cards like credit that displayed their worth.

As they stepped through the crowd, his eyes wandered from those playing machines to the people playing cards and roulette. Jack wondered why Lucky had gone through so much to bring them there.

As they were guided up a few more steps to a side hall, they passed a few doors, and the two brothers stopped. Massive double doors made of carved oak were knocked on hard by Christopher. The door opened to a large executive office. Black leather furniture, crystal glasses, and an abstract painting of a bright green three-leafed shamrock above a fireplace decorated the office. A few men dressed in the same black suit and green ties Michael and Christopher wore surrounded a desk. When Jack heard a voice project from between them, he somehow already knew it was Lucky's.

"You kids are drenched," the voice said as the surrounding guards began to separate. "And soaking my carpet too. You must've met Nessie. Someone go get them some fresh clothes and food." Unlike the guards, his voice only had a hint of an accent but a saltier gruff tone.

"Sure thing, Lucky," replied a guard. They all left, leaving behind a woman with a stony facial expression in an elegant white dress who was barely taller than Sonny. Jack noticed a thin gold bracelet dangling from her wrist as she kept her hands folded together. She stood next to what appeared to be an empty leather chair behind the desk. Jack scanned the room for the source of Lucky's voice but failed. No speakers or any other equipment could be found. He was sure it was a man's voice he heard, but only the woman seemed to be left with them.

"That thing outside is named Nessie?" Jack directed at the woman, unsure who else to speak to. "Like the Lochness Monster Nessie? I thought that was just a legend…and from Scotland?"

"A lot of legends have some truth to them, and with enough good fortune on my side, I was able to win her for a month from Phoenix after he had her rescued in Scotland," his voice came again from the chair. The woman stood beside it and gave the smallest hint of a smirk but remained utterly silent. After exchanging looks with Sonny, Jack stepped closer to the desk and peeked over into the chair.

"Why are you even helping us?" Jack craned his neck as he peered over the desk. A man, not more than three feet tall sat in the leather office chair. He was barely tall enough to see over the wood, the size of a large stuffed doll, but alive and nicely dressed in a black suit with an open collar and a shamrock on his lapel. A gold ring with an emerald stone covered a portion of his pinky finger. His hair was short and whitish gray fading from a dark brown, although, like the Spirit of Independence Day, he seemed more spirited and stronger than his age may show. As he stared back at them with a raised eyebrow, he passed a gold coin between his knuckles.

"Just good business," Lucky admitted. "Because of your actions at the hotel, I had the good fortune to have my party in the dining hall last ten days, followed by the world not ending so you could say I'm in a grateful mood for now."

"Well, that's kind," Sonny said to the short-statured man. Jack waited, hoping she wouldn't say anything insulting about his height. "So that creature Nessie IS a girl. I had a strong feeling of that. Is this woman your wife?"

Jack sighed in relief. Sonny questioned him like it was an interview. Lucky placed the coin on his desk grinning. "No. Cassandra is my most loyal guard."

"She's a guard?" Jack scoffed at her thin frame, but immediately knew he'd made a mistake.

The woman's eyes narrowed, and before he could blink, she had him pinned against the wall with a tightly bound gold wire cutting into his throat. Lucky simply sighed. "Let the kid breathe Cass. I'm sure he meant nothin' by it. Why don't you play nice and find them a couple of Green Apple Mint Fizs. If he messes up again, I'll throw him in the trunk myself, all right?"

Swallowing hard, Jack kept his head still as much as he could until Cassandra released him. She wrapped the gold wire around her wrist until it contracted back into a bracelet. Eyeing Jack cautiously, she walked out of the room and closed the door gently behind her. Lucky gestured for them both to sit. Jack took a seat, rubbing his neck where the wire had been pressed against his skin.

"That how she usually greets people you invite?" Jack questioned.

"One dangerous dame, she is." Lucky grinned. "I wouldn't tempt her, or you might end up sleeping with the fishes like Francis."

Jack rubbed his neck. "What happened to Francis?"

"Don't worry about Francis, he's no longer with us. This is about you." Lucky glared at them.

Sonny sat down, politely next to Jack. "Actually if you don't mind me asking, why exactly are we here?"

Lucky turned his chair to face them, interlocking his fingers. "I've been in this position for just over ninety years. Built an empire based on the trinity shamrock and its meaning to create this fine casino. Throughout the years a group of trustable spirits have gathered in secret to do what's needed to preserve a proper balance and do what the judges won't or can't. A union based on the good of the two beings."

"What exactly do the members of this union do?" Sonny asked.

"Started with the first generation spirits," Lucky continued. "I was a third gen Saint Patrick's Day spirit when I was chosen. First of my line to be raised and die in the states. Last time the union gathered was thirteen years ago to capture Trick. As unfortunate as it is, Sandman's return will need the union's cooperation again, through you."

Lucky raised himself from his chair and walked around to the front of the desk, which took many more strides because of his size. What Jack hadn't noticed until now as Lucky came closer to them was a small yet severe scar on the right side of his face. It was a deep gash that held many years of aging and made him look even more like a mobster.

"What would the union need us for?" Jack asked, trying his hardest not to stare. "You're holidays. You have to be able to handle him, right?"

"Not that easy kid. The Sandman's abilities are strong. Too strong for us to just overpower him. He can force someone's mind to imagine anything and believe it's true. Quicksand pulling you deep down into the ground where you could be trapped for eternity, your most frightful nightmares becoming real and attacking everyone you ever cared for. And the dream sand causing you to sleep for weeks, months, or even years without knowing you're committing crimes, like puppets. But it's even more dangerous than that."

"What do you mean?" Sonny asked.

Lucky strolled over to a small black bat in a glass case on a shelf. "False hope. Many citizens believed his methods made the city better against who they thought were the real enemies. Several dislike the special treatment holiday spirits get on upper clouds, and he kept the judges from harshly punishing dreamers for bringing items from this plane."

"Those sound like good reasons for a new leader to me," Jack commented.

"Trust me, nothing is so simple." The spirit turned back to them. "I can't say what the judges do is always right or allude that things are perfect, but it was much worse when the Sandman rose. A dreamer taking an item from this plane to your world could be disastrous for both. Some punishments may seem harsh, but his were far worse and unjustified. That's one reason why there are four judges and not one. Make's me appreciate my casino that much more. Anyone can move up the clouds with proper luck, and I can live in all the levels, keeping my ears open. Everyone has a chance."

He stared at them, intently like he was describing precise instructions. "He'll need to find and sacrifice three spirits to create the sands. Spirits who fit the characteristics of each sand and then he'll replace his shell. We all need someone less likely to draw his attention to power kid. We need you to stop him before it happens."

"My dad needs my help!" Jack argued.

Lucky held his quiet demeanor. Jack couldn't tell what he was thinking as the spirit adjusted the ring on his tiny pinky finger and strolled around the office. He flicked a switch, and his fireplace ignited, and flames danced in his eyes. "A few years after I became a holiday spirit, the Sandman planted an idea in our heads. He made us believe we were all nightmarish versions of ourselves who attacked each other without restraint. I was only able to resist due to a lucky investment in my newly purchased beverage company and a new test product. A new recipe was developed that weakened the effects. Took it just before he took control of Phoenix and pelted me with hourglasses. That's where I got this scar. That's what got me the nickname Lucky too. Constantly reminds me to keep friends close…enemies always seem to be closer."

The door to the office creaked open. Cassandra and another guard walked in with two green Fiz drinks and fresh clothes for Jack and Sonny. They politely took a sip of the Green Apple Mint Fiz. Seconds later, Jack felt a warm surge through his body. It rushed quickly from the inside as if removing any weaknesses. They accepted the clothing as they towered over Lucky, who flipped his gold coin in the air with his thumb nonchalantly.

"Since Phoenix is still in his infant state, Father is temporarily in command of the union," Lucky stated. "He asked me for this favor. Break you out of the J.A.C.K.'s custody, provide a list of safe places for you to hide from them, and help you locate the Sandman to clear your name. Cassandra will show you where you'll be staying for the time being. Now, my job's done, for now, so you kids get outta here. I've got work to do. Go get some rest. You'll need it."

Weeks passed by fairly quickly. It was the most prolonged rest Jack had had in quite a while, although every day he became more anxious. It reminded him of being in trouble at school but fearing more than detention. He was sure any day now the cloud keepers would find them hiding in Lucky's guest rooms of the penthouse. Every day seemed to take longer to pass as he thought about them. Between that and worrying about his father, he'd never felt more trapped.

The last few nights he and Sonny had repeatedly been over an escape route prepared by Lucky. The altitude seemed to be affecting Sonny more as she'd been getting more headaches over the last week, occasionally ripping pages from her notepad. Lucky's guards explained it happened to dreamers when adapting to the city. The green Fiz drink helped settle her pain quickly, although Jack only ever felt faint dizziness.

Other than that they were mostly left alone. Lucky took care of his business affairs secretly and without question by anyone. Rocho slept on a cushion in the corner of Jack's room when he wasn't in his flashlight form. Jack never had a dog before but felt an immediate attachment to him. If it were possible, he felt the need to take care of his flashlight more than ever. Sometimes Cassandra would walk by the door when Jack and Sonny were going over notes, glare at him with squinting eyes, then step by as if nothing at all had happened.

"Did you see that?" Jack asked Sonny.

She lay on the floor, her hand propping up her head as she read notes. "See what?"

"She just walked by giving me that look again!" he explained.

"I assume she still doesn't appreciate the day you insulted her," Sonny noted.

"That woman is crazy!" Jack shouted, partly laughing. "I'm telling you, she's gonna kill me!" He couldn't remember the last time he'd really laughed at anything.

Sonny closed her notepad and clicked her pen. All of the notes she had taken appeared on the walls of the room with dates in different colored ink. The pictures the aspiring journalist had taken looked like a police stakeout connecting data to the snapshots with lines. Information lined the walls in a way she had grown accustomed to, forming around the room's nightstands, lamps, and dressers. The list of suspects she'd copied from the detective displayed in silver. She looked at a green list and diagram positioned above the couch. It showed the penthouse, a route to a back closet, and a list of step-by-step escape directions.

"We should go through it again," suggested Jack.

"We have been through it," Sonny stated reluctantly. "Several times actually. I'm sure I could maneuver the escape route in my sleep, and Lucky has fortune on his side. I have no doubt the escape route is covered."

"It's not good fortune or luck that helps him," Jack said in frustration. "He seems lucky because he finds a clever way of doing things. And I hate just sitting around here waiting. The J.A.C.K.s already came once since we've been here and we haven't heard from them since. Three weeks are gone now, and I have no idea what that *jerk* Teddy did with my dad. Why are we still even here?!"

Sonny put her hand on Jack's shoulder. "Okay. We'll go through it again."

Just then Cassandra stepped into the room clutching a folded white note. Reluctantly, she handed it over to Jack and returned to the doorway, where Lucky had walked in accompanied by the brothers Michael and Christopher. They hadn't seen Lucky since the first night they escaped the headquarters. He removed the sunglasses from his face as if he'd just been on a leisurely drive. Michael stood to his left, carrying two sacks by their shoulder straps, and Christopher stood on his right with two covered food dishes. Lucky stood between them with a small black alder wood container with a glass inlaid top firmly in his tiny hands. Through the top, Jack and Sonny were able to peer down at the gleam of a gold coin.

"Hope you two got enough rest while you were here." Lucky squinted up at them both. "Gotta hunch it may be your last ones for a while. The sacks are a gift from Holly. Had to convince her red would be harder to hide, so she changed it to black. I took the liberty of having lunch brought up for you."

Sonny's pleasant smile became a broad grin as she caught the lingering smell from the plates. "That wouldn't be hunter's pie and coddle soup, would it?"

Lucky raised an eyebrow at Christopher who chuckled automatically, answering Lucky's questionable expression. "Lass got a bit of the Emerald Isle in her boss." Christopher placed the plates down.

Lucky looked over Sonny. "From your grandmother's side, right?"

Sonny nodded impressively, but Jack held up the folded note Cassandra handed him before they could go any further. "What's all this for?"

No one spoke for a moment. The brothers glanced at each other as if Jack made a monumental mistake interrupting the holiday spirit. It was difficult to tell with her stone face, but it seemed as if Cassandra was attempting to smile yet forgot how as she slyly unclipped her bracelet. Jack began to take a small step back until Lucky snapped his fingers. He pointed down at their feet, and Michael dropped the bags. Glaring at Jack, Cassandra reconnected her bracelet disappointedly.

"The note you were handed is actually a list," explained Lucky. "Ten hideouts approved by union members to help you, however, a few are being watched too heavily. Normally you would head to Father's Lane, but as the J.A.C.K.s know of all your acquaintances, it'd be idiotic for you to try. You should instead head to the spirits less known to you personally. Mother is your first stop." He pointed to her name on the list.

The list had half the names already crossed out. Along with Father's, the crossed out names included the spirits of Christmas, Valentine's Day, Saint Patrick's Day and of course

New Year's Day where it all began. The hideouts not crossed out were Mother's Avenue, Bicentennial Village, Plymouth Meeting, the Fiz Factory, and Shadow Manor. He wasn't sure why the Fiz Factory was on it, but Jack almost laughed when he noticed Mr. Shadow's home was listed. It'd be the last place he'd want to be caught in and the last person he'd ask for help.

"You'll have to travel down to Cloud Eight to get to Mother's." Lucky went on as he adjusted his tie. "Her neighborhood's just passed the Fool's Circus, opposite Father's Lane. She'll offer you help when you get there and a place to stay. This will help you on your way."

Lucky lifted the lid of the black alder wood box. Jack reached inside and hesitantly pulled out the gold coin. It was similar to the coin Lucky had been known to shuffle between his knuckles. The size of a half dollar, it had an embedded clover on one side, and an *L* on the other. He examined it thoroughly as it glistened.

"That's interesting," Sonny said, snapping a new picture of the coin and briefly blinding Jack. "Are we supposed to spend it?"

"We've only now been able to access the high-security vault," Lucky continued. "Just shine a bit of light on it, and you're good, kid. With so many eyes on everyone, can't afford to make mistakes. It will only work for a short period but should get you where you need to go. Questions?"

Jack went to speak, but Lucky carried on anyway. "No? Good. I've got old business to take care of. Those sacks have supplies in them. No need to fret though kids, every cloud has a silver lining."

He removed his sunglasses from his suit pocket. Placing them on his face, he turned, flipped his personal coin in the air, caught it, and exited the room. His guards followed, closing the door behind them. Jack studied his new gift. Sonny sat across from him on the couch and began eating the Irish hunter pie.

Placing the coin in his pocket, Jack sat down to eat beside her. As much as he knew he should, he didn't have much of an appetite. Instead, he picked up the sack and searched its contents. It was a single strapped black book bag with several zippered pockets. Before he could examine it further, Rocho's ears perked up. It was the slightest flicker, but it caught Sonny's attention, who pointed it out to Jack.

Jack watched Rocho's head spring from the cushion. The pup tilted it to the side then walked over to the closed door. Jack wasn't sure if he had to go outside, as he hadn't in the last three weeks, but the door appeared to attract him unusually. Without warning, Rocho began to do something Jack hadn't seen before. The gold strip down his back had started to fizzle like electricity as he growled at the door then barked repeatedly.

"What's wrong with him?" Jack asked, just as a loud bang shook the penthouse abruptly. He immediately picked up Rocho, changing him back into the flashlight and placed him in his pocket to quiet the pup. Sonny grabbed one of the sacks lying on the ground and went to the door. Opening it slightly, they were able to decipher the commotion.

"Jurisdiction Approved Cloud Keepers, open up NOW!" yelled the detective. "We have a warrant signed by the judges to search the property. We have reason to believe escaped suspects are here. Cloud keepers have orders to use physical force on the property to find them if necessary!"

A scurry of several pairs of boots hitting the ground followed the loud bang, spreading in multiple directions. Jack could hear them marching toward them, just as distinct and rapidly as he felt his heart pounding. The entire plan left his mind, and instead, he stood frozen, clutching the gold coin in his palm tightly, preparing for the moment they'd be caught in the study. Fortunately, Sonny was as ready as she was quick and grabbed Jack by the hand just as she had many times before.

"We can't be caught by them, so stay low and stay quiet," she whispered. Jack barely had time to grab the second sack sitting on the ground before she dragged him through the doorway. He stayed as low as he could. Every step he made seemed to squeak ten times as much as the cloud keepers searched throughout the casino, getting closer to the guest rooms and office. The door they needed to reach was at the very end, in Lucky's trophy room. If they could make it in without being caught, they would be fortunate with a head start out. However, Jack's hand was shaking badly, and it was his misfortune to drop the coin.

"There they are!" yelled Cloud Keeper Mathews.

The only thing Jack could see were several blue illuminated badges pointed in their direction as he picked up his coin, then bolted down the hall. Stumbling into the room, he ran into a shelf, knocking over a few awards Lucky had won over the years. As soon as they were inside, Sonny pulled open a dark closet door, shoved Jack through, and locked them both inside. *It won't be much longer*, he thought. Sitting in the closet waiting with baiting breaths, he imagined the detective approaching with his squad ready to take them.

The soles of the J.A.C.K.'s shoes tapped on the hardwood as they searched the room he hid in. Cloud Keepers were flipping tables, shelves, and sitting furniture in search of them. The detective noticed the closet from across the room. He motioned for the cloud keepers to surround the door on all sides. A short countdown got the squad in position. And finally, the eyes of the detective focused just before an abrupt turn of the handle, and the closet door swung wide open to reveal…boxes. Boxes of plaques, badges, and trophies, leaving nothing else but a frustrated expression on the investigator's face.

Jack imagined all of this and sighed with relief as he and Sonny stood outside, feeling the fresh night air for the first time in three weeks. Lucky's plan had worked much better than he could have hoped. He and Sonny had pushed the heftiest boxes aside where a small trap door could be found behind it. Crawling through, they'd located a small cylinder area they were able to stand in containing a line of buttons. They pressed the number eight key firmly, waited a moment, and then exited the televator. He looked back at the Out of Order sign swaying on the televator door and couldn't help but smirk at Lucky's cleverness.

Sonny appeared pleased with how fortunate they had been using the escape route. Jack still didn't consider it luck but couldn't argue the results. He peered out at the hard brick road of Cloud Eight, where they would travel to the next safe house. Removing the list from his pocket, he checked the first name on the list. Mother's Avenue would be their next destination. They would just have to figure out the best way to get there unseen.

A patrol of J.A.C.K.s were walking up the road. Sonny pulled her sack's strap over her shoulder and lead Jack behind a jewelry store until they passed. He went through the red bag to check what supplies they were given. Even with food, blankets, a sleeping bag, Fiz bottles, and extra clothes inside, there was somehow extra room inside it. He maneuvered some items out of his pockets to put inside. The list was first, then the bottle from the cruise ship, and then the coin caught his eye.

"Wouldn't happen to have any idea how we're getting to Mother's?" Jack asked.

"Not exactly," Sonny whispered as the last of the patrolling cloud keepers disappeared around the corner. "Lucky stated it would be after the circus tents, but that's not much to go on. I'm not sure how large Cloud Eight is but if it's nearly as big as Cloud Nine with so many large homes, searching out in the open isn't the brightest idea."

Jack usually had an impressive memory, but after their escape, he couldn't recall precisely what Lucky said about the coin. *Something about being good to go…and puppets,* he thought back. It annoyed him how difficult it was to remember with so much going on. Sonny looked at him as if waiting for an idea, but Jack just continued to examine the coin like it was a toy from his childhood.

A flash from Sonny's camera followed by sirens broke his concentration. "What are you—?" Jack began, but stopped once he noticed the glitter the coin produced in his hand. It shimmered a bit and flakes appeared above it momentarily then vanished. Reaching for his detective's flashlight, he shined its light onto the coin, bringing it closer to the lens cap.

The closer he brought them together, the more gold flakes were produced from the coin. Fixing it entirely over the lens, a prism-like rainbow shined through, hitting the ground. A yellow path jetted out in front of them as if painted onto the bricks, stretching throughout the street, but then faded quickly. Sonny watched it all as if forgetting what she was previously doing.

"Oh perfect, we have something we can follow now," she said brightly.

At first, Jack hadn't caught on to what she meant. Holding the flashlight and coin in his hands, he could see a glimmer through its tail end. Jack held up the magnifying glass end of his flashlight to correctly see through it, and the yellow path became perfectly visible onto the bricks again. He shook his head, rolling his eyes as he peered through. "I can't believe we're seriously following a yellow brick road? Really?"

Tilting her head as if she didn't understand the reference, Sonny pointed at the coin. "It's changing."

Jack stared, noticing it as well. The top part of the coin's gold began diluting and showing a small silver portion as if the gold had melted. Returning it to his pocket, he placed the sack onto his shoulder and started following the path with his flashlight's lens. It was far into the distance, but he could just make out the very top point of a circus tent seemingly a few miles out. Colorful light bulbs danced in a breeze on the brim while soft comical music projected out.

As he gestured to go, Sonny didn't follow. Instead, she stood staring down an alley, the yellow path bypassed. Jack couldn't tell what she was doing. It was like Sonny was waiting on a bus to pick them up. He took a few steps back behind her where he could still be hidden in case cloud keepers came.

"You should probably see this before we continue," she relented, showing Jack her notepad. It was the picture she had taken just moments ago of a boy. The curly jet black hair, pale skin, and brown eyes were unmistakable holding the green flashlight. The words *Wanted: Jack Taylor* appeared below with a reward from the J.A.C.K.s.

Jack took the notepad from her and glared uncertainly as his mouth fell open. "Where did you get that?"

Sonny pointed down the street to her right, shrugging her shoulders. "I'm a journalist. I seek out the truth, and sometimes, it just finds me to report. It seems this is a new truth."

Jack peeked around her curiously, locating the source, and understanding how difficult it may be to hide now. Beside the small tavern promoting the epic battle between the Autumn Grizzlies and the Summer Sharks on January 26, his eyes widened as he realized just how many people would be after him. Every street was crowded with cloud keepers knocking on doors and questioning business owners. The blue and white lights of their vehicles and badges lit every alley and doorway in the area, showing a hundred wanted posters plastered on multiple walls with Jack's face glaring back at them.

Chapter 6
Mother's Intuition

"Are they still behind us?" panted Sonny.

She and Jack hid behind a gnarled tree of a small park of Cloud Eight. "No, I think we lost them," Jack breathed heavily. They had been running for the better part of an hour. The path they followed blinked red occasionally, warning them of danger and changing to a safer direction. Someone was trailing them, and it became more dangerous with every close encounter.

Taking their newest glowing path out of the park, they were sent down a rocky dirt road. Jack discovered tracks along the trail. They came from the large wheels of a stopped wooden carriage in the distance traveling in the same direction. It looked abandoned from their vantage, but they were careful not to speak unless absolutely necessary to avoid any unwanted attention. Every kick of a rock or bristle of tree branches would force them to look in every direction. The last few hours of silent thinking and checking over his shoulder didn't help Jack's mood at all.

He gazed up at the mountain of tents they were approaching drizzled with sparkling lights around the brim. It was nearly a mile away but so massive it'd be impossible to avoid. The closer they stepped, the more the music drowned out any other sounds around them. It was the same tent Lucky described they would come upon before reaching Mother's Avenue. The trail went up the hill between a few trees and painted wooden carriages with steel cages promoting circus acts.

After an exhausting climb, Jack stopped, resting by the broken down carriage. Images replayed in his mind like a slide show of all that had happened. He tried to connect what he learned from his detective books and watching shows with his father to what was happening to him now. *If I'm being framed, it would be an enemy*, he thought seriously. *Teddy is the obvious person, but he'd have to work with someone for an alibi, and they would need a distraction. Someone close to me like Lucky and the detective mentioned. From Luminista's note, Father would be obvious but would he really set me up? There's no motive, but there's no alibi either.*

Sonny had just caught up, not nearly as out of breath. They were near the four open partitions of the giant tents when she snapped Jack out of it. "Are you all right?"

"Yeah, just thinking of something Lucky and the detective both mentioned," Jack replied as the thoughts dwindled. "Something about puppets..."

"You two shouldn't be out in the open like this," a man said and startled them from behind the carriage. It was difficult to see his face with night rushing in quickly through the land. He cranked heavily on a wrench, working on the axel before peeking around it. Wiping his hands on a stained rag, he stood up. He held a strange combination of a gray mechanic's jumpsuit, muscular build, and a clown nose on his face. None of it helped Jack feel any safer. "The Ringmaster's been waiting for you."

"Who are you?" Jack asked carefully, keeping his distance.

"Work for the circus." The man smiled largely squeezing his nose. "I'm a clown. Can't you tell?"

His smile seemed forced like he hadn't done it naturally in quite some time. It made Jack uneasy and more willing to leave the situation. Sonny made a movement from behind. Her face went stern, and Jack had a feeling she remembered his dislike toward clowns.

"The Ringmaster's in the center tents with the acrobats." The clown stated returning to work on the wooden wagon wheel. "Like I said, he's been waiting for you."

Sonny led them up the hill, while Jack cautiously followed, watching their backs. Stepping into the tents, they appeared even more gargantuan and spacious from the inside. Acrobats tumbled in the air by trapeze leaving a trail of blue, green, and red blurs struck with sparkling silver stars lingering in the air. They practiced flipping over prominent sharp spikes and tumbling through floating glowing rings. The sight of the acts alone caused Jack's heart to skip a beat.

They witnessed clowns parading foolishly in costumes of oversized pants with splashes of color, dotted shirts, silly wigs, and ridiculous makeup. They sprayed each other with high-pressure hoses bursting with gallons of water. Some practiced in darkened areas with neon face paint and juggling rings.

Others were fired from cannons into enormous custard pies or rode around in miniature vehicles as fire brewed from the exhaust on cyclone track. Jack walked further inside, stunned as it raced around the ring, then along the walls, vertically to the ceiling, and finally after a large loop, up a ramp and onto an oversized whoopee cushion busting with confetti and resonating with sound rumbling the ground.

Various sights of both delight and fear came into view from the sides. A beautiful woman in a silver one-piece garment with hanging crystals and a feathered crown balanced atop a mammoth-sized pink elephant with long black curled tusks. She tossed knives taking aim at a moving target. A man either bravely or foolishly performed the dangerous act of walking a tightrope hovered high above an open cage of low growls. Lions made entirely of steaming molten rock roared and clawed in a fury awaiting him to plummet. Warnings not to try the acts at home flashed through Jack's mind.

A band near the edge of the center ring played the music in waves that lured them in from down the hill. Oddly enough, every performer they could see appeared more depressed than the last. Ultimately, it made their extraordinary acts and performances seem rather dull. The benches surrounding them were completely empty as if it were only a rehearsal, but it didn't take long before Jack realized people had simply chosen to leave or had not shown up at all.

Stepping off the final platform, Sonny spotted him first and alerted Jack. A man held a frozen expression on his face imitating a grin. The familiar long white coat dropped down to his ankles. Curly black hair framed his charming yet hidden face. Within a short period, Jack could see Sonny weakening to familiar feelings.

"Doctor DeLuca?" she asked surprisingly. "What are you doing here?"

It wasn't who Jack expected at all. The Spirit of Valentine's Day turned toward them pleasantly. The white drama mask hiding his real face appeared complacent. He held a small jar in his hand, tightening the lid. Inside was a small floating bone connected to the nerves of a left arm. Jack tried his hardest to control himself and not allow the spirit's nature to make him jealous as it had before in his villa.

"Well, I see you two are doing well amidst all the trouble I've read about," the doctor stated as he turned back to his patient. "I don't normally do house calls, but I found this to be a special situation."

"Situation?" Jack checked the folded paper listing the approved hideouts he received at Lucky's Penthouse. Deluca's Laboratory was crossed off, leaving Jack to wonder why the spirit was there with them in the circus tent. "What do you mean?"

"Well, I'm here for a therapy session," he admitted.

The doctor stepped aside where they realized the ringmaster had been sitting. Atop a wooden stool rolling down his sleeve was another spirit. The spiky blonde hair, smiley face tie, and colorful yet pale polka-dotted suit were unmistakable even amongst his dreary outlook. It was a spirit Jack had not expected to see again and was somewhat unsure how to react to.

"Wowzer...that really did sting a bit." The spirit flexed his arm.

"The April Fool..." Sonny said simply. Jack's wide eyes focused on the man sitting on the stool, holding his left elbow gingerly. He stepped back and felt something squish onto his sneakers. Closing his eyes, he hoped it wasn't what he thought it was, and luckily found a wad of chewed pink candy instead.

"So what's the news, gumshoe?" the April Fool smiled. "Any clues?"

Jack removed the gum from his sneaker. "Is this another trick?!" He could feel his flashlight warming as if begging to be let out.

"No, no tricks," he answered. "Not anymore, anyways. You should know, I'm only here because of you."

Jack and Sonny exchanged looks with each other and then the doctor. The April Fool Spirit's voice was raspy as if he wasn't used to speaking. The doctor seemed uncomfortable in the situation, but it was hard to tell beneath the mask. The facial expression was rigid. Jack couldn't help but stare at the jar, the doctor slipped into a black medical bag. The Spirit of April Fool's Day continued to rub his elbow as he placed it into a sling and nodded at the doctor.

"It's alright, Doc," the Fool said dryly. "I understand patient-doctor confidence, but you might as well tell them. I owe them my trust at least."

Doctor DeLuca's eyes met with the Fool's from beneath his mask before explaining. "I've been studying a physical therapy technique for the last decade or so to help emotional issues. Barty has been depressed since his return from containment, so I've removed the ulnar nerve and small bone near his humerus as a therapeutic tool."

"You mean you've removed his funny bone?" Sonny laughed.

"Yes, exactly, that's very astute of you," the doctor stated." Luckily there's no actual surgery like my old days."

The April Fool stood up and looked from Jack to Sonny with admiration. "I've spent the last thirteen years in a prisoned maze, on a large inescapable island, protected by the elite cloud keepers, and the worst beasts imaginable. Every move I made was watched by oracles, and every day, my spirit grew weaker."

"Most of us were quite surprised he'd lasted." The Valentine's Day Spirit made his way towards the exit. "Another few months and I doubt we'd be having this conversation. I believe his innocence in the matter is what kept him going. You are definitely a strong spirit Barty... I'll leave you three to talk."

"How exactly did it all happen?" Sonny had her pen out before anyone realized. "We witnessed a film of you and Trick fighting just until he vanished with you."

"I've thought about that night, so many times, for a while I thought it was all a nightmare I just couldn't wake up from," the spirit continued. "I admit now it wasn't smart to follow him alone, but I couldn't let him escape. A holiday symbol challenging me at my own talents—maybe it was my arrogance throwing me off. More issues for Mr. Shadow, who got enough grief every year as it was. When he wrapped himself and vanished that night, I was able to land a hand on him. He brought us to an abandoned building of a sports team here in the city. Trick hit me with everything he had, but I was able to dodge or block most of them. He wasn't nearly as strong without his sister. That sword he had never landed, but it wasn't until I got distracted for a moment when he walloped me with his rotten egg bomb. Next thing I knew I couldn't move. My arms and legs were too heavy to lift, I couldn't speak, and the only thing I could see was Trick changing into a costume, of me."

Jack finally came around and looked at the spirit with sympathy, understanding why the circus felt so depressing. "That must've been really horrible to deal with."

"It definitely wasn't pleasant," the spirit confessed." But the worst part was looking into a reflection and not seeing my own face. Gotta admit, a mask permanently fixed to my face from a holiday symbol all about costumes wasn't a bad prank...I did not see that one coming."

A few blue and pink elephants trampled into the ring lead by a handler. Sonny rarely looked up as she took notes of everything the spirit said. Five acrobats were helping each other stretch, while a bunch of clowns blew up new whoopee cushions. Jack realized another show would be starting soon.

"It's good that you're out now." Sonny paused, writing for the moment.

"Because of you two," he said thankfully. "This is why I wanted to see you. I overheard information that I think would benefit you."

"Help us, with what?" questioned Jack.

"Help you find the Sandman and clear your names like you did mine," he answered. "My jokes haven't been nearly as funny as they used to be, but I didn't vanish into that endless well, thanks to you."

The mechanic clown ran into the tent from outside. He was dripping in a mixture of grease, sweat, and dirt but was noticeably more cheerful than before. He stopped in front of the ringmaster and pointed towards the entrance panting. "People...coming...down the hill...a group...a real audience maybe?"

"An audience?" The Fool blinked a few times in surprise. "They must've heard of Presto's guest appearance tonight. Unbelievable, yet uplifting. Ready the others and make sure if Lucky shows up the elephants do not try to juggle him again."

There was a scuffle as the circus performers prepared for the incoming patrons. The spirit gingerly adjusted the sling

~ 133 ~

supporting his elbow and directed Jack and Sonny out. "You two should walk with me to the side exit. We don't need anyone seeing you with so many wanted posters displayed."

In just a few minutes, cages were set up, rings were re-lit on fire, and safety nets were removed. For a moment, the April Fool's Day Spirit seemed a bit happier, and it appeared to uplift the spirit of the show as well. He escorted the young detective and journalist outside, making sure no one noticed them leaving.

Outside the massive tents of the circus' production, they stood on the declining grassy hill in a warm breeze. It overlooked a pleasant-looking neighborhood a few miles away. Per Lucky's instructions, Jack assumed it was Mother's Avenue where they were headed to next. From the side exit, they could securely see a mob of people walking up the hill.

A million thoughts ricocheted into Jack's head at once, like pinballs. He was already apprehensive about trusting the spirit, still playing with the possibilities of another mix up in prison. Sonny, however, appeared as if she were merely taking notes from an instructor. Removing the sack from her shoulder, she impatiently waited as if receiving a reward for good behavior. If he were honest, Jack would admit her carefree nature was what sometimes annoyed him the most about her, unable to let things go so quickly himself.

"What exactly did you overhear?" Sonny asked eagerly, preparing her pen.

"I know you can't be caught here so I'll be as brief as I can." His smiley face tie flipped in the wind, making them look as if they were frowning as he spoke in hushed tones. "Prisoners on the island are held in enclosures along the borders. A small area of space barely large enough to stand and lay in was my home for those years. A triangle window with bars was just about the only view we get. I was foolish to go after Trick alone, but that same foolishness had me stationed beneath one of the island's watchers."

"Watchers?" Sonny asked.

"Yes," he continued. "The oracles on the island who watch over prisoners. They can basically predict the moves we make before we make them, like connecting a thousand different pieces together and discovering the most obvious puzzle. Even when you change your mind, they can envision where it will all lead, like an extremely thorough fortune teller."

Fortune teller, Jack thought to himself. Something was tugging at his mind sharply but he couldn't fit the pieces together. Certain words triggered his memory like a flashback of moments. He couldn't understand what he was trying to connect. He did remember something a holiday spirit had said before.

"Mr. Shadow once mentioned the prison Trick was supposed to be taken to by you," Jack blurted, not fond of even mentioning the Halloween Spirit or his old symbol again. "He told us two small islands were separated by a larger one where they were watched by people with special abilities."

"Exactly," Barty went on. "Although, I'm pretty sure the two small islands are a misdirection making the prison difficult to find. We were taken so far below, it's impossible to tell where we actually were because very few ever leave. I do know the oracles are stationed at the highest portion of the real prison. That's why I was able to hear one of them as clearly as I hear you."

The people attending the circus show had reached the top of the hill. There were only a few dozen, but it was enough to make a ruckus. Most appeared to be the same people Jack witnessed on the first cloud walking the street. They entered the tents like a slow herd in one swift motion. If he didn't know any better, he could have sworn it was a mob, but without pitchforks and torches. As curious as he was, he tried to remain focused on the spirit's story.

"A little over a year ago, I heard this watcher whispering to herself above me, repeatedly like a record skipping." The spirit placed his healthy hand into his pocket and shuffled with an object. "She did this for a few days, possibly a week. Unfortunately, I couldn't tell how much time exactly inside the cell. I wasn't sure if she was in a trance or not, but it was unusual. Since oracles can freely transfer their thoughts from this world to yours, she could've been. It wasn't until her daughter came in that I understood what it all meant. They were the same three letters over and over again."

"What were the three letters?" Sonny asked excitedly.

"...J.E.T.," he responded, glaring at Jack as if studying his reaction to his and his father's common initials. "Once her daughter entered the chamber, she began saying it louder as if it were uncontrollably the only thing she could speak."

"How do you know it was her daughter?" Jack asked, staring at the ground, thinking hard.

"At one point she called her mother while pleading with her during a visit," the spirit answered. "According to the daughter, the cards advised her to visit immediately. She kept pleading for her to tell her what the letters meant. There was a long pause while I sat in the corner, listening to the conversation above through the small crack of a wall. Then her mother told her three words. The last three words I ever heard from her. Japan. Elder. Tailor."

Finally, it all came together. The oracle on the island talking to her daughter. The connecting flight to California. Even the Spirit of Father's Day had stated a different fortune teller had begun these events with a fortune cookie in Japan. The pieces finally came together for Jack.

"Luminista's mother," Jack said softly, lifting his head up. "If she can transfer between the planes freely, she must've known what would happen and gave my dad the cookie. But when did he send her to see me?"

"After he crossed over," the Fool finished. "He spoke to the oracle here. Once I learned of your father's initials and the names of his buildings, it all became clear. And I knew I had to help you if I could."

Jack felt his pocket growing hotter as if someone lit his pocket change on fire. He brought out the flashlight, wincing. "Ow, Rocho," he spat as he grabbed his side.

The pup changed quickly, barking as he leaped from his hand, urging them to follow. Looking behind them, the tent was filling with patrons who were beginning to get rowdy. Music played from the circus band, and before they realized it, performers were rushing in to control the group.

"That's my cue," The ringmaster said, enthusiastically holding his hand out to shake. "I hope this helps."

Jack cautiously grasped his hand and felt a shocking surge. It was weak but unexpected. Enough, however, for him to pull his hand back quickly. He looked from his hand to the man in front of him. The spirit smiled slightly, removing a hand buzzer from his finger.

Tossing the buzzer to Jack, he smirked. "Years ago, that woulda knocked you right on your rump. Unfortunately, my pranks have been unimpressive lately, but perhaps you'll have a foolishly unparalleled and unorthodox use for it." With that, he went into the tent and welcomed the audience in a booming voice.

Rocho barked and persistently pawed at the ground, forcing Sonny to turn and close her notepad. "We should go before someone from the crowd spots us."

Jack swayed slightly feeling the springy grass beneath his feet. He held up the buzzer noting its brass finish as the trigger lit in an electric blue. The young detective slipped it onto his middle finger with ease and it practically vanished into a standard thin ring. Waving his hand, judging its surprising weightlessness, he adjusted his sack onto his shoulder and followed Rocho down the hill.

Over an hour passed trudging downhill before the two dreamers were forced to stop. Their stroll down the hill was long and quiet. Sonny seemed able to tell Jack was deep in thought as she hadn't disturbed him. The moon was high over their heads now, shining brightly onto plants and through tree branches. The sound of the Cloud City clock tower chiming eleven times could be heard from seven clouds below.

Rocho was well on the trail sniffing to lead them to Mother's Avenue. He stuck his tail in the air and small snout onto the ground. Street lights lit up as they followed swiftly down a winding trail that shortly turned into a lovely paved street. When he started to slow and whimper, they stopped. His green fur suddenly became dull, and the gold strip began to flicker and fade.

"Aw poor pup." Sonny kneeled down beside him. "What's wrong with him?"

Jack ran up to him, quickly holding Rocho's tiny head up with a finger and stroking his fur. "I don't know. Maybe he's tired? Been walking for a while."

Rocho paced the length of the street's edge, avoiding the lampposts. Between the branches and leaves of trees atop grass blades, he began encircling an area covered in the moonlight.

With a bit of extra effort, he opened his mouth wide allowing his tongue to hang out and took a large bite of moonlight. Teeth marks were clearly visible where he bit, chewed, then swallowed, followed by the devouring of the rest until the moonlit area was completely gone.

He did this to multiple moonlit areas. Each spot he chewed and swallowed. As he ate, his fur became brighter, the gold strip glowed, and his steps grew stronger. Before long, he was back onto the street, bounding and ready to go.

"Well, he seems happy," Sonny stood. "At least he doesn't require batteries."

Jack chuckled agreeably as they chased behind him. Revived with newfound energy, he sprinted down the final hilled street. After a blur of street lamps behind them, they were almost to their next destination and hopeful for a safe place. The time passing had given Jack a moment to think about something new. He wasn't sure if it was due to her concern over Rocho, the random theories she spouted, or the unusually satisfied grin on her face, but without realizing it, Sonny had caught him staring.

"What is it?" she asked finally.

He was caught off guard. "Nothing really, just… I was wondering why you decided to come with me."

She didn't answer right away, but her usual grin never left her face. "I've never really had a lot of friends. I think my father ignores me because I remind him of my mother. He's been depressed for a while, and most of the kids my age think I'm weird."

"Well, you are weird." Jack smiled uncertainly.

"Thanks," she replied all the same. "I guess I felt like helping you would be like having a friend."

He paused, momentarily, unable to gather the correct words to respond. Months had passed since he last spoke to any of his friends outside of school. Even longer since he really wanted to talk to anyone. Once his father died, he kept to himself the majority of his time. It wasn't until now that he understood how alienated he made himself.

Before he knew it, the moment had passed as they approached Mother's Avenue. The view from the circus hadn't put the neighborhood they arrived to in a proper perspective. From far atop the hill near the tents, they overlooked a line of ten houses outside a single street across ten more houses. They connected to a bend of another set of ten and another in a large square. White picket fences joined end to end protecting the outer barrier of homes. Dark roofs on pale yellow and white houses all surrounded the biggest home in the middle.

"It looks a lot like Father's villa at the hotel but bigger…and pinker," Jack noted.

Now that they were closer, they could see the strange perfection of Mother's Avenue. The street led into a grand gated entrance that remained open. Pink flower beds surrounded yellow houses. Bushes of violets lay around the white ones. Perfectly tended lawns were overlooked by a grand front porch. Fireflies hovered at eye level with a pleasant glow swaying with the motion of dangling wind chimes. The loudest chiming came from the largest house in the center.

"Three guesses which one belongs to her?" Sonny noted.

Mother wasn't one of Jack's favorite holiday spirits, but he knew they had better chances of surviving with her help than without it. "Let's go. The longer we're outside, the longer we're exposed."

Stepping through the gates brought unexpected attention. With each stride, Jack could feel more and more pairs of eyes watching them. One or two women peeked out of their windows, while others sat on a swinging bench of their front decks. Jack assumed they were Mother's symbols and appeared pleasant enough. As far as he was concerned if they weren't chasing him, they couldn't be too bad.

Sonny removed a piece of paper from her notepad and began folding it in half followed by the corners, making Jack curious. "What are you doing?"

"You'll see soon," she responded casually.

Trailing Rocho around the neighborhood, they followed the trail to the most substantial home in the center and were led up a set of stairs to the front door of the only pale pink house. The pup pawed at the door then sat firmly on the welcome mat wagging his tail. The house was Victorian style and three stories tall with broad windows. Plots of red and white roses grew on the sides. Sonny went to knock on the door when it sprang open, and Mother stood in the doorway.

"Lovely, aren't they?" Mother eyed her roses approvingly. "The red ones represent the mothers still with us, and the white is for those who've passed."

Sonny paused at this just before finishing her final fold of the paper. Jack needed a moment to take in Mother's robust stature. She appeared to be slightly taller, leaner, and carrying more jewelry around her fingers than the last time he was in her presence. An apron flowed from her waist unmarked and freshly cleaned, covering her orange and white dress. The small glow around her rosy cheeks was more prominent, and unlike Father, she appeared refreshed. Sonny presented her with the folded piece of paper. It wasn't until now Jack realized she'd made a paper flower.

"Oh my." Mother brought her hands to her chest and then accepted the flower. "It is so lovely to have children like you around, thank you. Come in, come in. Except him, no pets inside sweetie, they track dirt."

Jack lifted Rocho up and returned him to the flashlight form. He was able to whisper *nice job* to Sonny, which she blushed to in response before entering.

The inside was almost as sickeningly sweet in decoration as the smell they inhaled upon contact. Fresh baked cookies, pies, cakes, tarts, bread, and more all seemed to mix together as if the spirit had been baking all day for their arrival. The living room had several pink, white, and purple floral decorations on sofas and paintings. Through the hall, Jack could see a restaurant-sized kitchen fit for a staff of twenty. However, it was the dining room she led them to. A place of silver tea sets, pink floral decorations, and delicate white laced linen draped over round tables. She welcomed them in as if seating a dinner party.

"Please sit," she gestured. "I have been expecting you two, baking and waiting for your arrival."

Sonny sat down in an empty chair at the table where folded napkins, teacups, and a crystal container of wrapped chocolates sat atop. "That's very kind of you."

Jack sat beside her as Mother left to tend to a final dish in the kitchen. "I don't know how long I'll be able to stare at all this pink while we hide out," he admitted as he glanced at a calendar of kittens in a flower pot. The date of January 24 was brightly illuminated almost naturally but even it was in a pretty pastel color of purple.

"It's not so awful." Sonny glanced around playing with chocolate from the glass container in her hand. "It does vaguely remind me of my grandmother's house."

The mention of her grandmother teetered on Jack's mind. He had traveled with her for over a month and yet never asked much about her. Deeper issues had been brought up previously such as the relationship of her father who ignored her, the mother who abandoned her for reasons Jack still didn't know, and why she was afraid of small dark spaces. The more he thought of it, even her last name was a mystery to him. Information he now believed he may need to know someday as she slipped the chocolate into her pocket, and Mother returned.

"Did you see her new appearance?" Sonny said to Jack. "She seems almost youthful and more good-natured."

"Oh, you've noticed?" Mother carried an apple pie, followed by several other plates of baked goods, meats, and cheeses hovering around her. "Foresight of my holiday's popularity this year is blessed by Anna herself. Love how much stronger it makes me."

"Anna?" asked Sonny hopefully. "Who is she?"

Mother placed the pie down along with all other treats at once. Sitting across from Jack and Sonny, she placed a napkin on her lap gently. "Anna is the woman who began the Mother's Day holiday for her mother, Anne. Anne herself, like many of us mothers, was very talented. Along with being a mother, she was a social activist during the Civil War. Mother's Day really is an incredible holiday to thank all mothers who love, teach, pass on skills, and protect their children. Just today, one of my symbols completed the maintenance of her muscle car."

Jack raised an eyebrow in surprise while Sonny jotted historical notes. "How exactly does your holiday's popularity make you stronger?" he asked.

"Holiday terms," she answered. "Holiday spirits are chosen by the judges and provide their title for a term of 500 years. Easier for some than others. When I was alive, I couldn't have children, so I fostered and adopted many. They became doctors, lawyers, teachers, engineers, even an astronaut. Passive and prominent abilities are bestowed, and the popularity of the holiday increases it. Pure nature of the holiday dear, except for Phoenix, of course, he's so much older than I am."

"What happens after their terms?" questioned Jack.

"Retirement for most, few continue the title, a very limited few are promoted to higher duties when available." Mother stood cleaning meticulously, holding a plate of cookies, glancing at the untouched snacks she prepared. "You two are so thin. Eat something already. So much responsibility on you children already, I'd rather not send you on your way without a proper meal."

Jack began taking a few bites of bread and cheese before realizing what Mother said. "Wait we're not staying here? Isn't this one of the hideouts?" He scavenged his pocket for the folded note and skim the list.

"You were meant to yes, but I have the feeling it'll be temporary now sweetie," Mother corrected. "With Father being unavailable for you to stay with, I am here for your protection. Unfortunately, as much as I'd like, it won't be safe for you here with me long."

Sonny glanced at Jack for a moment then to Mother. "Why is it not safe here?"

Mother stared into Sonny's eyes for several seconds before responding. "Are you all right honey? Something about you seems dreadfully off. Are you sleeping well?"

Sonny shrugged, lowering her pen. "I think so..."

"Hmm, you seem almost nervous or perhaps you've had bad headaches. Oh, that reminds me, one moment." Mother entered the living room, and Jack immediately felt his own mother's presence when she turned. He had to remind himself it wasn't actually his mother. The guilt of leaving her at the Blue Mountain Hotel urged itself into his mind. He tried not to let it affect him, but he suddenly missed her a lot.

When Mother returned, she carried two masks similar to the one Dr. Deluca wore hovering in front of his face. These, however, both had unmoving expressions and a different color. Instead of being white, these were flesh colored. She placed one atop the table in front of each of them.

Jack took the mask placed in front of him, examining it. "What's all this about?"

"It's rude to speak while eating dear, no one will understand you." Mother sat at the table. "As far as the masks, these should calm any nerves you have about hiding in sight. Father offers general advice to people. Supposedly what he's good at, so they say. Honestly, I'm not sure how a shrimp of a little man like him can advise anyone but no matter. I, however, as I'm sure you've heard, offer the beauty of intuition. I can feel what you feel the same way I knew you'd arrive today, and just how I know, you won't be safe here very long. Father may know best…but Mother knows better."

"So where do we go now?" Jack asked. "The entire city could be after us by now. Why did Lucky send us here?"

"For the help of course," Mother scolded. "Help only I could provide. I spent hours finding the materials and creating. I swear children never appreciate handmade gifts anymore. These masks will hide your faces for a while. You'll look nothing like yourselves when you wear it, and no one will ever know who…"

She stopped midsentence briefly followed by a knock on the front door. She excused herself. Jack and Sony exchanged a look of panic before the door was eased open. A woman stood in the doorway wearing gray overalls with oil stains. Her matted hair was in a ponytail tied with a handkerchief, and protective goggles covered her eyes. Even with this, she was still quite stunning. She spoke quickly and too softly, addressing Mother for either of them to hear. After their conversation, the door was shut promptly.

There was an eerie silence followed by a steady beat of steps marching in unison. A glow danced in the window like a movie Jack had seen just before villagers burned a monster. The gleam grew brighter, and several women shouted, followed by the roar of a car engine.

"Is everything all right?" Sonny asked. "Who was that?"

"One of my symbols," Mother answered promptly with a look of worry. "A single mother. The mechanic I spoke of, well she's the do it all type. It seems we have less time than I realized. She just informed me of a group heading this way."

His heart began racing as he grabbed a mask and stuffed it into his sack. "Who? J.A.C.K.s?"

"No, it's much worse." She stepped away from the door and peeked out the window. "Far too peculiar the clowns would be so far from the circus."

Jack immediately knew something was wrong after she said it. "The group walking into the April Fool's tent. They weren't there for a show were they?"

Mother turned toward him, and their eyes met. "My symbol told me there are rumors the Sandman is capturing holiday spirits and turning everyone else into sleepwalking followers. You need to take the masks, find your way through the kitchen and head to the last hideout anyone would search for you."

As she turned away from him, Jack could feel the warmth of protectiveness as if she were actually his own mother. "What about you?"

"I don't want to hurt you by mistake," she warned. "Go somewhere safe and blend in. I will stay and protect the avenue. Don't worry darling, every cloud has a silver lining."

Jack made an attempt to persuade her to let them stay. "But..."

"Don't argue with me, young man, do as I say!" she responded sternly. "And bundle up, it's getting chilly out."

Jack looked to Sonny for guidance, who was only able to shake her head disapprovingly. He knew she would stay if he didn't force her to leave, so he found the exit through the kitchen. It all seemed somewhat familiar to him as Sonny followed closely. He turned to see Mother near the front door, ready to open. Her dress became tighter, and the necklace around her neck expanded near bursting capacity. The glow outside the window grew brighter than ever as if a hundred people were carrying torches or swinging lanterns in the night. The shouting had dulled, and he couldn't hear the car.

The last thing he witnessed before pulling Sonny outside was Mother swelling like an enormous balloon. Her height alone was enough to reach the ceiling, and her massive girth blocked the doorway. Her meaty fingers were squeezed by her rings. Tables were knocked over along with lamps. The walls shook and trembled as she braced herself. Jack knew something big would happen the moment the door opened.

Once outside, Jack could hear the murmurs of a large crowd with the crackling of that unique glow outside the house. When the front door was finally opened, it was followed by an unfamiliar voice. Jack and Sonny ran toward the white fences to escape. An argument erupted in the house, but they could only clearly hear Mother's protective yell.

"I will not let you harm my children!" she cried.

Jack and Sonny ran through the backyard as a haze appeared surrounding the house. A large force slammed into the ground abruptly causing the roof itself to shake and tremble. Streetlamps went completely dark for a moment. Black inky lightlessness swept through houses and the roads like smoke. The avenue gave the impression of an immense black hole.

When the lamps relit, the streets were visible once again, and the dust cleared. Together Jack and Sonny ran past trees and up the hill heading toward the next closest area, Groundhog Day Tunnel. Just before climbing over himself, Jack turned to hear the subtle yet abundant sound of a woman loudly snoring, and he sighed with familiar guilt.

Chapter 7
Unsafe Houses

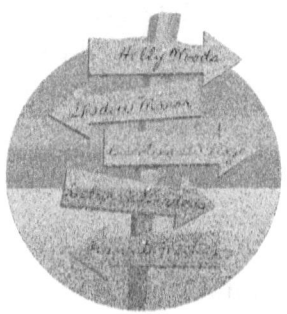

"Hurry, before they see us," Sonny whispered. "Behind this tree."

"It's too dark." Jack searched through his sack in frustration. "I can't find it without light!"

They'd traveled through the cold passing the rocky roads of Groundhog Tunnel all night. They regularly checked behind them for fear of being followed. Jack was still unsure who exactly had attacked Mother, but knew they weren't cloud keepers. After what she'd done to protect them, he hoped she was safe. Thoughts of his own mother flooded into his mind and washed into his vision. His eyes became blurry with tears, and he couldn't tell if it was because of the cold winds blowing into them or the memories.

Wiping his face with his sleeve, he leaned against a tree, hiding from sight and breathing heavily. He rummaged through his sack relentlessly, avoiding the use of his flashlight determined not to be spotted. With his hard breaths, the foggy white air leaving his lips still would've been easy to see, so he tried to calm himself. They'd been running for what felt like all night, and the exhaustion had started to affect him. With a final sigh, he plunged his hand deeper inside the sack.

Sonny looked in every direction while Jack studied their exit. The bank of elevators for Lucky's Casino was within view but guarded by two cloud keepers. One was thin and quiet while the other was pudgier, and from the amount of hot air leaving his helmet, very talkative.

He turned to Sonny, who was still looking for any followers. She'd acted quickly in Mother's home following Jack. None of it seemed to affect her as much as him. The sprint through the backyard, hurtling over the fence, the hour that followed running, or the cold they embraced now. He wasn't sure if it was strong stamina or her mentality, but he began to admire it. She stood firm through it all as if she still held no doubt it would all work out properly in the end.

"Got it," Jack whispered as he removed the flesh colored mask from his bag. He looked it over curiously. There were no strings or straps to fasten it to his face. He looked at Sonny, who was staring into her mask as well. Peeking around the tree to check on the cloud keepers, Jack placed the mask over his face and felt the bonding instantly.

Immediately he tried to remove it. He felt the stiff plastic structure latch itself onto his skin. Shortly after, he could hear bubbling as he rubbed the cheeks in pain. His skin felt hot, followed by burning like cooked meat. It became so severe he dropped to his knees in grunting agony, tightening his lips as not to make a peep. Through the eyeholes, he could see Sonny suffering the same. She turned in pain with her head down covered in her hands. Her fingers scratched at the brim trying to pull the mask off, but it only bonded tighter, bubbling and hissing.

Seconds later, the bubbling quieted. The hot surges and pain ceased. Touching his nose, forehead, and chin, he felt the changes. Sonny's head was still down, but she turned standing confidently. Her hair and body went unchanged, but her face had been transformed completely. Her nose was rounder, and her ears were smaller. There was a significant puff around her cheeks, making them stick out slightly, and her eyebrows were thinner. The changes were subtle, but enough she didn't look at all like the same person. If Jack hadn't seen it himself, he would never suspect her to be the journalist he'd been traveling with.

An unpleasant thought occurred to him. While securing his flashlight from his sack, he quickly held the lens up to his eye, scanning Sonny. "The J.A.C.K.s have visors that work like my flashlight. At the hotel, I could see through Trick's disguise."

"No issues then?" she asked.

"No, I think we're clear." He stood up, taking deep breaths, but their talking had alerted the guards. The pudgy cloud keeper approached them cautiously. "Hey, what're you two doing out this late after curfew?"

"Curfew?" Jack asked. "What curfew?"

The cloud keeper rolled his eyes. "Where you been kid? It was announced three days ago. Could have you two thrown in just for my amusement, all that's gone on. People doing strange things like standing in the middle of the street for hours. Confused how they got there, always the same excuses and random attacks in the middle of the night, or people disappearing altogether. That's why everyone's been told to pair up. Where were you two heading to this late?"

Jack was caught off guard. He went through the list of safe houses as they ran from Mother's, but there were only two clouds left they could hide on. The Fiz Factory seemed like the only option, but now with their new masks, they could return to Cloud Nine. They'd spoken briefly of the J.A.C.K.s after them and the possibility of Teddy still at Phoenix's Estate. Bicentennial Village, Plymouth Meeting, and Shadow Manor were all on the same cloud. Jack had trouble thinking of a convincing excuse. Luckily Sonny recovered faster but with an unexpected destination.

"We're on our way to Cloud Nine," she replied. "We have a friend waiting in Shadow Manor."

"Shadow Manor?" he bellowed, rubbing his chin. He exchanged looks with the thin guard who shrugged. "If you're going to see that heartless old man, that's punishment enough. Go on, get out of here."

Aside from a sideways glance, Jack bit his lip as they followed the obnoxious cloud keeper to the elevator. The other J.A.C.K. remained silent, glaring at them as they walked by. A stooped man in the corner backed away timidly from them as much as he could. Jack recognized him as a spirit Father had pointed out before. The Spirit of Groundhog Day, he was told, was afraid of his own shadow and rarely ever left his home. Keeping his distance in the corner, it looked as if he'd become even more shaken up.

Rubbing his folded arms as he held them close to his chest, he softly muttered repeatedly to himself, "A storm is coming, hide." This mumbling followed them as they jetted up to Cloud Nine.

The spirit was the first to leave when the elevator doors shuttered open, still muttering to himself as he walked quickly down the hall.

Jack peeked up at the night sky. "It's not even cloudy out," he said to Sonny. "You know what I mean, no storm clouds."

Sonny stared at the sky, as well. "Not all storms are wind and rain, you know." Several people were walking together toward the town center like a parade. Wanted posters hung between sections with Jack and now Sonny's picture plastered. The masks seemed to be working as no one looked twice in their direction. Sonny began walking into the hall when Jack stopped.

"So what was all that about?" he snapped. "Why did you tell them we would go to Shadow Manor of all places? You know he hates me!"

She smiled and put a hand on his shoulder. "I noticed. I'm sure no one expects us to go there. I told the cloud keeper that so he wouldn't grow suspicious of two teenagers walking around late at night. How many of us do you think there are here?"

Jack had to admit she was right. Even with a disguise, there couldn't be many who fit their description. Any suspicious behavior would bring unwanted attention to them if they weren't careful.

Whispering in his ear, Sonny leaned in close. "Look around. No one is watching us for once. We can go to any of the hideouts without being chased now, like Bicentennial Village?"

Jack hesitated but reluctantly nodded in agreement. He continued nodding unconsciously as he recognized the tattered suit and shaggy hair of a spirit in a corridor of the hall, clearly hiding his face with his coat. He hadn't seen Father in almost a month, but he appeared more worried and tired looking than ever. Jack wondered if the cloud keepers had ever caught up with him. He went to approach him, then remembered his disguise. If he was going to find his actual father without being caught, he had to remain unrecognized.

As the Spirit of Father's Day remained covered, Jack followed. There was a suspicious behavior he displayed that tugged on Jack's instinctive nature. Father kept his head low and stayed in the shadows, but Jack could still see the worry in his eyes when he turned. As carefully as possible, Jack crept along the walls. Father stopped and started speaking to a short person, cloaked in crimson red. With his back to them, Jack tried to overhear their brief conversation.

"I need to know if you are with us or not," he heard Father whisper. "We've seen this before. Too many of us are behaving differently, and you know why."

"And why would you think that would have anything to do with me?" Jack heard the other voice say. It was the voice of a young boy's, but a tone Jack recognized as if it were thoughts in his own mind.

Father whispered lower. "Because family is a strong bond, and your protégé may want you with him. Lucky and the other union members need to know you are with us and safe. After what your butler has told the cloud keepers about Theodore's disappearance, you must know of his involvement. The Sandman could be latched onto any of your staff now. What do you plan to do when they come after you for the fourth sand?"

"I have been around longer than any other holiday spirit," the young boy said sternly. "The Sandman's job was to put children to sleep nightly. Most do not realize when the hourglass is broken dreamers are the easiest to latch onto. Spirits are too strong, but a dreamer will allow him to take over when they sleep, build an army, and find three spirits to restore himself. If any of my staff has been latched onto, it was Theodore. It was dangerous for me to leave my throne, but your message seemed urgent. I know what he wants, and eventually, he'll come for it, and soon after Cloud Nine. As I always have done in my lives, anything I must do, I will do, even if he *was* my best friend."

Attempting his hardest not to look suspicious, Jack bent his head lower. Father walked back toward the elevator while the boy strolled back toward the town's center, and Jack was able to catch a glance. He had an average build for someone his age with a short blonde mop of hair. It was strange seeing someone so young just after what Sonny had mentioned about a lack of teenagers. From the angle, it was hard to tell who it was, but the voice he heard with the tone of an older man lingered in his mind unexpectedly. The crimson red robe and matching slippers were a definite giveaway.

"Phoenix?" Jack deduced as Sonny caught up. "I knew I recognized the voice, but I didn't expect to see him grow so fast in a few weeks."

Sonny started coming down the hall. "What is he doing away from his throne? I thought he didn't leave."

It was yet another question he couldn't answer. Jack didn't understand why after last year's near ending of all existences he would risk leaving his home and throne to see Father. "I think it was about protecting the spirits in the union. I think they know the Sandman is latched onto Teddy. He was the only dreamer there when the hourglass was broken...and I think the Sandman was Phoenix's protégé."

"What?!" Sonny's eyes went wide, but it didn't last long as she caught Jack staring at something new. The thought had already been pushed out of his mind when his eyes found another spirit he'd just left.

"Mother?" He watched her exit the elevator behind them.

"What is she doing here?" commented Sonny.

Jack shrugged his shoulders. The Spirit of Mother's Day walked by with a gray wash over her eyes. She paid no attention to Jack or Sonny. He couldn't tell if she was unable to recognize them beneath the mask, but she walked by without a glance in their direction. A line of people followed behind her including several from the circus tents and the April Fool, all with the same blank expression. They stepped through the crowd toward the cloud's center. The hour was late, but with the number of people out, Jack was determined to find out why so many were gathering.

The inner circle of Cloud Nine between the twelve paths was abundant with spirits. A few hundred had arrived in what appeared to be some sort of meeting. Streetlights hovered above each route. Mother and those who had followed were standing together. Many had the same dreamy look in their eyes as if staring at nothing. Father looked Mother over suspiciously before lowering his head disapprovingly. Shortly after, he exited down the hall.

Echoing from the first cloud, the clock tower chimed twelve times. It was now midnight, and the group began to settle. Sonny stood behind Jack, and they each kept their heads low to avoid unwanted attention. The cold winds swept in, but no one made the slightest shiver. The crowd had gathered into a large circle around a single spirit. He appeared darker and more tone than Jack remembered as he addressed them all with tattooed muscular arms and a gruff voice.

"I'd like to thank you for coming out tonight and serving this great city with pride and resilience," the Spirit of

Independence Day said with cold eyes. "It is our civic duty to protect what we care for most. Our freedom is in danger as long as the terror, Sandman, remains uncontained. We must do what we can to assist the J.A.C.K.s in locating the ones responsible for releasing this horrible spirit and bring them to justice!"

The crowd nodded in agreement with Redd. Many looked as if they were ready to take matters into their own hands. Sonny took a few pictures of the group until Jack waved his hand for her to quit. No one glanced at them, but the rapid flashes were distracting.

Redd made two fists as if preparing for a fight himself. "The cloud keepers are doing what they can but need our loyalty. The detective has released statements that young Mr. Taylor and his partner are only wanted for questioning. Many of you believe they are guilty. Either way, we need to band together to get them back into custody for their personal safety. The toymaker was the first reported to go missing after the celebration, and now there is evidence to believe Presto the Illusionist never appeared for his performance."

The illusionist, again? Jack pondered to himself. *Luminista's magician card. I wonder...*

A rush came over Jack as the spirit held up an item he'd seen before. It was an enlarged wanted poster displaying Jack and now Sonny, with the green flashlight shown in his hand. The black leather jacket he wore was the same in the picture, making it simple for anyone who paid enough attention to spot him even with the mask. What was most upsetting, however, were the small boxes beneath their pictures. They were of any known accomplices he may come in contact with.

Lucky had been stamped captured by the J.A.C.K.s, providing a sufficient amount of guilt in the bottom of Jack's stomach. Beside that spirit were the marked photos of the spirits of Thanksgiving, Independence Day himself, April Fools' Day, and lastly Mother's Day. It hadn't been too long since he'd left them, but it seemed they had all already been questioned. Mr. Shadow alone had a question mark over his hooded face. The last few spirits including Father and Holly of Christmas had circles around their photos.

Jack wondered where Holly could be when Sonny gestured to where the April Fool stood. He was missing his arm sling he'd worn just hours ago and had the same absent stare Mother had. Sonny held up her notepad so Jack could see the list of names that remained for safe houses while the Spirit of Independence Day finished.

"Some of you may have opposing feelings about the city's structure, but we must put political differences aside." Redd stepped through the crowd with a stern, grim smile. "We must work together to find these former heroes. We will split into groups: one to the Spirit of Easter and the other to the Spirit of Hanukkah. From there we will branch out to the other homes, and be sure this cloud is vacant of them. Once through, we will influence the clouds below to follow. We together will do our civic duty and aid in their safe capture!"

They dispersed into their groups seeming ambitious. The hunt had begun, and Jack was running out of both time and safe places. He thought carefully about the events of New Year's Day and the Sandman. He remembered what the investigator had told him of a relative defeating him with a fourth sand. Now it made sense that the fourth sand was the infinite sand Phoenix carried. Now his newest concern was where Teddy could be. Finding him would not only clear his name but locate the Sandman and most importantly find his father all at once. His anger blocked out any fear he may have had before, but besides a slight dizzy feeling, it didn't affect his ability to think clearly. He knew after seeing what Trick was capable of as only a symbol he'd require all the help he could gain fighting a full powered former holiday spirit like the Sandman.

When Sonny tugged on his arm, he already knew what she intended to ask him, and he was prepared with an answer. "I memorized the list. I know where we need to go next."

It was rare to see Sonny's mouth slightly agape unable to find the right words. However, she regained herself quickly. "Well I had an idea, but where do you believe we should go?"

"Plymouth Meeting," he answered as he walked toward the path. "From their direction, it looks like the groups won't be back there for a while. I'm not sure what the circles around Father and Holly were meant for, but with Father hiding, they are probably looking to question them too."

"Do you think we'll be safe hiding there?" she asked skeptically.

Jack stopped and turned suddenly clenching his fists. "No! I'm not hiding anymore! If the Sandman or whoever wants to find me, I'm not just waiting around to be the prey." He spoke loudly, but most of the crowd were either just out of earshot or had left entirely.

"So what are you planning to do there then?" Sonny asked in a hushed tone.

He walked with a focused look toward the rocky path of Plymouth Meeting. "To find more hunters."

It was well after midnight when Plymouth Meeting finally came into view. She didn't say it, but Jack was sure Sonny had to be as tired as him. They went over the list of suspects she'd copied from the investigator to remain awake. Ignoring their own names, the aspiring journalist managed to list Lucky, Father, Presto the Illusionist, Phoenix, the toymaker, Nina, and Butler

Morris, who Sonny snickered at. She occasionally would scribble notes on the matter then scratch them out. After weighing the possibilities of the listed suspects, they agreed they needed more clues. Presto was still on the top of Jack's list, and he wasn't sure how much evidence he had to support it but had a theory the illusionist could've been the distraction in it all.

He could feel himself dragging with every step he took. The path was long, settled between hills where buffalo either slept or grazed. It was rough as if no one had made it safe for travel yet. The only evidence he found that it had ever been used was a set of footsteps, but even they were headed in the opposite direction.

Hiking up the final hill, Jack discovered Plymouth Meeting. Smoking wreckage floated near the beach's end. A wooden sixteenth-century ship with full white sails and the large metal anchor was docked on the shore a few hundred yards away with a large hole in the hull. The starry sky danced on the ocean's surface behind it while damaged wooden planks drifted around the brim of the beach. The ship and two of the masts holding the sails had been broken violently. The steering wheel, along with other debris, littered the water.

Sonny looked past a short ledge of land over to the ocean. "Where do you think she is?"

Jack simply shook his head. There was no sign of the holiday spirit, Nina, anywhere. Even in the dark without Jack's flashlight, walking onto the mainland, they could clearly see movement. A few turkeys spread throughout the grass were flapping their wings wildly. Some ran rampant in panic while others nibbled on corn, beans, and squash that had fallen to the ground. Smoldering piles of tent left over from a brutal battle continued to smoke. Plenty of tables, benches, and food had been warped from the mixture of heat and water, but no people were left.

Seconds later, Sonny had already hopped down to the beach near the ship's side, rummaging through the broken wood and taking notes of what she found. Jack stuck to the burnt remains on the grass. Weeding his way through the turkeys wasn't as difficult as he thought, although they were heftier than he realized. A few steps in their direction would cause them to flutter away.

The ground was littered with food, plates, and spilled drinks. A feast had occurred moments before the disruption. As Jack investigated, the young detective noticed one unusually large bird tugging on something like a worm. The more he inspected it, the more he realized it wasn't a worm but a thin wire. Once the cable was dislodged, the turkey ran away, and Jack could see what it was attached to. It was a foot long piece of wood, but different than the others lying about. It was lighter in color and weight with rounded edges, smooth surfaces, and a metal staple fastened to it. For some reason, it was familiar to him, and Jack remembered two items the investigator had bagged previously.

Jack reached into his coat pocket for his flashlight, when Rocho surprisingly leaped out barking as if unable to stand still any longer. "I really wish you would quit doing that," he said to the pup.

Rocho circled a few spots and sniffed with his nose stuck up in the air. There were moments where he passed the same area curiously, and his tail pointed straight. His eyes became droopy beneath the green fur, but he shook his body quickly and growled. When he started to bark repeatedly, Jack could tell he had found something. He stayed close while following the barks.

Jack searched the area unable to see anyone around, not even Sonny, who he assumed was still near the ship. Rocho stopped short of a small mound on the beach. He pawed the pile, scratching away the sand to reveal an electric blue weaving of string, beads, and feathers. As Jack bent down to pick it up, he analyzed it carefully before understanding what it was.

"Is that a dream catcher?!" Sonny startled Jack.

He snapped his head around quickly to find her sneakers and jeans damp up to her knees. She appeared worried and shivering, brushing off black ashes from her shoulder. She looked from Rocho on the ground to Jack and brushed the hair out of her face as if waiting for an explanation.

"He just dug it up a second ago." Jack examined the delicately woven blue netting around the willow hoop. The white feathers and beads sparkled as if it had permanent raindrops laced throughout. If he held it at the right angle, he could see the slightest hint of the letter *J* in the netting.

Sonny shook her head. "Doesn't seem frightfully important. It'd probably be best to leave it."

"Kinda think it was meant for me," he responded as he opened his sack. "Besides it might help, having a dream catcher against the Sandman, you know?"

Sonny was acting particularly strange over the matter, fidgeting while she disagreed. "It might as well be stealing! It doesn't belong to us, and we're not thieves. We should really just leave it here."

Before he had a chance to respond, Rocho's head started drooping. In that brief moment, he began wavering, and his eyes blinked uncontrollably until closing completely. Finally, with a loud thud, the pup flopped to the ground dozing soundly.

Stuffing the dream catcher into his sack, he kneeled down to Rocho. His tail was curled around him, and the light green fur of his chest and stomach rose and fell gently. Other than that he was very still. Jack put his ear to his snout then lifted him into his arms.

"What's wrong with him?" Sonny asked.

"It's okay, I think he's just asleep." Jack switched him from his arms to his hand. Once Rocho had returned to a flashlight, Jack stared at the ground. Though he couldn't clearly see it, he had a feeling as he yawned there was something beside the late hour causing him to yawn. "We need to move. Get out of here quick. I think the Sandman's been through here."

Every Cloud Nine home they traveled to held a similar fate. The home for the Spirit of Hanukkah was a large Jerusalem town where a festival of lights took place. When they arrived, however, the area was in ruins. Houses lay in shambles, lamps were shattered, and some roofs and bushes were still burning. Other homes were just as bad. Rebirth Caverns had crumbled, leaving clumps of fur and a bow tie left from the Spirit of Easter's symbolic bunny. The homes of the Spirits of Passover, Ramadan, and Kwanzaa were all left the same. More destroyed homes, pillars knocked over, and villages ablaze, all as if a fight had occurred but no people. Just remnants of the Sandman's dream dust.

With Redd leading groups to chase them and have them locked up, Jack knew better than to go to him. Examining the list, however, few options were available. Lucky had been arrested by cloud keepers, and Phoenix's Estate was the site of the crime. Just before he was ready to head to the most unwanted of the final hideouts, Sonny had an idea.

"Perhaps we should head to Bicentennial Village?" she suggested.

She had remained relatively quiet over the last few hours. Jack assumed it was the depressing sites they'd seen lately. They'd traveled miles from each path dodging the herd of people chasing after them. Jack wasn't sure if this was a brilliant idea or the sleep prying crazy thoughts into her mind.

"To Redd's?" Jack asked. "You really think we should ask for help from the guy chasing us with a mob?"

"Of course not, but he was on the list of safe houses," she debated. "What better way to find out his real loyalty to the union than searching his home?"

Jack mulled it over silently for a moment before speaking. "Okay fine. Might be the only safe house not wrecked by the Sandman." Sonny sprang with surprised rejuvenation, while Jack trudged on behind.

He doubted the decision the moment he made it but didn't say anything to her. He found it strange how upbeat she'd suddenly become as he stifled a yawn, wondering what time the clock tower last chimed.

The outlet of the brick road they march onto was like stepping back in time to the eighteenth century. The path divided into two long rows of old official government houses, like a post office and courthouse, surrounded by homes. They stood similar to Mother's neighborhood, but with a much older colonial style. Street lamps were lit by torches, and horses were sleeping in a barn near the entrance. They walked around a large metal pole with a roped pulley. Jack assumed it was for the flag that had been taken down for the night. With so many old buildings, he wondered if someone would run out yelling about the "British coming" any second.

A taller building at the very end stood alone closing the street. The words *TOWN HALL* were etched on the white stone front beneath the roof. It was quiet, and there seemed to be no damage to any of the buildings. A set of stairs led up to two heavy wooden doors. A marble version of the Statue of Liberty stood on the left side while a marble Lady Justice stood on the right, blindfolded and holding balance scales.

It remained eerily quiet, walking up the steps of the empty street. Jack felt a shiver up his spine as the moonlight reflected from the face of Liberty. It appeared as if her eyes were following him. He tried to promise himself this statue wouldn't move, but he scanned the grounds for better shielding spots just in case. The moment they reached the doors, he tried pushing, but it didn't budge much.

"Is it locked?" Sonny asked as she put her hands against its rough surface.

"No, I think it's stuck," Jack responded, pushing hard. "Like something's behind it."

Together they pushed hard on the dense wood until it finally pried open just enough for them to squeeze through one at a time. Sonny stepped through first followed by Jack, who immediately understood why it was such an effort. Like the other Spirits' homes, this one too had held some sort of struggle inside. Debris from fallen pillars, broken podiums, and burnt wooden benches were thrown around the floor. From the looks of the room, whatever had happened had been contained inside this building alone.

Jack bent down using the magnifying glass handle of his flashlight to inspect the floor. Just as he suspected, grains of sand were sprinkled about the grounds glittering with false innocence. Gunpowder residue was mixed in, stinging the air with the smell of sulfur. A pile of broken ceiling raptors sat against a closet door. On the walls, portraits of presidents and patriotic banners had fallen to the ground, and the flag had been singed.

"This doesn't make sense," Jack muttered as he stepped over a banister. He brushed his hand through his curly dark hair, hoping a proper thought would give him a clue.

Sonny stared up at the rafters and spun in a slow circle. "Hmm. I would say he's either been attacked by the Sandman and now wants to protect us, or abducted and cloned as an evil twin." Jack looked up at her questionably before they caught eyes, and she carried on. "Never underestimate the cloned evil twin theory."

A loud thump forced him to bounce to his feet. Sonny wheeled around, quickly facing where the noise occurred. Muffled bangs like knocking with pillows, shook the boards leaning against the closet. Jack turned on his flashlight, shining the beam at the pile. Someone or something was calling out from behind the rubble.

"Help me," Jack said, and he began tossing the boards aside.

"We don't know what's in there," Sonny pleaded. "What if it's a trap?"

"What if someone needs our help?" he turned with determination in his eyes. "It could be my dad!"

She reluctantly helped him move the heavy pieces blocking the door. It shuddered as the banging became more abrupt and the muffled noises became more acknowledgeable. Sonny stood on one side while Jack reached for the handle. The voice inside became clearly audible just before he opened it. "Is that...?"

The door burst open in a flash of gray, leaping onto Jack with fury in a white top hat with stars, red bowtie, and overalls.

"In defense of the nation and of our forefathers, I will not mop gently into the night. May justice be cleanly served through purity, bravery, blood, and bleach!"

The rush pushed Sonny back, and she dropped her notepad. Jack fell to the ground, tackled by the man. The white hair beard puffed out from his face and hat. He stood over Jack enraged, holding a mop by its wood stock firmly pointed at Jack's forehead. Raising the shaft above his own head, the man made a quick motion to strike when Jack blurted out a name.

"Usher Sam!" Jack yelled from the floor.

The symbol halted but kept his mop pointed at Jack, threateningly raising an eyebrow. "Who are you?"

"Jack... Jack Taylor," he answered, remembering the mask was hiding his face. "Don't you remember us from the theater room?"

The symbol lowered his mop slightly. "Taylor? You don't look old enough to be the architect..."

"That's his father," Sonny interrupted from behind the door. "You don't remember last year?"

Sam lowered his mop and put his hand on his head as he looked around the room. The top hat slowly changed into a gray cap matching his overalls. He now held the appearance of a janitor. "I've been confused lately. Apologies, my appearance has been changing at random lately. Utility Sam at your service." He held out a hand for Jack to take, helping him up from the floor and brushing him off with a small whisk broom.

"Utility Sam?" Sonny asked snapping a picture of him.

Sam stood proudly with his mop in hand. "That's right. Fixing, mending, and cleaning away the filth, bringing purity with a fresh lemony scent."

Jack scanned the destruction left in the building and was thankful it wasn't his own room. He politely picked up Sonny's notepad and noticed a few pages ripped out as he handed it to her, accounting it to the drawbacks of using a pen over pencil. "Do you know what happened to Redd?" he asked the Independence Day symbol.

The symbol paused in his cleaning with a hinting mix of anger and regret. "There were only a few. My spirit and I were preparing orders for this year's celebration. He seemed a bit off, but I assumed he was just excited for the fireworks arrangement this year. That was until they came strolling in as if hovering above the floor, sand falling in their wake."

"The Sandman?" Jack asked. "When was he here? Did you see him?"

"I assume it was, but no, I did not see him," Sam stated as he threw down his mop. "My holiday spirit shoved me into the closet when they entered to protect me. I could only hear the explosions, knives hitting wood, the building falling, and those people shouting."

"That's awful," Sonny expressed. "Did you hear anyone say anything?

The symbol shook his head. "All I remember was fighting to get out. Thought I heard someone with a bad cough, but that's about it."

Sonny pursed her lips and continued her writing. The mop Sam picked up became a broom as he swept the piles. Jack glanced at the doors. He tried to imagine the actions that had happened. The Sandman was gaining followers fast. If he had a chance at all of figuring this out and finding Teddy, he would need every piece of information possible.

"Did anything else happen that would help us find them?" he asked. "Anything at all?"

There was a change as Sam swept and the broom became much, much shorter. "Before the fighting began I heard those who came in mutter something about Holly. Redd Rocket's always been protective over her."

As he used the tiny broom, he swept some rubble to the side and found a rolled parchment. It was white but thoroughly aged, although there were no rips or other signs of wear. Sonny stared at it questionably while Jack recognized its appearance. "Is that the Declaration of..."

"Freedom," Sam finished. His bowtie had changed to a catcher's mask while his overalls separated at his waist. "Looks similar to Independence but different entirely. Wish I'd had that earlier."

He tossed the parchment to Jack. Sam pulled down a catcher's mask over his face and swept the space below him with the small broom. Jack watched, rolling the parchment tightly and placing it into his sack as Sam completed changing. The symbol looked at them both as if they were walking to the mound.

"Ready to play ball?" Sam asked. "Great American pastime. Umpire Sam is ready to play."

Jack squinted at Sonny. "We should head to Holly's and see if she's all right."

"Absolutely," she agreed. "Thank you for your help, U.S." Sam continued sweeping, muttering baseball terms as they exited, as he slowly changed back into Uncle Sam.

Jack led Sonny out of Bicentennial Village, returning to the cloud's center. They rushed down a white, snow powdered path between tall pine trees toward Holly Woods, a name that was immediately obvious through their trudge between two grand forests. Atop each tree was a small formation of holly with its snow-covered red berries. Jack knew holly didn't normally grow on pine trees, but also knew very little was improbable in this plane.

Jack had grown almost as fond of Holly as he was of Father. His heart raced as he hurried down the narrow path of pine trees, hoping she was safe. It finally opened up to an epic circle of cabins larger than most of the Cloud Nine homes. A massive forest barrier far too thick to see through protected the town on all sides. Snow fluttered from the sky onto a few dozen wood cabins creating a thick layer that clung to the roofs. Green wreaths hung on doors with red bows like traffic lights and frost stained each cabin's candlelit window.

In the center, a broken shamble of ice crystals, wood, and glass of someone's home now laid crumbled together in a pile. The pieces projected out like javelins where a large section had imploded. Snow flew in from above, and Jack noticed a lifeless form lying on the ground being buried in the fluttering snow. He could feel his heart thumping in his throat as they rushed down the hill, almost tumbling in their hurry. His fearful worry peaked as he sprinted through the snow drifts as he realized they arrived too late.

Stepping over the spiked wood and glass blanketed with soft snow was difficult as they occasionally slipped. Jack had no problem ignoring the cold atmosphere as he harvested newfound anger once he witnessed the mass lying on the ground. An older man, with a white beard, strong in stature, wearing a white parka and hunting gear lay face down in the snow. He and Sonny quickly bent down and brushed him off as Claus struggled to stand up.

He was bruised all over, panting hard, and barely able to stand on his own. It took several seconds for him to open his eyes. Glaring at Sonny and Jack, it took a few seconds, but eventually, it appeared he was somehow able to see through their disguise, and a single word was uttered. "Massacre."

"Who?" Sonny asked.

"And where's Holly?" Jack asked.

Claus continued to stare uncertainly as he regained himself. "I tried…to fight them off but…there were too many…spirits with cold eyes. Holiday spirits fighting each other controlled like puppets. They took her." His head dropped down as if ashamed.

Sonny held a confused look. "They're moving fast like a plague avoiding the groups. Do you have any idea where they've taken her, or who was leading them?"

Claus finally stood on his own, shaking his head unable to meet their eyes and instead feeling the ground. "The snow is still soft here, not much time has passed, but it was a blur all the same. Mother, the April Fool, a few others not acting themselves. I tried to protect Holly, but they overpowered me, destroying her home and leaving me here. I remember a wheezing figure over me, but I couldn't tell you who. I used every hunting trick I know but wasn't strong enough. Not alone."

Jack remained quiet. Several thoughts ran through his head. Familiar feelings of resentment bubbled inside him like those he had so long ago when his father was unable to come home. "You should've done more," he said quietly.

"Jack?" Sonny voiced, shaking her head.

"She was just here!" he pleaded, tears swelling his eyes. "My father was probably with them! You should've fought harder! You should've found others to help you! We could've found a way to save her. I can't lose anyone else!"

It was quiet. Neither the symbol nor Sonny spoke. A few flakes of snow fluttered in through the broken roof followed by a chilled wind of the night. Only the distant jingling of bells could be heard. Jack turned as he felt the urge to punch something and apologize all at once. His frustration had boiled over and was unleashed at an unintentional target.

"I should wait outside for my brother to return," Claus said finally.

Jack marched over to an undamaged portion of Holly's home. Grabbing his head with both his hand, he yelled loudly, balling his fists. Squirrels that had scampered inside scurried back out into the woods from fear. Sonny tried placing a hand on his shoulder, but he quickly stepped away. "I didn't mean to yell," he admitted.

"I know," Sonny replied, stepping closer.

Jack paced. "Just feel like I should've been here sooner. I could've done something for her, for them... For my dad."

"I know," She replied, stepping closer.

Jack shook his head. "I should've never gone into Phoenix's vault or left the J.A.C.K.s' headquarters. Teddy's doing his best to frame me. If I'd stayed focus on my dad, maybe this could've been avoided."

"I know." Sonny stepped within inches of Jack.

He paused, taking in a deep breath and calmly looking up at the ceiling. Above them, hanging in an archway were a few shrubby green leafed twigs with small white bulbs. Jack stared at them, curiously before turning toward Sonny.

"I think I'm so mad because it's my fault and I think...I think...that's mistletoe," he noted as he stared at the plant above and scratched his head curiously. His eyes fell from the ceiling to Sonny.

Her eyes followed the decoration down to Jack's eyes, and she replied softly, "I know." Their eyes began to close as they leaned into each other until a distinct sound of bells jingling grew louder.

"Do you hear that...?" she stopped. "...sleigh bells?"

Jack turned, surprised to hear the scuffling of hooves landing. Eight impressive reindeer outside the broken wall were harnessed together and shaking a bit of snow off their antlers. They appeared healthy but were panting. Together they pulled a large red sleigh with bright gold bells into the town's center. Over a year had passed since he'd had any positive thoughts about Christmas and even more years since he'd believed in the person stepping off the sleigh at that moment. The white beard, red suit, and immense black boots were prominent along with the enormous belly and sparkle in his eyes.

Santa stepped off the sleigh and into the soft snow but with more haste than a man his size would be known to carry, calling out for his other half. "Claus?!"

Claus marched in from the left with a defiant look in his eyes. The two men stood apart. One robustly powerful and the other weakened and thinner, yet they complemented each other like different sides of a coin. "Santa... Did you lose them?"

"No," he answered as he stared at Claus's bruises. "They did in fact return to the town center but vanished in a way I haven't seen in a century. Like an illusion. We won't be able to rescue her without the North Star."

A little further away, Jack noticed an enormous Christmas tree complete with decorations and broken gifts lying in shambles on the ground. A shimmering green substance he assumed was tinsel, or broken ornaments lay beneath it. A blinding flickering light Jack had seen before hovered near the ceiling. The same he'd seen in Holly's villa. Sonny walked over, looking at the light hypnotized like a moth.

"No, don't step there!" Claus snapped. The room grew darker. Everyone turned to where Sonny now stood. Jack felt as if it happened in slow motion. A swirling mass of sand rose from the shimmering green ground. Hands formed separating the field and grasping onto anything within reach. It was a trap.

Jack scanned the room quickly for something to pull her out with but only found a jar. He'd almost been pulled into it himself before stomping on a green hand. Gripping the container tightly, he could feel the base of his middle finger vibrating. His hand started to rumble, and he could see the hand buzzer suddenly changing the jar into a can. A shower of fake snakes shot out from the canister. They attacked the sinking pit, distracting the hands. Claus and Santa stood on either side, beating them off once Sonny was free.

"It's quicksand!" Claus yelled over the grains.

"Go, we'll find a way to stop it!" Santa yelled as he pulled a giant candy cane out of his red sack and tossed it to Claus. "We have to save the tree's light!"

For the second time, Jack had been forced out of a spirit's home, unable to stop an attack. He followed Sonny back up the hills as fast as he could, but her long legs seemed to keep her just a bit further ahead. He couldn't remember how many times it had been that he passed the center of Cloud Nine, but he started feeling dizzy. Exhaustion was settling in. He shook his head furiously, trying to stay awake, unsure where she was leading them as his eyelids began to feel too heavy. As they carried on, he searched his sack, taking a few bites of food, but nothing boosted him enough to wake up. Digging deep into his pockets, he found the small bottle from the cruise ship he'd never taken that read *Drink Me*. He remembered it was meant to reduce the effects of dizzying high altitude from their trip on the iPlane.

Unfastening the cap, he drank the contents and immediately felt his eyes pop open. His mind felt instantly at ease. Walking by a rickety old fence next to a worn train station, he shook off the exhaustion and realized where Sonny was leading them.

"We're not really heading to where I think we are, are we?" he asked.

"It's the last safe house of Cloud Nine anyone would search for us," she argued. "It may be the only place remaining on this cloud for us to clear our heads."

Shaking his head in disagreement, he followed her down the mossy path to Mr. Shadow's home. He realized the Sandman had infiltrated the neighborhood watch group who'd been following them, but still didn't know if the Independence Day spirit was one of them or just unwittingly leading them. They'd been fortunate not to be caught by the group yet, and he wondered if the coin Lucky had given them really was charmed, as well as showed them paths. Either way, leaving the open area, Jack thought would be the best plan they could hope for. If that meant asking Mr. Shadow for help in finding his father, he'd do what he needed.

Trudging on in the late hours of the night, the darkness somehow seemed to settle in even more toward Shadow Manor. Jack gagged as he inhaled the strange mixed smell of rotten eggs and ash. The muddy path stuck to their shoes with each stride. On either side of them, dead grass and mud clung to skeletal beings marching through sunken swamps throughout the woods. They didn't seem to notice Jack and Sonny as they pried their bones from the muck.

As they walked past, bats would leave the trees they hung from, shaking the branches abruptly. An occasional howl of a wolf or hoot from an owl kept them alert as they continued. The sound that irritated Jack, however, was the wailing, as if from a ghost or someone being tortured, just out of earshot. Anytime he would turn toward the source, it suddenly stopped, then begin again as he walked farther. He could already feel the chills move over his skin from the holiday spirit's presence, much like the long-legged spiders crawling on graves. They were close.

Sonny was first to approach a set of tall rusted gates attached to aging blood-red brick walls. The gates creaked loudly as she pushed them open and entered a fog-covered courtyard surrounding the spirit's home. Several other homes lay beyond it. However, all appeared abandoned and incredibly worn with age. *Or perhaps haunted,* Jack thought, *like a horror movie.* Cauldrons sat just beyond the doors of each one filled with something he couldn't see from a distance.

The largest house in front of them was an eerie castle at least three times larger than the one in Mr. Shadow's villa. Dark grand windows reached from one story to the next, absent any light at all. Torn flags waved in the win, and gnarled tree branches scratched on the window's surface. Dual towers peaked high into the night sky, and the doors held the imprint of a dozen grim faces from tortured souls carved into the surface. A pumpkin, big enough for both Jack and Sonny to kneel in, sat on the porch. It held a grotesque face they'd become use to after their last venture through the poisonous pumpkin patch.

He was hesitant to approach it, but after a diminishing glance at Sonny, Jack climbed the steps of the castle. Oddly enough, no odd gasses or strange liquids spewed out. Instead, it was filled to the brim with candy. Sonny took a handful without caution. "Never know if we may need it," she explained.

"I wouldn't be surprised if he left it here for me to choke on," remarked Jack, taking some as well. He knocked hard on the door and waited. No stir or sounds came from inside, and beyond the windows, everything appeared to remain motionless. Jack tapped a few more times, followed by Sonny's impatient tugging at the handle. However, the inside continued to be just as quiet, and the door stood firmly still.

"Do you think he left?" she asked.

Jack looked up at the peaks then down at the windows to the side. Reaching for his flashlight, he accidentally dropped Lucky's gold coin but paid it no mind as he noticed an undraped window on the ground floor. Gesturing the beam of his flashlight through it, it shined brightly but was still too difficult to penetrate very far inside the inky blackness of the room. The few items he could see were a tall staircase in the center and a shelf with two framed photos. The strange thing was he recognized someone in both pictures.

"There's no way," Jack whispered.

"What is it?" Sonny walked over and looked into the illuminated portion of the window. As she peered inside, she didn't ask any questions. In fact, she said nothing at all. Her mouth remained agape for a moment until Jack clarified his own shock.

"I remember seeing the first one on the cruise ship," he stated as he looked at the photo of a young girl and an older man. "I'm not sure who the old man is, but I'm sure I've seen that little girl before." He changed the beam to the second photo. "The weird thing about the other one is that same old man is in that picture again, but with my neighbor Mrs. Johnson."

Sonny turned her head, quickly staring at Jack as if she'd never seen him clearly before. "You know her?"

Jack nodded slowly. "Yeah, she lives across the street from me. Wait, do you know her too?"

Before she could answer, the flashlight had fallen from Jack's hand and changed into the puppy. He yawned widely as if just awakening followed by shrill yelping. His barks created an even brighter light into the castle. A shadowy figure inside became slightly more visible. Jack could tell it wasn't Mr. Shadow, but it was the shadow usually following him and at times would roam freely without its counterpart. Currently, it appeared to be making gestures, mimicking Mr. Shadow walking toward the door as if leaving.

Sonny smiled as if a brilliant notion had entered her mind. "I believe he's telling us Mr. Shadow's left."

Jack sighed and reminded her of their situation. "That doesn't really help us find a safe place."

"Well, we have to find a way to get to him," she persisted. "He may be in trouble if he doesn't know about the group, and might have a few answers for us."

Jack rubbed his eyes and looked at Rocho, who was now licking the coin on the ground. "It's like we're walking in circles. How would we even find him? I don't think the shadow is exactly allowed out to play."

In a flash Rocho sprinted toward the rusted gates, barking. A newly illuminated path became visible with each bark directing them out. After picking up the coin with little gold remaining, Jack glanced at Sonny, who beamed approvingly and made her way out. "Beginning to think he may be smarter than you."

Within a few minutes at a blazing speed, Rocho had led them down a new path. There was warmth from the horizon. Very little light emerged, but they could feel dawn approaching. Compared to Shadow Manor, the road to Deluca Gardens seemed like its complete opposite. Flowers were blooming beautifully and lively, leaning toward the direction of the rising sun. Instead of a swamp, a large field of fresh grass shaking off the winter cold lay on either side. An army of Roman statues were planted in artistic demonstrations. Ponds held fish with tiger and zebra stripes that leaped in and out. Between them were species of plants. Jack had never before seen. Some plants snapped at passing insects with their large thorny vines like tongues. Some appeared to have hard orange petals shaped like pineapples. The leaves would come apart and regroup to rest on a new tree branch. Others resembled tiny twig people leaping into the air and diving into the dirt in a manner that left their bottoms sticking straight up that then sprouted flower buds.

Rocho led them in following the cobblestone path to a long building. It looked very much like a two-story hospital with the majority stretching to the left. A portion to the right side, however, was entirely transparent, with several windowpanes creating the entire surface of walls like a greenhouse. The closer they came to the building, the more the path Rocho showed blinked until it curved around to the right side and ended. The sun's rising rays made portions inside simpler to see into as they stopped between a few bushes, noticing movement. It was a spot that would give them an advantage as the doctor stormed outside the hospital.

"I advised you before, once we began the therapy we could not stop," the Spirit of Valentine's Day babbled. "You could be flooded with emotions you are no longer prepared for. It's simply too dangerous."

Before he could see him, Jack felt the chills and immediately knew who the doctor spoke of.

"There is far too much danger to keep those memories outside my body now." Mr. Shadow had followed the doctor into the courtyard. "The Sandman is coming for each Cloud Nine spirit, and I can't help but see their faces. Having those memories returned to me now may be the last moments I have with them."

The doctor opened the door to his greenhouse. Jack could see the plants inside, along with three jars on a shelf. A beating heart he'd seen before, and a small nerve he recognized as the April Fool's. The other was an unmarked jar Jack had never witnessed. Before the doctor stepped inside, he sighed. "Henry, you've been my patient and dear friend of mine for several years. I have done my best to treat you as any other patient even during the years people thought the worst. However, I cannot in good conscience end your therapy so early."

Mr. Shadow's eyes beneath the hood were barely visible, but Jack could see the desperation in them and feared what would happen next. The spirit of Halloween caught the doctor's glance at the greenhouse. Making a gesture with a single bony hand, Mr. Shadow made a jar from the greenhouse appear. It was filled with a clear liquid solution and a small portion of brain. It was labeled, but Jack was unable to read to whom. Sticking his right hand into the air, the spirit caused a pumpkin handled sword to materialize.

"If you refuse to do it, then I will take matters into my own hands," the Halloween spirit stated flatly.

"Henry, no!" The doctor held up his hands, pleading with more urgency than Jack had ever seen. "Those memories are not yours. Memories of love are held in the heart, not the mind! Please, don't do this."

The hood over Mr. Shadow's face shook. Dr. Deluca calmed himself and gestured to the greenhouse. "If you feel this strongly that it would be safer with you, I will return the therapeutic tool to you. It's the heart on the shelf. I was nearing a breakthrough perhaps within the year. Love is…very powerful. I hope you remember as much as you miss them, we can't go back."

Mr. Shadow slowly handed the jar to the doctor and dropped the sword, making it vanish into black wisps. "I wouldn't be doing this if I didn't believe it was pertinent. All of the uncertainty lately, I've heard rumors a holiday spirit is leading his sleepwalkers."

"I've heard this too," the doctor agreed. "Father's name keeps coming up. That and a wheezing voice, although I have my suspicions of a dreamer being the vessel. I ran into another…" The spirits entered the greenhouse, and Jack couldn't hear their conversation any longer. The low rumbling of Rocho's growling grew louder behind him. Only the spirits' silhouettes could be seen inside. Just as he went to get closer, Sonny made a motion to stop Jack from standing.

"What are you doing?" he asked. "I thought you wanted to talk to them. It looks like this place hasn't been attacked by the Sandman yet."

"I believe it's about to be." She pointed over their shoulders to where a large group of people stretching all the way back to the entrance stood in perfect formation. Among them were the Spirits of Christmas, Groundhog Day, April Fool's Day, Mother's Day, Easter, Hanukkah, Kwanzaa and nearly every spirit they'd come in contact with.

Redd stood at attention towering over them both as he led the entire parade of holiday spirits. Raising his eyebrow, he grinned at Jack and made a statement before throwing sand into their face. "Welcome to the new spiritual order."

Chapter 8
Déjà Vu

It was a chilly morning, like most during the winter season. The wind blew hard, rustling the branches of bare trees throughout the neighborhood. Frost stained the windows of cars that lined the steep streets like the dust of white spray paint. There was no snow on the ground, but the dark clouds above looked as if they were debating the urge to allow it. A few stars were left, but they were close to fading completely. The orange glow of the sun against the dark-blue sky slowly peeked above the horizon as if it were waking from a long sleep.

The area was practically empty, except for the widow, Mrs. Johnson. She was a plump, talkative woman with graying red hair who began each morning with a walk around the neighborhood. Her husband had died over six years ago, but she continued their ritual every day as if he were still alive, jogging beside her with each step she took. As usual, she wore a shiny pink jumpsuit with matching hat and gloves.

After jogging in place, she'd stretch her weary bones, take a few deep breaths, and close her eyes, willing herself to go on. A few steps out of her front yard and she was on her way. The shiny pink fabric reflected the sun's rays brightly as she turned the corner.

In the house across the street, Jack lay awake in his upstairs bedroom. He woke up, startled by what seemed to be the most realistic dream he'd ever had and was unable to sleep any longer. Rubbing his eyes, a room he had become so familiar with came into view at a most unexpected time.

It was his bedroom just as he remembered it. The room was still dark; the closed window blinds blocked the light from outside. Clothes littered the floor from the previous night's packing. His surrounding walls were painted the same sky blue, and the signed poster of his favorite football player still hung across from him. Scattered papers, pencils, and school books sat on the desk that stood in the corner.

The small metallic-green detective's flashlight his father left him was still held between his fingers, although he didn't remember picking it up. He couldn't stop himself from thinking of his father looking at the gold engraving. It all felt so very real, causing him to wonder if it was. Everything was exactly the same as he remembered it months ago, and he began wondering if he'd simply had a long dream. So detailed and fresh in his mind, it made it more difficult to tell if he was currently sleeping, or had finally woken up.

Through the magnifying glass of the flashlight, he could see the ceiling fan, unmoving over his head. Almost unconsciously, his thumb ran up the side of the flashlight, and to his shock, it remained powered off. Seconds later, however, the lamp in his room had been turned on, and after his eyes had adjusted, he noticed his mother standing in the doorway.

"I think you might need some new batteries for it." She smiled pleasantly in her red turtleneck sweater and black pinstriped pants. Jack made a motion to hide it but stopped himself. He felt as if he hadn't seen her in quite some time. Looking at her properly, she didn't appear upset by it at all. His last memories of her, she hadn't been so tolerant of his flashlight, accusing him of dependency, but today she seemed almost cheerful. Something Jack hadn't seen often.

"Yeah, I guess it just died on me," Jack muttered at the lifeless device.

"We'll stop to get more on the way," she replied. Her bronze skin stretched into a pleasant smile. "Come on now, it's time to get ready. You don't want him dragging you out of bed."

Jack lifted up the sheets, slowly catching on to what she said. "Him... Him who?"

She returned a puzzled look as if he'd asked something bizarre about squid for breakfast. "Sounds like he's already on his way up. He's been excited to take you to his hometown after so much time working."

Glaring at his mother with a dazed expression, Jack had a hard time understanding who was walking up the stairs. The strange thing was each step felt unbelievably familiar, like echoes of memory. He almost felt angry at himself for even allowing the unfeasible thought to enter his mind. But with every step, his heart beat a bit faster, and he was reassured again and again. Although he was sure it had been over a year, he knew precisely who the steps belonged to.

"Car's almost packed up hon," Jack's father stepped into the doorway addressing his mother. "See you're still in bed, son. Better hurry, your mother's got breakfast ready. We gotta go soon."

Jack rubbed his eyes in disbelief, and they became blurry immediately, filling uncontrollably, but the sight of his father was too much as he remained standing there. The curly dirty blond hair, and brown eyes hidden behind thin framed glasses. Before he could grasp how it was possible, Jack leaped out of bed and wrapped his arms around his father. After what felt like months of searching and so much longer without him, he was able to hold onto someone he was so much like. At thirteen years old and still growing, Jack stood less than a foot shorter than his father, which forced him to look up several times before the young detective could truly accept it. He knew if it were possible, he'd never let him go again.

"Everything alright, Jack?" his father asked as he hugged him back.

"Yeah." Jack wiped his face only now realizing how wet his cheeks were. "I'm fine, just feels like I haven't seen you in a really long time."

His father sighed and kneeled down to look Jack directly in his eyes. "I know I haven't been around nearly as much as I should be, but starting today, I promise that'll change, all right? Deals have been made, and now I'll have plenty of time with the family."

Jack smiled from ear to ear nodding, as his mother beamed down at them both. Everything felt perfect. Making his way to the bathroom to get dressed, he made a final decision. If what was happening really was a dream, he didn't care. If the Sandman could cause all of this to be his new reality, he would rather stay asleep in bliss than awake to a nightmarish truth.

Walking downstairs, Jack felt odd, looking around his house. The usual depressing rooms from photos he'd become accustomed to were now refreshingly alive and cheerful. Gifts surrounded the tree, along with stuffed stockings on the wall. A gift from Jack to his father lay in front, like the drum major leading a band of presents. Strangely enough, he felt he had been through this day so many times before, but this time had changed. His father was with him and rippled everything else, making all the difference.

During breakfast, he ate with both of his parents as they discussed which routes to take. The smells of bacon, eggs, and toast coursed through the room delightfully. There were no tears and no awkward moments of silence, just a family preparing for a short holiday vacation away. As they ate, Jack's mother asked about the batteries needed for his flashlight. For the first time ever, he'd forgotten all about it as it remained upstairs. Having his father physically around him, the flashlight seemed less necessary, but before leaving, he retrieved it off his bed and carried it downstairs.

As he skipped a few steps as he secured the flashlight into his duffle bag, the kitchen caught his eye. As he'd remembered this day so well, he wondered what other details may have changed, particularly other people around him. Stepping into the kitchen, he opened the top drawer curious of his mother's hidden photo. Extending it fully, he revealed oven mitts and pot holders but nothing else. Stepping out into the living room, he placed the duffle bag over his shoulder. He noticed the picture frame sitting on the highest shelf of the room. All three of them were smiling in their matching Christmas sweaters a few years prior. Leaving to join his parents, Jack grinned with excitement.

The sun was higher in the sky now, and the remaining dark clouds had started to separate. Some of the frost had begun to melt off the cars on the street, making the windshields appear joyfully tearful.

Walking to the driver's side of the car and opening the rear door, he noticed the unchanged events occurring in his father's presence. No one else seemed as thrilled or even felt his father had left their lives, which made it easier for Jack to accept it too. His parents waved to Mrs. Johnson, who had finished the second lap of her jog. She panted as she made her way to the car, removing her gloves, rubbing her brittle hands together. The suit remained just as stuffed as always.

"Good morning Taylors, Merry Christmas," Mrs. Johnson beamed. "Leaving out so soon? It's early for you all, isn't it?" This time Jack's father went to speak, but Mrs. Johnson didn't give him much of an opportunity. "Seeing Jackson off to a business trip?"

"No, not this time, Ella," Jack's father answered. "After a long month of moving, I'm taking the family to my hometown. Showing my son where I grew up."

Mrs. Johnson went to speak but looked too choked up. Jack thought of the last time this happened. She'd been upset about her husband, and something clicked in his mind about a framed photo inside a dark castle, but he couldn't remember the connection.

"Is it the 21st already?" the kindly neighbor continued rubbing her hands. "I can't believe it's been a month since your company moved you, folks, here. I do miss my husband so very much. You should spend as much time together as possible."

After their conversation with their neighbor, they wished Mrs. Johnson a Merry Christmas and climbed into the car waving goodbye. Jack was seated behind his father while his mother sat in the passenger seat and buckled herself in. She glanced at him briefly, and their eyes met for a moment. This time she smiled simply. "Have everything sweetie?"

Looking from one parent to the other, he nodded. "Yeah, I have everything I need."

As the day went on, more and more cars joined theirs on the road. Like packs of animals smelling meat for the first time, people hurried from store to store for gifts, holiday foods, and everything in between. This time, however, everyone seemed more cheerful and generally more polite as they shopped. Several waved delightfully to their car as Jack and his family drove by.

Except for a stop for lunch, they continued on the road for hours just as before. The further they traveled, the more these new memories pushed out Jack's previous ones. From the cars going by with out-of-state license plates to the people waiting at the bus stop, they all became less familiar – almost like he'd imagined it all, to begin with. Even a kid who looked excitedly through a store window pointing at a toy gave Jack the feeling he should remember him. Over the last few hours, it'd become new experiences. It wasn't until he smirked at a department store's Santa chasing his hat on the sidewalk that he heard strange whispers.

The sleepwalkers are ready… Jack barely heard in his left ear. It caused him to turn and peer out the window. "Huh?" he asked, unsure where it came from.

His father looked at him through the rearview mirror. "I said the buildings in the area probably look familiar. Your Aunt Linda lives not too far from here in Westchester. Do you remember?"

"Oh, yeah," Jack nodded, shaking off the odd moment. A little over a minute later, he heard another whisper in his right ear wave in and out as if breaking through barriers to get to him.

...toymaker said they were unrecognizable, behind masks... Jack turned to his right. "What is that?"

Both his parents turned for a moment, but it was his mother who spoke. "You mean the radio? I can turn it down soon if you'd like honey, we're nearly close enough anyway."

Jack wondered what she meant by "close enough" but didn't press the issue as it left his mind quickly. The radio did seem louder than his mother usually kept it as if she wanted to drown out road noise — *or possibly something else* he wondered. The holiday music made it difficult for him to concentrate very well on anything. The closer they came to driving by the exit to a familiar rest area, the harder it was to remember anything from the Holiday Hotel or Cloud City at all.

A few more minutes passed, and a final whisper entered both his ears at once like rushing waters. *...Using the illusionist to follow their locations, so keep her safe until she wakes. Chain that sleeping dog and let Teddy know the flashlight hasn't been found yet.*

"Did you hear that?" Jack asked. "What was that about a toy maker and Teddy?"

His parents glanced at each other for a moment. Shortly after, his father began speeding up. They said nothing to Jack, but the voices he heard were clear. "A toymaker, Teddy, and an illusionist," he said to himself, making mental notes. His parents continued to ignore him. The more he thought about it, the more his head hurt as if two sides of his mind were fighting.

His view through the windows became sketchy as random images of another world came into sight in the distance. Patches of ground had changed into the somehow familiar streets of a cloudy city. He could feel himself being marched into a shop filled with wood that just as suddenly switched back to the inside of the car. Outside the windows, images shifted in and out, gradually allowing Jack to witness a young blond girl with ink-stained jeans struggling to free herself from two large men. Sand trailed behind them as they held her arms and dragged her forward. She spotted Jack and yelled out to him silently before being dragged down, beneath the ground. Whether it was the car driving by so quickly or the figures beside her, no sound left her lips, and he was only able to read the formed words…*wake up.*

In a panic, he placed both hands on the sealed window and watched as all three disappeared. His father was driving much faster now, racing down the highway. Buildings and trees whizzed by in a blur as other cars appeared to practically leap out of the way. He pounded on the window when a name wedged itself into his mind. "Sonny!"

His parents turned around with such haste, Jack thought they'd broken their necks. Both faces flickered in and out like a skipping movie momentarily revealing two different appearances. A louder clearer voice coursed into his ears as if yelling. *What did he drink?! He's beginning to wake!*

He reached for the door handle as his mother turned to stop him. "Honey, don't be so hasty. Wouldn't you rather stay here with us and be happy?" she asked Jack with pleading eyes.

His father looked at him through the mirror speeding even faster. "We're almost there, son. In a few seconds, everything will be the way it should be. You'll forget the bad, and can finally have what you've always wanted. A father who's alive and has time for his son."

Jack hesitated. *A second chance,* he thought to himself. It was what he wanted more than anything to go back and really have his father back. Alive again as if he'd never left them. Looking at the woman, he thought of how his mother would feel if he never returned, losing both her husband and now her son. Then he thought of the spirit of Mother's Day and her sacrifice, and it made his decision easier.

"I don't trust you," Jack said defiantly. "This place will never be real. I am not your son, and you are not my parents." Swinging the door open, the two figures lunged for him, but Jack was able to leap from the speeding car just before crossing the city limits.

Falling to the ground, he closed his eyes and braced himself for the hard road's impact, but it never came. Instead of an abrupt hit into the field, all of his memories reemerged, and his eyes snapped open to a new scene. A blurry image of a large printer working loudly above him came into view. He could smell the strong odor of ink and wondered if Sonny were around. He was lying on the ground in a dimly lit room where papers spewed out of the machine and landed behind him onto a neglected stack. The stack had grown into a pile ready to topple over. It wasn't until he read the headline of the papers as they continually spilled out that he understood where he was.

"Cloud City News?" he read in a whisper. "Celebrate the holiday of the day, "Spouse Day," and appreciate your better half, while we bring you news of the next game in the Eclipse Tournament."

He wondered if the date were actually correct as he couldn't account for the last few days. Black and white news articles littered the walls like the writings from Sonny's notepad. Before lifting his head off the ground, he remained still and listened intently, ignoring the ruffling of pages being printed for anyone who may be near him. The only other sound he heard, however, was a distant muffled murmur of people.

Raising his body slowly, he checked around him to locate what the source was. A single door with a small tinted window stood in the corner. On a table to his right lay a flesh-colored mask, his sack from Lucky, the birthday card Luminista had left him, and Rocho lying asleep in a locked cage. It appeared whoever brought him in hadn't emptied his sack fully as it was still lumpy.

He was reluctant to stand up as he noticed something, or actually, someone was missing. He didn't see Sonny anywhere, and none of her things were in the room. After scanning the area, he crept to the door silently. Pausing for the right moment, he peeked through the window for a glimpse of who was inside. Behind the door, he was able to spot Teddy standing beside the Spirit of Father's Day. Jack remained below the window listening as Father and Teddy kneeled speaking to another person he was unable to see clearly. Only the person's hands were visible as he sat in a chair with a piece of string tied to his middle finger like a ring. Placing an ear near the door, Jack tried his best to listen for clues to where Sonny may be.

"I have unfortunate news, sir," Father apologized in his usual caring voice. "The latest group used the last of the dream sand we carried between the other two dreamers. It seems the boy may wake up soon if we don't gather more sand from the sleepwalkers."

"I could've easily taken care of this without as many problems," Jack heard Teddy's familiar voice state smugly. "I've been under Phoenix's employment for years, and he never suspected a thing. If I hadn't been preoccupied fixing my remote using spare parts from your player's glove, we could've switched the hourglasses secretly. We'd be finished by now, and my employer and I would have my totem, dork."

Jack heard Father stand to his feet. "I have grown the Sandman's power immensely with the army of sleepwalkers under my care. Those who haven't been put to sleep still trust me and will be easily convinced to his ways, kiddo!"

Teddy scoffed. "You were supposed to remain close to the dreamer who took my flashlight. He trusts you. You could've easily gotten it back from that thief. And if it weren't for your misguided advice, we would've known my fifty years on this plane would make my shell unusable. The Sandman would already be at full power if we didn't need to find the new one."

"Enough!" There was a pause followed by wheezing breaths. The hidden man was clearly struggling to breathe. "Do you two have any idea how difficult it has been to survive in this shell? All of that wood dust has destroyed these lungs. This form is weak, and I grow tired of it! We have grown ever closer to having the entire city under my rightful control. The strength of the spirits will empower me soon, but timing has become critical for our success. They will pay for denying me. Now, where is the girl being held?"

Jack listened intently to Father as he answered. "We placed her somewhere safe where she won't interfere until the sleeping effects clear. She was more accepting of the dream sand. Once the J.A.C.K.s and the rest of the city have been put to sleep, she'll be transferred to the final ceremony plot. Perhaps she'll know where the flashlight is, and we'll be done with him."

"Good," the wheezing man responded, coughing. "It will all begin soon. The nightmare sand will aid me once I am at full power, and these spirits will feel our vengeance as they discover what real fear is as they tear each other apart." He laughed in a cold deep wheezing voice like a chainsaw chipping on steel.

"The games begin soon. Grab the boy while we gather more dream sand from the sleepwalkers. It won't be long before my strength is refilled, and I won't need them any longer. We must keep the boy under as long as possible until we can access the new source. Once he wakes, Teddy, you will have your flashlight along with the freedom you were cheated so long ago. Then the boy and his father can be disposed of. I'll have no need for the cloud keepers to chase him any longer."

Jack remained crouched down beside the door, panicked they would come through any moment. He made his way over to the sack that lay on the table as quickly and as low as possible. The young detective needed to escape, and Rocho was still locked away in the cage asleep. Rummaging through his bag, he looked for anything that may help him. Inside were a few packages of food, a sleeping bag, the dream catcher, a bottle of Green Apple Mint Fiz, the now mostly silver coin he received from Lucky, and the freedom parchment from U.S. that shined like foil. Strangely enough, he also found Sonny's striped pen inside as well. The mask still sat beside the sack, waiting to be used.

The handle to the door started to twist. Jack quickly stuffed all of his items back into the sack and clutched the freedom parchment in his left hand. With his right, he reached through the bars of the cage and gingerly touched Rocho with as much of his palm as possible. Instantly it changed the slumbering pup into his reliable flashlight, making it possible to slip it between the bars. A single ball of light had appeared in the magnifying glass handle like a tiny sun. Jack remembered this had happened in the hotel; the flashlight acquired three glowing balls in a day's time from lying in the sun at Dr. Deluca's Villa. He assumed during his time asleep, they must have been left in the sun. The door suddenly sprung open, and

Father stood a few yards away, scowling as he discovered his hostage.

"Where do you think you're heading son?" he asked as he unraveled one of his striped neckties threateningly. His eyes made contact with the parchment, and he ran towards Jack impressively.

Jack backed up to a wall as Father came after him, brandishing his tie like a whip. Instinctively, he made a throwing motion with his flashlight, and the ball of light flew out and landed in front of the holiday spirit. The sunny ball blinded Father and created a distraction with a pop. Jack continued clutching the rolled up parchment as it began glowing. A pulsing aura radiated from the center the closer he came to the wall. Jack could feel the absence of a solid surface as he reached back. As Father remained sightless, the article littered wall felt like vapor behind Jack and his eyes widened as he took a deep breath, stepping backward through it.

Instantly he appeared on the other side. The early morning sun felt warm on his skin as if he hadn't felt natural heat in weeks. He heard the loud slicing of the Father lashing on the other side of the wall in front of him like dozens of claws. It was followed by several voices yelling. He knew they would all be coming after him. Frantically, he checked the signs of the street he'd appeared on, hopeful of losing his captors somewhere safe. "Civil Circle," he read aloud, discovering his location to be on Cloud One.

Digging into his sack, he found the gold coin and shined the flashlight's beam onto it. "Come on, give me somewhere safe to go," he pleaded as he peered through the magnifying glass lens.

As if answering a prayer, the yellow path could be seen through the magnifying glass lens stretching through the streets toward the outermost ring. Just before departing, he heard a side door around the corner burst open followed by a host of several footsteps. Plunging his hand into the sack, he grabbed the mask, and shoved it onto his face, enduring the bonding process as he dashed up the streets.

He followed the yellow path as it twisted up Cloud One, changing direction in an instant and confusing his chasers. Sprinting toward the outer ring of the bottom cloud, he could hear the footsteps growing more distant. Flinching in pain at the mask's final bonding stages, he was led into the crowded street in front of the bank of elevators of Lucky's Casino. People wore jerseys, carried flags, and wore headgear supporting their team of choice. He was able to easily slip between the shuffle of growling people sporting their Grizzly bear ears and those with Shark fins strapped to their backs. He felt his heart beating through his t-shirt as he spun in place, searching for the new hideout. Finally spotting a colorful sign atop an expansive building, he rushed over to the Fiz Factory.

He prepared to knock on the colorfully bubbled door when he recognized a familiar plaque to his right. *J.E.T. Enterprises*, a plate with the initials shared by both his father and himself, gleamed, bolted in gold on the factory's wall. Before his hand was able to brush against it, the door opened slightly as if compelled to do so. A scurry of shouts formed around the corner, splitting the crowd looking for Jack, and his mask began sparking wildly. In a panic, he dove inside and closed the door securely, throwing the malfunctioning mask onto the ground.

A scatter of shouts and shoving could be heard outside the walls. Jack listened for Teddy, Father, and others searching through the crowd and then continue through the streets. Inside the factory, machines crushed berries, grinded herbs, and liquefied rare minerals as they streamed down conveyer belts.

They were mixed, creating different colorful solutions in large mixing bowls on his left side. To his right, a vat of bubbling silvery liquid turned to steam rising high above and gathering together into thick dark cloud-like masses. The clouds carried the shiny mixture over the factory, hovering above an array of funnels. Beyond the machines in front of him, several people in white jumpsuits and goggles sat in booths aiming pressurized cannons, shooting the mixes at the clouds until they burst and rained down fizzing liquids into the funnels below. At the end of the cycle, they poured the rainbow of mixed cloud rains into individually labeled Fiz bottles. They sizzled freshly inside the containers as they were sealed, packaged, and hauled away.

Jack stood astonished, watching the shower of his favorite orange island cream flavor flow from cloud to bottle. At his feet, his mask smoked and bubbled, contorting its features and producing strange odors. He picked it up, wondering if he'd be able to use it again. A short man wearing a uniform like the others walked over to Jack. A gold circular seal was pinned to his chest. Removing a glove, he stretched out a hand.

"Mr. Taylor, earlier than I expected you'd be. I'm Frank, the factory's supervisor."

Shaking his hand cautiously, Jack's eyes glimpsed the familiar seal. It was the same seal embedded onto his coin, and the same one decorating the casino's penthouse. "The Fiz Factory is owned by Lucky?"

"Of course it is," the supervisor yelled over a bursting purple cloud cascading Fiz overhead. "It's a bit loud here on the floor. I'll show you to the office!"

The Fiz Factory supervisor escorted Jack to the left of the machines, where a flight of stairs could be taken to the second story. His office was tidy with a standard desk, chair, and plush sofa in front of a large window overlooking the factory. The

Lucky Corporation and Fiz Factory logos were displayed behind the desk proudly. Frank kindly offered Jack a seat on the sofa, which Jack accepted but remained alert in case the manager had intentions to turn him in.

"The Lucky Corporation is fortunate to have a hand in quite a few lucrative businesses," the manager stated. "Your father designed this building when the owner first became a holiday spirit. Not many felt the need for business ventures in the afterlife; however the boss has always believed in bringing happiness with his ideas. Having a purpose seems to help."

"And getting paid for it of course," added Jack.

Frank shrugged. "Well he is a businessman but Lucky respects us and pays his dues. The good news is, since your father helped him when others doubted his ambition, he has chosen to repay it with safe housing."

Jack checked behind him wondering how secure the factory could be, how long he would be able to hide out and wondering where the Sandman planned the ceremony he overheard. Mostly, he speculated how long Sonny and his father would last before it was too late.

"Well, I should get back to work," Frank exited the office door. "I'll leave you here to do what you must. Feel free to use whatever's necessary and if there's anything you need…"

"Actually," Jack interrupted, "I could use a history book of the city…and a bottle of Blueberry Fiz."

Books will take a few minutes," the manager replied. "But Blueberry Fiz? That we have plenty of."

Over the next hour, Jack scavenged the book for information of the Sandman as he drank the Blueberry Fiz hoping a bright idea would spring into mind from what he read. It was only the second time he'd sampled the particular flavor, but he knew it would help him think clearly and see connections quickly.

After reading about the Sandman's last attempt at control over the city, he discovered how he used three sands to enslave citizens, absorb the strength of the holidays, challenge the four seasons for power, and influence Jack's plane of existence. It described how his mentoring friend was able to defend the fourth sand and his courage to capture the Sandman in the hourglass. Unfortunately, it didn't have any details on how he did it. Photos of the Sandman seemed to mock him as he turned each page. The only useful information he discovered were a few tools people used to defend themselves like dream catchers, focused energy drinks, and how he planned to influence the two worlds.

Outside the office, the loud cannon bursts and ingredients splashed together, but inside it remained incredibly quiet. Occasionally, Jack peered out onto the employees below. He still wasn't sure exactly how long he'd been asleep but knew at least a few days had passed according to the newspaper printer. He was somewhat occupied by recurring thoughts of Sonny. She had been with him for the better part of a month, and now she was missing. He'd gotten used to her being around, and now that she was missing he felt just as alone as when his father died. Jack had grown used to bouncing ideas off of her and knew if she were with him, he'd have a better chance of surviving.

The factory became quiet, which Jack could only tell by the missing clouds no longer hovering at the windows. Without the distracting images, he was able to stay focused on his two tasking problems clearly. The image of Teddy stuck in his mind more vividly than anyone else in that back room. *He was right there*, he thought to himself. It made him angry to think of the dreamer so freely taking his father, using his remote. He still had trouble deciphering where his father and Sonny were being held. Whether it was the beverage or the quiet, he focused on what he learned from the conversation and what he witnessed, as if Sonny was still there to talk to.

Three people were talking in the room. The spirit of Father's Day, Teddy, and a third who had a wheezing voice and string wrapped around his finger. The detective had mentioned the Sandman using people like puppets, and Luminista warned me not to trust Father. The person wheezing said the girl would be transferred to the ceremony plot after the game. He must have meant Sonny. Maybe the games meant something to do with the fans outside in sports jerseys.

He stared at the gold seal of the Lucky Corporation behind the desk and felt the drink affect him as a chain of ideas came together. Details of the night he escaped with Sonny from Lucky's Penthouse became more natural to identify. *There was a sign,* he recalled, *next to the wanted posters.* He racked his mind mercilessly, trying to remember the information on the sign. "It was a tournament between the Summer Sharks and Autumn Grizzlies on…the 26th!" The date seemed off, but with the crowd of fans outside, it only confirmed his suspicion, and he realized he had in fact been asleep for days.

Frank walked into the office with a bag lunch and a couple of miniature red and yellow bottles. "It's nearly noon, I thought you might be hungry. How's it all going?"

Jack gathered one of the books and his things together into his sack and placed it over his shoulder. Bracing himself and hoping it would function correctly, he put his mask over his face. "I think I may have a clue of where they're headed and hopefully a defense."

"Well I thought you might enjoy these samples of our Fiz flavors," Frank offered. "They're remixed versions of our

Strawberry Crush and Citrus Burst flavors we are releasing this spring. I should warn you, it's not safe to mix them. They're pretty potent to you dreamers already. We've been working on mixing them into a rainbow versioned Fiz with the best complimenting flavors, but the results have been…unpleasant. Still a few kinks to work out."

Jack accepted the samples into his sack and thanked the factory manager. Heading outside, he found the streets were still crowded as supporters for both teams funneled into the elevator. A few J.A.C.K.s walked between them and passed out wanted posters with Jack's real face on them. People with an expressionless face and gray eyes surrounded the area standing very still. Jack had his suspicions of them the moment he caught a glance. He could only hope the mask was working correctly and remained that way.

Posters and banners hung on buildings, and lined windows displayed information of the tournament on Cloud Two. Before he made a step forward, he felt his mask spark uncontrollably again. "No, no, not now." He looked at his reflection in a nearby window. The face changed slightly, reforming to another. As the sparking slowed, someone noticed.

"Over there!" he heard one of the sleepwalkers yell. Jack did what he could to get lost among fans scrambling to the elevator. Sleepwalkers made their way toward him as he attempted to hide his face. Luckily, the elevator jetted up as they watched sourly.

When the doors opened, Jack was the last to leave. He poked his head out of the elevator, scanning for anyone who may be waiting for him. After deeming it was safe, he proceeded out into Cloud Two of the city. It was similar to Cloud One concerning the inner layer of circles containing shops. However, it also had random national holidays like

National Soup Day, the current celebration of Spouse Day, and sports stores filled with merchandise of all the teams surrounding them—like the Wolves, Eagles, Moles, Scorpions, and Rabbits to name a few. In the distance toward the center of the cloud, banners of all sixteen teams were draped atop the outside ring of a gargantuan open-sky arena. It was reminiscent of ancient Rome's gladiatorial fields modernized, like a futuristic football stadium. With a stone image of the sun atop one side, the moon on across from it, massive projection screens, and enough neon lights to outshine Las Vegas, the size wasn't the only thing dwarfing other arenas.

A line still stretched half a mile away but moved quickly as the pre-game announcements were being made. Jack could feel the mask continue to glitch. He needed to hide, and time was working against him as was his luck. Cloud keepers were stationed at the visitors' entrance of the arena and one, in particular, walking toward him was the investigating detective. He patrolled the line with one of his cloud keepers speaking barely loud enough for Jack to hear.

"We need to be sure that every cloud keeper is paired with another," Jack overheard the investigator say. "I don't want any of our people falling to the effects of the Sandman or any of his followers. If the rumors are true, an underground army is being built. People are rebelling, turning to his puppets."

There it is again, puppets, Jack thought as he remained casual in the line. *Why does that bring up a red flag? Why does the inspector keep using that term… And why do I talk to myself so much more without Sonny here?*

"Well, the Spirit of Saint Patrick's Day believes Taylor's innocent," responded the cloud keeper. "He was lucky again.

Released on a technicality. That monster of his ate the warrant when we went in."

The inspector stopped a short distance away from Jack, who turned away. "Not entirely unexpected. I would agree with him in that aspect except the dreamer did breakout under custody, and I firmly believe guilty people do not run. He's hiding something or someone."

The preshow could easily be heard beginning in the arena as fireworks, and a performance of flying creatures with fur Jack had never seen before swooped in and out of formation above. The line was quickly getting shorter as cloud keepers scanned fans and searched through bags using their badges for anything peculiar. Jack continued to listen as he edged closer.

"All of the players and referees have been checked," the cloud keeper carried on. "We should be able to focus on the danger outside."

The inspector's sunglasses gleamed in the sun as he turned. "The Sandman is dangerous in different ways. He's a powerful spirit and a politician with strong ambitions. The spirit won't simply force followers once he gains power — that would just cause a rebellion. No, he prefers to make deals. Give the people something they desperately want until they rely on it and fear it'll be lost. If enough people need him, they will be loyal. He won't need an army. There will be nothing left to take."

He stepped closer to Jack, who quickly turned around to face a store shop. As he did, a man about his height bumped into him while rushing toward the gates, stumbling to the ground. Immediately, Jack's mask began sparking again and reforming all at once. The man who ran into him began scrambling away on the ground with a curious and frightened look on his face. Both the detective and cloud keeper alternated glances between the man and Jack before scanning him. It wasn't until Jack noticed his new reflection in the window that he understood why. His face now looked identical to the man who bumped into him.

Without hesitation, Jack ran toward the arena's entrance weaving in and out of the line but made a detour to avoid the cloud keepers at the gate. Separated by panicking fans, he gained some distance as he tried to walk casually around the outside of the arena to where a side entrance stood. Yet when Jack pulled on the doors, he realized they were locked and refused to budge. He quickly removed the freedom parchment from his pocket but found no matter how much he tried to step through, the glimmer had gone and the wall remained solid. Jack couldn't count how many times he'd been chased and cornered in the last month, but the young detective desperately hoped to find a way out of this one. He could hear the clomping of boots getting closer. Shouts came from both directions. Jack kicked the door in frustration, and to his surprise, it swung open.

"You're late. It's about time you showed up," a tall man in a gruff voice said as he looked down. He wore a strange material of light metal armor plates covered in thick brown fur on his shoulders, arms, chest, and legs. A helmet with dark visor and bear ears covered his head and face, but Jack could easily guess who it was.

"Morris?" he asked, wondering more who the Grizzly player thought he was with his new face.

"Tour Guide Morris," he corrected. "My brothers should be ready soon. You're the replacement, right? I know coach said you were short, but I didn't think you'd be so scrawny. Must make you better for running righ'? Well get in, only a few minutes left and we gotta get you into gear 'fore we play the Sharks."

"Wait, Sharks?!" Jack exclaimed as he was pulled into the locker room.

It usually wouldn't have taken long for Jack to be dressed, but his hands trembled while fastening every strap. Once the armor had been secured and his helmet securely placed over his head, a brown jersey displaying the Grizzly Bear team emblem was pulled over the protective chest plate. It presented a white number five on his back with the name Roberts. He assumed it was the name of the player he ran into. A unique black glove was affixed with a balled trigger in the palm of his right hand. He wasn't sure exactly what it was for yet, but both Tour Guide Morris and Butler Morris had one. He watched the final brother, Banker Morris, warm up. This brother was much more robust, wore glasses, and was a head shorter than his brothers. He would occasionally pause to calculate angles then adjust his form. His glove was in his left hand as he practiced lobbing a ball at the wall with a loud sound. His math was impressive as he ricocheted a ball into various buckets much stronger than his siblings.

Jack stood somewhat nervous, unsure how to even play the game, and worried over the Sharks. Banker Morris seemed to sense this when he walked over to Jack. "Nerves?" he asked Jack, who nodded. "Well, I crunched the numbers, and the odds are on our side. No worries, every cloud has a silver lining."

"Why does everyone keep saying that?" Jack asked, attempting an older voice.

"City slogan," Banker Morris answered. "Always something positive waiting to come out of it."

"Will the coach be here today?" Jack asked.

"Actually, we haven't seen him in about a week." The Grizzly player put his head down. "Not sure if he's still hiding from the J.A.C.K.s or caught by the Sandman. We appreciate you coming back on short notice. I know you haven't played in six months, but coach said you healed well. Didn't think she'd be out for so long but that glove explosion was bad."

Father's disappearance made it all the more real for Jack that he'd been betrayed. He looked at his glove, hoping Teddy hadn't tampered with his. Still nervous about the game, he quickly asked for some tips. "If I needed a twenty-second refresher lesson on how to play what should I know?"

Banker Morris laughed. "Just stick to running the gold and silver as fast as you used to, and we'll be fine. T.G.M. won't be far from you, and he's got all the information on the Sharks. Butler and I will be blocking in the back for you. It'll be a great game!"

There was an announcement, and all three brothers began swinging their arms, punching the air, and stretching their legs. "Let's get to it fellas!" Tour Guide Morris aggressively hyped as he led the team out of the tunnel. "Grrrrrizlies!!"

Just before he followed, Jack removed the two sample Fiz drinks from his sack. "Silver linings," he said as he stared at the Red and Yellow Fiz samples. Ignoring the factory manager's warning, he chugged both before catching up with the team.

The sun was blinding as they exited the tunnel and were greeted by booming cheers throughout the arena. Fans waved flags high in the stands, supporting the Grizzlies on one side and the Sharks on the other in the oval stadium. It was easily large enough to be occupied by most of the residents of Cloud City. Protective walls ten feet tall dropped below the stands separating them from a vast field split into three sections.

Smaller sections on either end held broad soccer style goals placed in the rear and separated by a red line. The part in the center was covered in fresh green grass triple the size of the goal zones.

An announcer's box floated above the center where large speakers projected out with a man's voice. "The Grizzlies have now taken to the field with tremendous applause. Two of the four remaining teams will go head-to-head today in week four of the Eclipse Tournament. The Morris brothers are looking beastly strong and their star runner, returning after last year's injury, number five Corey Roberts, is looking healthy."

Four people appeared on the other end, walking out of the gates toward them as the announcer continued. "The Sharks have entered looking very dangerous as they enter the field. This crowd is getting relentless as the brother/sister team of Juel and Saniyah debut with their cousins. Former three-time champion of the Raging Roadrunners, Jayla will join this year's sure to be rookie of the year Noelle. Coach Maya has been making some major improvements to the team's already impressive roster and conditioning this year. This will be an incredible match."

Jack followed from the rear as both teams joined the center field. He could feel the Fiz samples course through his body, making his muscles and skin feel as if it were on fire, but not painfully. Each step felt lighter and easier out on the field. The four members of the Sharks' team stood tall and lean like swimmers. A male and female stood for each position. They each wore similar helmets to the Grizzlies however theirs had a small gray fin near the back. The protective pads on their arms, legs, and chest were flexible leather instead of hard metal plates. Fins lined their arms, and their feet and gloves were slightly webbed.

A referee wearing a black and gold striped shirt and transparent helmet with visor floated from the announcer's box, greeting them in the center with a silver coin. "This side is heads, this side is tails," the referee's voice projected as he brandished a sun and moon side of the coin. "Grizzlies, call it in the air!"

The coin flew up, and Tour Guide Morris called out, "Heads!"

"It's Tails!" the referee's voice echoed through the stadium as Shark fans cheered. "The Savage Sharks will choose central zone. The arena will be set for Summer Sands. The match begins in sixty seconds. To your goals!"

Jack and his teammates jogged to their zone of the field where their team name was displayed. Jack had to slow himself down. Before he realized, he was nearly twice the distance of his team. The Sharks went to their zones, and once the center was cleared, it began to shudder. The land began to rotate like a giant cube on a rotisserie-style axel. The teams watched as the field changed from a frigidly cold, ice-covered landscape, to a green area with flowers and trees like a park, and finally to a desert oasis. The new sand covered landscape absorbed a considerable amount of heat that Jack felt immediately. In the very center was a large pool of water he desperately wanted to dive into.

The brothers huddled together as Butler Morris began talking strategy. "I've combined the information T.G.M. has on the Sharks with my organization skills to compile what their best strategy will be. They use their summer gloves to project heat into the pool and create a fog they can hide in. The water is their strategy, so try to stay clear unless necessary. Stick to the land and use the autumn gloves to shake things up and it'll break up the fog so they'll have nowhere to hide."

The referee suddenly went completely transparent and floated up above the arena. Soaring over to the left side of the pool, he placed a gold ball and to the right a slightly smaller silver one. Once clear of the central zone, he made his final announcements. "I want a clean game. Remember no direct glove contact with each other. Every goal is worth ten points. The first team to get twelve goals before the time expires wins. This match is set for three thirty minute periods."

The fans exploded in support of their team. Floating numbers appeared above the center field counting down the time. "Ten seconds to go!" the referee warned. "Sharks ready?!... Grizzlies ready?!"

The Grizzlies spread out in their zones. Their blockers, Banker Morris and Butler Morris, stood on either end while the runners, Tour Guide Morris and Jack, stood between them ready to sprint. Jack's legs shook, and his eyes were wide beneath the mask and helmet staring at the Sharks, just as the referee placed his hands in the air, and the countdown reached zero. The crowd went insane as the referee's arms sliced through the air. "Begin!"

The first period went by in a blur as Jack tried to understand the game. The visor of his helmet recalled the paths of the gold and silver balls as they were hurled into the air, but it was still hard for him to follow the quick movements. The Sharks were extremely athletic as their runners rocketed up the field scooping up the balls and diving into the pool. Just as Butler Morris advised, they used their summer gloves to hide in the pool's fog.

Tour Guide Morris proved to be very fast, Jack assumed from so much time walking the city. He sprinted down the field with his long strides at alarming speeds but Jack kept up easily.

It was clear the tour guide was talented as he ran up the walls, scooped up a ball, and used the autumn gloves to create sloping pillars of sand. He was astonished as Tour Guide Morris would flip from the sand pillars and launch the ball into the goal zone. Jack's heartbeat dangerously fast as he zoomed down the field, but it was his talent for launching the ball midfield and slamming into his opponents that impressed his team.

By the end of the first period, the Grizzlies were only down by ten points. The blockers had done well protecting the goal, but Jack was losing speed quickly. With only one runner actively scoring, they were unable to keep up with the Sharks' attack on the field. Luckily for Jack, still disguised as the former player and keeping the Sharks unbalanced, they weren't too hard on him, primarily blaming it on his lack of conditioning for so many months. After a short break, the second period began, and he felt his arms losing their strength just before they were on their way again. Unfortunately the last of the Fiz had worn off, leaving him feeling weaker and slower than ever. On the contrary, he felt as if his body weighed twice as much.

"I still can't believe we don't have the coach here," Banker Morris complained. The thought had crossed Jack's mind as well, but of course, he was hoping the coach would show up for another reason.

"We can't worry about that now," Tour Guide Morris replied, tired and sweating. "What we need is a good plan that will split their offense and defense."

"The hibernation plan," Butler Morris suggested.

Banker Morris shrugged his shoulders. "Do you think it's smart to go all in so early? Low success probability."

A broad smile came over Tour Guide Morris's face. "We're already behind. More harm could it do?"

With Jack being new to the team, the brothers advised him to stay at the goal, which he was only too happy to do. The moment the game resumed, all three brothers sat at their zone and remained still while the two runners of the Sharks ran toward them. The Sharks picked up both balls coming toward them and yet Jack had trouble understanding his team's strategy, not until just before the Sharks reached their zone.

The Grizzlies sprang to their feet. Plunging his fist into the ground, Tour Guide Morris shook the sand around both runners causing them to sink while his two brothers rammed into them with massive force. The balls sailed into the air, and the Shark runners slammed into the walls. Now it was three on two, and the Grizzlies rushed down the arena like bulldozers. Once they reached the Sharks' zone, Banker Morris created two pillars from the ground that slanted sideways toward each other. Butler Morris ran up one side with great agility while Tour Guide Morris climbed the other like an animal. As they leaped crossing paths in midair, they threw the balls into the net, forcing the Sharks' blockers to collide into each other.

"Goooall!" the announcer proclaimed. Much of the crowd cheered and applauded. The Shark runners were only now able to stand up but still led with a score of sixty to fifty. Once the balls were reset, the Sharks attempted a similar play, using all four members. Diving into the pool, they created a fog extremely heavy and awkward to see through. Jack remained at the Grizzly zone while his teammates chased into the steamy clouds. When the mist cleared a single Shark came sprinting through with both balls.

Jack was the only one in his way. He could barely keep himself standing due to the beverages after effects. His mask began sparking inside his helmet, and without thinking, he started banging it with his ungloved hand. A shock surged through the helmet when he suddenly remembered the hand buzzer still attached to his finger. An idea quickly came to mind as his opponent grew closer.

Just a little more, Jack thought to himself as the runner gained speed. Just before the Shark player threw, Jack joined the hand buzzer with his gloved hand until it began sparking. Concentrating hard on his targets using all the strength he had left, he jumped as high as he could into the air and pounded the ground with his hands. Two pillars of sand shot from the arena, spiking the balls out of his opponent's hands like cannons. Sailing over the other Grizzlies, the Sharks, and the pool, they landed in the Sharks' zone and without blockers, they slowly rolled into the zone.

"Goooal!!!" the announcer proclaimed. The referee's whistle blew, and the crowd erupted in cheers at the play. Jack fell to the ground in excited exhaustion as his teammates ran over and lifted him into the air.

"Shot was amazing!" Tour Guide Morris congratulated. His brothers cheered on as a timeout was called. The celebration was short lived as cloud keepers appeared on the field. They were led by the detective who escorted the Grizzlies' real teammate Jack had been impersonating.

The referee became visible again, floating from the announcer's box. As everyone, including his teammates' attention, was focused on the J.AC.K.s interruption, Jack slumped away into the locker room to regain movement away from the commotion. He shed off the Grizzly gear as quickly as possible and got into his regular clothes and leather jacket. Jack tossed his sack over his shoulder and placed his flashlight in his pocket. Just before he was able to escape through the backdoor, he heard a voice. It echoed through the arena loudly. One he knew did not belong to the detective but recognized.

Pushing the door open slightly, he poked his head out to see the entire stadium had gone quiet while the investigator, cloud keepers, referee, and even the real teammate lay on the ground mid-field. Four people stood among them, and Jack was finally able to place a person with the mysterious wheezing voice he'd heard earlier. The mousy hair hung over his eyes like a mop plopped onto his head. Dust covered his overalls while the tightly wound string remained around his finger as if he were still controlling puppets.

"My friends ease yourselves, I am not here to place any harm onto you," the toymaker wheezed to the fans. "On the contrary, I am here to offer you gifts."

The fans in the arena began looking around murmuring in confusion, unsure if this were all part of the show or not. Father stood on one side of the toymaker looking at the confused expressions of his former team cruelly, while Presto the Illusionist and Teddy stood with their arms folded, still wearing the chauffeur's uniform from Phoenix's mansion. As they looked out into the crowd, several holiday spirits among others approached the field from the Sharks' locker room, all with lifeless gray eyes. The sleepwalkers took their places around the walls of the arena as the toymaker continued.

"The holiday spirits who've led have not held your best interest," the toymaker continued. "They choose to place themselves on the highest clouds in the city. They believe themselves above you. I believe I am among you. One of the people who believe we are all equally valuable in my shared vision of a better afterlife. They make you feel lowly by asking who are you, to be greater than you are? Who are you to be important? Who are you to do the unimaginable? Who are you to do the unthinkable, the impossible, and the incredible? Who are you to be a spirit of National Soup Day, Grandparent's Day, or Grilled Cheese Day, and feel just as important as Christmas, Thanksgiving, and Easter? Who are you to be stronger, more powerful, and more important than you are? Well, I have a better question… Who are you not to be, when greatness waits? Allow me to lead this and future generations to a better place. As these holiday spirits grow weaker in their slumber, I become stronger. Their sacrifice will empower me, and we will topple the judges and become part of a proper society. One where I can make your most fantastic dreams come true, the way they were meant to."

The sleepwalking holiday spirits approached the center as Jack closed the door slightly, making sure he wouldn't be seen. He was able to understand now why so many rumors of wheezing were heard — he assumed from wood dust in his shop. The odd piece of wood from Plymouth Meeting Jack found a turkey pulling attached to a string, and finally, the bowtie evidence found by J.A.C.K.s hinted toward the puppets, and now the young detective knew why. The creepy toymaker was involved, and now he knew it was the Sandman speaking through him.

His speech was just as the detective described it. He was a sly politician with dormant yet powerful abilities. His offer, unfortunately, seemed to appeal to quite a few fans. It made Jack think of the small bit of time he was able to spend with his parents only hours ago. He shook his head, pushing the thoughts out and remembering none of it was real. Jack observed, wondering if the illusionist was also under his spell or the distraction that set the plan in motion. Impatiently he waited to see what the toymaker would do next as he opened his arms wide to the entire arena.

"What is real and what is not, are only illusions to the mind. Reality can be whatever you choose it to be. My gift to you is a sample of what I am willing to offer. In the end, the choice will be yours to decide."

His sleepwalking followers removed hourglasses from their pockets, cloaks, and bags that contained a sparkling sand Jack recognized. It was the reddish-tan dream sand he was all too familiar with. At once, they all smashed them to the ground, causing it to mix with the sand of the summer desert arena. Some fans in the stadium tried to run, but there were far too many who chose to stay and made it too hard to escape. An explosion jetted up high above the field. It spun quickly and turned into a monstrous hurricane, whipping around the stadium and dousing everyone in dream sand. Panic ensued by the crowd, and Jack was forced to pull the door closed just as it was pummeled by sand for several minutes.

As he held the door tightly, the sound began to settle. Once the winds had calmed and the door stopped shaking, Jack reopened it. A lull of simultaneous breathing eerily crept through the crowded arena. Dust still fluttered down like tan snowflakes onto the field. Near the Grizzlies' zone, Jack could see his former teammates lying on the ground as if they'd collapsed instantly. Besides the sleepwalkers, only Teddy, Father, and Presto remained standing with the toymaker in the center as he wheezed a short snicker from the corner of his grin. A second voice projected out of his mouth speaking along with his that sounded nothing like the mousy-haired toymaker. "Have them all collected and taken to the ceremony... A new season has just begun."

Chapter 9
The Lost Valley

Through the small slit opening of the stadium's locker room door, Jack could see the Spirit of Father's Day, Teddy, and the plump mousy-haired toymaker stalking the grounds. The illusionist leaned against the opposite locker room doors with his arms folded. Their group of spirits turned sleepwalkers followed every order without hesitation. Jack was disappointed to see Holly, Mother, Redd Rocket, Nina of Thanksgiving, Dr. Deluca, the April Fool, and even Mr. Shadow, along with a few dozen others from Clouds Nine, Eight, and Seven.

Once the sand storm had cleared, the toymaker strolled around the arena with a smug expression, clearly delighted by the results. "These new recruits will be more than enough. Use the quicksands to transfer the new pawns. Once I am free of this pathetic shell, I will finally recover the final hourglass from the man I treated like a father."

Jack struggled to remain quiet while watching the sleepwalking holiday spirits sprinkle green sand atop the slumbering fans. He'd seen the tiny glittering grains before during their short period in Holly Woods grasping at Sonny. The sleepwalkers continued to gather handfuls of green sand from pouches and sprinkled it onto the people pleasantly dreaming. Spots of the sand grew thin green arms beneath them, separating the ground abruptly. Tugging onto pant legs, ankles, and shoes, the arms brought each fan halfway beneath the stands as if they were stuck in small portals. The players and cloud keepers on the field were dragged partly beneath the ground similarly. Then, as if cruelly chained together, they were hauled and tugged following Father and the sleepwalkers out of the arena.

Limbs of the people being towed made long paths in the fallen dream sand. As the sleepwalkers marched on, they occasionally kicked up clumps of it that cautioned Jack against going onto the field, possibly falling into the same fate. Gazing out into the stands, he noticed one fan wearing a partial skull mask over the top portion of this face. He recognized it was Luminista's friend the witch doctor he'd met his first day in the city. He was being dragged along with the others without any restraint or struggle. Jack assumed his mask made no difference in protecting him. Looking at the players laying on the field, and the J.A.C.K.s' protective gear, he felt sure the helmet wouldn't aid him either.

As the toymaker and Teddy waited for the last few people to be carried out, Jack made a motion forward but stopped. Wherever they were headed would lead him to Sonny, and possibly his father, but he needed something to protect himself from being put to sleep. Searching the locker room for medical kits, Jack found nothing useful. He checked for something similar to the type of medicine Dr. Deluca would provide or a gas mask, but unfortunately, the supplies were limited.

I need a doctor or scientist or someone who knows something! Jack thought to himself as he rummaged through his sack. *Even Lucky's Factory would be a blessing for...* Mid-thought, he paused and started digging further into the bag. Somehow he was able to fit most of his arm inside as if it had expanded with so many objects. It was much deeper than he recalled, forcing him to shuffle objects around. After removing Sonny's pen, the other Fiz samples, and a handful of candy he'd picked up from Shadow Manor, he found it. The bottle of Green Apple Mint Fiz Lucky had given him surfaced. He remembered something vague the witch doctor said to him about healing properties, and the warm feeling he gained at the casino's penthouse while drinking it.

Snatching a towel from a nearby locker, Jack doused it with the green drink. Keeping the mask on, he wrapped the towel around his face like a bandit tying the back into a secure knot. Breathing slowly, he could taste the strangely delightful mixture of sour apple and mint. His tongue felt the slightest bit numb as he inhaled the cold air into his lungs. Peeking out of the door, the last few fans were still being dragged through the sand out of the arena's other entrance leaving an easy trail to follow. The holiday spirits and Teddy had already left. Jack secured the towel over his face, stepped back onto the field and followed the path, keeping a safe distance.

The clouds above began forming dark patches overhead from the center. Thunder resonated from beneath his feet traveling up and throughout the city like the sound of giants wrestling on the ground. Every step forward, he found the remaining sand seeping into the ground. As he followed the dragging fans, he wondered if the sand was somehow the cause of the weather shifting. Lightning flashed from the cloud below him, causing the trail to illuminate briefly. Above him, he could see a similar effect. The clouds were suddenly pulsing with energy long after the lightning flash, and he knew a strange storm was coming.

Minutes passed as he kept his distance, sneaking behind the last straggling fans. He followed them through the snaking streets of Cloud Two outside the stadium and around team stores. In his determination to stay hidden, he lost the line of fans and was forced to follow the remnants of sand to the cloud's edge where the trail went cold. The streets were bare, and the sky grew darker the longer he stood. A cloudy formation protecting the city towered behind him, leaving few possible directions.

The trail ended in front of an abandoned shack. The aged split wood of the door and store's exterior were unfamiliar, but Jack recognized the team name on a jersey blocking one of the windows almost immediately. *The Mighty Moles.* He remembered Tour Guide Morris's informative rant of a team no one supported anymore. The dark interior was impossible to see into, and the closed sign dangled from a broken string on the handle. It dawned on him how simple it would be for the Sandman to hide from the J.A.C.K.s here so often.

Pushing the door open as quietly as he could, he stepped inside and examined the old equipment of a team long forgotten. The store itself was small, barely bigger than his bedroom at home and clearly too tiny to hold an arena of fans. With the clouds growing darker every moment, less and less sunlight lit the area. He found himself searching rampantly near the register, dressing room, and old trophies for a clue of how they'd all vanished, toying with the possibilities of Presto using his illusions.

Further inside, a slam startled him. A shuttering sound came from the very rear of the store where a layer of dust had been picked up into the air. Rushing to the back, he found himself staring at three solid walls but no new doors. There were no new exits, but a few storage boxes of unsold merchandise surrounded an empty portion of flooring. The strange arrangement was enough for him to question the spot as he and Sonny had escaped similarly in Lucky's Penthouse.

"Where are they going?" he asked himself, using his flashlight to point at the slightly raised floorboards. Once again, it happened. However, he was able to fully witness it this time. The floorboards were lifted a few inches from the ground and then slammed back into place. Using the tips of his fingers, he pried heavily on the wood until it budged enough for him to flip it open. Sliding the merchandise out of the way it revealed an underground stairway. It was dimly lit, and the trail of sand had reappeared. None of the fans were in view, but a short gust of persistent wind explained why the hidden entrance continued to slam shut.

Venturing down below, he could still hear the echoes of the slamming floorboards behind him, and the shallow breathing of the sleeping fans among the twisting slithering sand somewhere beyond. The dimly lit stairwell delved further down, occasionally flattening out. His flashlight was helpful but didn't provide enough light much further ahead. Neither did it give any clues to where he was headed. However, the longer he traveled, the more he was sure he already knew.

After what felt like miles of traveling down the staircase, it became level. A familiar card lay on the ground. It was the ace of spades the illusionist had used in his first act of Phoenix's New Year celebration. He attempted to examine it, but the moment his fingertips grazed, he felt as if he'd fallen straight down. Dropping the card, Jack found himself in an entirely new underground plot. It was vacant and much shorter than the previous tunnel. A small ladder led up where he could see an opening through a new floor. It allowed much more light into the shaft where he could climb out. Stepping up the ladder, he poked his head up and discovered his assumptions were valid. The long underground stairwell and the illusionist's card were used to bypass the winding road and elevator system altogether. It brought him to another shop many had abandoned on Cloud One. And the toymaker's store was just as eerie as he remembered it his first day into Cloud City.

Inside, the store was dreadfully quiet with wooden puppets posted on surrounding walls, and some dangling from the ceiling by their strings like chandeliers. Some were fully clothed with different hats or hairstyles with prominent personalities, while others were still freshly carved and expressionless. Their motionless eyes stared at Jack like hundreds of cameras watching as he stepped through. He tried to shake off their protruding gaze long enough to see how dark it became outside. The storm clouds grew violent, occasionally brightening the sky with lightning and making the puppets' grins more twisted than ever. If it weren't for those brief patches of sunlight through the clouds, Jack would've thought it was night already.

Cautiously heading out onto the familiar road of Cloud One's outer ring, he quickly felt a denser, harder surface as if the cloud had pulled in much more water. Scanning around the other buildings was like watching an old western before a shootout. The entire district was vacant. No sight of the

Sandman's victims could be found. He tried using the magnifying glass lens of his flashlight, but something in the ground blocked any view of the trail. Jack was only able to see a blend of gray cloudiness. Random splatters of wet sand against the buildings and some familiar echoes followed him as he searched for the stadium victims.

A few ripped pages of yellow paper were found scattered among the streets with writing on them. Kneeling down for a closer inspection, Jack realized they were from Sonny's notepad. *She doesn't have her pen to write with… Is she leaving me a trail?* Feeling the dry pieces of paper, he knew they hadn't passed from there very long ago. As he stood, he quickly discovered their newest location by merely looking over the buildings.

A large black swirling funnel projected out in the distance, separating the upper clouds like a tornado made of thick oil. Sprinting past the buildings through the inner circles, Jack became more aware of the conversation he overheard in the Cloud City newsroom. The ceremony the three of them spoke of behind the door, breaking free from the weak body, and the tunnel to the toymaker's store. As the whispers grew louder, he knew exactly where he'd heard them, where he'd find Sonny, and with any luck his father before it was too late.

Nearly a month had gone by since he'd looked over the guard rail. The valley rumbled beneath his sneakers as the twisting funnel swirled from the ominous well several yards away. Being so much closer, he could see the dark mass was made up of so many spirits swirling together, lacking energy. What was left of them spiraled high above the well like a power source feeding into the cloud below it. Echoes projected out around him as if they were all trying to speak at once. Incoherent muttering rang in Jack's ears forcing him to hesitate just before tossing his sack over the rail. Ignoring the warning signs, he vaulted over and landed safely inside the valley.

He approached quietly feeling as if he'd walked onto a military base. Thousands of sleepwalking fans and a team of cloud keepers stood in several rows wavering in their hypnotic state. Dozens of holiday spirits were aligned in front of them holding small hourglasses in their hands. They all held the same glazed-over gray look in their eyes as Teddy and Father stood on their sides and the toymaker before them all.

"Over a century…" the puppeteer wheezed as he motioned to the holiday spirits, "…I was encased in an hourglass by those who I thought were friends for over one hundred years. By you, who place yourselves above the rest of us. Even by those, I considered family. Forced into confinement after a swift process and just as quickly wrongfully judged. And for what reason I ask? Aspiring to be greater than the role chosen for me? Surpassing their expectations and creating new services for something better than they could offer?"

He coughed while walking among them as if disgusted to look in the spirits' direction. "I made promises intending to keep them. Years of planning, preparation, and struggle went to waste for reasons your weak and feeble minds couldn't understand. I had the vision to change the city into personal paradises, a dreamland for everyone, and a justice system for the better! Well, now you will understand firsthand how much better that vision is. You chose to blindly obey your judges' direction, and now with my sands, you'll obey mine."

Keeping close to the ground, the thick layer of fog surrounding the well helped hide Jack from the crowd. The black mass expelling from the well drowned out his rustling footsteps as he drew closer to the toymaker and his sleepwalkers. He felt the echoes calling to him as if craving his living energy. Attempting to keep his distance from the source, he tried to shake off their chants, but this proved to be complicated. Peering out from behind a mound of dirt, Jack was able to see the toymaker and the events unfold. The Sandman's broken hourglass lay pieced together on the ground connected to wires. Following them with his eyes, Jack realized they all lead back to the well a short distance from him. *The power source...* he thought.

The repaired hourglass began illuminating. Waves repelled out like visible sound as the hunched toymaker stood over it. The ground rippled with each pulse, faster until it waved like water. The toymaker stood up straighter, smirking, and Jack could see him grow stronger as a separation started within. His plump mousy body began to shift into something else. Glimmers of a leaner, regal looking man were produced beyond the flesh wearing a brown suit. Light illuminated out surrounding his splitting body, and he shouted up to the clouds above with a merciless grin.

Near Jack, the well swallowed the funneling black mass down like a vacuum and a surge of energy propelled out of the hourglass. It was now that the hourglass refilled with black sand. The shifting form of the Sandman stepped out of the toymaker's side as if the puppeteer were made of glue, reforming from the separation then collapsing on the ground. The waves radiating from the cracked hourglass ceased, leaving a sizzling sound and a few wisps of smoke.

As the toymaker lay painfully curled on the ground, the Sandman stood proudly taking in the first deep breath of his newly created body. His shoulder length brown locks of hair contained a few gray strands of an older gentleman but matched well with his pointed nose and dangerous yet intelligent sleepy eyes. Jack tried to use his flashlight's handle to see closer, but it didn't help. Swinging the sack in front of him, he was able to dig through and locate Sonny's pen. It took a few tries, but he maneuvered it enough to rediscover the camera function and zoom into the scene.

Stretching his neck, the Sandman pulled down the collar of his suit, and Jack could see three hourglass tattoos emerge. Each one held different flowing sand. One of a reddish-tan, one green, and a final blue one. His eyes drifted down to the man on the ground before him.

"Such a pathetic and fragile form," he spat, shoving the shivering remains of the toymaker with his socks. The color of his suit shifted shades as lightning pulsed in the clouds. Although they shimmered in color matching the sands on his neck, Jack soon noticed just how similar the material was in design to his mentor's.

"What would you like done with him?" Father asked.

The Sandman sneered. "He's served his purpose. The illusionist should be returning soon with the final hourglass and our final guests. Have him sent in first."

Father promptly directed two sleepwalkers to assist. They proceeded to lift the toymaker by his arms and drag him over toward the well. His dusty overalls hung from his shoulders, and Jack noticed the defeated look of terror in his eyes. He was forced to watch in quiet horror a short distance away as the toymaker was thrown forward and left inches from the well. He could only muster to shake his head no as it happened.

The toymaker's arms flew open, and his head was forced up. Dark vapor swirled around him, grappling his arms, legs, and neck. His eyes and face became sunken, followed by his stomach, arms, and legs until his entire body was a thin frame. With a final yelp, his body was reduced to black ash, leaving a ball of glowing greenish-white energy absorbed into the well. It quickly turned black as it melted into the others, and the cloud pulsed darkly below it. The Sandman took on a gleeful appearance as if the well were still powering him directly.

It was a hard scene for Jack to watch. He struggled with his fear and anger, stuffing a few contents of his sack into his pockets while he thought of something he could do. Rocho still remained unchanged from his flashlight form no matter what Jack did, and he assumed the pup was still asleep from the sand. Watching Teddy, who'd been responsible for his father's disappearance, infuriated Jack the most. As much as he attempted to, he didn't see his father or Sonny anywhere, and the towel over his face covered in Fiz was drying. He knew if he didn't act now, he'd have no defense left. Just as he reached his hand over the dirt mound to climb over, a black sheet floated into the area. After whipping around the valley, it fluttered near the holiday spirits, and Presto appeared, snatching it through the air.

"There was a problem, sir," he addressed the Sandman. "The sleepwalkers I took with me fell quickly to the spirit's defenses. A group of the city's cloud keepers remained with him. I was able to dispatch most of them, but he's been locked away with the final hourglass in a secure room of the estate."

Teddy snickered quietly to himself, but both Father and the illusionist seemed frightened. The Sandman's eyes narrowed as he sighed, frustrated. "I will not have my victory tarnished… If you are incapable of handling the J.A.C.K.s alone, then the holidays shall be sacrificed another way. Have them assist you and bring me what rightfully belongs to me!"

"I'm afraid it's worse than that," Presto stated apprehensively. "The J.A.C.K.s inside aren't the biggest problem. The security system of the estate has a multi-step process that can't be bypassed, built directly into the mansion's 365 rooms. It randomly changes, and the cloud keepers have secured him inside one that continues to move as I enter a new door. It can't be tracked or disabled. Only one person understands how it functions, but he refuses. And I'm afraid my magic and your sands are useless in this matter."

The dark holiday spirit held an annoyed expression as if he already knew who it was. "Bring them to me NOW!"

With a few waves of his cloak, Presto made two people appear, and Jack was already to his feet when he spotted them. His father and Sonny arrived kneeling on the ground with their hands bound behind their backs.

"Let the girl go, I've never even seen her before now," he heard his father yell selflessly. His face was beaten, and his glasses were broken. Jack had waited so long to really see his father, but not in this manner. Sonny's head was held down, so her blond hair blocked her face. He was afraid to find out if she had been put to sleep or worst.

"Aw, Mr. Taylor," the Sandman remarked. "My associate here tells me you refuse to aid me in my vision of a new peaceful society."

"This isn't peace," Jack Sr. argued. "You promote lies as truth to the blissfully ignorant while you use them for your own greed. You make people sleep forever in a happy fantasy while you use them to affect both planes. You've brought war to a city that has done well without you for a century."

The former holiday chuckled. "War would indicate both sides have a fighting chance, architect." Lifting a single finger, green sand wrapped around Jack's father. It quickly snapped him to his feet and then into the air. "I do indeed use the sands to influence followers, but I assure you the final decision is all their own. Loyalty requires a certain amount of spark, to begin with. I simply provide the gunpowder.

Twisting his hand as if it held an invisible ball, the Sandman caused blue sand to rise from the ground, tracing Jackson's arms, legs, and chest. Within seconds his eyes were as big as tennis balls as he witnessed, what Jack could only assume, was a nightmarish scene. His father yelled for the Sandman to quit, and his hair began turning silvery white.

"You're an architect," the Sandman said in calm anger. "You know how the system designs work. Tell me how to get inside, or I will make these nightmares come to life, and you'll beg me to put you into that well."

Jack couldn't wait any longer. Before he was able to form a plan, he ran over to the group, removing his mask and face wrap. "Let them GO!"

A moment of stunned resolution passed where no one spoke at all. It wasn't until Jack dropped the mask onto the ground that he noticed Father narrow his eyes in recognition, and Teddy's mouth dropped as the old dreamer focused on the flashlight he'd been searching for over the last fifty years.

"And the junior, just in time to save the day," the Sandman acknowledged, dropping Jack's father harshly to the ground. "I see you've finally discovered the details."

"Wasn't too hard to figure out," Jack spoke through gritted teeth. "Not a hard trail to follow and the only dreamer left here dumb enough to work with you is that one." He pointed to Teddy.

"Well done young Taylor, well done," the Sandman replied amused. "We've tried providing you with the courtesy of a beautiful dream like the others after such a horrible year, and yet you wouldn't accept it as reality. If you won't accept my hospitality then perhaps you'll like another side. Holly,

Redd…welcome the boy into my good graces by showing his father the holiday spirit."

"Wait," Jack held up his hand. "I'll go. Send me to the vault. I knew a lot of my dad's building designs, and I got passed the software on the iPlane. Let them go, and I'll do it."

The Sandman released green sand from his other hand that entangled Jack and bound him. "What makes you think I need you?! I have all the leverage I need in your father."

"Because…I have more to lose," Jack said as he looked between Sonny and his father. "Be smarter in this century, send me."

The Sandman twisted his hand angrily, and the green sand squeezed Jack tighter then flipped him onto his head and pulled him closer. He came within inches of Jack as he hung suspended by green sand. "Now, I'm curious, exactly what is it you plan to do if I decline and put you back to sleep?" The Sandman waited with his ear near Jack's mouth, who only struggled upside down.

"What? No witty remark or clever responses?" the holiday's eyes narrowed. "I'll assume that means you are finished. You have however provided a sufficient reason to keep you conscious for now. Presto, send them away."

The last thing Jack witnessed was the cloak being pulled from the illusionist's top hat. It was tossed over Jack easily, and when he emerged from beneath it, he felt his arms and hands freely able to move again. Lifting himself off the ground and removing the sheet, the young detective found himself in a familiar white room. A ruffling of the cloak from behind alerted that he wasn't alone. Jack hastily removed the cover from the moving figure, assuming it was his father when he found someone else beneath it. "Sonny?"

"This is an important moment for you young Mr. Taylor," the Sandman's voice echoed inside the room. He could hear his father fighting for them to be freed somewhere near him. "A historic moment indeed when I finally combine the infinite sand to my hourglass and own this city."

Jack glanced at Sonny, who was now rubbing the dust from her eyes, then at the door behind them. There was no speaker for the voice to come through. He could only assume it was magically projected through the sheet. His sack lay on the ground with it, and he was grateful as he wasn't sure what he may need.

"Get this taken care of and your father and friend, along with you, will be freed," the former holiday spirit continued. "Almost poetic, having you return to the scene of a crime you were framed for. If I were you, I'd hurry. No telling how long your father will hold out."

Jack glared at the sheet as it lay silent, then around the room. It was one of the vaults he'd found following the black sand hourglass. "Are you all right?" Jack asked Sonny.

"Of course," she said as she brushed her hair out of her eyes. "You didn't think you would be rid of me so easily did you? Not exactly sure what has happened, but I'm here."

Jack nodded and lifted up his sack. All of the items he had before were inside. The candy from Shadow Manor, the gold coin, and the flashlight were all found. Scanning the room, it was otherwise bare. With only one door to go through, Jack turned the knob and peeked inside.

Beyond this door, he found a new room. This one was similar but with three more doors, one on each side of the room yet with small red sensors near the handles. Sonny followed Jack inside and closed the door behind them. Before he could stop her, the room shifted then spun, and it wasn't until the movement stopped that the light near the handles turned green.

"Oops, I think the doors only unlock once they're all closed," Sonny said as she inspected the handle behind them. It too had turned green. Reopening the door, she caused all others to immediately relock themselves. What Jack was really disappointed by was the door they'd just entered now led to a completely different room with two new doors.

"We can't go back," he said, closing the old door and inspecting the three new doors of his current surroundings. He attempted using the gold coin with the flashlight, but after blinking paths appeared in every direction, he realized it wouldn't be of any help. "There's no way to track the room when we go through a door."

"Seems similar to a maze, like the candy labyrinth," Sonny stated. "Shouldn't be too difficult, you love puzzles correct?"

"The Labyrinth…" Jack nodded, opening a new door across from him. The room was too dark to see inside, even inches in front of him, but he heard water suddenly stop flowing. He turned on his flashlight and spotted a door made entirely of ice. Sonny followed, entered with him, and shut the door, and the lights instantly came on. They were across from three new doors all frozen, but once the door had closed, they became liquid and possible to walk through.

"Maybe I should continue without you, and perhaps find the correct path quicker?" suggested Sonny.

Jack removed the sack and placed his hand inside. "Too risky, we could both end up lost. Not sure how many doors this next one will lead to, and we may never find each other. But, we can't keep going through random doors either. You did remind me of something important." Jack removed a piece of candy he'd taken at Shadow Manor from his sack.

Sonny smiled. "Perhaps some fairytales can have life-changing lessons?"

"Maybe your random theories and ideas aren't ALL insane," Jack responded.

Over the next hour, they went from room to room, leaving a piece of candy near every doorway they passed through. After closing the doors behind them, new ones became available. Every room held differences, beyond the original. Doors made of fire they couldn't cross until the previous entry was closed, rooms with doors on the ceilings, that Jack had to lift Sonny through, and rooms with a dozen doors of spikes in a long hallway. Some were more puzzling than others, causing them to walk through color-coded portals that would lead them back through a matching portal of the same room. It wasn't until they went through the odd colored one that they were able to continue somewhere new. A more difficult one required them to use a clock on the ceiling where the time would indicate the only usable door in a circle every five minutes.

Jack was lucky to have the flashlight even without Rocho awakening because of two rooms without any light and a rotating floor. For every few doors that were closed, the rooms shifted, and they would be forced to revisit a place they'd already been to. After going through half of his candy, they became hopeful of finding a room they'd been in, as well as a door they didn't need to venture through again. It wasn't much longer before his candy stash was low, but a room with a reinforced door was finally found.

As he surveyed this new room, he realized the door wasn't the only difference there. No candy was found, and a tablet-sized monitor similar to the one on the iPlane was fastened securely to the wall. Half the screen displayed cloud keepers on guard inside, while the other held a passcode prompt. Chattering could be heard briefly through the door, but once Sonny joined Jack, the secured room went silent.

Looking into the monitor, Jack understood the similarities of this room and another he'd found before. Made to look empty or complicated to deter thieves, the shifting rooms were actually very similar to his father's panic room. A simple facade made to shield the real room. Although he was relieved they'd found it, he had mixed feelings about assisting the Sandman. He debated internally on what to do, and Sonny appeared to notice as she took his shoulder.

"Do you really plan on helping him?" she asked.

Jack turned to her. "I don't know what other choices I have."

"But Phoenix…"

"I know…but my dad, and you," he interrupted. "Too many people depend on me, and if none of the spirits can fight him, how am I supposed to?"

"Well, we can't just give up either. We have to think of something better than this," Sonny pleaded.

"I know." Jack checked the tablet on the wall, and the look of the cloud keepers prepared to defend Phoenix. "I'm working on that."

Inspecting the tablet, he thought back to each of the other times he was forced to enter a passcode. He tried to think of his father's panic room and that the system was possibly personalized. The code for the cruise ship made sense to him concerning the type of vessel, so he did his best to focus on the issue in front of him remembering it was built for Phoenix.

Occasionally he glanced at the four J.A.C.K.s waiting on the other side, feeling guilty of what he needed to do. The passcode prompt requested an eight digit code with a forgotten passcode hint:

"Dates following each other like twins, separate a year by moments." Jack read aloud.

"Dates…like the fruit?" Sonny inquired.

"I doubt it," Jack responded as he tried the code 01/01/00/00. An error alerted with a buzz. "I thought it may be the first new year, but that's not it."

"What about the twin portion of the hint?" she suggested. "Perhaps all tens, elevens, or twelves."

Jack tried each of Sonny's suggestions, having none of his own. After receiving an error code for each one, a new alert displayed. It was a two-minute warning. A warning that would seal the door permanently from access unless unlocked from the inside.

"You gotta be kidding me!" Jack yelled. "We have two minutes left."

"Well think, what do we know about the new year?" Sonny asked as the seconds trickled away. "Something we haven't attempted."

Jack tried his best to think of anything new to enter, but nothing came to mind. The countdown made it even harder to concentrate, and the pressure mounted higher. He patted his pockets, hoping for something to help him. The only item he'd appeared with however was the dream catcher still in his back pocket and his flashlight.

"Jack…sixty seconds," Sonny reminded. "I don't mean to rush you, but if you're waiting for dramatic timing, I believe you're good to go. Why are your eyebrows scrunched like that? Do you have a plan?"

"Maybe," Jack said as he placed the dream catcher back into his pocket. Using his flashlight, he shined the light onto the keypad for a short period and then used his magnifying glass handle to examine the keys. "The heat from the flashlight should help show any traces left from the buttons pushed the most. There should be smudges or fingerprints, especially with all the sand in an out of the vaults…like these." Jack found the numbers zero, one, two, and three all with slightly darker keys than the others.

Sonny checked the monitor. "Not that I doubt you at all, but there are only thirty seconds left. Just letting you know, you may want to enter that code now."

Four beams of red light flipped down from the corners tracking their movements, and Jack scratched his head, thinking hard about the hint. "That can't be good. Red lights never seem good in these situations." His fingers fumbled over the keys as he brushed over them. "I have the numbers, but I don't know the right combination."

He repeated the hint in his head, remembering Phoenix sitting in his throne the night at the hotel, then at his celebration in his home, and the code used on the iPlane. With fifteen seconds ticking down the image of two iPlanes came to mind along with an idea as if whispered into his ear, but he knew it all along. "December 31." He said with each firm punch typing in one, two, three, one, followed by zero, one, zero, and one. "January 1."

The red lights from the ceiling tucked themselves away. A green acceptance bar illuminated on the tablet monitor and a new door became outlined waiting to be opened. Jack could see the cloud keepers preparing for the coming ambush through the monitor and knew he didn't want to be around for what happened next.

"I did what you wanted!" he called out to the Sandman. "Take us back before I relock it!"

There was a moment of silence followed by the door behind them opening, yet it was Presto and the sleepwalkers who glided in. "In chess, you always send the pawns in first," the Sandman's voice echoed. Presto once again threw his cape over Jack and Sonny's heads, but this time he wasn't as surprised to arrive in the new environment.

They had been returned to the valley where his father still lay crumpled on the ground. It was as if they never left, however many of the holiday spirits were no longer present, and neither was Presto.

"You've done well." The Sandman greeted them personally, with Jack's father before him like a ransom. "It won't be long now before they return with the item that's rightfully mine. You should count yourselves lucky to witness such greatness."

During their transfer back, the dream catcher had fallen from his pocket. Teddy stood scowling at Jack, and his father still seemed shaken but awake. The flashlight fell from Jack's hand as he helped Sonny up. It rolled onto the gravel, shining its light through the dream catcher. The shadow of its netting covered a portion of the ground as the Sandman strutted over to Jack confidently. He seemed to notice it as he stepped closer, looking between them both.

"Would that be the item that shielded you from fully accepting my dream sand?" The spirit gestured to the blue dream catcher. He opened his hands, causing the green sand to lift himself away from the ground. "More myths I intend to rid the world of. It won't help you when I have all of my abilities. You cannot save yourself from the progress that will happen. What made you think you could stand up to me when so many have fallen? Tell me, do you think yourself special or worthy boy?"

Jack stared at the small portion of land the Sandman had lifted himself inches in front of above the dream catcher's weaved shadow. "No, I think of myself as detailed oriented." He scrambled over to his flashlight, and snatching the dream catcher, covered the lens with it quickly. The shadow halted the Sandman in midair. The green sand fell to the ground, and the Sandman remained frozen caught in the shadow's netting.

"What is this?!" he raged. Jack could see him struggling, caught in the combination of his flashlight's beam and the dream catcher. "You can't hold me here for long! Sand is everywhere! I am everywhere!"

"I know," Jack replied. Presto reappeared with the small hourglass of white sand and moved toward Jack, but he was quick to respond. Before Teddy, Presto, or any of the sleepwalkers could stop him, Jack had switched his target to the broken hourglass on the ground. The motioning sand inside paused, and the swirling ceased.

While the Sandman floated back into the valley, in a quick motion, Jack flung the hourglass into the empty well. "No, STOP!!" The Sandman caused green sand to appear from the ground, throwing Sonny back, but it was unable to touch the effects of the dream catcher's weaving. He then switched his focus on Jack producing several beasts from his blue sand as headless horsemen, vampire bats, and flying clown-faced gargoyles chased and tried to stop Jack, just as the well swallowed the cracked hourglass.

Seconds later the creatures made of blue sand fell to the valley mid-run. Jack could see the dazed expression leave the faces of several spirits. They blinked as if waking from a long night's sleep, shaking off the remnants of the reddish-tan sand clinging to their clothing and their gray eyes becoming natural again. Finally, the Sandman himself began to show cracks on his face and hands. Pieces of his newly formed shell began to flake away like burnt pieces of paper as he balled his hands into fists. He stared into Jack's eyes, reaching out at him in anger until the last few frail parts of his shell finally collapsed onto the ground in a clump of ashes and withered away.

The holiday spirits stirred in confusion while fans from the stadium began to murmur about their whereabouts. The J.A.C.K.s made a commotion, and Jack realized there were still issues to be resolved. "Freeze!" the detective yelled. He again appeared woozy from the dream sand but sturdy enough to point out Teddy and the illusionist. "You two are coming with us for questioning. Someone get over to Phoenix's Estate immediately."

Presto waved his cloak in an attempt to escape while Teddy pointed his remote control at the cloud keepers. Before either of them could make their final movements, the cloud keepers had thrown powder from their pouches at them both, and they were surrounded in a transparent bubble. As much as Presto struggled with his magic, it made no difference inside. Teddy banged on the plastic-like enclosure but gave up shortly, glaring at Jack mutinously.

Surprisingly, the Spirit of Father's Day hadn't made a move yet. He appeared just as confused as the other spirits scanning the valley he found himself in, and Jack wondered, or possibly just hoped, that he too was under the Sandman's effects. Getting to his feet, Jack was glad to see Sonny standing unharmed. His father was finally freed from the illusionist's restraints and able to sit up.

Jack spoke in barely a whisper over the crowd of people. "Dad...?" He wondered if it was really him or some residual effect left by the illusionist. His father had been badly bruised, but his hair color had returned, and he was smiling as Jack slumped forward. For a moment, he stood staring at him before believing it was real, and finally, he fell into his father's arms.

"It's all right son." Jack's father kneeled, soothing his son, brushing back his curly black hair. "I've got you. It's all just a bad dream now."

It took several hours, but the city began to resume its standard daily actions again. The dark clouds receded back to their fluffy white allure. The dreary skies returned to its beautiful natural blue, and the city itself felt alive again, instead of the slow murmuring slumber it had been trapped in. Lucky returned to his penthouse, managing his businesses while the other holiday spirits reclaimed their respective duties, cleaning up their homes. The infinite sand was returned to Phoenix who, still in his child phase of life, willingly gave it up rather than see any more cloud keepers harmed. Father, however, was still being held on suspicion, but it was widely believed his actions were being forced like the others. Rumors spread quickly that Teddy and Presto would be detained until judgment. Everything seemed to be working out well, almost too perfectly, Jack thought at times.

The citizens seemed eager to help fix up and move on from the Sandman's fallout. Once Sonny had been cleared medically by the witch doctor, she assisted in the cleanup and was finally able to meet with Nina and discuss journalistic principals. Jack was happy to spend the remainder of the day with his father. A celebration was being planned on Cloud Two at sunset by the investigative detective once the arena was clear to thank Jack and Sonny for their newest heroic actions in defeating the Sandman. Although he was grateful to have his father back, it all seemed too familiar, and the Sandman's defeat still felt unsettling.

He sat on a bench in the locker room of the arena, waiting to be announced when the door creaked open.

"Hey, son." Jack's father entered the locker room, dressed sharply in a new suit and glasses. "I just spoke to Sonny on the other side of the field. Bright young girl. A very *different* way of thinking."

"Yeah," Jack replied. "Strange to say the least."

"Well people thought my ideas for a flying ship were strange along with a few of my building concepts," his father responded as he looked at him cautiously. "They seem to work well here. Is something wrong?"

Jack stared at the door then back to his father. "I'm not sure if any of it really matters. Even after stopping Teddy, you can't come back with me, can you? I don't want to leave you, especially now."

A hard knock on the door interrupted them, followed by the door being pushed open again. "Two minutes 'fore it starts," Tour Guide Morris warned before closing the door behind him.

Jack Sr. walked his son over to the exit hall. "The hardest thing I have ever done in my life was leaving you and your mother. The hardest thing since my death is watching over you, unable to let you know how proud I am."

"Proud?"

"Of course," His father reassured, grasping him by the shoulders. "You and your mother depend on each other now more than ever. You have to remember you're not the only one dealing with a loss, son. She still believes I've left you both. It's your job to let her know that I'm still here looking over you two, and I always will."

They marched onto the field to surrounding support of applause. Streamers rained down, along with confetti, and balloons rose in the sky. Jack felt as if he'd returned home from a war as he spotted the Spirit of Independence Day sitting with Holly, clapping. More people had shown up than during the tournament, now that several holiday spirits were freed. Sonny walked in from the opposite side. Her minor cuts were bandaged, and she smiled brightly as she stepped toward the center. Tour Guide Morris stood waiting in the vast green field on a small stage, to help them up as the detective prepared to introduce them and the crowd calmed.

"After sacrificing so much to solve an old mystery at the renowned Holiday Hotel, these holiday heroes have proven their worth once again," the investigator called out. "Not only did young Jack and Sonny save his father, but they saved us all from the nightmare spirit himself, unfooled by the sleepwalkers and unmoved by dream sand and its alluring effects. As a proud servant of Cloud City, I'd like to thank you both on behalf of us all."

The tour guide shook their hands firmly followed by the detective as Jack and Sonny took the stage. The applause was deafening, and after exchanging a surprised look with Sonny, Jack smiled, and they waved in appreciation. His happiest moment, however, was the look his father gave him while patting him on the back beside him.

Jack's broad grin and happy demeanor were short-lived, however. As he looked back at the supportive crowd, he noticed a small flicker in the audience like a movie skipping. New images appeared and vanished just as quickly. "Did you...see that?" he asked Sonny.

She continued waving and smiling and grabbed Jack's hand to do the same. He waved awkwardly and looked back at his father, who mouthed a short sentence to him and nodded. *Everything you wanted, right son?* Jack backed off the stage with his hand on his head.

"No, no...this doesn't make sense. Unless..." Jack held his head. As much he tried not to believe it, the whispers began to flood like waves all over again. *Jack, wake up!* More and more flashes of hooded figures appeared in the audience and finally, looking objectionably at his father, he was forced to admit it. "I'm still asleep."

Chapter 10
The Puppet Master

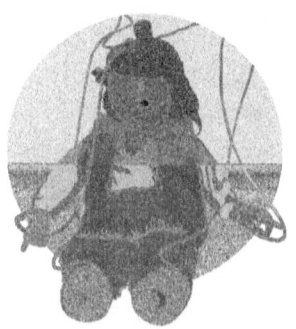

Jack stood awkwardly on the podium as the crowd before him continued to cheer. Although his feet were planted firmly, he felt his knees weaken under the new revelation. The man beside him grinned broadly, falsifying himself as Jack's father. The young girl posing as Sonny appeared oblivious to anything abnormal. What should have been a deafening sound of applause surrounding him in the arena was instead drowned out by his own thoughts as he watched the mistakes of this nearly too perfect illusion flash in and out.

"Wake up, wake up!" Jack repeated to himself. He stepped back from the podium, but the crowd continued to applaud. It was hard for the young detective to accept that he'd never really woken up. He understood now that the escape of the previous dream with his parents both at home, and the disastrous plane crash he believed never happened was untrue. More troublesome than that, it was an elaborate trap to lead him into this more believable dream that he'd trusted. Only now he had no idea how to wake up, or if he even could. Worst of all, it meant somewhere the Sandman was still roaming around.

"Jack, where you headed son?" the man impersonating his father asked. "This is what you wanted, isn't it? You're a hero. I'm here for you."

The dream version of Sonny held out her hand for Jack to take. Without thinking, he started running. Sprinting toward the doors of the locker room, although he was sure it wouldn't help. He knew he was still trapped within his own mind manipulated by dream sand, but being away from his father and Sonny made it easier to see how false the scenery really was.

Running across the green field, he attempted to think of what he went through recently and which parts, if any, actually happened. *It was before the eclipse tournament, before the Fiz factory, and before the printing machine.* Getting close to the locker room doors, he was unsure if anyone was chasing him, but he continued running and remembering. *It was before the dream of home, before the family trip and before waking up in my bed. What happened before that?*

"...have the numbers." Jack heard a voice say. It was distinct and loud as if someone were standing right next to him. More evident than any sound he'd heard at all lately. A voice he recognized but only barely. He was positive; it was real. Going through the doors of the locker room, he found himself alone. No one had followed him. Sitting on a bench, he found his sack still filled with the items he'd gathered. Going through them helped him think back.

He found the remaining candy and tossed them aside. However, Lucky's coin, Mother's mask, and the dream catcher from Plymouth Meeting triggered memories immediately, and he heard the voice again. "…record these numbers. One, two, three, one. Zero, one, zero, one."

Jack instantly recognized the numbers as they loudly rang in his ears. *The code from Phoenix's vault…* He remembered. The more items he pulled out of the sack, the more he remembered the moments just before he was initially put to sleep. As he removed the dull freedom parchment, he recalled their visit to Bicentennial Village, Holly Woods, Shadow Manor, and finally to Deluca Gardens where they'd been ambushed by a group of sleepwalking spirits.

It all seemed to run together as he remembered the moments watching Mr. Shadow argue with Doctor Deluca, and the voice came through again. This time he recognized it instantly as Teddy's. "Let him wake. We're only waiting on the girl now anyways."

Teddy's voice washed over Jack, and he became angry hearing it. He could feel the parchment grow warmer as he gripped it in his hands, but ignored it as he focused on the voice. The paper became lustrous and shiny again as he held it, providing a soft glow. Jack held onto the sound, pleading to wake up. With his eyes closed tightly, he repeatedly told himself to wake up and the parchment pulsed slowly. "Come on…wake up… Wake UP!"

"Who's there?" a second voice awoke Jack to open his eyes, startled. He was surprised to find himself out of the locker room, but he couldn't decipher where this new area was. Jack sat on the floor against a wall yawning. His eyes stung horribly as he tried to open them only making out a few blurred images. A monitor above his head beeped, with numbers illuminated.

Using the wall as a brace, he tried to stand, but his legs had no strength, and he fell immediately. Above him, he felt a wire dangling attached to a sensor stuck to his forehead and yanked it out forcibly.

"Who's there?" the voice asked again with a distinct accent.

"Jack...Taylor," he said, still lost, rubbing his eyes in a panic, and reaching out in front of him. The wire dangled behind him, and the monitor went blank. "What's wrong with my eyes? Why do they hurt so badly? Why can't I see straight?"

"I doubt you've used them in weeks," the man stated. "I'm surprised you're awake at all...or even alive."

"Weeks?" Jack repeated, confused. He coughed as if his throat were severely dry. Being asleep, the dreamer had no way of telling how much time had passed, but he found it hard to believe it would be nearly so long. Using the sound, he discovered the direction the man spoke from, although he still couldn't make out a distinct picture. A blurry outline to his right suggested a figure covered by a hood was hanging by his wrists, confined by thick chains. As Jack's vision adjusted, he noticed the ripped and stained white lab coat, just outside the metal bars he was locked inside.

"...Dr. Deluca?" he asked, forcing a dry swallow, coughing again to clear his throat. "What happened to you?"

The Valentine's Day spirit sputtered for a moment. "Sleepwalkers. And you at my home."

"Me?" Jack strained to look at the spirit.

"Yes...and your friend, before we were overtaken," the Doctor added. "I should never have stepped outside the hospital, but a friend needed my help. There were just too many to fight off. Too many friends to see hurt. I don't know what's happened to him since then, but they seemed intent on taking him with less harm."

The way the spirit spoke made Jack wonder how long the doctor had been shackled to the wall. He could hear the unusually raspy tone of the doctor's voice and wasn't sure if it was because of his weakened state, or their environment. The young detective crawled over to the cold metal bars of the cage he was locked inside of and peeked out. It was dark, but he could make out work benches, carving tools, several boxes of parts, a tiny cage across from him, and a calendar on the wall although it was too dark to see the date. A few objects hung from the ceiling. Tools were covered in a thick layer of dust, but he couldn't tell exactly what kind. Jack was sure he was in a workshop, and at first glance, he assumed it was some sort of sand, but none of it retained the reddish color he'd seen before.

Searching his pockets, he discovered his flashlight, Lucky's coin, and other items had been taken. A crash of thunder struck loudly followed by lightning and the tiny splatter of raindrops. He could see the dark skies light up through a distant pair of windows to his left. It caused a gleam against the faces of hanging dolls. Jack instantly knew from their strange smiles and the lifeless eyes of several puppets that he was in the toymaker's store. His eyes lingered over to a small mass beside him on the ground. Although his vision wasn't perfect, he'd seen this same image before.

"Sonny..." he whispered, shaking her. "Sonny, wake up." Her chest rose and fell with the rhythm of her breathing. He kneeled down beside her, making sure she wasn't hurt. The blond hair lay carelessly on the floor as her head rested on the paper, cut fingers of two delicate hands. Just as before, he shook her shoulder, but she didn't wake. Looking around the room, he spotted a white drama mask beside his sack as well as the flesh-colored masks, then returned to quietly speak to the doctor.

"They took your mask too," Jack guessed. "Why did they bother covering your head with a hood?"

There was a pause as if the spirit were trying to remember ever wearing a mask. "Before my death, I was a soldier of the Roman Empire. The king at the time banned marriages, believing it made soldiers weak to have a family, and that the empire should be all that we fought for. A brave priest performed marriages in secret and was imprisoned for it then sentenced to death."

Jack listened, remembering the story of Saint Valentine but remained confused. "Okay...but what does the priest have to do with you?"

"The last marriage he performed before his death was mine," the doctor wheezed, muffled by the sack. "The night before his execution, he sat in jail, waiting for daylight to peek. It was the same night he performed a final miracle as well. The jailer who kept him had a daughter named Julia, who was blind. The priest was able to heal her and give her the gift of sight. Later that night, he performed the marriage ceremony, and we were married."

"So you wouldn't marry her while she was blind and you have to wear the mask as punishment?" Jack assumed.

"On the contrary, I loved her very much whether she could see or not," the spirit admitted. "Even without sight, she could still see me completely. She will always be lovely to me, no matter her challenges. Her father refused permission unless I could find a way to provide the miracle and give her something she wanted. That was to see me as everyone else did. For years I studied basic medicine as a soldier, mostly plants and minerals, but of course, nothing worked. I refused to give up even after marriage had been banned. We were meant to be together, and she loved me as much as I loved her. When I discovered the priest's sentencing, I begged him to heal her, and in exchange, I agreed to prove my love for her the rest of my life. A debt I continued to give even after my life as the second spirit of Valentine's Day."

Jack inclined his head. "And the mask?"

"The mask is used because of the strong motivational aura I provide from my presence that is nearly uncontrollable around dreamers," the spirit replied. "The will of both love and jealousy for a soldier can be dangerous and strong. Gives a soldier something to fight for whether it's love for their country or their family. "

Jack stared at the mask mulling over this new information from the spirit. Valentine's Day had always seemed too mushy to him,, but he never put much thought into how much people would struggle just to be together. He started to wonder what his father was willing to do to win his mother, and what he'd be willing to do to rescue his father. "So you two were married and lived happily ever after?"

"Happily married, yes we were," the doctor explained. "I was killed in battle a few months later. Now the Sandman and these chains may be the issue that keeps me from her in the future."

As he processed it all, Jack had more and more questions. "When was the last time the toymaker was here?"

The head of the sack turned in Jack's direction. "The toymaker?"

"Yeah," Jack responded curiously. "The wheezing voice. The string and wood I found… The Sandman is hiding in the toymaker, isn't he?"

Even with his head covered, Jack could see the doctor shaking his head, confused. "The Sandman must find a dreamer to host in. Until those three sands are refilled, he can't survive without one. The toymaker is merely being used for his shop because of its seclusion. The dust here would easily affect anyone, honestly. Surely the reason you've been coughing too."

Jack was quiet for a moment remembering his dream was only that, a dream. However, some of the facts seemed to still make sense to him in theory. "So that would mean Teddy… " Jack began. Before he could finish his thought, he heard a low growl from the small cage across from him just beyond a curtain. It was too hard to see inside, but a pair of eyes began glowing. Jack backed up to the rear of his cell, but the eyes continued staring at him, growing brighter in the dark workshop. He kneeled down to protect Sonny. It wasn't until he heard the high pitched yelp that he recognized who the eyes belonged to. "Rocho?"

"Who woke that dumb dog up?!" A boy rushed into the back room, holding a small remote firmly. He pointed it in different areas controlling a few lights to switch on. It took a moment for Jack to adjust to them, but once his sight improved, his focus was immediately on Teddy. It was the first time Jack had really seen him face-to-face without a disguise. His clothes had changed quite a bit from the cuffed jeans and T-shirt he wore in the portrait fifty years ago. Now Teddy wore khaki pants, a dark hoodie, and leather bike gloves with the fingers uncovered. He continued wearing the same baseball cap Jack recognized although this time he hadn't bothered tilting it down to cover his face. As he approached Jack's furious gaze, he grinned with the same smugness he always held. "So everyone's new favorite dreamer finally woke up?"

"Am I?" Jack mocked angrily. "Seems like you keep putting me asleep because you're scared to face me."

Teddy smirked as if waiting for a gift beneath the Christmas tree. "Don't try to goad me. I might look fourteen, but I've been around here longer than your dad. I'm sure you'll get plenty of rest now that we're almost done with you." He pointed at the monitor above Jack's head.

Jack glanced up, but the monitor remained without a display. "Where are you keeping my dad, and what did you do to Sonny?!"

"Not the brightest detective, are you?" Teddy's smile broadened, and he glanced behind Jack. "She's asleep just like you were. Suppose something helped you wake up sooner."

Sonny remained curled on the ground, sleeping innocently. The effects still hadn't worn off of her, but she appeared unharmed. Unlike Jack, who'd been relieved of all his items, she still had her notepad in her pocket.

"What about my dad?!" Jack inquired next.

"Safe, for now anyway," Teddy responded coolly. "Now, how about you tell me what you did to my flashlight after you bagged it?"

Jack backed away slightly from the metal bars trying his best not to glance at Rocho. He wondered how the green fur and gold stripe weren't a dead giveaway but assumed a flashlight being turned into a dog by a little girl would be a stretch even on this world. Until he could find Sonny and his father, he decided to play casually. "What makes you think I would tell you anything?"

Teddy proceeded to step over to Rocho's cage extending an antenna just over three feet long from his remote control. "What was your dream about?"

"What? Why do you care?" Jack asked.

Rotating a knob on his remote, he pressed a button and electricity surged through the metal rod. Brushing the cage with the antenna, Rocho yelped in pain and backed away from the bars as sparks flew from them. "What did you dream about?" Teddy demanded, slamming the cage with the remote's antenna again.

"Leave him ALONE!!" Jack yelled back.

"Tell me what you dreamed of." Teddy continued to wave his remote over the cage, and Rocho's whimper became worse as he slumped onto the floor.

"STOP!!" Jack pleaded, attempting to remember the events from his last dream. "I was in a newsroom, and you were behind a door talking to the spirit of Father's Day and the wheezing spirit everyone's been talking about, all right!"

Teddy lowered his remote slightly. "Father?... You must have some serious daddy issues ditz. Keep going…"

"Well I escaped after overhearing your conversation of a ceremony once the tournament was over, and I went to a safe house," Jack continued, worried about the pup's condition. "During the tournament, there was this storm of dream sand, and afterward, I found a tunnel under the Mighty Moles sports shop."

Teddy snorted. "Humph, least you got part of it right."

It was challenging to differentiate the dream from reality, but Jack continued, still unsure why Teddy cared. "I followed it back to this toy shop, and went to the Lost Valley where I found you, Father, some sleepwalkers, Presto and…"

A loud CRACK interrupted Jack followed by a new set of footsteps from the front of the store. They reverberated in the shop like tap shoes. Every step closer felt like the second hand of a clock ticking away until he finally entered the back area. "Here, I arrive to gather the security code, and I hear my name being praised," Presto said slyly as he shuffled a deck of cards in an arch from one hand to the next. The toymaker stepped beside him, standing by the doorway as if guarding it. The same sleepy gray look appeared in his eyes that Jack had seen on several sleepwalkers, and he wheezed slightly with each breath.

"You'll get them when I get my totem." Teddy pointed over to the cage. Jack was locked into. "He was just telling me about his latest dream experience and mentioned you."

Presto's smile widened. "Is that so? Well, the last of the cloud keepers have the room secured occupying the sleepwalkers, so I have a moment to spare. What has his subconscious unconsciously discovered?"

They both looked at Jack, who wasn't sure what they meant. He gripped the cold bar with his left hand still regaining strength in his legs. "What about my subconscious?"

Teddy looked over at the spirit of Valentine's Day who'd remained quiet beneath his hood. "Why don't we have the good doctor explain it to you?" Jack could see the doctor's breathing become slower, the closer Teddy strolled over as if bracing himself for another strike.

Teddy raised his sparking remote within inches of the hood, then at the cage. "You know what I'm willing to do to your friends when I'm forced to Doc. What's your theory on what his subconscious is saying?"

Presto held an evil smirk as if he were preparing for a bedtime story. It was difficult for Jack to watch the doctor, but he listened intently, as he explained. "While you dream under the effects of the dream sand, your mind pieces together small bits of information you may normally ignore. The sand keeps you in such a deep sleep, your mind created a logical reality for you to survive in. For instance, the Spirit of Father's Day was never voluntarily working for the Sandman. He's only recently been under the same dream sand that many of the spirits have endured. I know because I tested him, just before he made contact with another spirit of the union."

"That can't be," Jack argued. "I was warned not to trust Father, and I overheard him talking to Phoenix about choosing sides. And the detective said if I was being framed, it would be someone close to me. I realized Presto was the distraction at the party to set me up, but..."

Both Teddy and the illusionist chuckled. The doctor lowered his head and sighed dejectedly. Presto hopped in the air, clicked his heels together, and landed gracefully. "News flash kid, I wasn't the distraction. You were."

"Me?" Jack went on guard. "No, you were doing magic to the side, and everyone was watching you. You were distracting them!"

"Oh, I was still performing," Presto agreed. "But it was on you. When I hypnotized those dumb cloud keepers, I used a subtle phrase that also triggered you. *Beautiful, shake hands,* remember?"

It took Jack a moment to remember as it felt like months had passed. Then he realized at once how it all occurred and understood the investigating detective was correct about him all along. "B.S.H. — the black sand's hourglass initials. They're the same. The investigator was right. I was a part of it," he said mostly to himself.

"A simple suggestion and your subconscious couldn't help but follow it into the vaults, where Teddy *accidentally* left the door unlocked," Presto continued. "A bit of dream dust on Butler Morris so he'd follow orders and we were set. I am just that good, but that's not the best part."

"What else happened in your dream?" Teddy demanded.

Jack reluctantly went on, wondering what else he could have missed. "After I followed you guys to the ceremony, I found all of you torturing my dad, so I made a deal to get into the vault. I had to figure out some numbers to unlock it before you would…let him go."

"And finally we come to my favorite part," Presto twirled his hat. "All thanks to you."

"No." Jack pleaded against the bars. "It wasn't real, you couldn't have…"

Teddy pointed his remote at the monitor above Jack's head and pressed a side switch. The numbers Jack used to unlock Phoenix's vault in his dream displayed on his remote. Jack traced the wire he removed moments earlier, leading to the monitor, realizing just how far Teddy was willing to go.

Switching the monitor off, Teddy grinned, amused with himself. "Only Butler Morris had the alarm codes, and you saw more of it at the party than I ever did as a staff member. And now, you know why we don't need you asleep."

"Why are you such a jerk?!" Jack yelled, turning back to the bars. "No one forced you to cheat in the challenge. It's your own fault you're stuck here, no one else's!"

"Look flake, you weren't there. That challenge was a joke!" Teddy argued, brandishing his remote threateningly at Jack. "I finished what I had to do, but the *all-powerful* judges don't like being beaten at their own game. When I have my flashlight, the Sandman gets his code. He'll put the judges in their place for what they put me through. What they put a lot of dreamers through. What gives them the right? My employer told me what I have to do to get back, so why don't you just give up what belongs to me?"

"Your employer…" Jack spat angrily, biding time. "You mean the Sandman? Surprised you're willing to work for anyone at all. Thought you could do it all by yourself? Why hasn't he shown up yet? Or is he as cowardly to come out as you were?"

Teddy looked furious but subsided as Presto stepped forward. He flashed a dangerous look at Jack as if he was personally offended. Tossing the top hat on the bench, he vanished and appeared a short distance from Jack who stood vigilant behind the metal bars with his arms folded. "I'm not a kid. The boogie man's not real, and you don't scare me."

"You don't know what fear is, boy," Presto corrected. His eyes had gone dark, and his voice became a dangerous low growl. Jack noticed Teddy stepping away from the cage as the lights flickered, but the illusionist's voice lingered as purple wisps radiated around him. "I *am* the Boogie Man."

He vanished from Jack's sight as the lights flickered off, and the toymaker's shop went completely dark. He couldn't see very much at all beyond the cages, except the dangling figures of the puppets mounted from the ceiling creaking. Their twisted grins seem to smile directly at him. The lifeless eyes of every doll hanging from wires, sitting on workbenches, and those still being carved seemed to follow him. Another loud crash of thunder followed a bright flash of lightning, and every doll disappeared at once.

Jack backed away from the cage, almost stumbling over Sonny, who was still lying on the ground. The strings dangled freely as if the puppets had been cut free, and spots of the workbenches that should be covered with wood dust were clean. He turned his head quickly as he heard scurrying to his right. Then to the left, he heard clawing and dragging on the floor. Tiny patterns of footsteps like rats continued in front of him. Whispered, child-like laughter followed from every direction, starting softly but getting louder and faster, mimicking his heartbeat.

A second crash of thunder and lightning lit up the area around his cell, and Jack could see dozens of wooden puppets surrounding it. Several walked toward him as if possessed, some without legs but with a single eye, so their empty socket stared as they dragged themselves closer to him. When the shop went dark again, he lost sight of them, but the whispering continued. A third flash of lightning and they were even closer. The twisted grins of those with mouths enclosed on him on all sides as Jack backed away to the very rear of the cell. The legless puppets stretched their arms out toward the bars as they grew closer and closer from all three sides until the room went dark a final time.

There was a long stretch of darkness this time. Jack could feel his heart pounding through his chest as he searched left and right, but couldn't see anything as if he'd been thrown into the ancient well. The scurrying and scratching sound ceased, and the room became silent so that only his rapid breathing could be heard. Then a final flash illuminated the backroom. Jack nearly leaped out of his skin as every puppet appeared inside his cell, staring up at him with those lifeless eyes, and their smiles larger than ever.

"All right, quit it already," Teddy called out from the darkness. Jack couldn't see him, but he heard the illusionist's cackling laugh as the lights flickered back on. Jack remained against the wall. The puppets had returned to their various places as if they'd never moved, although a few from the ceiling were swinging slightly from their strings.

Presto reappeared and leaned next to the Spirit of Valentine's Day smugly. "What?… I was just starting to warm up." His eyes were still darkened, and a hint of the purple wisps left his jacket as if a power were begging to be released within him. "Didn't even bring out the clowns yet."

Jack's breathing slowed as a new revelation developed. "You're his symbol. You're the Nightmare King," he said, still looking at the ground.

The illusionist bowed with his arms outstretched. "Most powerful symbol still around. Almost a century passes, and you're the first to figure that out. Not bad."

"We don't have time for this," Teddy stated as he pointed to the doctor. "We have to get him and the other two hourglasses ready for the Sandman's return."

Teddy began moving the gray curtain positioned behind Rocho and across from Jack's metal enclosure. The pup was still lying on the ground trembling, but it seemed mostly from fear of what Teddy may do. What Jack witnessed next he hadn't expected at all. Behind the curtain was another room hidden containing several shelves. Without seeing the entirety of the inside, he could easily assume there were nearly a thousand hourglasses. Each hourglass was barely bigger than two stacked soup cans. The figures he could see trapped inside, however, were much harder to miss.

There were over a thousand miniaturized major and minor holiday spirits, from the April Fool to the spirit of National Grilled Cheese Day. They were all detained, trapped inside with just enough dream sand falling to cover their legs. Some, like Redd Rocket, banged on the glass or slammed into it with their shoulders while a few, such as Mother, shouted in protest. Several, however, sat in their individual hourglasses with common defeated expressions. Jack assumed they had been in there longer than the others.

"What are you doing to him?" Jack asked as Teddy and Presto prepared the doctor. "Leave him alone. You practically have the whole city asleep by now. Leave the doctor alone."

"We don't put the holidays to sleep, dork," Teddy mocked. "No holidays would mean no holiday celebrations when I get home... We copy them."

Jack didn't exactly understand, but they began ignoring his mercy pleas. Teddy wheeled out three larger hourglasses, each nearly half full except for the last which was empty. The first had the red tinted dream sand Jack had seen so many times before, along with a spirit. It took him several seconds to see through the falling granulates, but after a long gaze, he recognized the man as the cowering spirit of Groundhog Day. The same spirit he'd seen entering the elevator on Cloud Eight. The second held darker blue sand and the holiday spirit buried to his waist beneath it Jack recognized almost immediately.

Mr. Shadow kept his composure even in his reduced form. The blue sand piled onto his hood, yet whether by force or by magic, his face still remained hidden in shadow. It wasn't until the hourglasses faced Jack's cage properly that the Halloween spirit made any move at all. Jack assumed something new must have shaken him, as he placed a bony hand on the glass unexpectedly. Whether it was him being locked in the cage or the doctor he'd argued with before, Jack couldn't tell.

With a wave of his hands, followed by a snap of his fingers, Presto forced the chains shackling Dr. Deluca to obey his command. Unbinding from the wall, the chains carried the doctor over to the third hourglass, where he instantly appeared inside of it. Teddy shoved a metal disc, just large enough to stand on, out onto the floor. Adjusting a switch beneath it, he slammed his palm on a center button and waited. After only a few seconds, Jack watched as green sand rained down and filled the hourglass from above the doctor. Sand began rising from the disc, twisting and filling into legs, then a torso, arms, and finally a head. A lab coat draped down from his shoulders and quickly formed into a mirror image of the Valentine's Day Spirit but with gray eyes. Presto directed the copy to take the doctor's mask, and a moment later he'd left the store.

Jack was shocked by the scene. Sand continued to fall onto Dr. Deluca within the hourglass, but he didn't move. The hood hung over his face solemnly, as the glittering green grains poured over him. With the doctor apparently so weakened by the Sandman and the sleepwalkers already, Jack turned away, unable to watch the spirit submitting to defeat.

"What's wrong with you?" Jack squinted at Teddy with a new level of disgust. "Even if you find a way to get back to our world, it won't be the same. Decades have passed, and the Sandman will probably put the entire world to sleep, or worse. You're being used."

Presto's eyes danced between both dreamers before he resumed securing their newest hourglass. Teddy had fastened a metal brace together to hold them but stopped after Jack's statement. "Still don't understand how it works, do you? When I go back, it'll be like I never left. I'll be fourteen and home. Whatever the Sandman's planning is going to happen. There is no stopping him, and no reason to either. Unlike you, I prefer the dream if it means going home… Seriously, what would you do to get your life back?"

He wouldn't admit it out loud, but Jack felt he understood where Teddy was coming from as he returned to finishing the metal braces. Jack wasn't sure how far he'd have to go to rescue his father, but he was positive he'd do everything possible. Glancing at the cage Rocho was locked in, Jack wondered what other options were left. Although it wasn't a particular favorite plan of his, he thought a negotiation may be the only way to save the lives he cared about most.

"What if I made a deal between us?" Jack suggested. "Gave you the flashlight, to let us all go. That's all you really want anyway, right?"

For the second time, the illusionist stopped and glanced between Jack and Teddy as if wondering what he may choose. Jack noted the uncertainty as a clear sign of mistrust from the Sandman's symbol. Jack was sure Teddy would decline, and knew, if for some reason, he decided to go along with Jack, it would either be a trick or someone would likely stop them. That distrust the young detective hoped may at least be enough to delay them into fighting each other. At the very least, he believed that Teddy would ensure his safety as long as the flashlight's whereabouts were unknown to him.

"I already made my deals," Teddy responded without turning his head. He completed his work on the brace, powering it with his remote. Presto returned his attention to the three larger hourglasses, floating them to their respective places in the metal braces. Twisting his right hand, each one locked into place and powered on with a small hum.

"The Sandman is still inside of you. He needs you more than you need him," Jack pleaded in a final attempt. Yet something unexpected happened. Both Presto and Teddy began chuckling. It was a relatively manic laugh then Jack ever expected, and vaguely reminded him of comic book villains so much it annoyed him. "What's so funny?!"

"You still think I'm the dreamer the Sandman is using?" Teddy sneered. "I wasn't the first one to touch the hourglass, ditz."

"You're not the dreamer..." Jack said, taken aback. "No, you're lying. You'd have to be, who else..." He stopped midsentence remembering every moment following the black sand hourglass. The moment they'd left the hotel and the idea to access the hourglass on the cruise ship. Following it to Phoenix's Estate where he'd been hypnotized and framed. Jack went through the events in Lucky's Penthouse, that flowed into Mother's Avenue, where the spirit gave them candy and the masks. Then their return to Cloud Nine where they'd traveled to Plymouth Meeting and found the dream catcher and puppeteer pieces among the debris. His memories raced back quicker as he recalled thoughts of other homes they'd inspected including Light Festival, Rebirth Caverns, Ali Pillars, and Imani Park and how they continued to be followed. The strange events in Bicentennial Village when he'd been tackled by Uncle Sam, to Holly Woods where the trap had been left, and then to the locked doors of Shadow Manor. It all struck him suddenly with precise detail until their final moments of capture in the doctor's garden. Even the door alarm buzzing in Phoenix's estate, and the ripped yellow pages now made more sense. The sleepwalkers had always been so close.

As he worked backward connecting the dots, he remembered their first moments on the cruise ship, and finally the first time he'd ever seen the black sand hourglass. "It was her. She touched the hourglass first on the roof of the Holiday Hotel, and it stung her hand. That's why she dropped the pen on the cruise ship. Morris broke the hourglass while sleepwalking with his gloved hands and it went into..."

Jack turned in his cell away from Teddy and Presto to look at the sleeping mass on the floor, yet Sonny was no longer sleeping. She stood face-to-face with Jack. Although the rest of her seemed just as usual, her eyes appeared to be in a deranged state as she unwrapped the piece of candy she'd received from Mother's and placed it into her mouth. Jack could only glare at her disappointedly, wishing he'd paid more attention to it before. "…and Sonny doesn't eat chocolate," he finished.

She raised her hand to Jack's chest, and he instantly slammed against the cage walls. Black sand fell to the heels of her sneakers as she controlled him. Jack was then dragged up to the ceiling until he was hanging in the air like so many of the puppets surrounding them. When she spoke, two voices left her lips as if a much more dangerous person hid beneath the other. "Didn't I warn you, it's always the butler?" A devilish grin spread across her face.

Chapter 11
Silver Linings

$\mathcal{S}$and dripped from the sleeve of Sonny's up-stretched arm as she kept Jack pressed against the ceiling. He could feel the pressure-weighted against him with so much force, he was sure he'd go through the bars any moment.

"Sonny…let me go." Jack struggled. However, her twisted smile remained, and she only seemed to relish in it as she pushed him up further. Rocho began growling insistently in his cage, but no one seemed concerned.

"Took me weeks to ease myself into her mind, but the results have been satisfying," she said to Jack as if he were a new toy. "My temporary shell should've been Theodore but unexpected issues and all. She was stronger than I'd anticipated, much like an older mind, but no matter. I despised hiding away for so long, yet my patience paid off. My thoughts soon became hers, and now I have her under full control."

"We were able to follow the trail you left us, master," Presto bowed respectively.

Sonny whipped her head toward him so quickly, Jack thought her neck would turn and break completely. "Aw, my loyal Nightmare King. No accounting for haste I see. It took you long enough to find us at the Penthouse. All those ripped yellow pages; I had to be so careful *he* wouldn't find them leading you to us. And those incompetent copies of yours were only meant to put *him* to sleep, not me!"

"My apologies, master," he cowered slightly. "It took longer than we expected to gather the proper spirits for the sands. We needed the J.A.C.K.s to continue chasing you."

Teddy cleared his throat. "I did follow the directions from your original notes. The metal braces have been built to proper specification. There should be no issues."

"And the three hourglasses are prepared," Presto added. "The final two spirits were more difficult to capture. The sleepwalking copies didn't expect to find them together, and we certainly didn't expect to find you there as well master, but you were kept out of danger, I assure you."

The Nightmare King motioned to the three hourglasses, and they turned toward the cage. "The Spirit of Groundhog Day worked as well as you depicted for the dream sand. Shadow was a more difficult capture but seemed to be distracted. However, the nightmare sand poured quickly with him as expected. The doctor was much easier once we captured his friend and covered his head, but it took time to weaken him enough for the quicksand."

Sonny glanced over at the hourglasses and then overlooked Presto. "So this is what you've become in my absence. My symbol is now a lowly form of entertainment for the holiday spirits who doubted my brilliance and shunned me into capture for nearly a century. And an entertainer of all things. You were meant to replace me as a holiday, but I wonder if you're at all worthy now."

The symbol approached the cage gingerly. "Master, I only did what I needed to survive. This persona was an easy transition to fool the naïve spirits, but I only did it to see to your release. "

"Don't belittle my intelligence," she argued. The twin voices became eerier to Jack as she became angry. "I know how you crave attention. I designed you into royalty for a reason. The king of all symbols, a strong symbol to support my efforts should not be treated as a mere fool."

"I promise, I will do better," he assured.

She slowly returned her gaze toward Jack with an annoyed expression. "Good help and all that, you know? I do hope you understand. None of this is personal Jackson, merely a means to an end. I did offer you an alternate reality, but you decided to reject my generosity. You will learn to accept it one way or another, or you will simply go insane, incapable of telling reality from the dream."

Jack remained against the ceiling with limited movement. "Sonny…please fight it."

She shook her blond head. "Begging does not become you dreamer. Where are we with the fourth hourglass?" she directed to Teddy.

"The last few J.A.C.K.s have apparently hidden Phoenix in a secure location of his estate and used an inaccessible code to lock them in," Teddy responded.

Sonny dropped her arm and subsequently, Jack. He fell to the cage's floor, hard like an anvil, but she ignored his groaning as her attention was diverted. "My mentor. Always with the dramatics."

"I have withdrawn the code for you," Teddy carried on. "There's just the matter of my flashlight I need from him, and it's all yours."

Her eyes wandered over to Jack lying on the ground clutching his jaw and lingered for a moment as if reading his mind. Then after scanning the shop, bypassing the room of holiday spirits trapped in hourglasses, she stopped and smiled. "I've grown weary and weak in this shell. I believe it's finally time I greet my fellow holidays as one of them before my ascension. Open the cell. I know where your totem is."

There was a loud crash from the front entrance that shook the shop. Glass and wood shattered inside as if a rhino had rammed through it. The sleepwalking toymaker was blasted to the side and left collapsed on the ground along with several of his puppets. The storm raged on with booming thunder and rain swooping inside. When the wood debris cleared, Jack was able to lift his head enough to see Claus covered by Santa's red coat, he assumed to shield from the rain as he stepped through the shop's newly enlarged entrance. With the woodsman's leaner body, the coat dwarfed him a bit, but Jack was sure there was something different about him as he dropped the red sack to his side.

"Release Holly and the other spirits," he said flatly. There was no ultimatum, nor argue in his tone. He stood tall with the wind rushing at his back as he made his passionate demand with implied consequences.

"Perfect time to regain my honor," Presto whispered as he walked towards the symbol of Christmas with an expression Jack hadn't seen before. It was as if he were preparing for the last finale he'd ever perform.

Every step forward seemed to melt a piece of his clothing. Violet wisps rose from his legs, hands, and shoulders as his tuxedo pants bulged out with more muscle. Another few steps and his chest and arms expanded massively like a bodybuilder ready to burst through his suit. More steps forward and his shoes had become indigo metal plated boots that clank against the wooden floors. His plated leggings followed, along with the hardening of his chest plate, his plated spiked shoulders, arm guards, and gloves. The wisps formed a cape that unraveled from his shoulders down to his heels. Finally, when he was within a few feet of the Christmas symbol, a horrific demonized helmet with tiny bone-like spikes around the sides covered his head. The top formed into a crown-like piece with black diamonds, and his eyes held a vicious, blood red glow.

When his armor completed forming, he was respectably bigger and taller than before. Jack watched astonished as the illusionist had become a demonic knight in heavy violet armor. He worried Holly's protector was strongly outmatched this time, and that it was his angry words that set Claus to this unfair battle. He watched the last few wisps form into a large double bladed sword that the Sandman's symbol dragged on the wooden floor, creating a long carving. Looking from his crown down to his terrifying armor and cape, Jack understood why he was named the Nightmare King.

"My sleepwalkers already defeated you once Claus," the Nightmare King stated flatly in a much more monstrous voice that matched his appearance. "Strong holiday spirits have been trapped, I've embarrassed your legacy, and now I can only assume you've come to be put to sleep after your failure to protect her? You may have been the first great symbol, but *I* am easily the strongest left in this world."

"Wrong." The Christmas symbol removed his hooded cloak. "*We* are stronger than you could ever be. And you just made our naughty list."

There was a drastic change in his appearance since Jack had last seen him. His face was fuller beneath the white beard tied into a point, and he wore the same red hat usually worn by Santa. His body was just as large as the Nightmare King's with bulking muscular arms and chest but beneath a ripped red sleeveless vest with white trim. White padding covered one of his shoulders clasped down by a large leaf of holly. A metal skeletal reindeer head matching his bracelets made up the buckle of the belt that held up his red loincloth so he had the appearance of a barbarian warrior. Yet, what struck Jack the most was the familiar white shard in the center of his chest that seemed to radiate throughout his body with a bright glow.

The Nightmare King's bold attitude hadn't wavered, but there was a hint of surprise as he stared at the shard. "The North Star? Father Christmas, together again."

Jack's head shot up at the word *father*. He attempted to lift himself up, but he was still dizzy from being slammed so hard. Instead, he rolled over onto his back and listened carefully.

"My brother's sacrifice made us stronger," the Christmas symbol replied, pulling the gold rope to unbundle his red sack.

"It won't be your last sacrifice, Santa Claus." The Nightmare King dashed at the newly combined Christmas symbol and swung his sword up in a single motion. The symbol of Christmas was ready to counter as he pulled a long double-edged ax with a candy cane striped handle from the red sack. The word *Naughty* gleamed on the blade as the barbarian parried the Nightmare King's swings. With his other hand raised, he pummeled the dark symbol in the face with roasted chestnuts.

The Nightmare King was stunned briefly but recovered quickly. Santa, however, was already charging. With an impressive blow, he hit the king sending both symbols piling through the walls of the storefront, and into the back where Jack was caged. Teddy was able to leap out of the way at the last moment, but the evil symbol was thrown back, tumbling through a wood bench. Floating himself into standing position, he stretched out an arm and the room dimmed into darkness once again.

Jack could hear the whispers beginning already. The only light that could be seen was from Santa's shard as he stood ready. The Nightmare King vanished, and the puppets shuttered and moved again. Santa Claus dropped his weapon and summoned his red sack to his hand. There were easily a hundred puppets rushing at once this time, and some joined together into more massive toys. With a hard pull of the sack's remaining gold rope, a thousand enveloped letters propelled out like throwing stars, striking the toys and sticking to the walls with razor sharp corners. Jetting out in every direction they bounced off of bars, hit the room behind the curtain and took out several attacking dolls. After being struck by twenty or so letters, the bigger puppets finally went down as well.

Santa dropped the rope, and the sack appeared empty as the lights flickered. Glowing green eyes could be seen behind him, followed by a second set, then four more, and then they doubled until a dozen surrounded him. Without warning, undead clowns with peeling makeup and juggling knives lunged at him. Two were able to knock him back as he ducked the next blow. Swinging his ax, he slashed through them as they fell into clumps of blue sand. Swiping low, he took out three more with a broad swing at their legs. With each swing, another went down until four undead clowns remained. With both hands, he struck the ax down into a clown's chest, and with a loud grunt, he caused the light shard to brighten the room, blinding the others. As they stood stunned, he yanked out his ax and spun, cutting through the remaining clowns.

The Nightmare King reappeared behind him swinging his sword with precision, but the Christmas symbol was able to dodge the first strike. The second struck part of his shoulder pad, and he was forced to spin around, ducking a third blow that hit the cage. Jack was rattled but still lying on the floor.

As Santa rolled back beside the cage, he seemed to notice the hourglasses containing every holiday spirit, including Holly, behind the exposed curtain. Little time was spent gazing before the Nightmare King crossed his arms into an X over his chest. He began multiplying himself as two, four, seven, and finally, ten copies of the king surrounded Santa, brandishing their swords threateningly.

Santa laughed with a jolly grin, a bit out of breath but still reassuringly. "You should've brought more. It might've been a fair fight!"

The evil symbol's copies attacked all at once. Their swords raised, they came within a few feet of the Christmas symbol, who stood defenseless and brought a single finger next to his nose. With that gesture, he vanished, along with the bright shard lighting the room. For a moment, it was quiet, and the copies stood confused as they stared at the empty spot. Jack looked to his side, unable to tell any of them apart when he noticed the table just beyond the cage that was smashed was the same one that held his mask and sack. The sack on the floor was a few feet away, but a few items had rolled out. As he tried to stretch his arm out, there was a loud painful yell.

One of the copies was being burned from beneath their metal boots and immediately destroyed into nothing, followed by another, then another, and another. Fiery coals spread out in a circle to burn the Nightmare King's copies, destroying them each in a furious pillar until only one remained. The dark symbol took guard. Slamming his sword into the ground, he kneeled, and violet wisps surrounded him as he began to reform again. This time he grew into an even more monstrous size reaching the shop's roof. Large leathery wings sprouted out along with sharp claws, scaly skin, and a dragon-like head, but with those same blood red glowing eyes.

Finishing his new form, the Nightmare King opened his mouth widely, and a furious growl resonated deep within as a purple fire began from his throat ready to expel. The glowing heat of purple fire rose from his throat but, before he could blow it out, the white shard appeared out of the darkness as Santa reappeared and leaped through the air. With a fist clenched back around a red stocking, he plunged his arm into the beast's mouth and released a mix of a hundred toys and candies until it began choking.

Withdrawing his hand, Santa landed on the ground surefooted beside his ax, as the beast coughed up toy trains and wrappers. Clenching his fists tightly in front of his chest, Santa Claus expanded his fingers as if he were holding a bowling ball in each hand, and the shard grew brighter than ever, radiating over his entire body. He began grunting as if he were pushing a heavy object until something formed in front of him and he yelled a name.

"Dasher!" he bellowed. A massive reindeer made of pure light galloped toward the monstrous dragon, struck it hard with his antlers and then vanished. More toys poured from its mouth, and it began changing back into the demon knight.

"Dancer!" Santa yelled next. Another reindeer made of white light sprinted forward, and the beast was struck again. Several more toys and candies poured from its mouth as it toppled back. The wings retracted, and the scales returned to armor.

Santa Claus yelled again. "Prancer! Vixen! Comet!" Each bolted out faster than the last hitting the Nightmare King with precision using their sharp antlers then vanishing. His previous form and armor had returned entirely, but there was a crack forming in the center of his chest plate.

Jack continued to reach through the bars of his cell for the freedom parchment that had rolled from his bag while witnessing the strain this new power was taking from Santa Claus as he yelled a third time. "Cupid! Donder! Blitzen!" he grunted as each one propelled out like a kick from his chest. Each one hit the Nightmare King hard, exposing the crack more and more until a hole was exposed. The dark symbol wobbled beside the cage, crutching on his sword when Father Christmas yelled a final time. The shard of the North Star became a blinding white light filling the entire room until Jack could only see the antlers of the last reindeer hitting the Nightmare King with a powerfully swift blow and the vanishing of a glowing red nose.

The dark symbol was propelled through the shop's wall and into the Birthday Blow Out store beside it. Streamers, cards, a few candles, and balloons drifted in through the hole. Santa Claus appeared tired but quickly picked up his ax. However, he wasn't looking at the spot the king had gone through. Instead, he drew his arm back, and with the last of his strength, he heaved the ax into the hourglass room. Jack had just grabbed the freedom parchment in time to cover his head and brace himself for the shattering glass.

But it never came. The young detective waited several seconds, yet the only thing he heard was the storm raging on outside. He clutched the freedom parchment firmly beneath him then peeked up over his arm. The hourglasses of the backroom remained unbroken with the spirits still inside. The thrown ax had been suspended in the air, inches from its targets. He noticed Santa Claus unmoving as well. It was as if he was struggling to escape, yet no one was near him. Finally, Jack strained to sit up and spotted Sonny lying on the floor a short distance away against the three larger hourglasses in braces. Except for the holiday spirits themselves still trapped inside, the larger hourglasses were empty of the colorful sand that once flowed. As both the ax and Christmas symbol were being dragged beneath the ground, Jack noticed the claw-like green sand glittering around them both.

"Not quite yet. Some things are about proper timing, while others are about style. I like to think I have both." The Sandman hovered inches above the floorboards slightly different than Jack had seen in the book or imagined in his dream. The pointy nose, intelligent sleepy eyes, and brown locks of hair were the same, but his clothes were different. He was in a pin-striped suit matching the dark violet of his symbol, black gloves, and dress shoes. It was covered by a long trench coat with a high collar shimmering with the colors of his three sands that changed depending on where you looked. The three hourglass tattoos on his neck simply confirmed that he had fully absorbed them all. Jack had been so occupied by the fight between the two symbols, he hadn't noticed Teddy already released Sonny from the cell. Now that he had his three sands, it seemed she was no longer needed, and he worried if there was anything of her left living.

With a single gesture, the green quicksand split the ax apart into several pieces like twigs. The Sandman then switched his attention to Santa Claus with neither remorse or satisfaction, as if handling a simple business transaction. The Sandman made a gesture, like prying an elevator open with both hands, and Santa Claus yelled soundlessly, unable to move his body as the quicksand ripped the two symbols apart from each other. Claus appeared weakened in his woodsman clothes to one side, as Santa appeared in his usual red and white clothing on the other in the same state. The quicksand grasped them both, dragging them below the floor until they were both swallowed, just as the shard of the North Star dimmed entirely.

"Sonny..." Jack whispered through the cage bars. "Are you okay?" He wasn't sure if she could hear him, but she made a movement in his direction. Behind the bars, he could heard rubble being pushed aside. A few more balloons drifted in through the hole, and the Nightmare King stumbled in, except he'd been reduced to his armor-less illusionist form. With his beaten appearance, much of the charm he held before had vanished. He raised his hands and brandished cards as if he were still fighting until he spotted the Sandman had fully returned, picking up his top hat.

"The years have weakened you greatly." The Sandman tossed the top hat to his symbol's feet. "I'd replace you right now if you didn't hold the tiniest grit of value to me for the moment. Gather the codes from Theodore, and return with my mentor's hourglass or do not return at all."

Teddy climbed out from beneath a turned over table after hearing his name. He walked over to the symbol timidly

~ 275 ~

adjusting his remote to display the numbers from Jack's dream. With a hesitant pause, he showed the numbers to the Nightmare King, who vanished immediately after a slight bow to the Sandman.

As if reading his mind, the dark holiday spirit turned to Theodore and gestured to Rocho. "I, of course, intend to keep my word. Your totem is in the tiny cage. I'm not exactly sure whose spell it is, but the dog can return to its flashlight form when held by the dreamer, so our arrangement is complete. Take your prize."

Teddy's expression quickly changed from fear to curiosity. He paused momentarily before turning his back but rushed over to the cage with haste to look inside. From the way he tilted his head, Jack could see the dots connecting for Teddy. Jack made the same movements when he found clues. He waited as Teddy noticed how similar the green fur looked, and the gold stripe, although not in words, were in the same placement and colors of the flashlight. Finally, after analyzing the pup, he opened the cage and grabbed him by the scruff of his neck.

"Tell me how to change him back!" Teddy ordered Jack. Rocho trembled in his hand.

"Leave him alone!" Jack yelled back. "I'm not telling you anything!"

"Tell me now!" Teddy demanded furiously. "Or I'll—"

"You'll do what?!" mocked Jack. "You won't hurt him, you need him. The last thing you'll do is hurt your chances of getting home."

Teddy went to respond but stopped himself. It appeared Jack was right as he hesitated again. The Sandman merely listened as he strolled inside the hourglass room, seemingly amused by the spirits who had him captured in the same manner as he waited. Pushing the pup back into the cage, Teddy approached Jack's bars and turned a knob on his remote and extended the antenna. "Fine, then I'll just have to hurt you instead."

Sparks flew in the air as he brushed the antenna against the bars, and the entire cage was electrocuted. Jack slumped to the ground when the shocks ceased, finally able to release the bars as Teddy yelled again. "Tell me how to change him back!" He brushed the bars again, but even lying on the floor of the cage, Jack still felt the painful shocks course through his body.

With every wave, Teddy demanded to know how to change Rocho back. Jack remained vigilant, only releasing a few painful grunts as he stared into the pup's eyes. He still felt as if the flashlight from his father held a piece of his father himself, and he refused to let it go. Between the painful shocks, his eyes opened just enough to see Rocho growling in his tiny cage.

It may have been the ringing in his ears from the shocks, but Jack swore he heard Rocho growl lower than ever. With every shock onto Jack's cell, the more tears formed in the pup's soft eyes. His fur began to stand along his neck and down his gold striped back. Sparks popped inside his cage as if he were being shocked instead of Jack. After several more waves, Teddy finally stopped as he heard something peculiar. Rocho's growl became loud like a pack of wolves about to attack. His tiny paws created small craters on the metal floor of his cage. He barred his teeth and clenched tightly as more tears filled his eyes, and yellow bolts of electricity surrounded his fur.

Teddy backed away from Jack as Rocho began growing larger in his cage. He expanded to the point of bending the bars as he rose from the size of a Fiz bottle to that of a boar. As the pup continued growing, bigger, the bars snapped, and his paws grew sharp claws that dug through the floor's surface. His teeth became sharp and fang-like, drool dripped from his snarling muzzle and his eyes narrowed. After all of his cuteness had vanished, and he'd enlarged fully, a savage bear-sized version of the dog remained. His bark shook every beam in the shop, as the last tear dripped from his eyes before he lunged at Teddy.

Jack was able to use the freedom parchment to pass through his cell's solid bars, just in time to cover Sonny. Teddy fell backward through the hole of the shop's side as Rocho crashed into Jack's former cell. Jack witnessed the Sandman finally turn to see the commotion.

Shaking off the impact, the bear-sized dog watched Teddy scramble out of the hole and over to the Sandman near the hourglasses. Teddy turned and aimed his remote at Rocho, but his antenna had bent during his fall and failed to work. Just as Rocho lunged again, Teddy dove into the hourglass room. The Sandman pelted red dream sand at the snarling dog who dodged each shot like a flash of lightning from spot to spot. Now within inches of the pup, the holiday spirit created a thick hardened wall of sand in front of him before vanishing. The overgrown dog plowed through it with ease and smashed into the room just as the Nightmare King arrived carrying a necklace.

"Sonny!" Jack shook her by the shoulders, still shocked by Rocho's transformation. "Wake up! It's about to get really bad here. We've gotta move now!"

She opened her eyes slowly. For a moment she was frantically yelling to be let go, shoving back impressively until she realized it was Jack who was shaking her. He'd never seen her in such a panic, but her expression quickly changed to relief after spotting him. "I thought... I killed you?" she said as she wrapped an arm around him. "So many thoughts became a forced suggestion… It was as if I was watching myself act, but I couldn't stop. Where are we?"

Jack helped her up as an hourglass containing a holiday spirit landed on the ground. "We're about to be in the middle of something nasty." Grabbing the sack from the floor, he pulled Sonny by the hand and through the store's hole. The calendar barely hanging on the wall caught his attention again as he ran by. The twenty-third of February was highlighted, but he ignored it and tossed Sonny through the gaping hole and into the store next door, finding cover behind a counter.

He called out for Rocho, but things only became more dangerous as the dog turned in one spot as if he'd lost Teddy in the room, yet still sniffed and scratched at an area. Once the knocked over hourglass hit the ground it shattered. Jack peeked over the counter, through both shops' holes to see the Spirit of Mother's Day appear, fully grown. She immediately took in a great deal of air and with incredible reserve, she released a mighty scream. Both Sonny and Jack were forced to cover their ears from the high pitched yell. He could only imagine the pain Rocho was going through. He witnessed the Sandman's symbol fly backwards past the hole, followed by the rippled sound of multiple glass shatters.

When the yelling finally calmed, Sonny started crawling pass, Jack. "Where are you going?" he asked.

"Well, I can't see very much from here, now can I?" she responded. As she crawled away, Jack reluctantly followed and spotted more spirits who'd escaped from their captive hourglasses including Nina, Holly, Redd, and Mr. Shadow.

"We will not stand by and allow you to destroy this city." Holly stood next to Mother, now also full-sized, and unfastened the red snaps that tied the red cloak around her

~ 279 ~

neck. "If we do not stop you from destroying these worlds, the judges surely will."

"I'm afraid you are far too late for that." The Sandman stood proudly with Phoenix's hourglass latched around his neck. He glowed as if the world around him bent from the mere presence of his aura. The white sand of the infinite hourglass had synced to flow at the same rate as the hourglasses tattooed to his neck. "I have planned for over a century how to expose and overpower the judges. Create an equal standing between the clouds and its citizens and a proper system, and now, the holiday spirits, the judges, and Phoenix will see just how far I've come. The choice is a simple one. Join me in my victorious dream to rebuild this city the way it was ideally meant to be."

"I don't have time for this nonsense." Mr. Shadow became transparent in darkness, and his cold voice crept out like smoke. "If the city needs to adjust it will, but not for you to rule over."

As the Sandman raised himself into the air, the roof of the shop was blasted off simply from his presence. The storm raged on above as his symbol addressed him. "I'm prepared to serve you, master, how may your king assist?"

The Nightmare King kneeled imploringly, but the Sandman appeared amused by the thought. "I will have you do what you do best. Entertain me."

With a wave of his hand, the Sandman flipped the top hat atop his symbol's head. It inhaled like a vacuum all at once. The dark symbol attempted with all his might to remove it. Magic cards flew from his hands as well as doves and red sparks as he tried to pry it from his head, but within moments, his head had been swallowed. As he flailed around with the top hat down to his shoulders, he was sucked inside even more. The Sandman gripped his hand tighter, so the hat was forced down, vanishing the symbol's body down to his waist. As he fell to his knees, the muffled sounds could be heard covered by the top hat's fabric. The Sandman clenched his hand fully into a fist, and it finally flipped up, swallowing the Nightmare King whole like a magic act.

He tilted his head toward the top hat lying empty on the ground as Jack, Sonny, and the holiday spirits looked on. "It's all a game of chess. Pawns protect the king." He resiliently summoned three sleepwalkers to his side. The copied spirits of April Fool's Day, Father's Day, and Groundhog Day appeared. "And I am the king."

Now that Jack saw them just a short distance from the real holiday spirits, he recognized the differences in their eyes even more. The Sandman stood above his three sleepwalking spirits with his arms held out. A dozen sand warriors appeared, risen from the ground. Each one towered behind the sleepwalkers and had boulders for hands. The Sandman presented them as if they were gifts. "How long has it been since you were asked to battle?" he asked Holly, Redd, and the others who'd been freed. "Any change of hearts?"

"For whatever reason, you thought we would side with you, you were wrong, Sandy." Redd balled his fists. "Let's be done with it already."

"Then each of you has already failed monumentally." Under his orders, the sand warriors stormed onto the holiday spirits without caution, who were forced to defend. Two sand warriors attacked Holly, who floated backward like a snowflake. She sent wreaths and stringed lights to bind and trap them. Mr. Shadow, in his shadow form, flew into a sand warrior, possessing it to attack another. Nina, in her pilgrim form, sent a massive spectral green ship sailing in from behind her, smashing four warriors at once then vanishing.

Redd was approached by three warriors at once who all changed their boulders into blades. Redd chuckled at their new weapons, retrieving the same large knife he showed Sonny at the celebration. "No, no, no. *This* is a knife." He plunged the blade down to the hilt into a warrior's side. Pulling it out, he dodged a swinging arm and moved to the next. The warrior began sizzling from his hip like a fuse until he was blown apart. Rolling between another warrior, he slashed its leg and kicked him into the other where they exploded into each other.

Jack and Sonny watched as they continued to fight. The sand warriors were mighty but were outmatched by the spirits. However, once they were all disposed of the sleepwalkers took their places. The spirit of Groundhog Day made a dark portal beneath him, dropping underground. The sleepwalking April Fool tossed two whoopee cushions between Holly and Redd, who were blasted in opposite directions. The copy of Father dropped his suitcase. Gears and panels expanded, blades etched out beneath, and three wheels unfolded until it became a massive black riding lawnmower the size of a bulldozer. Climbing inside it, he shot flaming bowling balls out that whizzed through the air. Within seconds nothing but the floor and a few beams were left in the shop.

Nina, in her Native American form, began chanting something Jack didn't understand. A blue glow allowed her to reflect the next wave of flaming bowling balls. Mr. Shadow removed a mask from his suit jacket and placed it on his face, changing his whole body into a werewolf. He chased after the April Fool copy, who seemed too agile and quick to be caught. Jack assumed the duplicate was unhindered by the years imprisoned or the missing funny bone like the original. He released chattering teeth onto the ground that emitted strange gas, causing Jack to restrain himself from laughing as it chomped after Nina. Redd sent a barrage of fireworks to attack them while Holly launched ornaments that popped all around the large lawnmower but was ineffective. With her eyes closed and her palms open, she summoned gingerbread men two feet tall to fall from the sky, kicking and tossing hardened gumdrops at the Father's copy. In a short period, the holiday spirits were being slowly overtaken, and the Sandman simply continued to look on.

The stones on Mother's rings flashed, but before she had a chance to use them, the copy of the Groundhog Day Spirit popped out of his portal, and the floor below her vanished. Both the surface and ground below were gone as she plummeted through the cloud with nothing to catch her. Jack wanted to react but wasn't sure what to do as he watched the spirit who'd recently protected him fall so suddenly.

A rainbow suddenly pierced the sky, blocking part of the falling rain diving into the portal. As the rest of the spirits were being capitalized on, a black tank-like limousine rushed into the wrecked shop and rammed into the modified lawnmower.

"Fortunately for you, I've arrived." Lucky exited the vehicle removing his sunglasses and adjusting his suit. "Michael, make it rain."

His associate Michael opened the trunk, and a black pot of gold coins was catapulted into the air. Just as the copied Groundhog Day spirit appeared from another hole to drop Redd, the pot of gold struck him back down, raining with coins and trapping him between portals. Nina continued to reflect flaming bowling balls shot from the lawnmower as they ricocheted off the floor. One struck Dr. Deluca's hourglass, but he remained half-buried in sand and broken shards. Even with his shorter stature, Lucky seemed dangerous as he stared up at the impressive machine Father's copy controlled. Snapping his fingers, the gears and wheels were propped up and entangled by thousands of stone-like shamrocks. Smoke erupted from the spokes as bowling balls jammed inside, and it came to a halt, finally blasting the sleepwalker away.

"Reinforcements, about time!" Redd cheered loudly. Raising his trembling fists in the air as if he were actually lifting something, a ghostly version of the Liberty Bell rose from the ground. Punching it with both fists, he sent it sailing at the sleepwalking April Fool. Sonic vibrations rang out, slowing his movement, allowing Mr. Shadow to lure him into a pumpkin patch of vines. Within seconds, the vines snapped together, pumpkins bound him tightly, and tombstones appeared, weighing him down.

Now that the bowling balls had ceased, Nina was able to rejoin Holly. Redd gripped the pumpkin patch vines and swung the trapped April Fool copy into the Groundhog Day's portal. As Mr. Shadow joined them, only the Sandman himself and the holiday spirits remained. They appeared worn but still ready for whatever came next.

A slow clap broke through the silence of the battle's end, and the Sandman was found floating down. "Well, I can't say I was entirely expecting you since our last meeting, Lucky. How's the scar healing?"

"Kept it as a reminder that I owe you one." Lucky removed his suit jacket and stood ready in his vest and green tie. He held up his favorite gold coin so that it could be seen clearly. "And I never forget a debt."

"Well put. Neither do I." The Sandman simply pushed his hand out in front of him, causing tiny green granules to propel out. A wave of sand rippled through, causing an eruption of several buildings on either side that blasted them apart. Jack and Sonny were forced to shield themselves, but his main targets were a few unbroken hourglasses on the shelves. More shattered, releasing several holiday spirits.

"You stand no chance, but I'm sure since you've all worked together before to refuse my rightful place in the past, you'll prefer to fall together now." The Sandman removed his gloves while the spirits stood ready, joined by the rest of the Cloud Nine holidays except Phoenix. They looked at each other in silent united agreement, prepared to make their final stand.

"The union defeated you once," Redd said as he pointed his knife at the Sandman. "We won't be ruled over by you."

Jack only now understood why the Sandman faced them all at once. He realized how arrogant Teddy had been, choosing to work alone in his challenge, and now he witnessed the same arrogance from this former holiday spirit. "He wanted them to be freed. He wants to prove he's better than the spirits that captured him."

Jack recognized a resentful look on Sonny's face that he'd never seen from her before. She observed as Lucky joined the others, but looked at the Sandman with a flicker of anger. "Well, I hope for some good fortune now that Lucky's arrived. No one deserves to be overpowered like he did to me. I simply wish there was more we could do," Sonny stated.

"Wait, wish…?" Jack tried to recall something important as the Sandman tossed his gloves aside.

"All right then, since you've declined my first offer perhaps you'll accept my second. I offer you all my condolences." The former holiday spirit looked upon them all as if these next moments would be business as usual.

Rain poured down from above, and thunder rumbled through the city as if the Sandman's anger were directly influencing it. Redd struck first, causing hundreds of fireworks to fall from the sky and mix with the rain, with sparkling colorful trails. A wave of the Sandman's hand and red sand caused them all to fizzle out. He sent compressed sand the size of sports cars through the air after Redd. Although Redd tried to dodge and duck them, three hit him one after another hard, and he collapsed. Jack couldn't tell, but it seemed he fell as if he were asleep. Holly sent ribbons after him like snakes, while Mr. Shadow tossed pumpkins that turned areas to stone. Lucky placed his hands on the ground turning the floor into rainbow patches. The patches caused rainbow arcs to leap from one spot to another, but none of their traps hit. The Sandman simply dissolved himself into a blue sand form. The ribbons snipped at him trying to wrap their long strands around him but grabbed at nothing. The pumpkins went through him as if he didn't exist, and he hovered right through Lucky's rainbow arcs.

Anna, the Spirit of Hanukkah, made bright crystallized lights appear over his head, as Nina went after him by tossing two dream catchers like tomahawks. The Sandman caused a wave of green sand to reverse the lights and attack the spirits instead as they fired one by one like missiles. Holly shielded herself and others with floating snow globes, but many took hits. Jack could see the Spirits of Kwanzaa and Passover with folded hands in prayer reviving Redd and others who'd fallen, while the real April Fool tried to fire back with his own peanut can pranks.

The Sandman reclaimed his solid body. Absorbing sand from beneath him, he changed his body into a four-armed, hardened sand warrior standing twice the size of the others they'd fought. "Is that really the best you can do?!" he roared in his hardened body. One hand formed into a sword, another into a spiked ball. The third changed into an ax, while the last turned into a sledgehammer. He swung at the holiday spirits, wheeling his massive weapons at them.

The Spirit of Ramadan floated blue crescent moons at the warrior giant, dissolving his body as he stepped on hidden Easter egg mines. None of it seemed to slow him as he struck each of them down with massive blows from his boulder weapons. Slamming all four arms into the floor, a field of green hands sprouted from the ground just like Jack's dream. They grabbed onto the holiday spirits, disabling movement and forcing them to struggle free, but more replaced those, and soon none of them were moving. It appeared the fight was nearly finished as Jack lowered his head and hoped something would happen when a blade sliced up carving into the rock giant from behind.

"No, we can do better," said the Spirit of Valentine's Day as he stood behind the Sandman's towering form. He leaped into the air arching his arms back, wielding a shield and gleaming sword. With a precision slice down, he struck hard, removing two of the rocky arms on a single side. After landing, Dr. Deluca slammed the Sandman back and swung his shield into his torso. With one side heavier than the other, the Sandman fell to one side off balanced.

The doctor stood valiantly with his brilliantly shining Roman sword, and shield gripped in his hands. It was the first time Jack had seen him without his lab coat or mask. He turned to face the Sandman in glimmering Roman armor. Half his face held scars from years of battle, but the other was flawlessly handsome beneath his dark locks of hair. Jack wasn't sure if it was the sprit's presence or the Sandman's arms being removed, but the others were fighting back against the green hands. Many of the hands withered back into the ground allowing the holiday spirits to free themselves. A new strength radiated from each of the spirits as they stood stronger than before. Redd was awake, and his arms looked larger as he joined a fellow soldier. Holly held an aura as bright as her North Star, and Mr. Shadow was able to summon his shadow behind him in a much larger version than usual.

Jack could feel it himself, and he grabbed Sonny by the shoulders. "I have an idea. I'll be back."

"Where are you going?" Sonny asked.

"I need to find fire!" he yelled back as he picked up a candle from the ground.

As the Sandman lifted himself off the ground, he leaned slightly to one side. Sand absorbed through his feet as he tried to regrow his arms, but Redd and the doctor were ready. They moved between each other as if they'd already seen what the other would do next. The doctor slammed the rocky form with his shield then planted it into the floor. Redd used the shield to launch himself through the rain and stab his knife's blade into the pit of the Sandman's arm. The arm was blown off as Dr. Deluca rolled between his rocky legs and struck his ankle, forcing the Sandman to fall to his knees. At once the two soldiers drove their blades into his rocky tors, so they stuck. He swung his remaining rock arm, but Redd ducked and grabbed the doctor's waiting sword from his stone back. The doctor removed the knife from his chest, and together they spun, slicing.

The Sandman fell to his last arm as sand poured out of his left side, and a large chunk blasted from the right. Redd tossed the sword to the doctor and watched him climb up the Sandman's slanted back. He sliced the nape of his neck with the sword and drove the knife blade into the top of his head as he leaped off. With the weakened remains of his body left, Redd drew his knife out, swung his arm back, and with a sharp uppercut yelled, "OORAH!" Fireworks rocketed from his fist into the Sandman's head, blasting him out of his rocky shell, and he crumpled to the floor.

He flew back nearly to the shop's entrance. Holiday spirits lined up behind Redd and Dr. Deluca as he picked up his shield. Holly and Anna's dresses fluttered with white auras, Mr. Shadow stood even darker with his shadow flexing powerfully behind him, and Nina stood proudly with both forms shifting into view at once. Imani and the other spirits all rose stronger than ever as they watched for their enemy's next move.

More thunder crashed through the sky as the Sandman shot up from the ground. His fists balled to his sides, and the first genuine smile appeared on his face. The rain separated, pouring around him, as if afraid to touch him. "Finally. Now that's the spirit!" he spat as he rose into the air. His trench coat fluttered, and all four sands swirled around him like discs. Green quicksand mixed with red dream sand to form two giant fists, temporarily blocking the rain as they slammed down on the spirits. Most were able to dive out of the way, but a few remained lying on the floor. Separating his hands, the sand followed the same motions dividing the spirits with two giant hands as he floated to the middle.

"He's combining the sands," the doctor stated to the others. "Anything he thinks of can become physical."

"All right then, let's stick to the source," Redd agreed. The Sandman walked between both sides as the green, and red sands mixed several floating weapons. As Redd and the doctor attacked together, two floating swords fought them back. Holly crossed her arms, and candy cane pillars spiked through the floorboards at slanted angles in a chain, but after swinging his arm, the Sandman caused saw blades to appear and sliced through them, attacking her.

The Sandman continued to produce more weapons with ease as Jack rummaged through the store. He searched for anything that would help him light a fire, but everything had either been damaged or dampened by the storm. Sonny turned around to see him pushing over a shelf. "Why are you looking for fire?"

Jack picked up a book of matches from under the tilted shelf, but they had been crushed by the weight already. "I need to light this candle. I have an idea if I'm right about the date I saw."

Sonny scanned the wrecked store. "What date, what are you talking about?"

"There was a calendar that was hanging on the wall," he explained. "I didn't know how long we had been asleep, but I think today's February 23. Today's your birthday."

Sonny shook her head, confused as lightning struck overhead. The battle continued on behind them as Lucky, although holding nothing, shot out gold coins like machine guns. He shot through every weapon the Sandman produced, freeing up his fellow spirits to attack. Before they could advance, the Sandman forced the blue nightmare sand into the quicksand, and three beastly winged demons with claws formed a protective triangle. The holiday spirits worked together, but these minions were much quicker than anyone else they'd fought so far.

Sonny continued staring at Jack as if he'd only told her the first half of a joke. "What does my birthday have to do with anything?"

"I remembered you telling the owner of this place," Jack reminded her. "The Birthday Blowout store is this store. Don't you remember what he said about the candles? The candle release black smoke if your birthday hasn't passed, white if it's the week of." He handed the candle to Sonny. "And lights fully if it's the day of."

The candle smoked but immediately went out. It wasn't entirely white or black but definitely an attempt at burning. "It's not lighting."

Jack took the candle back. Small white wisps formed and vanished. "I know, but I think it's all the rain. If we could get a real fire to dry it out, then maybe we could make a wish to stop the Sandman."

Sonny looked out at the dreary raining skies. "It's dark. It could be tomorrow anytime now. Time is running out on us, isn't it?"

"It always is, isn't it?" Jack looked back through the hole where the demons had gone, but apparently, it had taken out a few of the holiday spirits as well. Among them, Anna and the April Fool lay unconscious in a corner. The Sandman had split into four separate people, each one with a trench coat matching the color of his sands. Lucky sent shamrocks overhead with the weight of boulders after the green one, but he was hammered through the floor and fell to the clouds below.

The Sandmen moved between each other easily swapping targets. The one in red blasted two-holiday spirits and instantly put them to sleep at once. The blue one forced Mr. Shadow to attack Nina. The one in green released a fog around him that reached out, pulling in any holiday spirits near him. The one in white with the small hourglass around his neck, however, didn't move nearly as much. An occasional raised hand stopped Redd or another spirit from landing a blow as if he paused their movements. Jack could see Dr. Deluca watching the four of them just as he was, and he wondered if they both came to the same conclusion.

Lightning sliced through the air above them and diverted Jack's attention, but in that moment, he had an idea. Running closer to the hole, he squeezed the wick of the candle with his fingers, trying to dry it, then shoved it into his coat. Sonny followed him over, but mostly, it seemed out of curiosity. "Where are we going now?" she asked.

"Rocho!" Jack shouted over the battle. He could see the Valentine's Day spirit ducking between the green and blue Sandmen, making his way to the one in white.

"I don't think he's coming Jack," she replied.

Jack continued looking over at the back room he'd seen Rocho chase Teddy into. He needed to make sure the pup was okay, but there was another reason he needed Rocho. As Jack waited for the puppy to hear him, he noticed the doctor running at the white cloaked Sandman. He raised his hand to stop the doctor from swinging his sword. However, the former soldier had already hurled his shield, and it smashed into the Sandman's head. He lost his concentration, and the other Sandmen returned to him.

"If I could get Rocho over here, we could use him to spark the candle," Jack clenched his fists and looked up at the sky. "If we could just get lightning to—ouch!" He grabbed his hand in pain.

Sonny looked at his empty palm. "What's wrong?"

He shook his head but then paused for a moment and shoved the candle into Sonny's hand. He gripped the wick tightly, enduring the shocking pain. "The hand buzzer the April Fool gave me. I'm still wearing it."

The candle finally lit, just as the Sandman regained himself. There was a fury in his eyes Jack had never seen before. The last of the holiday spirits advanced onto him, but he sprang into the air, sand falling from his trembling body of anger. "NO!

~ 292 ~

I will NOT be defeated by you pathetic weak minded spirits AGAIN! " With his hands gripping the air, a wave echoed out, gradually turning the surroundings gray. It reminded Jack of his trip through the inside of the theater in the Holiday Hotel. Raindrops stopped falling midair. The holiday spirits threw everything they had at him, but it all ended the same way. The white sand around his neck pulsed as the waved etched closer and closer to the spirits.

"We have to stop him now!" Jack yelled over the crashing thunder.

Sonny kept closing her eyes and blowing on the candle, but it wouldn't go out. "Nothing I wish for is working. I wished for him to be destroyed, locked away again, and never released. Maybe we're too late, or...or need to get closer?!" She ran through the hole, ignoring Jack's pleas to come back, keeping her distance from the gray wave. Very little of the wooden floor remained, so she was forced to climb onto the cage that previously held them. Her hand hovered over the candle to block the rain that still fell, and she blew on the candle again. However, the small flame still burned.

Jack watched as the holiday spirits continued to back away from the Sandman's pulsing wave, but they quickly ran out of places to go as the buildings behind them blocked them in. Jack watched as parts of their bodies were being paused instantly in place, still holding their ground and fiercely facing their enemy. He glanced at Sonny, still trying to make a wish and then at the Sandman as lightning streaked over his head. It reflected off the broken glass on the ground, and Jack remembered something important a smug yet brilliant engineer in a turtleneck told him about fulgurite glass.

"Sonny, the lightning!" Jack yelled. "Use the lightning!" She struggled to hear Jack, but he, unfortunately, caught the

Sandman's attention. Sending a stream of nightmare sand in her direction, he knocked the cage over, and she began falling into the floor's gaping hole. Jack snatched up the sack, flinging it to the cage to swing over the gray flooring. He scrambled over to reach out a hand to Sonny, but she was already falling through. The cage was tipping over from his weight, and before he could rebalance it, the Sandman shot him with blue sand too. It propelled back as if it were unable to touch him but still caused him to fall in as well.

Tumbling through the air felt like a lifetime to Jack, but it had actually been for less than ten seconds. Blurs of gray clouds falling through the rain as he tumbled were disorienting enough, and after what happened next, he was sure he was dead. They smacked hard onto a surface, but luckily it was cushioned like a gel. The rainbow-colored road that circled during Lucky's entrance earlier lay beneath them. After recovering and checking where he was, he realized Mother must have landed there as well, but she was nowhere to be found. Jack grabbed a part of the cloud to lift himself up and felt a solid piece like a jagged javelin. It was silver and wiggled up and down, but was sturdy enough to support him. Sonny shook on the floor, holding her head, but when Jack went to comfort her, she screamed.

"Get me out, get me out!" she repeated. "Don't lock me in!" Jack could see the flakes of blue sand in her hair and immediately knew what nightmares she thought were occurring. He knew she feared small spaces but never asked her why. As she rocked back and forth, still gripping the candle, he tried his best to pull her out of it, still clutching the sack in his hand.

"Sonny, listen to me," he whispered in her ear. "It's not real. We're not trapped anywhere. I need you to listen to me. We're in the open sky, and we'll be okay. You're stronger than this. No one's got you trapped." Sonny's shaking slowed, and she began opening her eyes.

"Stretching the truth a bit now are we not, Jackson?" The Sandman hovered down to the rainbow road, glancing between the two dreamers. "Did you really believe that birthday candle would stop me? Did you think after all the time I spent remolding her mind, I didn't remember her birthday was today? I am far too strong to be beaten by the holiday spirits, and soon enough the judges will kneel to me as well. What threat would either of you hold to me?"

He left Sonny lying on the ground and directed his attention to Jack, raising his hand. "Unfortunately for you, I believe it's time you experience real fear."

The Sandman shot him with a blast of blue nightmare sand, and Jack quickly closed his eyes, yet nothing happened. Using both hands, the Sandman tried again with such a powerful, steady stream that Jack turned his head and squinted. When nothing changed, he took advantage of the moment. The storm raged on above them as Jack yanked hard on the jagged piece, freeing it from the cloud, and drove it into the Sandman's chest, where it stuck through his back. "Every cloud has a silver lining." Jack stepped back.

The Sandman staggered, but it appeared from surprise more than anything else. He laughed at Jack's efforts and looked down at the long jagged silver sticking out of him, forming dream sand in his hand. "The weak never seem to understand. Have you not learned anything yet?"

"Yes, I have," Sonny said as she stood behind him, gripping the candle tightly in her shaking hands. "Never be a victim again." As he turned to find her facing him, she closed her eyes and blew out the candle. Thunder rippled above, and Jack had the slightest moment to snatch the infinite hourglass from his neck before he and Sonny dove out of the way. The Sandman grabbed for his necklace then furiously changed to sand, yanking the silver javelin out. Before he could remove it, lightning parted the clouds, cutting through the skies and striking the silver spear, which lit him up like a beacon.

More strikes continued too brutally bright to watch. Jack could feel the heat radiating from the Sandman as he yelled, repeatedly jolted so it sounded as if he were gargling. Nearly a minute passed before Jack stopped hearing the strikes land along with the sound of sizzling metal although the Sandman had gone quiet in half that time. He secured the hourglass in his pocket. Looking back at the Sandman, where a new gleaming, completely glass version stood in his place with the silver still protruding from his chest and back. He didn't move, but Jack could see the slightest flutter of his eyes narrowing. Before he had time to react, a black limousine raced toward them on the rainbow road. Jack and Sonny scooted to the sides as it smashed into the newly made statue.

The Sandman broke into two pieces. The bottom half was stuck under the car, while the top just a few inches in front of it. The back doors opened on either side. Mother got out on one side and flattened her dress, while Lucky stepped out of the other side. He held the same black bat Jack had seen in his office. It was almost as tall as the spirit himself with clovers around the handle, balanced over his shoulder as he whistled and drank a Green Apple Mint Fiz. When they reached the top half of the Sandman's body, he nodded to Jack and Sonny and looked down at the glass figure. "Third time's a charm," the Spirit of Saint Patrick's Day stated. "Looks like today's my

Lucky day." With a single swing, he smashed the bat onto the glass Sandman, shattering the entire half into crystallized powder.

Chapter 12
The Judgment

Raindrops falling onto the windshield of the limousine fell fewer and fewer between. Jack stared out at the clouds, sitting comfortably on the cushioned wrap-around leather interior of the backseat. Gradually, the skies were changing from a nearly blackish gray slowly entering white. Sonny sat next to him jotting new notes in her notepad, shaking her head at the ripped pages. Lucky and Mother sat across from them, discussing the other spirits still frozen above, as they were all driven up the rainbow road Lucky created back to Cloud One's entrance.

Except for the occasional glance outside, Jack kept his focus on his sack sitting between the spirits. He was determined it wouldn't leave his sight until the cloud keepers arrived to secure it. Both holiday spirits assured him that they were safe as long as the dream catcher that protected Jack remained inside, and neither he nor Sonny touched it. It wasn't the most fabulous temporary container, but all they had available. Still, with the infinite hourglass around his neck, Jack felt obligated to protect it as well as Sonny, after what she'd been through. So he continued to oversee it as they sped up the road containing the Sandman's powdered remains.

Returning to the toymaker's shop, he felt the wind pick up, but Jack was sure it was only the exposed portions that made it feel that way. The shop and dozens of buildings near it were destroyed by the Sandman. Very few walls or beams remained standing. The shop, as a focal point, was practically a crater and all other buildings around were the resulting blowback as if a giant meteor landed. The toymaker himself was still lying near his store's entrance but snored loudly as Jack walked by. Most of the holiday spirits were still recovering from the infinite sand's effects, as Lucky's personal guard Cassandra continued to feed them the same healing Fiz drink she used to free Lucky. Portions of their body remained gray but were slowly wearing off, allowing movement.

Mother pointed Jack to the back room while Lucky stayed with his two favorite drivers watching the sack. He leaped over the spots missing floorboards until he reached the curtained back area. The moon finally peeked through the clouds as they separated, making it much easier to see where he stepped. Many of the hourglasses were still shelved, including some broken ones, with spirits either unconscious or unaware of their freedom. He was careful not to step on any fractured shards as he found Rocho much further into the back. He'd shrunk from the beastly bear-size Jack witnessed earlier, regaining his petite form, perhaps smaller than he'd ever seen the pup. His green fur was dull, and his eyes were not nearly as illuminating as usual. The streak down his back sparked like Jack's mask when it malfunctioned. He lay panting on the ground, still scratching at a piece of the floorboard.

"It's alright, Rocho." Jack scooped him up with both hands gingerly. "You were incredible. I've got you now."

The pup tried to bark, but little came out. Jack's words seemed to comfort him as Rocho's tail wagged happily. He licked a beam of moonlight and reformed back into the familiar flashlight. Inspecting the floor where the pup had been scratching, Jack could see a tiny gap in the wood broader than the others. Prying it open, he recalled a portion of his dream about a hidden tunnel leading to the Mighty Moles' sports store. The young detective hurriedly tugged hard on the wood already sure what he'd find and who he'd missed going in. It flew open on a hinge revealing a short staircase just as he dreamt, and it was empty. He took a step forward but was stopped immediately.

"Teddy is long gone by now sweetie," Mother said softly with her hand on his shoulder. "I'm so sorry."

Jack already knew before opening it, but he'd hoped somehow he'd catch him. He slammed the makeshift door closed, angrily turning. "It's my fault! I should've chased after him when I had the chance. Why didn't I follow him when I got out? I could've stopped him."

"Honey, you did everything you could," the spirit responded. "If it weren't for you and Sonny, this city wouldn't be the same." They both looked around at the broke, and smoldering debris and Mother waved her hand. "You understand what I mean."

"And if it weren't for you I would no longer be here." Sonny had stepped behind the curtain so Jack could see her clearly. "You pulled me to safety and woke me up from those nightmares. You helped me come back."

Jack exchanged looks from Sonny to Mother. He could see a glimmer of his own Mother in her as she stared back into his eyes, and it made him want to breakdown tearfully, screaming and fighting at the same time. "You don't understand. Teddy knew where my dad was. Not only did I lose Teddy again, but I have no way of knowing where my dad is or if he's okay!"

"He is okay, honey." The Spirit of Mother's Day pushed aside a mix of wood planks and rain. At the very back of the room, she picked up a shard of glass. It was possibly the only one still in a single large piece from the hourglasses. She handed it to Jack, warning him to be careful before telling him what it was.

"Your father was trapped in an hourglass, just like the rest of us. I could see him from the shelf I was being held on. He was pointing and drawing lines, but I wasn't sure at the time why. When Teddy tried to gather him and escape, he rolled out from his hands. He was able to breakout before Teddy used dream sand on him. I think it's a message for you sweetie."

She reached out to fix Jack's hair, but he was too occupied to care. The glass shard gleamed in the moonlight, but he couldn't see much more than a few smudges. After squinting for a moment, he sighed frustrated and lowered his hand. On the shelf, he noticed the tiny holiday spirits still in their hourglasses. The glittering sand at their heels, he remembered how much more of the world he could see through the totem. Using the flashlight's handle, he looked closer at the glass, examining the tiny lines written by much smaller hands. "This is bigger than you know. Return home. Protect the totem. I love you son."

~ 301 ~

He read it repeatedly to himself. He could almost hear his father's voice each time he went over it. It was simple to understand that his father wanted to protect him, but Jack had made up his mind months before. "I have to find him. I can't let my dad be punished to save all of us. He's died once already, I won't let it happen again."

"Teddy has taken him, children," Mother reminded them both. "We could explain what happened to the cloud keepers and have them help."

"I'm quite sure after everything you've done for the city they'd be willing to follow the tunnel," Sonny added. "Do you have any clues as to where he may have gone from there?"

Jack looked up at them both nodding. "He mentioned his employer telling him what he needed to do. Now, I really don't think it's the Sandman he was talking about."

"Why is that?" Sonny asked.

"There's no way they could've communicated," Jack explained. "You were the first dreamer to touch him in all this time. If Teddy wanted to, he could've found a way to free him from the roof of the Holiday Hotel last year, or even the past fifty years."

She clicked her pen. "So what are you saying exactly?"

Jack held out his flashlight. "He wants this. This is the totem Teddy's after so he can go home. It's the only thing he cares about. He's not leaving the city without it, and my guess is whoever he's working for is either here in the city or somehow getting him instructions. We just have to find out who, and how."

Sirens rang from a short distance away. Jack and Sonny exited the back room leaving Mother to release the other spirits on the shelves. Lucky stood with his guards, Christopher and Michael, and Cassandra. Together they administered Green

Apple Fiz to the holiday spirits speeding up their recovery from the infinite sand. A group of J.A.C.K. patrol cars pulled up hastily. Many of them contained yawning spirits Jack assumed were put to sleep by Presto. The cars waited with their blue and white lights swirling in the night.

It wasn't until Jack heard a motorcycle pull up that any of them exited their vehicles. The investigator arrived in his usual sunglasses, his trench coat flowing behind him as he rode in on a speedy looking white motorcycle with blue accent lights highlighting the engine. Moments after he dismounted, the seat stretched into a mane, the headlights and front became a shaking head and muzzle, while the body became that of a full grown white horse. It was the same white horse Jack had seen after their breakout from the J.A.C.K.'s headquarters. Steam spewed from the horse's nostrils like exhaust after it shook its head and tapped the ground with its silver hooves.

Jack quickly noticed how similar the change was in comparison to Rocho morphing from his flashlight. He wondered if they had both been changed by the same little girl and was possibly the reason the detective believed him at all. Ten cloud keepers stepped out of the patrol cars and followed the investigator as he approached Jack. They stopped in unison with their transparent shields ready, projecting from their badges. The detective held out his gloved palm to Jack and looked down at him through the dark glasses.

"The hourglass, Mr. Taylor?" the detective requested flatly. Jack had initially planned to deliver it to Phoenix himself, ensuring its return to the spirit. He hesitated, wanting to refuse, but after seeing Sonny nod her head, he reluctantly removed it from his neck and handed it over without a fight.

The detective looked over the remains of the area. After a quick scan, he was handed a lockbox by one of his keepers. Jack recognized him as Cloud Keeper Matthews, who'd walked Sonny and himself to the headquarters on New Year's Day. Before anything else was said between them, Lucky turned around casually.

"In my car, he's in the sack on the back seat. What's left of him anyways," he addressed the detective as if giving directions to a mall then returned to what he was doing.

The detective nodded to Cloud Keeper Matthews. He and two others went to the limousine. Seconds later, they called out for a proper container and secured the Sandman's remains inside. Jack watched as they loaded it into a new heavily armored hourglass, then inside a chained container, and finally into a vault. He was glad to see this time they weren't taking any chances, but something still bothered him about it.

"Why bother keeping him at all?" Jack asked as he watched the transportation process over again. "We should drop it in the valley well so he can't do this again!"

"Higher authority Mr. Taylor," the detective acknowledged. "Destroying his presence would mean destroying your plane of existence. Without the Sandman, even locked away, there would be no sleep. Like the two beings, we are bound by balance. However, it seems you have been busy since our last meeting. I would admit you have done an excellent job, although it was not your job to do so."

"What do you mean?" Jack argued. "I had to save my dad. We did what we had to do to stop the Sandman."

"You should have left this matter to us," the investigator rebutted. "The laws are set for a reason. Although what you did may be considered admirable and the city may or may not find it heroic, you put yourself in danger, and you've put all of its citizens in danger. The ends do not always justify the means,

Mr. Taylor. These acts may have unforeseen circumstances. As such, you two need to come with us."

Sonny's head shot up. "Where are we going?"

"To the J.A.C.K.'s headquarters for questioning," he responded, turning. "We need to debrief you. You are witnesses in this case."

Jack and Sonny were escorted up through the clouds to Cloud Nine. The city was peaceful as if it were finally able to rest. Although he was sure he'd slept for weeks, it made Jack feel tired as well. The patrol car climbed through Cloud Five, and he felt something poke him. Reaching into his pocket, Jack found the card left to him from Luminista. He stared at the last line for what seemed like ages. *Happy Birthday.* He wondered where she was now, and if somehow she really knew where all of this would lead.

Arriving on Cloud Nine, they were marched into the J.A.C.K.'s headquarters. Passing by the portraits, Jack took an unusually long look at Teddy's. Silently, he promised himself that he would do whatever it took to make sure Teddy never made it home. Cloud Keeper Matthews scanned Sonny's hand with his badge. The badge illuminated in red and he placed it in a clear bag marked evidence.

Next, the detective placed a small blue orb on the table. Jack and Sonny were asked to describe their experiences since their arrival in Cloud City. They were explicitly questioned about interactions with the Sandman and any possible affiliates. Jack was more than happy to tell them about Teddy. As they recalled the last two months of their stay, leaving out minor details involving Lucky and other holiday spirits who hid them, mist swirled inside the orb. The moment they were finished, the detective gathered it, marked it in a case also containing Presto's damaged top hat, and walked out.

After the debriefing, they were told to wait inside while the detective delivered the information to the judges. Hours passed just as it had the last time they were detained by the cloud keepers. Jack could see the holding cell behind them had been repaired. The window allowed the tiniest hint of sunlight through the bars, and he realized it was morning. Sonny sat beside him, going through her notes and writing information she had missed from the story. Jack felt the need to apologize to her as a cringe of guilt washed over him like a cold shower. The way he saw it, if she weren't there to help him find his father, she wouldn't have missed her birthday or been possessed by a vengeful spirit. He nudged her gently, but before he could say anything, someone walked in, and it wasn't who he expected.

"Sorry it took me so long to get here, but I've been waiting for the cloud keepers' approval to thank you for saving me, again." A young boy stood in the doorway, speaking to Jack. He appeared to be no more than one or two years younger. His face was friendly, and his hair was blond reaching the back of his neck, much like Sonny's. He reminded Jack of the kids who skateboarded in the parking lots after school. What really caught his attention were the pajamas and the hourglass around his neck, but Sonny seemed to notice it first.

"Phoenix?" she confirmed. He'd aged even faster than Jack would've guessed since he'd witness his meeting with Father. He smiled at them both pleasantly.

"Honestly, Sonny had more to do with it than I did," Jack admitted. "She went through the worst of it and was the one who really put the Sandman down, and missed her birthday doing it. She was strong enough to save all of us, including me. If anyone deserves to be thanked, she does."

A soft smile spread across her face, and she seemed to be at a loss for words looking at Jack. He nodded at her supportively as if to say *don't argue, it's true,* but what happened next he wasn't ready for. Wrapping her arms around his neck, she hugged him tightly. It was awkward for Jack, especially with the New Year's Day spirit standing behind him, and with the guards around. However, after a moment, he hugged her back and whispered in her ear. "Happy birthday, Sonny."

The detective walked in, clearing his throat, and they separated. Sonny wiped away a small tear. The detective disregarded the holiday spirit's presence altogether, as he slammed a folder onto his desk and removed his sunglasses in frustration. It startled the cloud keepers in the room, but they remained steady. After a deep breath, he sat down and looked between Jack and Sonny.

"I just finished the initial hearing from the judges," the investigator explained. "The spirit of Saint Patrick's Day among others arrived in the courtroom as witnesses to defend your roles in this matter. I should warn you now there is good news, and some unexpected bad news I must explain."

"What is the good news?" Sonny requested first.

"The Sandman was found guilty, of course," the detective explained. "After the New Year's Day spirit's testimony and the judges' agreement, he will be transferred to the island prison. A new system will be implemented there that will allow dream sand to flow while he is imprisoned. The facility is far more secure, so an incident like this won't happen again. And, the Spirit of Father's Day is already working with the Spirit of Christmas to reassemble the fragmented shard of her north star, so they may restore her symbol, Santa Claus."

Although relieved to hear Holly's symbol would be all right after the things he said to him, Jack dreaded what was coming next. "And the bad news?"

"To begin, I sent cloud keepers down the tunnel you reported the dreamer Teddy had escaped through." The investigator looked between them both. "As you predicted, it traveled to an end destination just below the Moles' former clubhouse. I assume the Nightmare King aided their transportation previously, however, we were unable to locate your father or the dreamer."

Phoenix lowered his head. "I can't believe I employed him through so many of my previous lives without knowing."

"We have officers stationed at the entrances, and all boarding docks are secured," the detective assured them. "Eventually we will find them, but I'm afraid that may be the least of your worries at the moment."

Jack rolled his eyes in disappointment. "What else could matter?"

The detective opened the folder on his desk. "Charges were brought up, and I'm afraid the votes did not come to your favor. One in particular of being an accomplice. As I've told you before we are all bound by the laws of the city."

"What do you mean? Sonny was a victim, not an accomplice," Jack argued.

"The charges are not on her, Mr. Taylor," he corrected. "As I'm sure you've noticed the cell you were held in has been rebuilt. The men employed by the Saint Patrick's Day spirit were released from the judgment of assisting your breakout. He was *fortunate* enough to argue it as a simple traffic collision and paid a fine along with damages. Defending your case proved to be a much tougher issue. Tests have proven your partner was under the effects of the Sandman; however your actions were entirely your own. As such, you, unfortunately, have three pending charges."

"This is ridiculous," Phoenix interrupted. "These dreamers are heroes."

"Regardless of my feelings, I'm afraid my attempts to persuade the majority of the judges have failed," the detective stated. "The law is the law. All you can hope for now is that your good deeds will persuade a lesser punishment."

Sonny responded before Jack was able to. "Punishment?"

There was another interruption as the door swung open once again. Holiday spirits poured into the J.A.C.K.'s headquarters. Some moved slowly still overcoming the Sandman's effects. Holly, Redd, Lucky, Mother, Father, Nina, Anna, and the April Fool, among others Jack couldn't see, crowded the doorway. They marched in arguing all at once, but between them all, he couldn't make out exactly what they were saying. The detective put his hand up to stop his cloud keepers from reacting.

"I got you the best defense money can buy kid, don't you worry," Jack heard Lucky promise.

"Good soldiers like these doing their civic duty should be rewarded, not lookin' like enemies when the history books are written!" Redd yelled.

"The judges must know of their contributions to the city!" Father advised.

"You're such a handsome young man if you would just stand up straighter..." Mother added.

The arguing continued until the detective held up his badge and shook it vigorously. A loud whistle pierced their ears until everyone went silent, and he was able to address them all. "People, please refrain from yelling. I understand and appreciate your frustration, but the decision is not up to anyone in this department. You all know the procedures as well as I do, and what's done is done."

"I don't understand," Jack stated finally. "What am I charged with?"

The detective removed the paper from the open folder he slammed on his desk and read through a list. "One charge of fleeing from custody, as well as endangering officers during a chase, and inciting mass panic from citizens. One charge of conspiracy against the holiday spirits, the judges, and the capital city itself. And finally, one charge for aiding in the escape of a previously imprisoned high-level political criminal, including hiding his whereabouts and interfering with cloud keeper investigations."

"He never helped the Sandman," countered Sonny.

The detective placed the charges back into the folder. "That's not the way the judges see it. By helping you, as you were controlled by the Sandman, Mr. Taylor aided the Sandman indirectly."

Jack brushed his hand through his hair. "I don't understand. What happens next?"

There was a knock on the open door. The brothers Michael and Christopher poked their heads in. "Lawyer's all set there boss," Michael interrupted.

"And how did she do?" Lucky asked.

Christopher grinned. "Brilliant. Stroppy at times even. She's got some neck, that one, but it's still a chancer."

"There's no coddin' with these judges," Michael added. "Nearly six bells. Better get goin'. You be sure to mind yourself lad," he gestured to Jack.

"Well let's get to it." The investigator waived two cloud keepers over who helped Jack stand and walked him past the spirits and out the doors.

He was escorted back down the hallway. Instead of turning, he was directed to the same swirling green portal he'd passed on his tour to Cloud Nine. It was taller than he remembered. The bars continued to cover it as they advanced toward it. Sonny, Lucky, Father, and the other holiday spirits followed behind them. The J.A.C.K.s stopped abruptly before the portals just beyond the thick bars and waited.

After a moment, one by one, the bars slid up. Lucky's personal guard Cassandra stepped out of the portal holding a briefcase in her hand. She looked down at Jack, raised an eyebrow, and continued walking over to Lucky. Jack covered his neck, watching until she passed. "Wait. Don't tell she's my lawyer?"

"Trust me, kid, there's no one better to keep you from that island," Lucky confirmed. "Might be the last place you wanna end up at. Best person to argue your defense."

"How did she defend me?" Jack asked. "She never talks."

She began unclasping her bracelet, but Lucky intervened. "Believe me when I tell you, it's the quiet ones that are most dangerous. She can speak at great lengths when needed."

"A little advice," Father said to Jack. "Be respectful, and don't talk back to them, especially the oldest one. He doesn't take jokes well."

Jack was sure he already knew better but didn't like the way the spirit added the last part. "Why the oldest one especially?"

"He's not exactly a fan of your father's," the Father's Day spirit divulged. "He hasn't been since your father refused to redesign the prison."

"Great." Jack was marched into the portal. He could feel himself being pulled up through a twisting green tunnel like a water park slide in reverse. Seconds passed, and he was pushed into a new building he'd never seen before. A dark dungeon-like courtroom with four tall pillars aligned in a semicircle draped in different colors down to the floor. One was grass green with black lines forming a flower, the next red with a black flame, a taxi yellow one displayed a leaf, and an icy blue one was centered with a snowflake. Deep alcoves were atop each one Jack nearly had to look straight up to see.

He was pushed forward by the cloud keepers up an aisle between several sets of benches to a podium. Oddly enough, it reminded him of a dream he'd had months before when he repeated the same day. There were no windows. Very little light was available from the torches lining the walls. Just beyond his podium in the center of a pit roughly ten feet deep, he could see a dark mound of boulders protruding up with patches of color matching the four draped pillars. Chains crossed over it bolted down on four sides and covered in a transparent dome. Jack wondered why a bunch of rocks would be shackled down when a pebble rolled down. He wasn't positive, but for a moment he was sure the mound was breathing.

Sonny, Father, and the other spirits stepped through the portal. They sat on the benches behind Jack, giving him encouraging words, but it only made him more nervous. "Where are we?" he asked, turning to Father.

"No one really knows exactly *where* this place is," Father whispered. "This place is hidden from the city to protect the judges. The little research I've gathered from Tour Guide Morris would place us in a courtroom attached to a castle. We're either on a distant cloud away from the city, or somewhere below an active volcano."

Jack wanted to laugh, but he wasn't sure if the spirit was joking or not. He pointed to the chained rock formation in the pit. "And what is that?"

"The elemental rock," he answered. "It was tamed a few millenniums ago. It's the power source the judges depend on.

They use a potent amount of dream sand to keep it subdued. Their power is sourced from the elements, and we holidays get our abilities from them, which is why it must stay alive. Simply put, the judges are the strongest beings left in the world."

A voice echoed throughout the courtroom, and everyone went quiet. "All rise for the four honorable judges, maintaining the balance in the eyes of the two all-powerful beings."

Jack stared up as shadows approached the alcoves atop the draped pillars. The torches around the courtroom went dim. A light shined down onto Jack overhead that he shielded his eyes from with his hand. He noticed the elemental rock shutter slightly then become still again. Each alcove lit with the color corresponding to their draped pillars.

A small flurry of snow fluttered the blue draped pillar, and an ashen, tall, older man floated out of the alcove. He was cloaked in the same matching blue that complemented the frosty gaze in his eyes. He stopped at the lip, so the draped pillar appeared to follow from his clothing. His white hair and beard were reminiscent of Phoenix in his old age. Jack could feel a fierce cold from him stronger than he'd ever felt before. Immediately he knew whatever this judge lacked in youth, he could easily make up for in other areas.

A few yards away from him, the next judge floated in. This time leaves whisked through the alcove as it illuminated in yellow, and a Middle Eastern woman appeared. She was stunning like Holly, but with flawless bronze colored skin. Shoulder length black hair fell against the hood of her robe as she folded her hands together. She rolled her eyes annoyingly as the next judge arrived. He slid out of the third alcove like a surfer, and Jack was sure he saw swimming trunks beneath his red robes. A wave of heat followed him as he settled in. This one was much younger than the woman a short distance away.

Complimented with a Pacific Island complexion, he seemed barely out of his teens, athletic, and carefree. Smiling as he brushed back his ocean, washed sandy hair; he winked at the other judges.

The final alcove lit in green followed by sprouting daisies and snapdragons. A much shorter judge floated out of the nook quietly in a green robe with the hood hiding the judge's face. After reaching the end of the pillar, this final judge removed the cowl and Jack instantly recognized her. Although the dirt was removed from her cheeks, the rainbow-colored eyes were clearly visible even at a distance.

"Spring," Jack said beneath his breath. It was the same young Asian girl who brought his flashlight to life. Her red, accented dark hair was just as he remembered. It was difficult for him to believe she was somehow judging his case. Recalling that day, he tried to remember the conversation they had. He remembered her fear of the old man catching her outside the temple. After seeing the oldest judge's grumpy expression gazing back down at him, Jack could understand.

"Be seated," the oldest judge directed the room, his voice was as cold as his aura. "Jackson Eli Taylor. The junior, correct?"

Jack wasn't sure whether he needed to yell up or not, so he just spoke regularly. "Yes...sir?"

"Do you understand the charges that have been brought against you?"

"I think so," Jack looked back at Lucky.

"All right then." The judge peeked further down the pillar at Jack. "I at this moment find you —"

"Wait!" Spring interrupted in a tiny voice. "Doesn't he get to say anything?"

The oldest judge snapped his head at Spring, and his shoulders froze over. The woman beside him gestured to Jack. "It's only fair. Let the boy speak."

"Fine," the elder judge grumbled and the ice shattered from his body. "Say what you must."

"Well, I really didn't mean to break any laws," Jack explained. "I was only trying to save my friends and my dad."

"And you thought you would be able to stop the holiday spirit alone?" the elderly judge interrupted. "Foolish decisions, just like the rest of this new generation. Must get that from your father."

"I had to do something," Jack pleaded. "The city could've been destroyed. I don't get why you weren't doing the same." The moment he said it, he immediately knew he shouldn't have.

"Direct defiance!" The old man's eyes were colder than ever.

"Do you know who we are?" the woman asked Jack. "We are the four seasons. We control the essence of both planes and oversee the natural fate of the world. Following each step in the cycle as it was set by the great beings. Spring into Summer followed by Autumn..." she gestured to herself.

"And Winter," the oldest judge finished. "Honestly, I don't know why you bother explaining anything to this boy. He's just as arrogant as that last dreamer and shortsighted like his father."

"Like Old Man Winter?" Jack asked aloud. "I'm guessing your short temper took out the dinosaurs too?"

Winter shook his head in fury, but the young surfer-like judge laughed. "Ha, it's funny because it's *so* true dude."

"Enough!" Winter snapped coldly. "It's time we vote on his punishment." He thrust three fingers into the air, so fast ice cycles formed overhead. He then looked to Autumn.

"Based on your charges, I believe it's the fairest option." Autumn held up two fingers and looked at the next season impatiently. "Summer?"

"Stop calling me that," he responded. "I told you I'm changing the name of my season to Max Heat." He held up two fingers as well, which left Spring to vote. She slowly raised one finger but sighed as if it no longer mattered.

"Fine." Winter shook his head. "We will reunite after the usual preparation time to decide where he will be sent. Until then, he will be held under cloud keeper custody. Case dismissed!" All four judges floated back to their alcove, and the illumination ceased. Only Spring lingered for a moment, looking at Jack before leaving. He still wasn't sure what the numbers meant, but he had a feeling it wasn't a good sign as he witnessed the expressions of the holiday spirits behind him.

Jack said quietly as he stepped away from the podium, "I'm sorry everyone. I didn't mean to lose it like that."

"It's alright son, Winter has a way of coldly attacking nerves," Father replied.

"What did they decide on?" Sonny interjected. "What did the numbers represent?"

"One is low level," Father answered. "Usually short term community service. A three, like Winter's vote, is for imprisonment on the island. The same decision the Sandman received."

Sonny took a picture of the room with her pen. "And two?"

Father cleared his throat. "Well, it's a good thing we have four months to train you before you compete."

"Four months!" Jack repeated. "Why? To compete in what?"

"To make sure you survive." Father put a hand on Jack's shoulder as all of the other spirits looked on. "You've been sentenced to compete in the challenge of four seasons. Come on, son, we've got work to do."

Case #1: *The Holiday Hotel*

Case #2: *Cloud City*

Case #3: *Season's Sacrifice*

About the Author

Christian N. Wynn was born in California, and his father's military service took the family all over the United States. For over twenty years he has called Delaware home. The personal experiences of his friends and family are often his most important inspiration for the characters and stories he creates, including the middle-grade fiction series, *The Jack Taylor Cases*. This series has been described as *The Hardy Boys Mysteries* meets *The Nightmare Before Christmas*.  Along with the *Jack Taylor Cases*, Mr. Wynn's future writing plans include a book series about strange summer vacations, a trilogy of children's books featuring warrior teddy bears, and a book of fables based on characters in the *Jack Taylor Cases* with the profits from the publication being donated to charity. When he isn't writing, Christian enjoys slipping obscure movie lines into conversations, collecting refrigerator magnets from his travels, and reading written works by Rick Riordan, Suzanne Collins, and Daniel Handler. He's also a Hufflepuff and a Los Angeles Chargers fan.

You can find more about Christian Wynn and the Jack Taylor Cases at www.jacktaylorcases.com.

www.jacktaylorcases.com
facebook.com/jacktaylorcases
twitter.com/jacktaylorcases